Hurricanes in Paradise

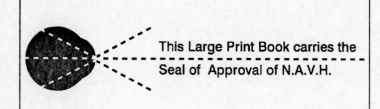

This Large Print Book carries the
Seal of Approval of N.A.V.H.

HURRICANES IN PARADISE

DENISE HILDRETH

THORNDIKE PRESS

A part of Gale, Cengage Learning

GALE
CENGAGE Learning·

Detroit • New York • San Francisco • New Haven, Conn • Waterville, Maine • London

Thorndike Press® Large Print Christian Fiction.
The text of this Large Print edition is unabridged.
Other aspects of the book may vary from the original edition.
Set in 16 pt. Plantin.

LIBRARY OF CONGRESS CATALOGING-IN-PUBLICATION DATA

Jones, Denise Hildreth, 1969–
    Hurricanes in paradise / by Denise Hildreth.
        p. cm. — (Thorndike Press large print Christian fiction)
    ISBN-13: 978-1-4104-4275-8 (hardcover)
    ISBN-10: 1-4104-4275-6 (hardcover)
    1. Resorts—Fiction. 2. Hurricanes—Fiction. 3. Female friendship—Fiction. 4. Bahamas—Fiction. 5. Large type books. I. Title.
PS3608.I424H87 2011
    813'.6—dc23   2011032413

Published in 2011 by arrangement with Tyndale House Publisher, Inc.

Printed in Mexico
1 2 3 4 5 6 7 15 14 13 12 11

*This book is dedicated to
anyone who has ever walked
through a hurricane . . .
and survived.*

1

Saturday morning . . .

The salt air of the Caribbean rushed through the open sliding-glass door with the force of a tropical storm gust and blew a picture frame on her coffee table to the floor, reminding Riley Sinclair that her second chance at life was just as fragile. Her bare feet stepped onto the warm concrete of the small balcony, and she leaned against the iron railing. Her pajama pants blew between the teal-painted slats as a soft curl swept in front of her face, its color as dark as the black tank top she wore.

She closed her eyes and breathed in, the oxygen traveling all the way to her toes. This was the smell she knew, the scent of her memories. She also knew the teasing dance that hurricanes played on the coastal waters. And this tropical paradise that she now resided in had avoided another close call in Hurricane Jesse. But rumor had it a new storm churned in the Atlantic. And though the Bahamas had avoided each storm this year, the mere chance was never good for business. She exhaled deliberately and released anything else that needed to go. The first prayer of the day was offered as the sun pressed its way through dissipating clouds.

When the discourse of her morning was over, she headed back inside to get some Dr Pepper, her new a.m. sugar kick of choice. The South knew how to grow its women proper, raise its boys to be gentlemen, and make its tea sweet. But Bahamians had no idea they were as southern as you could get, so sweet tea wasn't a readily accessible commodity here. So she had switched to Dr Pepper.

She knew that amount of sugar probably wasn't an ideal breakfast companion, but she figured if that was the only addiction she possessed after what she'd been through, she'd fared pretty well. She set her liquid sunshine down and turned the sleek silver shower handle upward to let the water heat up to just below scalding. When steam had taken over the shower door and made its way to the bathroom mirror, she entombed herself. As warm water cascaded over her, the low, melodic sounds of her hum reverberated through the stone bathroom. She closed her eyes and began to sing softly, letting the thickness of her alto voice take up the spaces the steam had left vacant.

The shower was over when she was finished singing. She dried off, dressed, and released her hair from a large clip; it fell to the center of her back as she glanced at her reflection in the mirror.

There were days she could see it. This was one of them.

Life had come back into her almost-thirty-nine-year-old face. It was as if she got younger with each day that moved her farther from her past. And sometimes, like today, she could actually see it in her eyes. They were alive. Even her laughter had changed. Okay, come back. And every time it arrived, she could feel it travel from somewhere in her gut. It was real. And it was wonderful. Yet still slightly foreign. But she was so grateful for it. And if it brought new lines with it, that was a fair trade. She'd trade the aged face of stress for a new one streaked with laugh lines as willingly as the gamblers here traded dollars for chips.

She gave her reflection a smile and pulled the taupe silk top over her head, then readied her face for the day. Now she was ready to face the biggest challenge of her day: waking Gabby.

The distance from her bedroom to Gabby's was three full steps. Though at five foot two, for her, it was more like five. Even though the condo was only a little over nine hundred square feet, she and Gabby didn't require much; plus it was right on the Atlantis property and a blessing of a deal for this season in her life. And it was peaceful. She was more than willing to sacrifice her four thousand square feet of turmoil for nine hundred square feet of peace.

The twin bed gave slightly beneath her weight as she sat down and pushed the curls that hid Gabby's tiny face. They brushed across the Cinderella nightgown and fell over her shoulder. Riley relished this brief moment without her mouth moving. Since Gabby had learned to talk, she hadn't stopped. That's why Gabriella had quickly been shortened to Gabby.

She leaned over and pressed her mouth against the soft skin of her little girl's face. Her words swept past Gabby's ear. "Time to get up, sunshine. You've got to get ready for school."

The tiny frame wriggled beneath the white down comforter. Long black eyelashes tugged at each other before they finally broke free and revealed eyes that carried as much variety of blue as the Bahamian ocean. Even though Bahamian waters could be as unique as aquamarine, as taunting as turquoise, and as regal as royal blue, they were the only waters distinguishable from space. Gabby's eyes were able to transform as well, but Riley could recognize them from space too.

Gabby rubbed her eyes with the backs of her fists. Her mouth opened wide as she yawned away some of her sleepiness. Then she rolled over.

"Come on, Gabby. You've got to get up." Riley rubbed her back. "It's a big day, remember?"

Gabby rolled over and forced her eyes open. "I'm going to the science museum today."

Riley stood up from the bed. "That's right. Are you still taking Ted?"

Gabby slipped quickly out of the bed, her tiny feet dotting the carpet as she ran toward her fishbowl, where Ted resided. "Yep. I'm taking Ted," she stated matter-of-factly in her distinctly raspy little voice.

She lifted his bowl and spun it around the room. Ted jolted from the rock he had been sleeping on, his stubby turtle legs rapidly trying to regain their positioning. "Don't you want the little boys and girls to see you

11

today on our field trip, Ted?" she asked.

Ted didn't respond. He was still trying to get back to his throne.

"Slip on your clothes, and Mommy will go make your breakfast," Riley said as she laid out some khaki shorts and a white polo. She hadn't told Gabby that they didn't have to wear uniforms today because it was a Saturday field trip to celebrate the end of this semester and to begin their three-week break from year-round school. She thanked God for school uniforms. They removed one morning battle. Pink ballerina outfits weren't the best attire for first grade.

Riley headed to the kitchen. "What are you hungry for, angel girl?"

"I'm thinking pancakes would be good!" Gabby called out.

Riley laughed as she opened the refrigerator door. She kept a flourless, sugarless pancake batter in the refrigerator most of the week. A friend had given her the recipe and Gabby had no idea they were healthy. Riley had no intention of telling her.

Gabby finally bounded into the kitchen and pulled out a barstool from beneath the black granite countertop. Riley turned over the last pancake and put it on Gabby's plate next to her glass of orange juice. She picked up her own plate and sat down beside her.

Gabby held up her hand as if Riley was about to intrude on her prayer. "I'll bless it, Mommy."

"Go for it."

Gabby folded her tiny hands, where pieces of her hot pink fingernail polish clung for dear life. "God is great and God is good. Let us thank Him for our food. By His hands we all are fed. Give us, Lord, our daily bread. Amen," she announced with a bob of her head.

"Amen," Riley echoed.

"Is Daddy coming to get me this week?" Gabby asked, half a piece of pancake hanging from her mouth.

"That's pretty." Riley laughed.

Gabby snickered and chewed wildly.

"No, he's coming next Saturday. You're going to spend the first part of your break with Mommy and the last part with Daddy." Gabby smiled wildly; then Riley saw the light slowly dim behind Gabby's eyes. For six, her mind worked way too hard. "Whatcha thinking?"

"That you'll be by yourself. I don't like you being by yourself, Mommy."

Gabby could still get her in the deep place. Riley set her fork down. "Angel girl, you don't have to worry about Mommy. I love it that you get to go see Daddy. And you need to spend that time enjoying him and Amanda, not worrying about me, okay? I've got a lot of things to keep me busy and I want you to have fun. That's what matters to Mommy. Okay?"

Gabby had stopped chewing and begun talking, her Southern accent as thick as pluff mud, keeping Charleston always before her. "But now we have to fly to get to you. Used to, you could just drive."

Riley placed her hand on Gabby's exposed knee that stuck out from her shorts. "But Mommy can get to you at any time if I need to. So you just know that. Mommy's not going anywhere. Got it? Not ever again. You can get to me anytime and I can get to you anytime."

Gabby's voice was solemn. "Anytime?"

Riley gave her a reassuring smile and wished for a six-year-old instead of a thirty-year-old. "Anytime. Now eat up. You and Ted have a busy day."

Gabby jammed her fork into a piece of pancake and stuck it in her mouth. Her muffled tones came through anyway. "Ted's going to be a hit!"

"A surefire hit."

When Gabby's form disappeared through the front door of St. Andrew's School, the

International School of the Bahamas, Riley could finally deal with the heaviness that Gabby's words had blanketed over her heart. She had spent the last few years climbing out of heavy moments that were as boggy and stinky as Charleston's marshes. Thankfully, she handled them much differently now than she had in the past. Now she plowed through them when they swept over her. She didn't avoid them. Nor did she stay in them. She simply put her head down and didn't look up until she got to the other side.

The second prayer of the day was made on the way to the hotel. And by the time she got there, one more moment had been experienced, grieved, and left. She was through existing. Even if living meant fording through pain, that was a journey worth taking. To her, living meant no longer hiding. Hiding had robbed her of years with Gabby, of her marriage, and almost of herself. No, there would be no more hiding.

Riley parked her car in the employee parking lot and headed toward The Cove, one of the exclusive properties on the Atlantis complex. This place took her breath away. She couldn't imagine a day that it wouldn't.

Towering palm trees swayed slowly with the subtle breeze of the tropical morning as she stepped into the porte cochere that welcomed guests at The Cove.

She passed a young valet. "Hey, Bart." They had become friends on her first day.

"Hello, Miss Riley. You and Gabby enjoying your weekend?"

She smiled. "So far, so good."

"So is this our week?" he said with his thick Bahamian accent, an accent that could move with such a quick cadence, she sometimes had to make him repeat himself.

"I'm thinking Friday would be great."

His huge white smile took over his black face. "Well, that's what I was thinking." The pitch of his voice rose. "I'll meet you at the end of the aisle."

"Don't be late," she chided at their little joke. Then laughed from deep inside. He had been proposing marriage since she'd arrived, even though he was probably twenty years younger than she was. But now he no longer proposed marriage, only the wedding date.

She headed into the Nave, the open-air lobby of The Cove, with its thirty-five-foot teak ceiling and magnificent sculptured lines. This six-hundred-suite tower was her responsibility. Her small heels clicked on the stone flooring as she walked through the expansive walkway, then softened when they met the deep wood that encased the stone. She walked into the glassed-in guest services offices directly across the hall from guest registration.

"Hello, Mia," she said to the newest staff member and her top assistant. Mia had arrived two weeks ago from Australia. The staff was as much a melting pot as were the guests who stayed in their rooms.

"Hello, Riley." Her face lit up as Riley walked by. "Busy week, I hear."

"Yes. A few special guests this week."

Mia's long blonde locks fell across her shoulder as she pulled a leather portfolio from her black Chanel bag. With the straw market at the port in Nassau where the cruise ships came in, Riley knew that fake designer handbags ruled in most of the Bahamas. But not so much here. Fake handbags were as scorned in this luxurious environment as husbands with laptops, but both sneaked in every now and then.

She followed behind as Riley walked into her office. Mia's long, lean legs bridged the chasm quickly. "So who are our VIPs this week?"

Riley looked down at the large desktop calendar to the names written in red ink. Three women arrived today. Three women whose arrivals had been preceded by slightly panicked phone calls: one from a detailed agent, one from a concerned parent, and one conference call from three loving and determined children.

"Let's see here; our primary focus will be Laine Fulton, the author. She's coming here to research for her new book."

Mia scribbled in her notebook like a diligent student. "I hear she's demanding," she said in her slightly frantic way.

Riley's ears piqued at her statement. In the two weeks Mia had been here, Riley had been slightly disarmed by her moments of childishness quickly diffused by an action of maturity. She couldn't figure Mia out. Her outward beauty was obvious. Her reactions not so much. "You have? How so?"

"Oh, I have a friend who hosted her at a property in Dubai. She used that as the setting of her last book. She said there are as many layers to Laine Fulton as there are characters in her novels."

"I prefer to think she's a woman who knows what she wants. And she happens to want things a specific way. I spoke with her agent this morning and —"

"Mitchell?" Mia interrupted.

Riley cocked her head. "Yes, Mitchell."

"That's her ex-husband. And I heard he wasn't her agent anymore," Mia responded matter-of-factly.

"Yes, well . . . okay." Riley shook her head. "Let's stay on our toes with her this week and make sure everything runs smoothly. Her specific room requests should have been taken care of, and it sounds like she'll be occupying a lot of my time. So if you could go make sure everything is in place, that would be great. Just in case I don't get to go back and check."

"No problem." Mia continued to write. "Who else?"

"We've got a young lady named Tamyra Larsen. She's a 'Miss Something,' but I can't remember what her title is."

"Not a pageant girl." Mia scrunched her nose and shook her head. "Really?"

"I'm sure she's delightful. And her mother called and . . . well, she sounded really concerned about her."

"So we're to babysit a beauty queen? I hear they all need babysitting."

Riley gave Mia her best smile. "We don't babysit, Mia. We take care of our guests. Plus, I have a daughter. I know what worried parents sound like, and this mother was worried. So, beauty queen or not, we need to keep our eyes on her."

Mia looked up. Her blue eyes held Riley's. "Consider it done."

"Finally, we have Ms. Winnie Harris."

"Ms. Harris?"

"Yes, *Dr.* Harris actually, but her children said she only uses that title at school. She's a principal at a high school in Nashville."

"Oh, that kind of doctor."

"Yes, that kind. And her children are really concerned about her because she has never been on a vacation alone. Her husband died three years ago and this is her first vacation without him. So it's our responsibility to make sure she is taken care of. And she made a special request *not* to be able to see the Beach Tower from her room."

Mia eyed her oddly. "Why?"

"I have no idea. We don't ask why. We just fulfill the requests." Riley patted her calendar and raised her head. "I believe that's it."

Mia closed her portfolio and stuck it back in her bag. "I'll go check on each of their rooms and make sure they are ready as soon as our guests arrive."

"Thanks. We'll catch up later."

Mia walked out of the office, and Riley sat down. She studied the three names again, making sure she had them committed to memory. She knew what it meant to a guest to be known by name. So she had made remembering a practice ever since she had gone into the hospitality business fifteen years ago. She knew there would be other guests that required her attention this week. But as of today there were only three that were demanding it. Whether they knew it or not.

Riley exited the elevator of the suite tower. Laine Fulton's room was ready to go. Everything she had requested, from the fully stocked liquor cabinet to the pistachios and the all-black M&M'S, awaited her arrival. Her entire bedroom had been rearranged at Mitchell's request, the desk placed in front of the sliding-glass doors to give a view of the ocean. Mia had done an excellent job paying attention to every detail. Now all Riley had to do was wait for her guests to arrive.

She headed down to the Cain, the adult-only pool, to check on Laine's poolside cabana.

A body glided up beside her. "Hi, Riley. Mind if I walk with you?"

She turned toward him, but she knew that voice. She and Christian Manos had worked side by side, he at The Reef, she at The Cove, for the last six months. Their virtually identical jobs brought them to a place of familiarity quicker than most. And that closeness had awakened things in her she hadn't felt in a long time. That's why she had taken to avoiding him. Her pace increased with the rate of her heartbeat. "No. Not at all." She pushed her hair back and turned to look into his beautiful, tanned face.

"Are you coming to the meeting this afternoon?"

She could smell his cologne. The breeze carried it right up her nose. "Umm . . . no." She blinked hard. "I've got a couple arrivals this afternoon that I've got to make sure get settled in okay. Mia is covering for me." She gave a soft smile.

"The luxury of revolving guests," he said.

"Yes, must be nice to have stationary guests." The Reef was a property of luxury condominiums with part-time residents instead of temporary vacationers.

"Very nice. But it looks as if it will prevent you from coming to the meeting. So does that mean it would prevent you from grabbing some lunch before?" he asked, stopping short of one of the poolside towel cabanas. His six-foot-one build towered over her petite frame.

Riley stopped too. "Oh?"

He smiled, the fresh sun on his cheeks. "Yeah, I just wondered if you'd like to have lunch. But it sounds like you're pretty busy. Seems like work is taking up all your time. So I guess maybe we could make it dinner, then."

She knew he could see her heart beating at the base of her neck. This was a date. A date offered by a man who did something to the increase of her pulse that even running a 5K didn't do. She knew she must look extremely awkward, standing there, mouth slightly open, but she wasn't sure what came after this. It had been so long.

"I'm thinking . . . you're wanting to say something?" The subtleties of his Greek accent were still present.

She shook her head to try to break her trance. He was almost too pretty to be a boy. And every time he got near her, heat rose to her face no matter the temperature. "Oh yeah, dinner . . . Well, sure. I guess . . . I think dinner would be nice . . . maybe."

He laughed, his white teeth taking over his face. Taking it over perfectly. And they were a stark contrast to his tousled black hair. "I'm thinking, 'Sure, I guess, nice, maybe' is not quite the response I was hoping for."

Riley laughed awkwardly. "I'm sorry. I . . . Well, you don't need to know all of that. But I . . . ." She breathed in deeply and sighed loudly. This was what she had been trying to avoid. "I'd like that. Dinner. Sometime. Yes. Sure. I'd like that."

He laughed again. "Okay, I'll take that. I was thinking maybe this evening."

She shifted on her heels, placing her hand awkwardly on her hip, and scrunched her lips. "Oh . . . this evening . . . well. That soon?"

He reached out and touched her arm. The hair on her arms shot to attention. She hadn't been touched with this effect in a very long time. Old Mr. Tucker, who directed housekeeping and loved to touch her arm, had never caused quite the same reaction.

"If tonight doesn't work, we can pick another night."

She knew if she hesitated, she'd talk herself out of it. "No . . . no . . . tonight would be great. But it's probably too late notice to get a sitter for Gabby."

"Bring her. We'll have a blast."

She studied his face. But the inflection of his voice had convinced her he meant it. He let his hand fall to his side. She resisted the urge to grab it and put it back. "Yeah?"

"Sure. There's this great little place over on Nassau. It's where the locals hang out. Is that okay? It's really casual."

24

"Gabby and I do casual very well."

"Can I pick you up at six thirty?"

"Yeah, six thirty will be fine."

He reached up and patted her arm again, grabbing it slightly as he did. "It will be fun. Thank you for saying yes."

"Sure. Yeah. No problem."

She watched as he headed around the walkway and back up toward The Reef. His brown leather flip-flops slapped against the concrete and reverberated on her insides. She bit her lip. "Sure? Yeah? No problem? Are you an idiot?" she whispered as she headed back toward her office. "You get asked out on your first date in fifteen years — by a beautiful man, no less — and you say, 'Sure. Yeah. No problem.' You are an idiot." She shook her head and turned toward the pool. Fear dropped with a thud in her gut. It pressed harder with each step she took. By the time she reached Laine's cabana, it had taken over, verifying one thing. She would not be going out with Christian Manos tonight. Or any night.

2

Saturday afternoon . . .

The customs agent nervously wiped at the black ink now smudged across the Formica countertop, glancing up at her with an awkward smile.

Tamyra smiled at him and simply held out her hand to retrieve her passport. "Have a great afternoon," she said as she walked toward baggage claim.

She didn't acknowledge the heads that turned as she walked out the doors. But she knew. She had turned heads since she was in diapers. She just drew people in. It was one of her gifts. She retrieved her two large bags and headed toward the exit, where a distinguished Bahamian gentleman stood with a sign that had her name written across the front in black block letters.

"Hello," she said, nodding at him as she exited. She glanced at his name tag, which read Roy Rogers. "Nice name." She chuckled.

His smile took over half of his cheeks. "Good American name, isn't it?"

"Your mother must have liked Westerns." He walked her toward the waiting car. "She loved Roy Rogers," he said, giving her a wink as he opened the back door.

"Well, you, Roy Rogers, are far cuter than the original," she said, patting the top of his hand that held on to the doorframe.

A flush of red was visible even on top of his black skin. "And you, Miss Tamyra, are a very astute lady." They both laughed. He paused a moment as if studying her. Then he spoke. "Did you know that these here Bahamian waters are known as healing waters?"

Tamyra felt the blood rush from her face. She was grateful she was sitting down. She gripped the edge of her seat.

If he noticed, he didn't let on. "But there's something else you need to know. A person has to believe healing is possible." He stopped as if to let the words sink in. "Enjoy your stay, sweet Tamyra." He closed the door.

Tamyra rested her head against the black leather headrest. Bahamian music filtered softly and rhythmically through the car. Why had he said that? What was the purpose? Did she look like she needed healing? Or was God so cruel that He enjoyed rubbing it in? She turned her now-furrowed brow to the window and forced her attention to the new world outside. But if she was honest, every day seemed like a new world. Nothing was as it used to be. Since the day she left the doctor's office with heartbreaking news, nothing about life or even her own body, her hands, her face, was the same. The only thing that remained the same was the callous soul of the world. It stopped for no one's pain.

Her family was worried sick. She knew that. But no matter how many times she had come to the brink of telling them everything, something held her back. She was here to continue processing her new life. For no other reason. Least of all healing waters.

The palm trees that lined the winding streets cruised past her. They looked as if they were waving. The car drove through the downtown area of Nassau, and she watched as visor-clad tourists ambled down streets on Caribbean time. Even though this was hurricane season and rumor had it one swirled around nearby, no one seemed to care. She certainly didn't. One could sweep in and wipe the whole place off the map and she'd be grateful. Remarkable what four words could do to change your life.

She swatted at the tear that burned its way down her face and turned quickly so the driver couldn't see her crying in the rear-view mirror. The ocean lapped at the sides of a concrete barrier that ran the perimeter of the road. It surged with force but then rolled back as it met the unmovable wall. Her tears did the same thing.

Her heaviness lifted slightly as the car pulled into the tropical and breathtaking setting of the Atlantis. The rich coral towers seemed to welcome her, and when the young man opened the door of the car, salt air rushed through as if it were desperate to reach the wounds in her soul.

She stepped out of the car and barely noticed the young Bahamian bellboys falling over each other trying to get to her luggage. They finally divided and conquered: one closed her door, one took her bags, and one led her to the hotel lobby. She stood in the lobby unaware of its beauty but completely aware of her aloneness. Her mother had begged to come along. Tamyra had assured her she needed a little more time away. But standing in this spectacular lobby with its modern bookcases, waterfall wall, deep black wood-grain floors and counter-tops, and contemporary sculptures displayed in uniformity inside bookcases, she thought of only one thing: she was all alone.

"You must be Tamyra." A petite woman whose Southern accent stood out yet whose olive features were complemented in this tropical paradise extended a hand toward her.

Tamyra shook the woman's hand. "Yes, I'm Tamyra. How did you . . ."

The woman was apparently already prepared for the question. "I'm Riley Sinclair, head of guest relations here, and I try to make sure I know everyone who is coming in for the week."

Tamyra felt as if she towered over the petite brunette. "My mother called you, didn't she?" Her hand went quickly to her hip.

Riley crinkled her nose. Obviously she was deciding whether she wanted to tell her the truth or not. "Yes, as a matter of fact she did. And I understand the ways of a Southern mother."

Tamyra closed her eyes and shook her head.

The woman spoke before Tamyra could. "But I'm glad she did. We've held quite a few pageants here through the years, so consider this your second home. And I wanted you to know that I'm here to serve you any way that I can this week."

"I don't require much. I just needed to get away. Clear my head and all that good stuff before I start this new season of my life."

"Well, I'm glad you've joined us. We've got a lovely room ready for you, and this is an ideal place to start a new season of life for anyone. I'll look forward to seeing you this week."

"Listen, Riley, I know my mother can be very pushy. . . ."

Riley reached her hand up and touched Tamyra's bare arm. It held the same warmth her own mother's had right before she left home. "Your mother didn't ask me to babysit you. It's my job to make sure my guests are taken care of."

Tamyra let the air come in and roll out in a deep and audible sigh. She wondered if her weariness was visible.

"I'd like us to have dinner together one evening if we could," Riley offered.

"Sounds great." Tamyra delivered the words with all the professionalism her year as a beauty queen had taught her. Whether she meant it or not.

■ ■ ■ ■

Tamyra handed the doorman a five-dollar bill after he dropped off her last bag. She barely noticed the marbled bathroom with its white modern bowls that sat atop wooden consoles with chrome fixtures. She couldn't have cared less about the luxury bath products that lined one of the sinks, inviting her to unwind in the bathtub or the marbled and tiled shower. She offered an unimpressed glance toward the breathtaking view of the Atlantic Ocean and the lighthouse that sat at the end of the peninsula of Paradise Island. The two flat-screen televisions that hung in the sunken sitting area and above the wall-length dresser across from her bed meant nothing to her.

Instead, she went straight to her carry-on and pulled out a small, padded fabric cooler. She carried it over to the hidden minibar in the console that separated the bedroom from the sitting area and opened the refrigerator door. She reached inside the bag and pulled out three bottles of medicine, each with a tag received from airport security. She had never walked through security with medicine before. Two months ago she wouldn't have had to. Her eyes scanned the labels as she placed each inside the refrigerator. The revelation of what her life had become was announced before her in dosages. When the third bottle sat firmly on the top shelf, she closed the door.

And as it closed, her grief opened. If her concrete barrier had been expected to withstand this torrent, it wasn't prepared. It gave way as quickly as a sandbag holding back a ruptured dam. And if anyone had been next door, they would have beaten the door down to get inside because her wails were so loud. But before any guest arrived, the grief had subsided and left her in a swollen pile on the carpet, asleep from the sheer exhaustion of her flood.

"Oh, my Lord in heaven, have mercy! I'm in the Bahamas," Winnie Harris said to the pilot as she stopped in front of the open cockpit door.

"Yes, ma'am, you are," he said with a wide smile stamped across his tanned face.

She shook her shoulders slightly as if a chill had coursed through her. She heard the stewardess laugh as she turned to walk the Jetway to the terminal and flung her monogrammed tote across her shoulder. The cream canvas of the tote wasn't as cream as it once was, and her initials were fraying. But shoot, she'd lived seventy-two years and not a single thing on her body was in its original state.

Her barely five-foot, slightly round frame bounced up the corridor of the airport terminal. She hadn't taken a trip in four years. Anywhere. Not even with the kids. Frankly, since Sam had died, she didn't find traveling worth the effort. But her kids had driven her crazy. Gave her this trip for her Christmas present, and she'd been dreading it for the last nine months. But here it was. And so was she. Right smack-dab in the Bahamas.

Her clear blue eyes darted upward and found the arrow pointing toward baggage claim. She pointed her body in that direction. She'd traveled enough to know her way through airports. Sam had taken her all through Europe; they took a cruise of the Mediterranean and had traveled doing mission work in Ukraine. She had loved it back then. But now it seemed useless. Plus, until this exact moment, she had never traveled alone. She hugged her tote tighter against her meaty arm as she made the resolution not to call her children this entire week. They had sent her out here, so they could worry sick about her until she got home.

She passed a mirrored wall and turned

toward her reflection. It sparkled. Her blue denim outfit was bejeweled and a declaration of her Nashvegas life. She ran her fingers through her snow-white locks, then patted her midsection.

Her body was also reflective of the years she'd traveled and the baggage she'd claimed. Her middle section had found companionship and she'd enjoyed the introductions. So, with no intentions of remarrying, she decided if her midsection made more friends along the way, she'd just see how far her elastic could stretch.

A picture of the Atlantis hotel was lit up on the wall in front of her. She caught her breath and turned her head. She and Sam had come here about fifteen years ago, and she didn't like going to places they had been. She still avoided Friday night movies, Saturday morning walks, and the Japanese steak house. She was content to put those parts of her life behind her. That included travel. Those desires had died with Sam. And so had a part of her.

She exited the terminal with her Vera Bradley luggage. Salty air blew over her denim as she walked into the Bahamian afternoon sun. It was thick and warm, and as it passed over her, so did a smile and a slight hint of gratitude. Her children, however, would never know.

"You must be Mrs. Winnie Harris?"

Winnie turned toward the nice-looking man and set her tote on the ground. She tugged at the sleeve of her jacket and pulled it off. "And you must be Roy Rogers," she laughed.

Roy reached up to help her out of her jacket. "I am. Are you ready for your car?"

"Thank you," she said, reaching for the jacket he now held. Her thick arms were now fully visible from her sleeveless pink polo. "This is silly, though. I can take a cab. My kids shouldn't have spent money on a car."

Roy leaned over and placed his hand on her upper arm. "They want you to enjoy yourself. Plus, it's not much more than the taxi fare anyway. Climb inside and relax. You're on Bahamian time now," he said as he moved his hand and opened the back door to a green 4Runner.

Winnie gave him a smirk and tilted her head. "You treat all the girls like this, Roy?"

"Only the beautiful ones, Miss Winnie. Only the beautiful ones."

She slapped him playfully and climbed into the car.

He held the door for her, and when she had settled herself and buckled her seat belt, he spoke. "You should know, Miss Winnie, that these Bahamian waters have healing in them."

"Now, don't go throwing some voodoo mojo on me or something, Mr. Rogers. I'm a good old Baptist girl, and we don't go for any of that stuff."

Roy's thick laugh came from his gut as his chest shook up and down. "No mojo, Miss Winnie. Just good, healing water. But there's something you need to know about it."

Her blue eyes widened.

"You can only find it if you're willing to face your fears."

She reached her hand out of the open car door and wagged her finger at him. "Roy, I'm not afraid of anything. I'm the principal of some of the toughest kids in Nashville, who tower head and shoulders over me. I just traveled all the way to the Bahamas at the age of seventy-two all by myself, and I'm trusting that you're putting me in a car that's going to take me to my hotel and not some side street where young boys are going to try and have their way with me. Even though I doubt any of them have had this much woman before."

Roy's laughter escaped again with a burst.

"But thanks for telling me. If I find someone who needs healing, I'll let them know they've come to the right place."

"You do that, Miss Winnie. You do that." His laugh was still audible even after he closed the door.

Her driver was a thirtysomething Bahamian native named Florence. Florence gave her a tour of the city as they wove through the roads of Nassau on the wrong side of the street.

"Ooh, child. You like to ride up people's butts over here, don't you," Winnie said as she pushed her body back into the seat as if that would create distance.

Florence laughed as she jerked the wheel and pulled them around a car that had been coasting in front of them. By the time Florence pulled up to the front of the hotel, Winnie regretted the fact that she had left her Depends at the house.

"Florence, any chance you're going to be my driver when I leave here?" she asked when Florence opened the door to let her exit. She wasn't asking out of hope.

"I don't know, ma'am. Never can tell what my schedule's going to be."

She patted the driver's arm with a slight tremble in her hand. "Well, don't rush back on account of me, okay, honey?"

"I'll drive you anywhere, anytime, Miss Winnie. You just call Roy and ask for me."

"Sure, yeah, absolutely. But I think I'll probably be staying here most of the time anyway. So don't sit around waiting for Miss Winnie, okay?"

Florence laughed and climbed back into the car while a young valet retrieved her things.

"Where's the bar, son? I think I need a drink."

He laughed. "You can take your pick, ma'am. There are quite a few around here."

She took in a deep breath and turned toward the lobby. The place was magnificent. Everything about it was modern elegance, yet timeless and classic. And it had a hipness to it too. She wished her students could be here. But she knew most of them wouldn't be able to comprehend it all. When all you know are gangs, hunger, and drugs, there are some things in life that your soul can't even begin to assimilate. Beauty like this was often one of them. Some of them still had trouble believing in her, and she was no beauty queen.

She walked into a large room where the front desk and concierge resided, the sound of the waterwall already washing away the stress. "My, my, my . . . look at this place."

"Are you Ms. Harris?" a brunette asked as she extended her hand.

"Mrs.," Winnie corrected. It was still Mrs. to her.

"I'm sorry about that."

Winnie patted the woman's bony arm. "Honey, not a thing to worry about. And aren't you a breath of Southern sunshine. Where are you from, darlin'?"

She smiled. "Charleston. I'm Riley Sinclair. I'm the head of guest relations here."

"Well, Miss Riley Sinclair from Charleston, I love the low country. Shrimp and grits, low-country boils. Can't you tell I know where the good food is? And speaking of good food, if we're going to apologize for anything, it needs to be the fact that you pass by food every day and don't eat it. You've been here too long."

Riley laughed again. "Well, I'll make sure I do better with that."

"You need to. Really, honey, men don't want to marry scrawny chickens. They want hens with breasts and thighs and meat on their bones. Not that I even know if you want to get married or not. Shoot, you might already be married, but if you're not, you really need to think about putting the fork to your lips, sweetheart. I mean seriously." She came up for air. Then drew her hand up quickly to her lips. "Now I'm sorry," she mumbled from behind her hot pink fingernail polish and then dropped her hand. "I tell kids what to do all day long. I doubt you needed to know a bit of what I thought."

"It's okay, really. You're right. I stay too busy. I probably do need to eat a little more."

"Did you come over here to tell me something before I blabbered like an idiot?"

"I came to tell you that we're so glad to have you. I will be here this week to take care of any of your needs. You name it and I'm here for you. I want you to experience every part of the Atlantis that you desire to."

"Well, I don't really need much of anything. I'm just going to enjoy my room and maybe walk on the beach a little here or there. Have me a piña colada or two," Winnie said with a wink, "and spend the rest of the week ignoring phone calls from my children."

Riley opened the folded piece of paper she had in her hands. "Well, you might be able to ignore their calls, but it seems like they've packed your schedule with quite a few things. You're swimming with the dolphins tomorrow —"

"I'm what? I'm not swimming with fish! If God wanted me to swim with fish, he'd have given me fins, not a life preserver," she said, jiggling the flesh around her waist.

Riley laughed. "Well, that's not all. You also have a day at the spa and tickets to a concert on Thursday night."

"A day at the spa I can do. A concert? Who's playing?"

"We have a special concert by Harry Connick Jr. on Thursday night."

Winnie raised her eyebrows and pressed her lips together. "I like him. He reminds me of Sinatra. I met Frank once, you know."

"Really? Ol' Blue Eyes himself?"

"Yes," she said, batting her own eyes at Riley. "He said my eyes were the most beautiful blue he'd ever seen."

"Well, I'd have to agree with him."

"My Sam liked them. Said they reminded him of the blue of the sky on a cloudless day. As if it were painted just for him."

She saw the shift in Riley's eyes. Compassion maybe. "I'm sorry for your loss, Mrs. Harris. Please, if there is anything you need, I'm here to serve you. I have a feeling you will enjoy yourself." She nudged Winnie's shoulder with her own. "And I have a feeling you're a mess."

"A perfect mess," she giggled.

As soon as she got to her room, Winnie

peeked out of the sliding doors to make sure they had honored her request. They had. There was no sign of the Beach Tower from her window, just the breathtaking ocean that only exists with this kind of beauty in the Bahamas. Seeing it now made her feel as if she were back on those white sands fifteen years earlier with Sam's hand in hers as he hummed their favorite song and they dug their toes into the cool sand.

She shook away the memory, scolded it like a ninth grader, and batted back at the grief that had shamelessly tried to reach the surface. She wouldn't allow it. She hadn't allowed it for three years, so why in the world would she begin today?

"Have you found your replacement?" Laine Fulton asked her assistant of only one month with her controlled tone.

There was stammering on the other end. She hated stammering. "It's not a multiple-choice question. Have you found your replacement?" Her words came out deliberate. "Because turning in a book cover without me approving the final copy pretty much guarantees you'll need to. So why don't you take this week while I'm away to find one. You can e-mail me résumés. I'll expect to see some by tomorrow."

Laine hit the End button on her iPhone. She pulled her Tumi carry-on behind her. Her black patent flats with wide silver buckles strode across the carpeted corridor in an unbroken stride. She stuck twenty dollars in the hand of a young man leaning on the arm of his luggage cart and told him to grab her bags. When he had pulled both of them off the carousel, he followed her outside.

The afternoon Bahamian sun quickly warmed her gray, skinny-leg 7 For All Mankind jeans and black Dolce & Gabbana tank sweater as soon as she exited the airport. When all your clothes were dark, mixing and matching was easy.

"I'm Laine Fulton," she said, extending her hand to the man holding a sign that bore her name. She reached into her pocket and pulled out a small black ponytail holder. Though her white-blonde hair barely grazed the top of her shoulders, she could still pull it back, leaving her bangs to brush the corners of her eyes.

"Welcome to the Bahamas, Ms. Fulton. A pleasure to have you here."

She caught a glimpse of his name tag and puffed air. "Thank you, Roy."

He gave her a smile and opened the car door, showing no response to her sarcasm.

She held his friendly black eyes. She wasn't sure why. She just did.

"Where are you from, Ms. Fulton?"

She hated small talk with strangers. "California."

He held on to the handle. "Oh, you have beautiful weather all the time. So is it work or pleasure that brings you to our tropical paradise?"

"All work. Always work." She whispered the last statement more to herself.

"Well, do try to fit in some pleasure, ma'am. There is much to enjoy here."

She placed her hand on the inside handle of the door. "I write the stories that tell others what they can enjoy."

"Well, when you're writing your story, be sure and let them know that the Bahamas here are known for their healing waters."

"Is that so?" she asked as she climbed into the car.

He held the door open a moment longer. "Yes, but there's a catch."

She turned her face toward him. "And what would that be?" She resisted the urge to grab the door from his hand.

"No one can be healed when they won't let go of their disease."

"Well, then let's thank God I'm not sick." She didn't resist any longer. She reached

45

for the door to pull it closed. He resisted at first, then gave her a nod and closed it for her.

Something brooding yet kind was behind his dark eyes. She watched him for a few moments, then turned to look out the window. When her car pulled up to The Cove, she was still trying to shake his words.

"Ms. Fulton." A brown-eyed woman addressed her as she stepped from her car. Her Southern accent would be certain to irritate her if Laine had to listen to it for the next week.

Laine reached out and shook the woman's hand. "You must be Riley."

"Yes, ma'am. It's a pleasure to have you here with us at the Atlantis."

"Please, no *ma'am* is necessary. Everything taken care of?"

"Yes. Everything is ready and waiting for you. I've already checked you in and have your keys." Riley gave her a smile and motioned for one of the valets. "Bart, take this up to Ms. Fulton's room." She handed him a room key inside a paper sleeve. "May I walk you up?"

"Sure. I'd prefer that." The air was balmy even in the open-air architecture. Laine could hear the ocean as if it were a subtle background to the elements of nature that surrounded her. "Beautiful place you have here, Riley."

"Thank you. We think so, and we're glad you chose this for the setting of your new book. We've never had a novel set here before."

"I know. That's what I do. I like to take people to places they've never been. My last book was set in Dubai."

"Yes, I heard. Sorry, I haven't read it."

"You're never supposed to tell an author you haven't read her books."

Riley laughed nervously.

Laine let her rest in her uneasiness. "Tell me about the architect."

"Jeffrey Beers was our interior architect. He wanted our guests to have a 'sensory journey,' as he called it. That's why you have everything encapsulated here, from the sounds of the ocean and the movement of the palm trees to all the earthy elements and natural colors."

They passed tropical foliage that surrounded a water garden and came upon Sea Glass. Riley motioned toward it. "This is our open-air lounge. It's sophisticated and a great place to relax with a drink or just a peaceful place to enjoy the ocean."

Laine could appreciate the detail, the

contemporary yet still-soft lines of the exclusive resort. She had traveled the world. She knew how to appreciate beautiful things.

Riley continued. "And this is ESCAPE. It's the first store location of Eva Jeanbart-Lorenzotti's. She carries some fabulous haute couture items, and it is all duty-free."

"Good. The government gets enough of my money."

"I don't know a person who would disagree."

They entered the covered foyer of the actual suites at The Cove. The ceiling was as high as the outdoor corridors. "Hey, Gerard," Riley said to a young man at the concierge's desk. "This is Ms. Fulton. Gerard will be helping to make your stay as enjoyable as possible."

"Oh yes, ma'am. Absolutely." He extended his hand. "It will be my pleasure, Ms. Fulton."

Laine accepted it and nodded her head graciously. "Nice to meet you, Gerard."

"And you too, ma'am. I am available to you 24-7. It's my pleasure to serve you this week."

"Well, thank you. I appreciate that."

Laine followed Riley to the elevators. As the door closed behind them, the small talk

48

Laine hated began. "You're from Los Angeles?"

Laine exhaled slowly. "Yes."

"I've only been there a couple times. It's very interesting. Completely different pace."

"It fits me fine." Laine paused for a moment, then took over the conversation. "So tonight I'd like us to have dinner at Mesa Grill; then tomorrow night I would prefer to eat at . . ." She stopped when she saw the slightly panicked look on Riley's face. "I'm sorry; did you not realize I'd need you with me this week?"

"Oh, well . . . yes . . . sure, of course. This week is about you, and I'm here for you. So Mesa Grill is fine."

"You're hesitating?"

"No, no. I'm not at all. What time would you like to go?" Riley pulled out her phone. "I'll make our reservations."

"I'm an early eater because I go to bed pretty early and get up before the sun. So let's say . . ." She looked at the white face of her two-tone Baume & Mercier watch. It was already two o'clock. ". . . six o'clock."

The doors of the elevator opened, and they walked out onto the geometrically patterned carpet in rich jewel tones.

Riley hesitated slightly again. "Sure . . . yeah, six will be fine."

49

"If you had plans, Riley . . ."

"No, no. . . . My job is to make sure you have everything you need. It's my pleasure. And you just let me know where you'd like to go tomorrow, and I'll make sure that we have reservations for those places as well."

"I was going to say, if you had plans, you needed to cancel them."

She watched as Riley's head snapped back slightly and her eyes widened. "Oh. Well, no worries, then. Because I didn't have any plans."

Riley slipped the key into a room at the end of the hallway and pushed the door open to one of the twenty-six coveted Sapphire Suites. Laine walked across the marbled floors of the foyer and into the expansive space of the seventeen-hundred-square-foot suite. She kept going until she looked straight out through the wall of windows in front of her. The azure ocean seemed to begin where her living room ended. It was as if she could step out the door and walk on the water.

"Do you like it?" Riley asked.

"It's beautiful. Thank you," Laine said as she continued toward the double doors that led into the bedroom. She noticed the desk sitting in front of the window and felt a thud in her chest. She stopped abruptly. "Mitchell called you?"

"Um, yes, he did. Why? Is there a problem?"

Laine chewed at the inside of her lip, then turned to Riley. "No . . . no. I just saw the desk."

"He said you like to look at the ocean when you write."

Laine walked to the entrance of the bedroom and spoke without turning around. "I'm going to unpack now. I'll meet you for dinner at six."

Laine could tell Riley got the message. She heard her feet stepping back onto the marble. "Well, I'll just leave your keys here on the foyer table. If you need anything before dinner, just let Gerard or me know. We'll be more than glad to bring you anything. No need to call room service or housekeeping. Just dial one and that will get Gerard, and two will reach me."

"I'll be fine," Laine said as she leaned against the doorframe of the bedroom. "See you at six." She still didn't turn around.

When she heard the click as the door closed, she set her Louis Vuitton canvas handbag at the doorway of the bedroom and headed back into the living room. She scanned the inviting tones of the cream sectional; the dark wood coffee table; and

51

the coral accents of sofa pillows, lamp-shades, and floor-to-ceiling draperies. The colors were similar to the tones the architect had chosen throughout The Cove and were all woven together in a large area rug that rested beneath them as their anchor and in the abstract, hand-painted artwork that hung on the large wall separating the master bedroom and living room. She walked around the sofa and pulled open the large sliding door. The music of the surf, the smell of salt, and the rush of warm air burst through as if they had been toddlers waiting to get inside.

She walked onto the balcony that wrapped around her suite and leaned against the iron railing. As she began to relax, her phone rang. Tension flared. When she reached the phone, Mitchell's picture stared back. She hesitated. It just made it harder. The more he called, the harder he made it. That's why she had fired him. She had to eliminate all contact. But he wouldn't quit contacting her. Her ruby and diamond ring, which was now the only ring she wore, flashed from her right hand as she hit Accept.

"Hey," she said, turning back toward the open doors and walking out onto the ve-randa.

"Desk okay?" he asked.

"Mitchell, you shouldn't have called them. Really. I can move my desk."

"But I know how you like it."

She sat in one of two cushioned teak chairs on the balcony, slipped her feet from her shoes, and placed them on the teak ottoman, her French pedicure greeting the sun. "I know you do, Mitchell. But I've got a lot of work to do this week, and really, I've just got to get all of this behind me. You do too. Please, I need you to leave me alone. You've got everything you need. I've taken care of you financially. Please . . ."

"You know this has never been about money. I just need to know you're taken care of, Laine. No one knows how to do that like I do. Sorry if this call disrupted your week." She could hear his hurt. "I won't call you again while you're there."

"I mean *not ever again,* Mitchell. Not just not again this week."

"You really want that? You really want me to never call you again?"

She heard the shift in his tone. But she steeled her voice. "Yes, Mitchell. I'm asking you to never call me again."

There was a long pause on the other end. She could picture him sitting there behind his desk, baby blue tie that matched the color of his eyes knotted loosely around his pressed, button-down white Oxford with his sleeves rolled up just below the elbows. One hand would be pushing his blondish-brown hair out of his eyes, hair highlighted by the sun from the weekends he spent out on their boat. His boat now.

"Okay, Laine. The next call will have to be made by you. But no matter what has happened to us, despite what brought us to this divorce, please know that I do and always will love you."

Laine felt the tears fall down her face. She leaned her head in her hands and waited until she could respond without revealing to him the fact that she was crying. "I know. Thank you. Good-bye." She removed the phone from her ear and hit the End button. It was finally over. Eighteen years of marriage. Twenty years of friendship. Six months of being legally divorced and it was finally over. And she was glad. At least that's what she spent the next four hours telling herself.

3

Saturday afternoon . . .

The alarms of slot machines dispensing clanging coins into metal containers matched the echoing in Riley's head as she walked through the fifty-thousand-square-foot casino that linked the two Royal Towers. Even though the skylights and windows tried to make visitors feel like the outside had been brought inside, Riley felt like the walls were closing in around her. She could tell that her week with Miss Merry Sunshine was going to be a thrill a minute. But she should thank her. Laine had given her an excuse to cancel her date. The word *date* hovered over her like flies at a Sunday dinner on the church grounds.

She walked through the Crystal Gate at the entrance of the casino. The thirty-thousand-pound structure made of two thousand pieces of handblown glass by designer Dale Chihuly didn't even turn her head. Usually she was mesmerized by the tower, as well as the million-dollar structures of the Temple of the Moon and the Temple of the Sun that sat on the floor of the casino. But now, not so much.

She walked into the ladies' room and slipped behind a slatted teak door and into a stall. She pressed her back against the door and tried to slow her breathing before she went in to see Max. He had called about an upcoming event that he needed to talk with her about. But between having a date, having to cancel a date, and being ordered to cancel a date as if she were a schoolgirl, she had been swarmed by unexpected and intense emotions.

Laine had afforded her a perfect excuse to get out of having dinner with Christian. She wasn't ready to start dating. It just wasn't time. Gabby needed her. She had a new job too, a lot of responsibility, and she needed to maintain her focus. She couldn't afford to be distracted. So she should appreciate a guest who demanded her undivided attention.

She stepped out of the stall, walked over to the mirror, and leaned against the sink to see if she could see any appreciation.

Not a lick.

She washed her hands, trying to wash

away the angst. She knew the feeling well. She knew the fears that lurked in the shadows of her soul because she fought them daily. They were many and they could be relentless. But for the last couple years, she had taken them one by one, stepped into the face of each one, and dealt with them. Yet today they felt like they had come in multiples. She cut off the faucet and reached for a hand towel. Granted, Christian's presence could make her spine tingle. And sure, he stirred up things inside her that she hadn't felt in years. But the last horror movie she had seen had done pretty much the same thing. And having to cancel their dinner for the sake of her job was proof that it just wasn't meant to be.

She raised her head, squared herself in front of the mirror, and gave her reflection a nod. It was settled. It wasn't time. Her heart wasn't ready. And it was a good thing. Because he probably couldn't handle her past anyway. Jeremy had been the exception to most rules. There were days she believed he was the only man with so gracious a heart.

Max stood outside his office, readers propped on the tip of his nose, as he thumbed through papers. The ends of his glasses were hidden beneath his wavy black hair, a symbol of his Italian heritage. "Riley," he said as she came into his view.

She hugged him. "Hey, Max."

"Good day?" he asked as he walked back into his office and laid the papers on the desk.

"Good day," she said with a sigh.

"Is Ms. Fulton here?"

"Just took her up to her room."

"Everything okay?"

"Down to the black M&M'S."

"Californians, New Yorkers, and us Italians, we love black." He laughed and sat on the sofa that ran the length of his wall. He patted a cushion. "How are you?"

She smiled at him and sat down. He loved her almost as much as he loved his own daughters. Her father had been his roommate at The Citadel; they had weathered pledge week, knob year, and four years of military service together. An odd pairing. A New York Italian and a Scottish Southerner. The waters ran deep and true and their debates ran long and passionate. Max and her father both had the gift of hospitality. Max chose to enjoy his in the hotel business, while her father took his to politics, where he was one of the longest-serving senators in South Carolina. Riley had the same gift. But since she had no interest in politics, Max had paved the way for her first job in the hotel business. When he moved to the Atlantis property and left South Carolina, both she and her father had grieved. But when her life fell apart, Max had been a steady voice. Loving. Compassionate. But true. He got Gabby into the international school. And he was another reason living had been worth it. "I'm good."

"Yeah?"

"Yeah. I'm really good."

He clapped his hands together, scooted to the edge of the sofa, and reached over to his desk to retrieve the papers he had laid down. "We've got a new contract from The Friesen Group. They want to hold their next convention here, and it's going to be a large undertaking. I'm finalizing most of the contract and will send it over to you later today. I want you to make sure all of the items pertaining to The Cove are on point. This is a big one, so I wanted you to know it was coming. We need to be on it promptly. If not, someone else will entice them to their property, and we want their money spent here. To help ensure that we get them, we're flying a group of their vice presidents in this Thursday just so we can make them feel special," he said with a wink.

"And special they will feel. I'll be looking for the contract and get it right to you."

"Go over it thoroughly. Then have it sent to legal and they will finalize everything tomorrow and get back with Friesen first thing Monday morning."

"Does Claire ever take a weekend off?"

"Claire thinks the Atlantis is her hotel."

"Well, by the way she runs legal, I think so too."

Max laughed.

"When can I expect the contract?"

"You'll have it on your desk before you leave."

"Then I'll have it sent to legal first thing in the morning."

Max stood. She followed. "Sorry you're having to mess with any of this tomorrow. I know it's your day off."

"It's no problem. With Laine Fulton here this week, I don't think there will be a day off."

"Well, she's a huge author. Best sellers every time."

"That's what I hear."

"Hopefully this storm out there won't mess anything up for her or our VIPs."

They walked to the door. "I had heard there was some trouble churning out there."

"September can be a brutal month for

hurricanes. But we've lived through worse, haven't we." He patted her on the shoulder.

She reached up and patted his hand. "We survived tsunamis."

Riley walked down the covered walkway that connected the Royal Towers and The Cove, past the spa, and headed toward the fitness center.

"Just pick up the phone and call him," she said, shaking her head.

"Excuse me? Did you say something?" a guest asked as she exited the fitness center, a ring of sweat around the collar of her dark blue T-shirt.

"No, um, no. Sorry. Just talking out loud, I guess." She walked hurriedly past the lady and pulled her BlackBerry from the pocket of her slacks, then dialed Christian's cell. She'd just as soon get it over with.

His voice came over the other end. "I can't take your call right now."

She felt her resolve weaken. Even his voice was beautiful.

"But just leave a message and I'll get right back with you. Thank you."

The beep that followed fortified her nerves slightly. "Hey, Christian, it's Riley. I'm sorry about tonight, but the author that I have in town is expecting me for dinner. And it

61

looks like I'm going to be pretty swamped with her all week. So, sorry, but I think dinner is out for a while. But . . . um . . . thanks. I mean, thanks for asking and everything. But I've just got to, you know, make sure my guests are taken care of and all, and well, yeah, I guess . . . well, I guess that's it. I'm rambling, aren't I? Sorry, I don't mean to ramble. When you have a six-year-old, every now and then you ramble. So, okay, well, then . . . I guess good-bye. Well, it's not good-bye; we'll see each other around and everything. But good-bye for a date. Tonight. Yeah. Alrighty, then. I'm hanging up now. Okay. Bye-bye."

She disconnected and stuck the phone back in her pocket. "Okay, you're an idiot twice. Twice in one day. Why don't you see if you can make it three? I hear that's a lucky number. And this is just the place for lucky numbers."

Mia was in Riley's office when she turned the corner. She stepped from around the back of Riley's desk. Her presence caught Riley off guard. "Hey, um, what's up? You looking for something particular?"

"Oh no, I was just checking on something for Mrs. Harris. I knew you had written her appointments down on your calendar, so I was just checking it to make sure I had it right."

"No problem. I actually wrote them down and gave them to her. And she's a character, let me tell ya."

"Well, they called to confirm her dolphin experience tomorrow, so I was just checking it with your time."

Riley slipped around Mia and looked at her calendar. "It's at ten thirty tomorrow."

"Good. That's what they have. Do you need me to assist you with anything for Ms. Fulton?"

Riley's brow furrowed as she pulled her phone out of her pocket and laid it on top of her calendar. "Um, yeah, there is. Could you get us dinner for two tonight at Mesa Grill, back table, something quiet?"

"Consider it done. Anything else?"

"Yeah, let's keep a good eye on Tamyra. Something's not quite right there."

"Will do. So if that's all, I've got a few other guests to check on. Let me know if you need me." Mia walked toward the door of Riley's office, then turned. "Oh, I did get an update on the hurricane. They said its course has been so erratic that they're not sure where it is going to make landfall, but they are saying if it follows its projected course, we're in it."

"Of course we are. With a week this packed, why not throw a hurricane on top of it?"

"I'll keep my eyes on it. We've already had quite a few cancellations for the week, though."

"Well, let's do everything we can to be prepared. There are always those determined few that won't leave regardless."

"Yeah, I hear they can be pretty headstrong when it comes to vacating early on a vacation."

"Can't blame them. I figure if they're willing to make the reservation during hurricane season, they're risk takers anyway."

Mia laughed. "Got quite a few of those here, it seems. See you later."

"Thanks, Mia. Great job. Really."

"It's my pleasure, Riley." And she left.

Riley looked at her watch. She had fifteen minutes to go grab Gabby. That would give her time to call Jeremy. If they were in the path of a hurricane, she didn't want her daughter in it.

Riley clicked the Weather Channel off and went back into the kitchen. Macaroni swirled in the hot, salty water like synchronized swimmers in a pool. "Angel girl. Come in here for a second. Mommy needs to tell you something."

Gabby bounded into the kitchen, wearing her pale pink leggings and pink leotard, and plopped onto a barstool at the counter. "I know. I know. Melissa's coming to watch me tonight. That's the only time you cook macaroni and cheese."

Riley laughed as she twirled the wooden spoon through the cloudy water. "Yes, and Mommy's very sorry. But there is something else I have to tell you. Daddy is coming in early to get you. He'll be here tomorrow."

"But you said he's coming in next weekend." Her voice began to tremble slightly.

Riley turned the burner off and set the spoon down in the ceramic spoon holder by the stovetop. She walked around the bar and knelt down, turning her body toward Gabby. She placed her hands on top of Gabby's stocking-covered legs. "Hey, I know. I know. But listen. It looks like there's a storm coming through here, and Mommy doesn't want you to be here for it. So Daddy is going to take you the first part of your vacation instead and I'll have you during the last part. It's like we're doing a swap!"

Gabby threw her arms up, her dramatic abilities about to be unleashed. "But my ballet recital is tomorrow night! I can't miss it! I'm the star!"

Riley stood and laughed. "You won't miss your recital, angel girl. Daddy is going to stay here for it and then you'll leave when it's over. So this way he gets to see it too."

Gabby's eyes widened, as if this might be a good trade-off. Then the crocodile tears ran effortlessly down the side of her small face. "But I'll miss you," Gabby said, biting hard at her lip, clearly trying to make her tears stop flowing.

Riley hated it when Gabby thought she had to be strong. She leaned over and wrapped her baby in her arms. "Hey, sweetie, listen. Mommy will miss you too. But you know what? When you get back, I'll see if I can take an extra day off and we can spend the whole day together." She tried to keep the lilt in her voice.

"But if I'm going away to be protected, who is going to protect you?"

Riley felt that one right in her chest. She hated that Gabby thought she had to protect her. "Hey, hey . . ." She held Gabby's precious round face in her hands. "Mommy will be fine. Remember I'm always protected. Right?"

"Yes, angels. They protect us both."

"Yes, so no worrying about Mommy. And if I have to leave, I will leave. But I have to take care of the guests here too. And some of them won't be leaving."

"You promise if it gets super bad that you'll come to South Carolina with me and Daddy?"

She held her baby against her chest. "I promise. If it gets super bad, Mommy will come to South Carolina to be with you."

The quiet was all around Tamyra when she finally opened her eyes. They burned as she blinked. She lifted her upper body off the floor and sat there in the strange hotel room. In front of her was a view of the ocean that would take most people's breath away. But to her it was just water beating against sand only to displace it forever. Just like she felt. Displaced. Two months ago she had known everything the next few years of her life held. A new job. A new husband. A whole new life.

Today she knew one thing about her life: it held death. Granted, death comes for everyone. But most people don't live with it as a vise grip around their necks. Most give it a passing thought when they hear of a friend's sickness or a parent's death. But it wasn't a passing thought for her. For her it was a neon billboard that never went to sleep. And the knowledge of it had displaced her. The mere revelation of her illness had displaced the ring from her finger, the man from her side, the people from the guest list. And the uncertainty of life had displaced her from living it. Right now she just wanted to survive it. Life, that is. Today. She just needed to survive today.

Her stomach rumbled. Her eyes blinked hard and turned toward the clock. Five thirty. She hadn't eaten in twenty-four hours. She pressed her hands against the carpet and raised her body off the floor while pain shot through her leg from the stationary position. She grabbed her makeup bag from her carry-on and walked into the bathroom to let warm water flow over a soft white washcloth. She wrung the water out and patted the wet cloth across her face. Her eyes were almost swollen shut. She pulled Visine from the makeup bag and tilted her head back, letting the wet drops flood her eyes.

She blinked as the drops careened down her face and then wiped them with the warm washcloth. She hoped her concealer was a miracle worker. She studied her tank top in the mirror and deemed it neat enough, even though the nap on the floor had been brutal to her shorts. She ran her hands down the front as a make-shift iron, studied her efforts, and declared them good enough. She grabbed the denim jacket draped over her suitcase and stuck her room key in her back pocket. When she had pulled three pills from the refrigerator, she walked out the door in search of dinner.

Laine looked at her watch. She had been sitting in the same chair on the veranda of her suite for almost four hours. Mitchell's words pounded afresh with each wave that crashed onto the sand. She had officially heard him say, "I won't call you again" well over three thousand times now. Her OCD wasn't a great traveling companion in moments like these. She lifted herself from the cushioned chair and walked over to the small refrigerator. She pulled out a bottle of Jack Daniel's and a can of Coke, grabbed a small glass from the velvet-lined drawer beside the refrigerator, and fixed herself a drink.

The ice cubes clicked together as her bare feet walked across the stone floor, onto the carpet of the bedroom, and into the closet, where the valet had left her bags. She had motioned him in earlier with a wave of her hand, told him to put her things in the closet, and had gone back to Mitchell's voice resounding in her head. She had no idea when the valet had left. When she stepped into the closet, she saw her clothes were neatly hung. He had obviously been there a little longer than she had realized. She selected a simple gray sweater that hung to her thighs and a pair of black leggings, then walked into the bathroom. She turned the silver shower lever to blistering and decided she might be a few minutes late. Laine Fulton was never late.

Riley sat at the bar and stared at the bubbles that swirled around in her glass of Dr Pepper, a lime bobbling against the surface. Her acrylic wedge heels clicked against the metal of the barstool as they moved to the music that filled the electric environment.

Riley sat snugly beneath a wooden trellis that held the goatskin covering above the bar. She looked toward the other end of the bar where a group of young men stood crowded together with their oxfords, crisp shorts, suntanned faces, and amicable spirits aided by the spirits they held in their hands. She loved to watch her guests; they came in with visible stress, and as each day passed, the tension flowed from their bodies. It was part of the magic that the Atlantis held. One of the men shifted slightly, allowing Riley to catch a glimpse of Tamyra seated at the bar.

Riley was relieved to see her. She hadn't realized that she had been slightly anxious over the well-being of the young woman. She glanced at her watch. It was ten till six. She ran her hands down her dark-wash blue jeans, straightened the bow that fell softly at the neck of her sleeveless purple silk blouse, picked up her glass, and headed in Tamyra's direction.

Winnie closed the book she had been reading and studied the picture of the majestic mansion on the cover. She had saved the book for her trip. When she retired from teaching, she had spent years catching up on pleasure. Now that she was back to educating, she didn't have much time for pleasure. So if she did nothing but read the ten books she'd brought along with her, it would be worth the trip. She turned the book over and studied the face of Laine Fulton. Fair-complected, clear green eyes, movie-star cheekbones and lips, almost-white blonde hair that barely clipped the top of her shoulders, and a soft smile that seemed to resonate contentment. She had been one of Winnie's favorite writers for the last ten years. Her novels were full of everything from intrigue to romance, and her range of characters as broad as Winnie's denim collection.

She got up and walked into her suite, setting the book down on the coffee table. She picked up the small frame that she had set out when she arrived. She studied Sam's face and smiled. Every time she saw him, it was as if she were seeing him for the first time. And she'd never forget that first time. It was a Fellowship of Christian Athletes meeting at the University of Tennessee, where they had both attended. She had gone because she had a fondness for both athletes and fellowshipping. What she never expected was Sam. He came in wearing a UT T-shirt, and when she saw his gorgeous green eyes, she sang a chorus of "How Good Is God." It wasn't until they had been dating for six months that he realized the only reason she had even attended that night was to meet an athlete. But by then he was so crazy about her, he didn't care.

When he took her to his hometown of Nashville, he introduced her to the Ryman Auditorium, Patsy Cline music, and bowling at the Melrose Bowling Lanes. He taught her what a real gentleman was, how a lady should be treated, and how to control herself until her wedding night. When the wedding night finally came, she attacked him like a kenneled puppy, and he had loved every minute of it. And for the last fifty years she had loved every minute of him.

She set the frame down and looked out over the ocean. She pushed back against the tears that rushed to the surface as she closed the sliding-glass door. It sealed off the sound of the ocean like a tomb and she sealed off her tears like she had since the day she had placed Sam in his. She glanced at the clock on the DVD player. It was 5:55, and her stomach announced it was starving. In the bathroom, she ran her stubby fingers through her hair and dotted her lips with some hot pink lipstick. She picked up her room key, stuck it in the Vera Bradley Raspberry Fizz handbag she'd brought, and wandered out in search of beef.

4

Saturday evening . . .

Tamyra's hand twirled the straw inside her glass of Perrier, and Riley knew she was completely unaware that anyone was around.

"Mind if I sit down for a minute?"

Tamyra's head darted upward, and Riley pretended not to notice the puffy eyes staring back at her. "No, um . . . sure . . . that's fine." She shifted slightly in her seat.

Riley pulled the stool out, set her Dr Pepper on the counter, and ran her hand across the tortoise-and-seashell top as she climbed onto the barstool. "How has your day been so far?"

Tamyra managed a smile. "Nice. It's beautiful here. The room . . . everything . . . just really beautiful."

"I'm so glad. Did you go out to the Cain pool today? It's our adults-only pool."

Tamyra lifted her glass and took a sip.

"No. It's been a really long week, so I took a nap when I got in." The Southern accent peeked out with her last words.

"You're from Savannah, right?"

"Yeah."

"Any layovers?"

"Just one in Miami."

"Well, hopefully, you'll feel better by tomorrow and you can begin to enjoy some of the wonderful things around here. But I'm glad you got out this evening; the food here is fabulous."

"I didn't realize how long it had been since I had actually eaten." She pressed her hands against her stomach. "I'm starving."

Riley watched as the corners of Tamyra's mouth rose. But nothing went with it. The heaviness was embedded in her like the seashells in the countertop. "Well, please know that I'm here to do whatever I can to make your stay all that you need it to be. I want you to enjoy every moment you're here. And I'll make sure your mother knows you're okay," she said with a wink.

Tamyra shook her head. "Good luck with that. You may tell her, but I doubt you'll convince her."

"Why, hello there!" Winnie's voice was both unmistakable and unavoidable.

Riley looked up and watched as Winnie

headed their way, the stones on her jacket catching the light and reflecting across Winnie's face. She could be her own disco ball. Winnie's face broke out in a captivating smile, stretching her hot pink lips to their maximum potential. None of the grief her children had mentioned was apparent in any measure.

"Hello, Winnie," Riley said, smiling at the white-haired, petite grandmother of five, her olive skin already pink from the Bahamian sunshine.

"Hey, Riley. Oh, baby girl, what a day this has been," she said, pulling out the barstool on the other side of Tamyra. "I sat on that balcony, looking out at the beautiful ocean all afternoon. I think I read twenty chapters from my new book. And it had nothing to do with how to keep a high schooler from becoming a hoodlum."

Riley laughed. "Winnie, this is Tamyra Larsen. Tamyra, this is Mrs. Winnie Harris."

"Well, how do you do, Miss Tamyra? Aren't you a beautiful young lady," Winnie said, extending her hand.

Tamyra reached her long hand out to Winnie's. "Thank you, Mrs. Harris. Nice to meet you."

Winnie waved her hand in the air in an exaggerated movement. "Call me Winnie, please. For this entire week I am boycotting *Mrs. Harris.* So just Winnie."

"Okay, Winnie."

Riley looked at her watch. It was five after six. From what she had been told of Laine Fulton, she was never late. She glanced over her shoulder. The group of young men had moved to their seats, leaving an empty bar and an unobstructed view of the entrance. There was no Laine.

"You have to be a beauty queen or model or something," Winnie said.

Riley turned back and watched as Winnie hauled herself onto the stool.

"You're just too drop-dead gorgeous. I mean seriously. You are a stunning young woman. Now don't think I'm being weird or anything. I have three beautiful children and was married for fifty years. But you look like a celebrity."

Tamyra ran her fingers down the side of her glass. "I won a pageant a little while back, but it's no big deal really."

"I knew it! I did. I knew it. Well, we'll keep those boys at bay for you," Winnie said, patting the top of Tamyra's hand.

Tamyra moved her hand quickly and responded with as much speed. "I have no interest in boys."

Winnie sat back in her chair; a slight look

77

of horror crossed her face. "Oh, honey. Don't tell me that."

Riley tried not to choke on her drink.

Tamyra corrected the misconception. "I mean I'm not *looking* for a man. I'm completely happy being single."

A puff of air exploded from Winnie's lungs. "Oh, thank God."

Riley knew she needed to intervene. "Tamyra, we'll let you enjoy your dinner. It was wonderful to see you, and remember what I said," she said as she stood.

Tamyra turned toward Riley. The gratitude was evident in her eyes. "I will. I definitely will."

"Winnie, come with me and I'll make sure they give you a great table."

"But this young lady doesn't need to eat alone," Winnie said.

"She'll be fine," Riley assured her.

But Winnie's attention shifted quickly from Riley. She stared at the entrance with a shocked expression. Riley turned to see what had captured Winnie so completely. Laine Fulton was walking through the door.

"Oh, my word, that's Laine Fulton."

Laine could read the lips of the woman next to Riley. She watched as Riley took the woman by the elbow and led her toward the

78

hostess stand. The woman never took her eyes off of Laine.

"Karin, would you make sure you give Mrs. Harris a lovely table by the window? Over there, by the beautiful picture windows." Riley nodded toward the far wall. "Then when you get back, could you take me and Ms. Fulton to our seat in the back?"

The hostess gave an exaggerated nod, picked up a menu, and took the bedazzled woman by the arm. "Right this way, Mrs. Harris."

Mrs. Harris didn't move. She just stood there. Eyes fixed on Laine. Laine gave her a small smile and a brief nod.

The hostess tugged her slightly. "Mrs. Harris?"

She finally removed her stare from Laine and gave her attention to the hostess. "Yes. Sure. Winnie. Please, call me Winnie."

Laine watched Riley exhale slowly as she turned toward her. She had obviously been nervous about the attention of this fan. "Hello. Did you get settled in?"

"One of the young men got everything situated for me, yes."

"I'm so glad. Looks like you got a little bit of our sunshine," Riley said, touching her own nose.

Laine patted her cheek with the back of

her hand. "Yes, I did."

"September really is a great time of year to come. Plus, it's quieter. Which is nice if you're willing to risk a hurricane."

Laine's brow furrowed. "Are you expecting a hurricane?" She had checked the weather before she left.

"There's a disturbance out there right now. But we'll just keep our eyes on it. We always know in plenty of time."

"Well, I've got too much work to do to worry about some wind and rain."

Riley raised her eyebrows.

"I've lived through the earth moving, Riley. I can handle a hurricane. So should we get sequestered indoors, we'll simply use that time to learn the *inner* workings of the Atlantis."

Riley's expression made it clear she hadn't bargained for so much of her time being taken up. The hostess interrupted. Riley looked grateful. "We have your table ready, ladies."

"Great," Riley said, her excitement a little too revealing.

"Right this way."

Riley motioned for Laine to go in front of her. On the walk to the table, Laine took in every nuance of the restaurant. It was filled with bold splashes of color: mustard yellows and royal blues. The fabrics contrasted in subtle yet whimsical waves from cowhide fabric–backed chairs to smooth red leathers all infusing the Southwestern touch chef Bobby Flay was known for. The grill sat as if it were a stage from where all the productions of the evening would flow.

The hostess pulled out Laine's chair. She sat, ran her hands across the soft white linen tablecloth, and turned the sleek contemporary silverware beneath her fingers. Everything on the table had clean and simple lines, allowing the food to be the center of attention.

Laine reached into her bag and pulled out a notepad. "Beautiful restaurant."

"We're told it is his best so far."

"I'd have to agree. I think I've eaten in most," Laine said as she turned her head toward the other side of the restaurant. She let her gaze wander among the diners as Riley's gaze followed her. There was a letting down that occurred in places like these. She could see it in the way people touched, discoursed, and laughed. Vacation bred relaxation. And it was evident all over the dining room. "Do you ever wonder about the stories behind people who dine alone?" Laine's eyes were on the woman who had been enamored of her earlier.

Riley turned quickly as if she knew who had Laine's eye. A huge smile spread across the woman's face when she saw them looking at her. Then she waved. Riley gave a quick nod and turned back to Laine.

"You know her."

"Yes, Winnie Harris. She's a guest. I've been asked to keep an eye on her for the week."

Laine sensed her uneasiness. "Really? Am I keeping you from her?"

Riley shook her head. "No, no. She's here on vacation. Her family just asked me to make sure she enjoys herself."

Laine nodded over Riley's shoulder again. "What about her? The stunning, young African American."

Riley didn't turn. Evidently she knew her too. The young woman paid them no attention. Her elbow rested on the table, her head in her palm, a menu lying in front of her. "Yes, she's another one I've been asked to take care of this week. Her family is concerned about her too." Riley ran her hands down the side of her place mat. "Truth be told, I am as well."

Laine saw Riley's countenance shift. "Is she in trouble?"

Riley shook her head as if she had said too much. "Oh no. I doubt it's anything like that. Just a concerned mother."

"Invite them to eat with us."

Riley let out a slight chuckle, then picked up her napkin and laid it in her lap. "Trust me, I don't think you would want that. Mrs. Harris over there is apparently a big fan of yours, and I'm not sure that you would have the opportunity to eat."

"You'd be surprised. Once you get people talking about themselves, you don't really have to do much talking. Plus, some of my best character ideas come from real people and real stories." Laine picked up the drink menu and studied it. She raised her green eyes above the top of her menu and locked them on Riley. "Invite them."

Riley fidgeted in her seat. "You're sure?"

"Invite them." She made it clear that this time it wasn't a suggestion. Laine needed an evening with strangers. She needed enough people to carry on conversations so she wouldn't have to. And one of them seemed like the ideal candidate.

Riley scooted her chair back and headed to Tamyra first, probably because she would be the harder one to lure. After what seemed like much coaxing, Riley and Tamyra walked over to Winnie's table. Winnie had her butt half out of her seat before they even got to her.

Winnie eagerly pulled at the leather chair on the other side of Laine and plopped down, bouncing slightly as she did. Riley tried to hide her snicker. Laine could tell Riley didn't think she knew what she had gotten herself into. What little Miss Riley didn't know was that Laine Fulton was a master study in people. And she had already discerned she really didn't like Riley Sinclair.

Riley couldn't understand Laine wanting to invite strangers to have dinner with her. But she had never really understood Californians. They wore black all the time or shades thereof. Apparently thought earthquakes and hurricanes were part of daily life. And thought anyone who had an accent different from their own held a slightly lower IQ. At least that's what Laine's tone seemed to imply.

"Oh my, what a delightful treat. I am having dinner with Laine Fulton," Winnie said, leaning toward Laine and patting her hand as if Laine might not even know who she was. "*The* Laine Fulton."

The waiter walked over, apparently aware that the dynamics of his table had just changed. "Hello, ladies."

"We've some additions," Riley said. "You

might want to let the other waiters know we pulled from two tables over there." She knew what it felt like to have guests change their minds on you.

"That's no problem. Can I get you ladies something to drink?"

Everyone paused and looked at Laine as if she should begin. She took the cue. "How about watermelon martinis for the table," she said, setting the menu down.

Winnie reached over and placed her hand atop Laine's again. Riley watched Laine's face tighten. Apparently conversation she could do; personal contact, not so much. She waited for her to pick up Winnie's hand and set it back by her plate. "Oh, honey. I can't. I'm Baptist. I always talk about drinking but haven't had a drop in my life." She looked up at the waiter. "Do you have sweet tea by any chance, darlin'?"

"No, ma'am. We only have unsweetened tea."

"You don't get any more Southern than this unless you want to go to Cuba. You'd think sweet tea would be everywhere," she said, pulling her hand back to her side of the table. Riley watched the muscles in Laine's face relax. "I'll have unsweetened. That's fine. Sugar is sugar, right, ladies?" she said, picking up a packet from the sugar holder and waving it slightly.

Tamyra spoke next. "I'll just stick with Perrier, thank you."

"And thank you for the offer, Laine. Honestly," Riley said. "But I think I'll just have ice water, if you wouldn't mind, Derrick."

Derrick nodded his head and turned toward Laine.

"Like I said, Derrick. I'll have a watermelon martini."

"Yes, ma'am. I'll be right back with your drinks, ladies."

"Well, I guess I don't have to worry about spending the evening with a bunch of lushes," Laine said. The ladies laughed in unison. "So you've never had a drink in your life, Winnie?"

Winnie looked at Laine. "No, sugar. Not in all of my years. I've thought about becoming a sop a time or two, threatened my husband with it for most of my marriage." She laughed softly. Riley watched her face. It shifted as if she was remembering. She shook her head slightly and her voice found its life again. "But no. It was against my religion for years. Now I just don't do it because I'm trying to keep my streak going."

Laine laughed. "Well, good for you, Mrs.

Harris."

Riley leaned back in her chair, almost grateful that she had been removed from being Laine's sole conversationalist.

"My friends call me Winnie. And I would love to tell my friends that Laine Fulton is now among them if I could. So please call me Winnie."

"Winnie it is."

Derrick returned with their drinks, and Laine ordered without asking. "We'd like one of each, please."

Derrick's head popped back. "Do you mean of the main courses?"

"No, I mean we'd like one of each appetizer. Then give us a moment to loosen our belts. Then we'd like one of each of the main courses and a sampling of the sides. And when we're about to bust, we'd like you to bring us one of each of the desserts."

Riley could tell by Derrick's expression he wished he were having dinner with them. He snapped his order book shut and raised both eyebrows. "One of each it is." He retrieved the menus and went off to do something Riley guessed he had never done: order every item on the menu for one table.

Winnie laughed like a giddy schoolgirl. "I've always wanted to do that since I saw that movie *Last Holiday*. Only I didn't want to have to be on death's door to finally have the chutzpah to do it."

"I'm glad I could make a dream come true and that you're not dying, so you can actually enjoy it."

"Plus, all you girls need to put some meat on your bones. I'll enjoy just watching each of you eat." Winnie raised her eyebrow at Riley but then quickly turned her attention back to Laine. "Have you ever been to Memphis, Laine? Best barbecue you'd ever eat. And Graceland." She reached over and slapped Laine's arm. "That's what you should do. You should write something about Elvis. Then come on down to Nashville and write about the Grand Ole Opry, drink some sweet tea, go to the Loveless Café to eat biscuits like your mama makes."

Riley watched Laine raise her eyebrows.

"Your mama doesn't cook biscuits, baby?"

Laine chuckled softly.

"Baby girl, come down to Nashville and let old Winnie introduce you to living. Where are you from?"

"California."

"Well, California is like another country. Come spend some time with me and you will be wearing rhinestones and singing 'Rocky Top.' "

Riley saw the shift in Laine. It was evident

she didn't want to be the one answering questions. "What brought you here, Winnie? to Paradise Island?" Laine asked.

Winnie stirred sugar into her tea. "My children were bound and determined I needed to get away. My husband, Sam, died three years ago. He was sick the year before that. And I haven't felt like traveling. They felt like it was time." Her voice softened.

Riley spoke. "Well, we're glad you're here, Winnie. Tell Laine what you do."

Winnie sipped her tea and crinkled her nose. "Just can't make it happen this way."

"Excuse me?" Laine said.

"The tea. You just can't turn unsweet tea into sweet tea. I don't care what they say." She set her glass back down. "I'm a high school principal. I had retired when I was sixty-five. Then the school board called me two years ago and asked me to come out of retirement. I had been home a year without Sam and I needed to get out. And the students needed me."

"I bet you're great at it," Riley assessed.

"You know, it's my gift. I've learned through the years what I can and can't do, and I can motivate people to see their potential. When I came in, it was the lowest-performing high school in the state. The No Child Left Behind program gave us two years to turn it around. When I arrived, they had a 67 percent dropout rate."

Derrick and a couple waiters began to lay down the appetizers in front of them. But Laine wanted more of Winnie's story. "What have you learned in the last two years?"

Winnie removed her eyes from the sweet potatoes they set in front of her. "I learned my babies were hungry. And a baby can't learn when he's hungry. So we make sure every child has breakfast, and then we fill each classroom with snacks. We feed their bodies so we can feed their brains. Last year our graduation rate was 78 percent."

Riley couldn't hide her shock. "You did that in two years?"

"In two years," she said as she scooped out some sweet potatoes and put them on her plate.

Each woman began to sample a little bit of everything. Amid *ooh*s and *aah*s as they tasted the various delicacies, they shared their impressions of the resort and discussed the weather — specifically whether the tropical depression would disrupt their week.

Finally Laine turned her attention to Tamyra. "So, Tamyra, right?"

Riley watched as Tamyra lifted her glazed eyes to meet Laine's. A softness fell across

Laine's face when she took Tamyra in. "Tell us about you."

Tamyra reached up and ran her fingers down the side of her glass. They pushed at the condensation until it made a clear puddle on the tablecloth below. "Not a lot to tell, honestly."

"Don't let her fool you," Winnie piped in. "This young woman is a beauty queen."

Tamyra turned her expressionless face to Winnie, then back to Laine. "I give up my title in two weeks."

Laine took a drink of her martini. "Happy?"

"Ambivalent."

"Know what you're going to do when it's over?"

Riley watched it all intently. Laine's questions came with the fluidity of a friend at a standing weekly dinner.

"Not sure what I'm going to do tomorrow, honestly." Tamyra shifted in her seat as Derrick and another waiter began to remove the emptied appetizer plates from the table.

"What would you like to do?" Laine pressed. Riley wasn't sure how far she'd get.

"Two months ago I could have told you," Tamyra said, putting her fork down by her plate and looking straight at Laine. "But six weeks ago, I sold everything I had, retreated to a friend's little bungalow in Cozumel and spent time reflecting on my life and my future. Then they moved back in and I wasn't ready to go home. A friend told me about the Atlantis a while back, so I decided to give myself one more week away from home, and this is where I decided to spend it. Next Saturday I'll go back home. And that is absolutely all I know today."

Riley moved her elbows from the table while they finished clearing the dishes to ready them for the main course. "You sold everything you had?"

"Everything but what I could fit into a rental car, because I sold my car, too."

Now Riley had questions of her own. "How does a young woman like you make a decision like that?"

"One day can change everything."

Winnie reached over and patted her hand. Riley could all but see her mothering rise to the surface. "Yes, it can. And it can all turn around in a day too."

Laine absently moved her notebook farther from her plate.

Winnie didn't miss it. "What do you write in there?"

Laine turned toward Winnie, removing her gaze from Tamyra. "In here?" She patted her notebook.

"Yeah." Winnie scooted up as if she were about to get something worth delivering to the *National Enquirer.*

"I write the details of what I see, the texture of the food, the ambience of the lighting, the feel of the room. My readers want to think they're here. So I bring them here with my words. That's why we're trying everything. I'm not sure what my characters may want to eat."

"You do that! I just got through reading chapter after chapter and you so had me right there, as if I could step out and touch the man-made shore of Dubai."

Laine nodded. "Well, thank you, Winnie."

"So you just let the story determine itself?" Riley asked.

She glanced at Riley. "I let the story take me wherever it wants to go."

Winnie wrinkled her nose. "So you don't have to know how it ends for your publisher to be willing to say he'll publish it?"

The chuckle came out as a puff. "I've sold thirty million books, Miss Winnie. I don't even have to tell my publisher what my story is about. As long as he knows I'm somewhere researching for a new book, he's happy."

Winnie laughed. "Of course he is."

Derrick and two other servers laid the

main courses on the table. But there wasn't enough room, so they agreed to serve them in two rounds. Winnie looked at the filet in front of her. "I was craving beef."

The main courses were half-eaten when Riley finally leaned back in her chair again. She was certain her stomach had never been so full. She was also keenly aware that Laine had barely had to talk. Winnie had carried most of the conversation talking about Laine's books, giving Laine ample time to down another martini.

Near the end of the meal, Winnie put her fork down and looked at Tamyra. "You don't eat meat?"

"I'm a vegan."

"You're a what?" Winnie leaned across the table, her blue eyes wide. *"Vegetarian,* I know. *Vegan,* I'm clueless. I teach kids who would be grateful for a pack of peanut butter and cheese crackers, and I come from a family who thinks fried foods are a food group. So help me out with *vegan."*

"We try not to consume animal products of any kind." Her expression didn't encourage further dialogue.

Winnie's furrowed her brow. "Does that include milk?"

"I try to stay away from dairy whenever I can. But sometimes it sneaks in there. I just try to eat food in its most natural form."

Winnie raised her denim-clad arm and pushed at the hidden hanging flesh underneath. "Probably why you look like that and I look like this."

For the first time that evening, Tamyra laughed.

Derrick came and served the desserts, which kept mouths full so that Winnie's groans of delight were about all that was heard. Until Laine had finished and decided to inquire of Riley next.

"And what about you, O gracious hostess." Laine's words came out slightly sarcastic. "Where did you get the name Riley?"

Riley exhaled slowly, grateful that was the question she asked. "I got it from our mayor."

Winnie's brow furrowed.

"Joe Riley. He's the mayor of Charleston and one of the longest-running mayors in the nation. And he is one of my daddy's good friends."

Riley caught Laine's raised eyebrows when she said the word *daddy.* She decided that was enough information.

"So your 'daddy' and the mayor go way back."

Apparently Laine wasn't going to let that be enough. "They graduated from The

Citadel together in '64. Then they both went to law school at the University of South Carolina. One became mayor; the other is one of the longest-serving senators in South Carolina. Daddy thought . . ." Riley paused for a minute. She had never been self-conscious about calling her father *Daddy* until right now. "Well, he thought I would be a boy. I wasn't, but he kept Riley anyway."

"That is a wonderful story of friendship," Winnie offered. "My daddy named me too."

Riley smiled, grateful someone else had a daddy. Must be a Southern thing. "He did?"

"Yeah, Mary Poppins came out in 1934, three years before I was born, and one of the main characters was Winifred Banks. My mother always bought my brother and sister a book a week, and one night when my dad was reading to them, he came across old Winifred. And that was that," she said, clapping her hands together, causing her rhinestones to catch the light and dance reflections across the table.

Derrick interrupted the stories with the bill and began to clear away the dessert dishes, his smile never leaving his face. The tip would be huge and he was already celebrating. Riley reached down and tugged at the waist of her jeans, hoping to give herself more room to breathe. Laine had taken notes throughout the entire dinner. Riley wasn't sure if they consisted of the conversation going on around her or the small bite of each item she had sampled. She hadn't missed one. Laine charged the bill to her room.

Riley spoke first. "Thank you for an amazing dinner."

"Yes, it was great. Thank you," Tamyra said.

"Sister needs a wheelbarrow," Winnie announced. "Yes, my big, broad behind needs to be wheeled right up to my room. The way I'm going to have to waddle out of here, these people are going to think I'm wasted."

Laine laughed and stood up from her seat. "You're each welcome. Thank you for sharing your stories. They were wonderful to hear."

"We're too famous for television," Winnie announced.

The laughter continued as they walked toward the entrance of the restaurant. Riley turned to speak to Tamyra. She wasn't there. Riley turned farther and saw her still at the table. Tamyra slipped what looked to be a pill in her mouth and took a drink of water. Riley turned quickly and followed Winnie and Laine.

Riley knew there were parts of each lady's story that had been kept to themselves. Tamyra had talked about her practiced parts. Winnie had told stories of her husband, her children, and her students. Laine had talked about basically nothing. Riley had shared briefly about how Max had talked her into moving to the Bahamas. Her story was just as strategically shared, but she was here for them, not the other way around.

Laine and Riley stood beneath the rainbow colors of the Mesa Grill sign. Riley could sense the shift in Laine's demeanor when the other women left. "I'd like you to meet me at nine in the morning in the foyer of the Royal Tower."

"Sure. Yes, nine is fine."

"I would like us to take a tour of all the property tomorrow. That way I can begin to document the history here."

"That will be great. I'll be there at nine."

Laine nodded, then hesitated slightly. "Well, good night, then."

There seemed to be something else. "Do you need anything else this evening?"

Laine shook her head. "No, I'm fine, thank you. I'll see you tomorrow."

"Tomorrow." Riley watched Laine make her way down the softly lit corridor of The

Cove. The ocean offered background music to what had been a pretty good day. She let the breeze wash away her frustration over losing her day with Gabby tomorrow. If Jeremy's flight wasn't coming in so early tomorrow, washing it away might have been a little harder. But she was learning. She was learning that control was an illusion, and she had a feeling that knowing that would help her get through the week.

She stopped at her office and picked up the legal papers Max had left for her. Mia had them waiting on her desk. The thickness of the folder in her hand gave her a sneaking suspicion there would be much partaking of Dr Pepper tonight.

As Riley headed out to her car, her mind analyzed Laine. She had been pretty amicable at dinner. But as soon as Winnie and Tamyra left, she had turned back into the businesswoman who had arrived that afternoon. Mia had been right: there were many layers to Laine Fulton. Riley just wasn't quite sure she wanted to know what lay at the center.

Winnie came in and sat down on the sofa, taking in a good hour of the news before she slipped on her nightgown. She ran her hands across the ivory lace at the edge of the scooped neckline. The blue satin felt like silk against her skin. She moved the piece of chocolate the evening housekeeper had placed on her pillow and set it on the bedside table. She climbed under the thick duvet and high-thread-count sheets and let her body fall against the mattress. It seemed to reach out and pull her in. The evening had been perfect. The day had been too, if she was being honest. But life was so different now. Even though moments could be enjoyed, there was still this feeling of something missing.

She rolled over and looked at the pillow next to her. It stared back at her, fluffed and perfect.

"It was a great day, Sam."

She ran her hands across the top of the pillow.

"But, oh my word, I haven't stayed up this late since, well . . ."

Her words were broken by a yawn.

"I met the writer. Laine Fulton."

She laughed.

"Yes, that's the one. You remember me talking about her. I've read all her books. She even said she'd sign the one that I have here. But she's sad, honey. The child has never had sweet tea. Wears black like she is in perpetual mourning and spends a lot of time avoiding questions."

She pulled the blanket up underneath her arms.

"The kids won't believe it when I tell them. But I'm not calling them one time while I'm here," she announced, sounding like a kid herself. "I'm letting them stew and worry about me."

She rubbed the pillow again and sighed heavily.

"I know it's not nice. But they were so demanding about this trip and I just didn't want to take it."

She rolled over on her back.

"Yes, I can say that I'm glad I came. I had a really nice day. And tomorrow I hear they think I'm swimming with dolphins. Though there's no way that's happening."

She rolled back over and patted the pillow again.

"Now, don't you laugh at me. I mean it, Sam. I'm not swimming with any dolphins. They don't need Blubber taking over the dolphin tank."

She chuckled softly, then leaned over and pressed her lips against the soft fabric of the pillow cover. The pillow dipped at her movement.

"I love you, Sam. I love you."

She laid her head on the pillow that would

serve as Sam's chest for the remainder of the evening. Just like the pillow at home had served as his chest for the last three years. The same tears that tried to make their way down her face each evening as she told him she loved him tried once more. And once more they were refused their journey.

Tamyra stood on the balcony of her suite. The wind whipped across her exposed body. The white tank top and pink sleeping shorts didn't cover much. She looked out across the ocean. The ocean she had paid no attention to all day long. Tonight it looked like royalty because the full moon hung over it like a crown of light. The moon cast its reflection across the white tips of the waves and followed them all the way to the shore, where they finally collapsed in a crescendo. To her, however, little seemed extraordinary anymore, even majestic oceans at midnight. And crowns were nothing more than a symbol of needed affirmation, restricted diets, and wasted years.

She ran her hands along the still-warm iron of the railing. Her long arms stretched out as far as they could until her cheek pressed against it. Her ears were dull to the crashing of the surf, the wind pushing through the leaves of the palm trees, and even the soft music that the evening house-keeper had started when she turned on the bedside clock radio. The warmth of the railing seemed to warm her entire body. The evening had been nice, she thought, as her mind replayed some of the conversation. She had said more than she intended. But Riley made her feel comfortable. Laine was very interesting. And Winnie was infectious.

Infectious. The word created a surge from her gut. Before she knew it, she was leaning over the toilet, dinner relieving her of its calories and wasting a hundred dollars' worth of medicine. When her body had expelled the evening's contents, she washed her face, brushed her teeth, and then stood in front of the mirror. Another surge made its way up through her soul. But this one was different. This time she simply leaned over the sink and let the tears make their way down the drain. Which was fitting because that's where she officially saw her life headed.

Laine had taken her time coming back to the room. The colors and sounds of The Cove moved through the open-air corridors with the fluidity of a symphony. The vivid blues that had wrapped their way through the halls that afternoon flowed into rich reds and magentas. A breeze from the ocean blended beautifully with the rhythmic music that played softly and the color that seemed to dance across the large columns that surrounded her.

She reached her room and slipped on her black silk pajama pants and black tank top. Pulling a wine cooler from the refrigerator, she unscrewed the lid and sat down on the sofa, grabbed the remote control and clicked on the television. She pounded her thumb mindlessly until it landed on the Lifetime network. A movie based on one of her books — Mitchell's favorite book — was just starting. She pointed the remote and clicked the TV off as if scolding a disobedient child.

She scrambled for her iPhone and studied it again. There was still no message from Mitchell, nor had there been the ten other times she had checked. There were ten voice mail messages alright. But they were all from her assistant, whom she was deliberately ignoring.

Mitchell didn't call much anymore anyway. But now she knew that he would never call her again. And it was driving her crazy. She controlled everything in her world. Her calendar on her iPhone was color-coded. Her schedule was planned down to her bathroom breaks. Her breakfast had been the same every day for the last ten years. She was a woman in complete control. And yet for the last year and a half, she'd had no control over anything, and she didn't know how long it was going to take until someone discovered how out of control she really was.

But Mitchell knew. He knew everything about her. That's why he had acted the way he had through their divorce, because he did know her. Mitchell's knowing her had never been the problem. The problem now was that she didn't feel as if she even knew herself. And she wasn't sure anything more frightening existed. She looked down at the wine cooler now perspiring in her hand. She mentally calculated how many drinks she had had today. Five. Was she out of control with that too? She lifted the bottle to her lips and took a long swig.

"I did that because I wanted to," she announced to the bottle now inches from her face.

She set it down on the bedside table, then pulled back the already-drawn duvet cover and curled up beneath it. She lay there, eyes wide-open, staring at the desk sitting in front of the window. After ten minutes she'd had all she could take.

She jerked the duvet cover off; her heels

pressed hard against the wood floor as she walked over to the desk. She tugged at it, trying to pull it to the other side of the room. With each barely successful heave, hot tears burned trails down her cheeks. "I want to work in the other room this week! I don't need a desk to work!" she shouted as she cried.

With the desk only slightly relocated, she collapsed in a raging heap on the floor with her hands still wrapped around the legs of the desk. After a few guttural and expletive outbursts, she stood quickly and swatted at her tears with her hand. She snatched a tissue up from the nightstand and grabbed the phone, pressing *1*.

A voice answered before the second ring. "Hello, this is Gerard."

She cleared her throat. "Gerard, this is Laine Fulton. I need my desk moved from out in front of my window."

"Absolutely. I will be there in just a few moments."

"Thank you." She hung up. He had not acted like her suggestion was at all strange. It was almost midnight. It should be strange.

She sniffed hard and plopped down on the edge of the bed. Gerard was in and out in less than five minutes. When the door closed, she stood in the middle of the living

106

room for a moment, the quietness sur-
rounding her. Then she went back into the
bedroom, grabbed a pillow and the duvet
from the bed. The comforter dragged on
the ground as she made her way back into
the living room and plopped down on the
sofa. Curling up like a baby, she pulled the
blanket up under her chin and looked into
her bedroom. Perfect. She couldn't see the
desk at all from here.

5

Sunday morning . . .

Laine rolled over and almost fell off the edge of the sofa. She gripped the cushion while the repercussions of yesterday's imbibing wreaked havoc on her bladder and her head. When she returned from the bathroom, she sat down on the edge of the sofa. The African tribal ceremony that played in her skull made going back to sleep out of the question. She squinted to try to read the backlit clock on the DVD player. It looked like a five, but she couldn't be certain. It was still dark outside, and though this was her favorite part of the day, she didn't quite feel like paying it any attention this morning.

She laid her head back down on her pillow while the drum solo pounded on her right temple. Expletives rolled beneath her breath as she pushed herself upright. In five minutes she was dressed and out the door.

Daughtry blared on her iPhone as she pushed the Down button of the elevator.

The elevator deposited her in a foyer of suites where two neatly pressed Bahamians stood as if waiting to simply greet her. She gave them a raised hand and headed out the door toward the ocean. Her pace matched the rhythm of the music that pulsated in her ears. She turned it up to try to blast out the pounding in her head. The four ibuprofen she popped had yet to infiltrate the front line of her marching band, but she ran anyway.

Periodic lanterns along the large concrete walkway dimly lit the roving pathway that coursed through the myriad of pools and over manicured lawns. She could hear the ocean and breathe in its salty air before it came into view. The moon was slipping away quickly and morning was beginning its push. She stepped from the path and her tennis shoes dug into the thick, damp sand, her weight pushing against her calves, propelling her farther down the beach.

The ocean's roar was able to make its way past both the pounding of the music and her headache. She loved the ocean. Its massiveness gave her comfort. A comfort that said there was something bigger in the world than her. Mitchell had been that in a way.

He had kept the predators at bay. Guarded her talent. Guarded her heart. And in one moment, everything that he had given her was washed away as quickly as the scampering crab that ran toward its hole in front of her. So now, more than ever, she needed to know there was something bigger than her. Even though the mere thought collided with her doubt.

A doubt that she pressed against as her feet sank deeper into the sand. She had always used the first run of the morning to clear her head, purge the chaos, and refocus her thoughts. But focused thoughts had been rare commodities the past year. That's why her latest book was six months behind, why four assistants had found their way through her revolving door, and why last night she had let three strangers join her for dinner. She hated dinner with strangers. Honestly, she didn't like strangers at all. Crowds either, for that matter. She had preferred dinners with Mitchell. Alone. But there was something she hated worse than strangers or crowds. She hated eating alone. That's why she made Riley come in the first place.

The sun thrust out the remnants of yesterday and forced her into today. That was when the words of the song "Home" that was playing on her iPhone began to register with her heart. *Home?* She didn't even know where that was anymore. Home had been with Mitchell. With no children, he had been everything to her. And she had felt displaced since the day she walked out of their home and moved into the St. Regis hotel. A year later she was thinking she might need to find a real place to live. But if she were being honest, the borrowed furniture, borrowed sheets, borrowed hand towels made her feel like she was just visiting, like maybe her old life might find her again, in spite of what she had said to him yesterday. Her heart knew he was the only home she had ever known and the only one she really wanted.

She jerked her iPhone from the holder attached to her waist, flipped open the leather case, and stopped Chris Daughtry mid-chorus. She stuck the phone back in its holder and dug her feet harder into the sand. She wiped at the sweat clinging to her brow and headed straight for the rising sun. That was when she whispered her gratefulness that it rose on the just and unjust alike. Otherwise, she'd be living in the dark.

Riley guzzled the glass of water sitting on her bedside table. She wiped at the sweat that was running down the sides of her face. If anyone had told her she would one day have a treadmill in her bedroom, she would have told them they obviously didn't know her well. She had always had a knack for decorating. She had even thought about becoming an interior designer and leaving the hotel business altogether right before Max called. But she had jumped at the opportunity to get away from the memories of her past and the whispers that had overtaken her city and her life. So treadmills in the bedroom weren't really part of the design aesthetic she had in mind for her new place. But when you had a little girl and no husband, trips to the gym weren't much of an option.

The divorce had changed so much about her life, and it was often the little things she noticed most. Days now had to be planned out in advance since Jeremy wasn't there to call when she forgot an important paper, left the iron on, or couldn't remember if she had turned off the coffeepot. There was no one there to help her with Gabby at night or to drive her to the doctor when she was sick. No, now she drove herself and Gabby everywhere; she made her own chicken soup when she was sick; and when a lightbulb burned out, she climbed up the ladder to change it herself. Life was different. It wasn't the one she had wanted, but it was the one her choices had made.

She grabbed a Dr Pepper from the refrigerator, grateful she had worked out so she could drink it, then took a quick shower and slipped into a burnt orange A-line sleeveless dress. She and Gabby had a Sunday routine, and today it was shot to pieces. They loved to go down to a little restaurant near the church she had found, share a bagel, and talk about their week. With her working most Saturdays, it had become "their" day. The quaint, nondenominational church Riley had found had been a tremendous source of community for both her and Gabby. Gabby had a lot more friends than she did, but she had met a few ladies and found some really good babysitters.

She turned the gold antique diamond ring on her right ring finger. Her grandmother had given it to her before she passed away and it was now the only ring she wore. It had taken a year before she was able to get rid of the ghost feeling where her wedding ring used to sit. She didn't know how an empty finger could feel so heavy. The day she had placed the ring back in its box and closed the lid, she felt like she had shut the lid of a coffin. A soft rap on the door caused her to jump slightly.

She opened the door to Jeremy's familiar smile. "Hey," she said softly.

"Hey," Jeremy responded. "She still asleep?"

"Yeah. I thought since we weren't going anywhere, I'd let her rest a little longer. Come in. Come in," she said, stepping back so he would have room to enter.

He walked in and hugged her. His Burberry cologne still hung on her clothes when he released her. His tousled brown hair was in charming disarray. His black flip-flops peeked out from the edges of his frayed jeans, and his baby blue button-down was tucked in only at the front of his jeans, revealing a blue- and black-striped belt. "I'm glad you let her sleep."

"You want something to drink? Did you get breakfast?" She pulled a granola bar from the cabinet.

"All good. I grabbed something at the airport," he said, sitting on the edge of the sofa.

Riley walked over and sat in the chair across from him. "How's Amanda?"

"Amanda's good. She's looking forward to seeing Gabby."

Riley couldn't help the prick in her gut.

She knew Amanda was precious, loved Gabby, had picked up a lot of broken pieces that she had left in Jeremy's life, but it still pricked her. Jeremy had given her the opportunity to come home. Had forgiven her. But she didn't. She couldn't. So this was good. He needed to move on and it was time she did too. "I know. Gabby is looking forward to seeing her."

"Your mom and dad are expecting her too."

"I know. Mom called twice yesterday and talked to Gabby, telling her all the big plans she has for them when she gets there. Good luck even getting to see her." They both laughed.

His face sobered. "You doing okay here, Riley?"

She smiled. His care for her had always run as deep as the blue bloods ran in Charleston. "Yeah, doing real good. You know how good Max has been to me. Gabby is flourishing, and I just can't tell you how much I appreciate you letting me bring her here. I know this is a sacrifice to all of us. So thank you."

"The best thing for Gabby is a mom and dad who are whole."

She nodded and stood. "She'll want to know you're here. She needs to get up anyway. Plus, I'm already later than I had planned, and being late isn't a good idea for me." She ran her hands across the top of her head and down to the tip of her ponytail as she reached for her bag on the kitchen table. She turned toward him. "I'm glad you're getting a do-over, Jeremy. You deserve it."

He stood and walked toward her. "Everyone should get a second chance, Riley. You are a wonderful mother, and you prove that every day. I'm grateful Gabby has you."

"Ahh . . . stop it." She laughed, swiping at falling tears. "I'm going to have to get ready all over again if you say anything else nice."

He laughed too and wrapped her in his arms. She let him hold her there. Those arms were as familiar to her as the dimples in Gabby's cheeks. Her body had molded a place in them for so many years, but now they felt different. Someone else had carved her own shape there. Riley patted Jeremy's back and removed herself from his hold. "Go see our angel girl."

"You sure you're okay?"

"Yeah, yeah. I'm fine. Really. Busy day. I'll meet up with y'all for her recital tonight. Not sure if I can grab dinner, but I will make the recital."

He patted her arm and headed toward

116

Gabby's door.

Riley closed the door behind her, took a deep breath, and reminded both her heart and mind to come to terms with the fact that Jeremy would not be part of her future. She knew it was inevitable, and she had never pursued him. But she had not been prepared for the emotions that would come with the arrival of his new future.

She pulled herself together on the car ride and freshened her makeup. As soon as she stepped from the car, Christian was on her heels.

"Hey," she said as she walked toward the resort. She knew what awaited her this morning and hadn't planned on starting it with this. She walked quickly, wishing she had seen him when she pulled in because she would have spent more time freshening her makeup in the car, hidden.

He stepped in line beside her. "Everything okay?"

She patted her face, thinking she had covered her surprise pretty well. Apparently not well enough. "Yeah, everything's good." She kept walking, shifting her purse and the envelope with the contract from Max to her other hand.

"Well, I just thought when you weren't home last night that something must have happened."

She stopped in the middle of the parking lot. "You came by?"

"Yeah, I came by at six thirty like we had planned."

"Didn't you get my message?"

He shook his head and stuck his hands inside the pockets of his blue and white seersucker pants. "No, I didn't get any message."

"I left a message on your cell that Laine Fulton needed me to go with her to dinner."

Christian shook his head slowly. "Sorry, I don't know what happened."

"I called you as soon as she asked me."

He shook his head again and shrugged his shoulders. "Crazy. Nothing came through."

"So you went to my house?"

"I did. The babysitter was there and I told her to tell you I had come by."

Riley raised an eyebrow. "She didn't mention it." Her look softened. "I'm so sorry. Honestly. I did call you." She started walking slowly toward the resort again.

He followed beside her. "No problem. I figured something had happened. I knew that Southern girls weren't the stand-you-up kind."

She reached over and touched his arm,

the white button-down crisp beneath her fingers. "Honestly, I would never have done that."

He laughed and patted her hand; heat rushed through her. "I believe you, Riley. Really."

Mia was standing in The Nave when they arrived. "Good morning, you two."

Riley withdrew her hand quickly. "Good morning, Mia."

Christian tossed up a hand. "Hi, Mia." He turned his attention back to Riley. "Anyway, it's no big deal. You called and I didn't get it. So, lunch today?"

Riley flicked her eyes toward Mia. She had her nose in her portfolio. Riley turned back to Christian. "I'm sorry, Christian. This week just isn't going to work. Ms. Fulton is expecting me at her beck and call all week. I think it's best that I make sure she has what she needs."

"So you're not just avoiding me."

Riley had no intention of being that honest. "No, just a new job that I can't afford to screw up."

He gave her a smile. "I respect that. Go get 'em, then. And I'll catch you this week somewhere."

She returned his smile and watched as he walked down the corridor. She hoped watching men walk away wasn't a premonition of the rest of her life. And this man — this one she didn't know what to do with. Not since Jeremy had anyone invoked the feelings that Christian sent blazing through her simply by being near. And now that Jeremy was moving on with his life, she had the opportunity to move on with hers. But that didn't have to mean with a man. She blinked her eyes twice, let out a deep exhale, and turned her attention back to where it needed to be. Not on men or lunch or dinners, but on her guests. That was why she was here. She turned and headed through the atrium to her office. Mia followed her.

"So you and Mr. Manos have a thing for each other?" Mia's heavy accent gave her words a dancing cadence.

"No. I do not have a *thing* for Mr. Manos. He asked me out to dinner. Dinner does not a *thing* make. And I honestly don't think this is productive conversation. We've got a busy day and I've got to get to the Royal Towers to meet Ms. Fulton for breakfast." She glanced at her watch. "And I barely have enough time to get there." She put her purse down by the edge of her desk, slipped her phone into the pocket of her dress, and started for the door with the contract in her hand.

"I need you to get these to legal. These are super-important papers. I've gone over them thoroughly, so we should be good."

Mia took the papers from her. "Sure, I'll be glad to."

Riley looked down at the envelope in Mia's hand; both her and Max's names were on the front. "Thanks. Again, they need to get there first thing this morning," Riley said, rushing out the door. "You'll make sure Mrs. Harris gets to the dolphin excursion?" she asked as she walked out.

Mia followed behind her. "I'll zip up her wet suit myself."

She laughed. "And make sure Tamyra knows I've reserved a place for her out by the Cain pool."

"I'll do it."

Riley stopped and turned toward Mia. "Thank you. I'm really glad you're here. I'll need you this week."

Mia gave her a warm smile. "It's my pleasure. I love it. All of it."

Riley didn't stop her steady jog until she reached the entrance to the Royal Towers lobby. She could see Laine's face from there. And it didn't look happy.

"It's five after nine," Laine said from her seated position in the foyer of the Royal

Towers. She sat surrounded by eight massive white stone columns that sat on top of large stone fish, looking like a bad version of Jonah and the whale. Vivid corals and aquamarine colors enhanced by live palm trees that dotted the marble foyer brought the tropics indoors. And Laine Fulton didn't seem to be enjoying any of it. In fact, by the look of those dark circles under her eyes, Riley was pretty certain that last martini might have done her in.

"I know. I'm sorry I'm late. I had a contract that I had to get out first thing this morning."

Laine stood. "It's really not important why. It's simply that you were. So can we get started?"

Riley felt the hair on the back of her neck bristle. This woman was a chameleon. Last night she wanted company. Today she was a piranha. "Sure. Absolutely. Where would you like to begin?"

"I'd like to start at the far end of the property."

And with that, Riley turned into tour guide and Laine Fulton turned into the most demanding of tourists.

Tamyra lifted her head from the pillow as if it held a weight on top of it. She leaned over and looked at the clock. It was a little after nine. She had been sleeping later and later over the last six weeks. A tiny red light was blinking on the bedside phone. She picked up the receiver and tried to figure out how to retrieve her message.

It was an invitation to the pool. A lady named Mia had reserved a place for her. She couldn't imagine spending an afternoon sitting by a pool. The thought of sitting around with nothing but her thoughts was in no way appealing. She had to do something active. Distraction had become her friend.

That is, until last night. Last night had been different. It was the first time since she'd found out she was sick that she had really forgotten. The mental torment had been silenced, at least until everyone had gotten up to leave, and then those repulsive pills burned like an out-of-control wildfire in her pocket. On top of that, the things that used to be mindless enjoyment — television, books, magazines, the Internet — all seemed a waste of time when you were dying. They seemed frivolous and trite.

When you're dealing with life-and-death issues, you're not too concerned with *People* magazine's pick for "sexiest person of the year." No, she cared only about essentials now. And last night showed her that one of those essentials might, in reality, be people. She had spent the last six weeks running from people — all kinds of people, even her family. But now she thought it might be her family she needed most.

One thing she knew she needed right now was food. In spite of all she ate last night, she was starving. Which in and of itself was a good sign, because she hadn't had an appetite in a while. She walked into the bathroom and pulled her hair up into a clip, piling it on top of her head. She slipped on a little sundress and some flip-flops and stepped into the hallway by the door.

Her cell phone sat in its charger on the foyer table, and it was also blinking red. She looked at it as if it were a bomb about to explode in the middle of her room. No one had this number. This was a new phone she had purchased for outgoing calls only when she had left Savannah. She hadn't even given the number to her parents. Sure, her mom knew where she was, but that was only because she had been in hiding from her for the last six weeks and didn't want to put her through any more torment.

She hit a button and the screen popped to life. The caller ID revealed that she had been found. The one person she had been trying to avoid had found her number. And if he could find this phone number, he was very likely to find her. She retrieved the message, and his voice sent fear rising from her gut. "I know this is your phone, Tamyra. I'm glad you've had some time away to clear your head. And I'm sure when you get back home, you and I will have a lot to talk about. And trust me, I will be waiting. You can't run forever."

The desire to eat was replaced by a wave of panic. For the last two months she had fled that voice. That fear. But in one moment every ounce of it was back with such intensity that she felt like she wanted to crawl out of her skin. She reached for the door handle and jerked it open frantically, half-expecting him to be standing on the other side. She had to tell someone what had happened. What could happen. But she wasn't even sure whom to tell. Riley? Riley had told her if she needed anything, she could call her. She darted toward the elevator and headed to Riley's office. A lady stood behind the large console in the office suite. She was talking frantically on a cell phone.

"I've got it under control, Mother." The lanky blonde's voice reverberated through the lobby. Her blue eyes darted up and caught Tamyra's. "I've got to go." She shut the phone quickly. "Ms. Larsen?"

Tamyra tried to pull it together. "Yes? How do you know my name?"

"I'm sorry." She laughed animatedly. "I'm Mia. I work with Riley. We make it our business to know all of our guests. Well, okay, that isn't completely true." Her lilting Australian accent lifted as she spoke. "We know as many as we can."

Tamyra tried to calm the racing of her heart before she spoke. "Yes, you left a message."

"I did. About the pool."

"Yeah, well, I don't think I want to go to the pool today. I'd really just like to see Riley." She scanned the office desperately. "Is she around?"

"Oh, I'm sorry. She's out with Ms. Fulton this morning. I'd be more than glad to help you."

"No . . . no. That's okay. I just really needed to talk to her. Do you know when she'll be back?"

"I honestly don't. I'm not sure what all Ms. Fulton intended for their day. But I assure you, as soon as she comes in, I'll let her know you wanted to see her."

"Thanks," Tamyra said, backing up toward the door. "I'd appreciate that."

"No problem. And you're sure there's nothing I can do for you?"

"No. No. I'm good, thanks." Tamyra headed back out into the corridor. Her fear followed right along with her.

Winnie checked herself in the mirror that hung over the long table outside the elevator. Not bad for her age. The red bathing suit was reminiscent of a sixties pinup model with its strapless cut and tiny halter string that wrapped around her neck to keep her girls remotely pointed northward. The red looked smart against her olive skin, and the skirt hid the cellulite on her legs. And the ruche . . . oh, she thanked God for the woman who had created ruche. It ran across the front of the suit and did its best to hide her midsection, the section of her body that was the celebration of both her womanhood and her nightly bowl of ice cream.

Her white sunglasses weren't quite as stark stuck on top of her white hair. She licked her red-colored lips and smacked them together in front of the mirror. Marilyn Monroe had nothing on her. She may have slept with a president but, hey, Winnie had slept with Sam. Winnie heard the ding of the elevator's arrival and turned; her monogrammed canvas bag full of books swung with her.

The elevator doors opened and the young woman from dinner last night ran smack-dab into her. She noticed a look of fright in those brooding dark eyes immediately. "Hey, hey . . . ," she said, reaching out to take Tamyra's arm as she came off the elevator.

Tamyra stood an entire head and shoulders above Winnie and looked down at her as she spoke. "Oh, hey, Winnie."

"What's wrong, baby? You look almost as white as me. And for you that's not a good thing."

She shook her head determinedly as if she were trying to shake something off. "Oh, nothing."

"You shake your head any harder and you're going to be in the hospital for shaken baby syndrome. Now, where are you going so frazzled?"

"I'm just going back to my room and —"

Winnie's hand flew up. "Ehh." The sound escaped her like the sound of a cicada. "No young woman as beautiful as you is going to be in a breathtaking place like this and live in your room. Go put your bathing suit on." She swatted her hand in the air toward the hallway.

"Winnie, I don't want to go to the —"

"I know you don't. I can see you want to jump out of your skin. I know what that feels like. I felt it for a couple years after my Sam died. The only thing is, I don't know why someone as young as you would want to do that. But you know what, I promise I won't ask you why."

She could see relief wash over the young woman's face.

"That's my promise. No questions. You can tell me only what you want me to know. But I'm good company and there's a gorgeous pool down there. So you and I are going to go spend our day by it. Now go."

Tamyra stood stoically in front of her.

"Go. I'll wait right here," she said, crossing her arms in front of her. She watched as Tamyra's shoulders eased back down and she finally nodded her head.

"You sure?"

"I'm positive. I'll sit and read and you can lie there and talk, pump music through your ear canals, or stare out into space. But I've learned sometimes it's just nice to have a body next to you. Plus, we'll order daiquiris," she said, raising her eyebrows up and down.

Tamyra's face relaxed, traces of a smile almost present. "You don't drink."

"Who knows. I'm on vacation. Maybe I'll

start." Winnie gave her a wink. "Now go put that beautiful body in a bathing suit so I can hate myself for the rest of the day."

"You're sure."

The girl was a slow one. "Go."

Tamyra inched backward. "Want to walk with me to my room? I'll just be a minute."

Winnie knew what fear looked like. "Sure, baby girl. I'll just sit on your sofa and wait for you. How's that?"

Tamyra's expression relaxed further. "That would be good."

She watched Tamyra as they walked toward her room. Winnie had spent years pulling young people out from underneath their burdens. Apparently some things never took a vacation.

6

Sunday afternoon . . .

Riley stood in the bathroom of the Mosaic restaurant and leaned against the counter. She was getting too familiar with the bathrooms around here. She had brought Laine back to The Cove for the magnificent lunch buffet but had come into the bathroom to try to get some relief from the pounding headache she'd acquired over the last four hours. She reached her hands up to the top of her head and tried to rub the throb away, but it just fell in rhythm with the movement of her fingers. She had spent the morning answering Laine's litany of questions and had covered only a fourth of the property. They would continue the tour this afternoon, and her evening would be spent catching Gabby's recital and finding answers to some of the tougher questions Laine had asked.

It wasn't Laine's questions that frustrated

her as much as it was the condescending, arrogant tone. Obviously sitting alone in a room writing books all these years hadn't honed her people skills. Riley was wondering how Laine had *gotten* a husband far more than how she had lost one. She pulled her phone from the pocket of her dress and held down the number 2 button.

"You okay?" A calming voice came from the other end.

"Teetering."

"Work? Gabby?"

"Everything. Long day."

"It's one."

"It feels like midnight. Jeremy got here this morning."

"I know. Your mother can't wait."

She laughed. "Just Mom?"

Her dad chuckled. "You know how I feel about that little angel girl."

"I've got this incredibly stressful client, Dad."

"Those kind usually have issues of their own, honey."

"Oodles."

"Might be a reason you're in her life."

Riley rubbed her forehead harder and chuckled softly. "I knew you would say that."

"You can handle this, Riley. You've

handled much worse than a stressed vacationer — which sounds like an oxymoron, if you ask me."

"This coming from a man who doesn't even know how to take a vacation."

"Well, at least *not* taking one keeps me from having stressful ones."

"Touché."

The line was silent.

"It's been a really hard day, Daddy. I haven't had one this hard in a while."

"Only one place to go on those truly hard days, angel girl. Only one place."

"I know. We've been talking."

"Good. Now go give this woman all that goodness that's in the heart of my girl. She's not on your doorstep for nothing, Riley. Remember, out of the comfort to spare."

Riley smiled, the fear dripping away. "I love you."

"You too, angel girl. Me and Mom will call you when Gabby gets here."

Riley closed her phone, took a deep breath, and exited the bathroom. She walked over to the buffet table where Laine was already layering her plate with seafood, cheeses, and salads. The influences of the Mediterranean were the foundation for Mosaic and came with the made-to-order dishes infused with the freshest of ingredients and cooked at the large square cooking center in the middle of the buffet.

Riley picked up a plate and covered it with every vividly colored food Mosaic had to offer. She followed Laine to a booth, where the punch of color in the red suede seat back contrasted sharply against the neutral tones of the restaurant and the black of Laine's dress.

Laine ordered a glass of pinot grigio and Riley ordered a Dr Pepper. If she could have made it a double, she would have. As soon as she sat down, her phone vibrated against her hip. It had vibrated all morning, another distraction in an already-busy schedule, but she picked it up anyway. It was Max. She always had to take that call.

"Excuse me, Laine. This is my boss. I'll be right back."

Laine gave her a nod as she picked up a shrimp and bit into it.

Riley walked out of the restaurant and into the open atrium. She stood across from the open doors of a sundries store and answered her phone. "Hey."

"Hey. I just talked to Claire. She's freaking out wanting to know where the contract is."

The vise grip returned quickly to Riley's chest. "Mia was supposed to take it first thing this morning."

"You didn't take the papers yourself?"

"No . . ." The time with Jeremy had pushed her schedule too much and she hadn't had time to do that and get to Laine on time. "No, I was running late and couldn't be late to meet Laine, so I had Mia send them for me."

"Those are important papers, Riley." His voice was more that of a disappointed father than a reprimanding boss.

"I know. I should have taken them myself. I have no excuse. I'll take care of it immediately."

"You need to look sharp, Riley. This first year, everything matters. And Claire . . ."

She rubbed her head again. "I know. I'm sorry. It won't happen again." She heard him sigh. She could see his furrowed brow and his deep, brooding black eyes. "I'll go find it and make sure it gets there myself."

"You know how much I believe in you, Riley." All frustration was now gone from his tone. She could hear his chair squeak.

"I do. And you know how much I appreciate it."

"How are things with the author?"

"I've been with her all day."

"Well, make her happy. Apart from this

contract, that is what is most important this week."

"I'll do it."

"Okay, I'm going back to lunch with my family."

"Have a great afternoon. Sorry you had to stop for this." She hung up the phone and paced for a few moments in the hall. Then picked the phone back up and called Mia.

"The Cove, this is Mia."

"Hey, Mia, it's me. Max just called, and legal said they haven't received the contract yet."

She could hear her shifting papers. "Oh, Riley, I thought it was supposed to go to Max. His name and your name were on the front. I thought he was sending it to legal."

Riley searched her memory frantically. She remembered seeing Max's name big and bold on the front. She had been so frazzled this morning there was a huge possibility that she had told Mia that. "Did you drop the papers off at his office?"

"Yes. I thought it was odd, though, that he wasn't there. I tried to call you, but it went straight to your voice mail. I figured you'd call to check in when you got a break."

"Well, they were supposed to go to legal. Claire is waiting on them and is apparently fit to be tied."

"Oh, Riley, I'm so sorry." Her voice was now slightly frantic. "I'll go right back and get them and take them over there right now."

Riley shook her head. "No, that was my responsibility. It was very important and I knew that. I should have taken care of it."

"Yes, but that's what I'm here for — to help you. I should have kept calling until I got you. Please let me go get them right now and take them."

"No, honestly, it's all right. I need to do this myself. I promised Max I would."

"Okay. But I am so sorry. I should have asked you twice this morning. I knew you were a little harried when you came through here."

"Yeah, slightly hectic morning. I'll see you shortly."

"Okay. See you later."

An overwhelmed feeling washed over her again, but she resisted, knowing that feeling would only lead her to a dark place. It was a place she hadn't been to in years and one she had no intention of ever returning to. Besides, she had no time for old demons. Not when new ones seemed so capable of finding her.

■ ■ ■ ■

Tamyra didn't notice the brilliant blue of the sky that hung like a tapestry over Cain, the nine-thousand-square-foot designed pool at The Cove. Nor did she pay any attention to the two infinity pools that sat elevated and served as virtual bookends. She was silently grateful that Winnie had rescued her from her own thoughts, but none of it would undo the fact that Jason had found her phone number. That in and of itself seemed impossible. And if he could do that, there was a huge risk that he could find her here.

"Are you Miss Larsen?" a beautiful Bahamian woman asked, the vibrant orange of her top a sharp contrast to the black of her skin.

Tamyra stopped in front of the small teak hostess stand that stood at the entrance to the pool. "Yes, I am."

"Come this way. Ms. Sinclair has reserved a place for you."

Winnie and Tamyra followed the woman's long legs, wrapped in flowing white pants, toward a large daybed with an awning-style covering that sat at the edge of the pool and stood elevated above the other lounge chairs.

Winnie stopped dead in her tracks. "You want us to climb up there?"

"They are remarkably comfortable, and we want you to have the complete experience here at Cain."

"The question is, do you want your other guests to experience me atop that bed?"

Tamyra couldn't help but giggle.

"I'm thinking the beached-whale exhibit isn't what you had in mind for your guests this afternoon."

The young hostess flashed a brilliant white smile at Winnie. "You, my dear, look breathtaking in that swimsuit of yours. You will be a model of elegance to all of us."

Winnie raised her eyebrows at the young woman and dipped her chin. "That is the biggest bunch of hoodoo I've heard in a long time." A smile broke across her lips. "But you can tell me that anytime. However, unless you have a crane to hoist my butt up on top of that thing, I'll have to pass."

Tamyra finally spoke. "Thank you, but we'd be more comfortable in a couple of the lounge chairs over there."

"You're sure?" the hostess asked.

"Yes, I'm positive. But please tell Riley thank you for us. It really is a kind gesture."

The hostess nodded and led them to lounge chairs that sat at the edge of the pool and down slightly from the daybeds. "How is this?"

"This will be great," Tamyra answered.

"Much better," Winnie said.

"I will have a server come over in a few moments to see if there is anything else we can get you." She left the ladies to themselves.

The music mixed into the natural sounds of the background — laughter, conversations, and cheers from the gaming pavilion behind them. Tamyra unfolded one of the towels a young steward brought them and laid it across her chair. She pulled sunscreen from her bag and covered herself in SPF 45, then lay down and watched Winnie wrestle with an umbrella.

She finally stood beside it, holding the pole in a victorious pose. "Could you see my red butt displayed atop that daybed? These people want to leave rested, not in need of therapy."

Tamyra laughed. "You are beautiful, Winnie. I hope I look half as beautiful . . ." She stopped midsentence. If Winnie noticed, she didn't say anything. The sun was warm and welcome against her skin. It was the first time in two months she had even realized it was there. But lying here in this beautiful setting, she couldn't help but feel it.

Winnie finally collapsed on the lounge chair with a thump. "I need a drink."

No sooner had the words come from her mouth than another beautiful Bahamian lady dressed in white shorts and a white shirt tied up around her midsection, revealing abs that Tamyra feared Winnie might scold, arrived with her tray and order pad. "Can I get you ladies something to drink?"

"I would like a piña colada."

Tamyra looked at her.

Winnie wriggled her nose. "Virgin," she said as she rolled her eyes.

"And for you, ma'am?"

"A bottled water would be great. Thank you."

Winnie didn't disappoint. "If you girls would get some sugar in you, then those stomachs of yours might not look like they were starving to death."

The hostess laughed. "I'll be right back, ladies."

Tamyra and Winnie leaned back in their chairs. Tamyra looked around at the bodies that surrounded them. There were all kinds. And the sun was worshiping each one.

She turned to see Winnie bolt upright on

her lounge chair. "I know she isn't!"

Tamyra looked across the pool and saw a young woman, probably in her late twenties, wearing nothing but the lower part of her bikini. She was sitting up with all parts alert, talking to the man and woman who sat next to her as if this were as normal as eating breakfast.

"I think I read somewhere that you could go topless out here," she whispered.

"She's showing her private parts to the world! And it's simply not appropriate."

"But it is okay. Here."

"But it's simply not ladylike and very unappealing. Who wants to eat out here with a strange woman's girls bouncing all around?"

Tamyra looked again. "Well, they haven't bounced yet."

"What would these people do if I set mine free?" Winnie asked, reaching for the strap of her bathing suit. "I bet I'd clear this place out in ten minutes flat."

Tamyra reached for her hand frantically. "Let's not try it today."

"What? You don't think these people would want to see my girls? Just because I can tuck them into the top of my britches doesn't mean they're not worth seeing."

Tamyra couldn't stop the outburst. The

laughter came from somewhere in the depth of her gut. She hadn't heard it in so long it sounded almost foreign. And before she knew it, tears were streaming down her face. Winnie was laughing too. And when their drinks finally arrived, they were curled up in two heaps of hilarity. The server simply left their drinks on the small teak table between their lounge chairs.

It was fifteen minutes before they could regain their composure. And somewhere in those fifteen minutes, with her back pressed against the lounge chair, legs curled up toward her mid-section, hands wrapped around her aching stomach, Tamyra's eyes caught sight of the sky, the brilliantly blue-colored sky.

Laine and Riley walked past the Lilly Pulitzer store on their way toward the casino. Laine had zoned out somewhere in the last thirty minutes, and Riley sounded like nothing but white noise in her head. She felt the panic attack as it wrapped its tentacles around her chest and crept up the nape of her neck.

Riley stopped at the top of the staircase leading to the casino. "Laine, you okay?"

Laine tried to shake it, but it seemed to grab her tighter. "I honestly think I've gotten enough information for today. I want to relax before dinner." She hoped she was convincing enough.

"Sure, yeah. Where would you like to go?"

She had to get out of there. "You just pick us something great and make reservations for six." She turned and tried to refrain from breaking into an all-out sprint.

"I can't tonight. I've got my little . . ."

Laine turned sharply. "I don't care what you have. Cancel it." She turned around just as quickly. She heard Riley's words in the distance and raised her hand to acknowledge them but never looked back. By the time she reached her room, she had broken out in a sweat. She went to the bathroom and pulled the small bottle of antianxiety pills out of her makeup bag. She broke one in half and stuck it in her mouth, then leaned down to scoop water from the faucet.

When her world collapsed, these attacks had started. She didn't know when they would show up, and lately they had been coming with more frequency, it seemed. She pulled her clothes off and dropped them right there in the middle of the bathroom floor. She stood staring at her exposed body in the mirror. She tugged at her skin, wishing she could shed that too. But it was there. It was a part of her, and no matter how many times she wished she could crawl out of it, there was no separating her from who she was.

The ringing of her phone startled her. She leaned down and tugged the phone from her pocket. There was a slight hope that tore through the vise grip around her chest. She turned the face of the phone toward her, and staring back at her was the number of her office. It was her assistant. Again. It wasn't Mitchell. She felt the hope sink and the panic escalate. He was never calling her again. She had made sure of it. She dropped the phone back onto the pile of clothes, walked into the suite, and pulled a bottle of rum and a can of Coke from her refrigerator. She poured herself a drink and took a long swig, letting it burn its way down her chest. If she couldn't will this thing out of her, she'd drown it out. Either way, it was going.

The umbrella had been covering them for a large portion of the afternoon. Winnie wasn't sure when she had fallen asleep, but two hours of slumber had overtaken her. She looked up to find Tamyra gone. She scanned the pool but didn't see her. Her snoring had probably sent the child running.

"Want a bottle of water?" Tamyra asked, extending one from her hand.

Winnie looked up, feeling a sense of relief at the young woman's presence. She took the bottle from her. "Thank you. I figured I had snored you out of here."

"You tried," she said with a smile. "But I just nudged you a little."

Winnie unscrewed the cap and took a long gulp. She shifted her body up on the cushion and looked across the pool. A young woman whose booty was toward the sun caught her attention. "I promise you that in this life there are two places I will never allow strings: in between my toes and up the crack of my behind."

Tamyra covered her mouth as she snorted. "Where do you come up with this stuff?" she choked.

Winnie giggled. "Baby girl, there's a lot more where that came from." She looked around to the other side of the pool and almost dropped her water. "Oh, my side. Oh, my side. I'm going to kill them. I promise if the good Lord brings the sun up tomorrow, I'm going to beat the living tar out of them."

Tamyra looked up. "What is it?"

Winnie stood, frantically grabbing for her towel and stuffing her things into her bag.

"I knew it wasn't about getting me away. I knew it. They can't leave well enough alone, can they? They've got to get their little mangy hands in everything I do. Well, I'm not going to have it, I tell you. I'm not going to have it."

Tamyra stood and reached for her. "Winnie, what is it? What happened?"

Winnie darted her eyes upward and over to the side of the pool. "That's what happened."

Tamyra turned. "What?"

"That. Him. The old man in the lime green bathing trunks."

"You know him?"

Winnie swung her bag across her shoulder and slipped her feet into her shoes. "He is my neighbor and he has the hots for me. I know it. He lost his wife a couple of years ago, and every time he goes to the mailbox or sees me sitting on my front porch, he smiles at me."

Tamyra covered her mouth.

"Go ahead; laugh. But I tell you he would have me hosting his dinner parties, given half a chance."

"And you've gathered this because he smiles at you."

Winnie furrowed her brow. "It's the way. It's always in the way, Tamyra. Their entire face smiles. Not just their lips. Their entire face. I'm seventy-two years old. Trust me, I know when a man has a thing for me." She turned and started toward the walkway leading back to The Cove.

She heard Tamyra behind her in a few moments.

"Sorry, baby girl. I just . . . well, I'm just very angry right now. My kids are little master manipulators. And I'm going to kick me some Harris booty when I get home."

"I'm sorry this has upset you so much, Winnie."

She turned to look at Tamyra. This morning the poor girl was a fright and now she was the one trying to give comfort. She reached for her arm. "It's okay, baby girl. I know I'm a lot of woman. I'll be okay. Don't worry about me. I'll just have to be very careful this week to avoid Mr. Albert Wilson. Because he is not touching this," she said as her hand displayed her body like Vanna displays a new puzzle.

"Would you like to have dinner?" Tamyra asked.

"I'll call you, baby girl. Let me pull myself together. I'm not sure what I'm going to do next." And she wasn't. What did you do with fear?

7

Sunday evening . . .

Riley collapsed into her office chair and turned on the sound machine that sat on the edge of her desk. She kept it on "waves." It fit the setting. She leaned her elbows on the edge of her desk and dropped her head down, letting her hands knead the knots in the back of her neck. What a day. Between Laine and the phone call from Max, she'd had to fight against old fears and old haunts harder than she had in a while.

"You okay?" Mia's voice came from the doorway.

Riley looked up. "Yeah. Long day."

"Sorry to hear that. Did you get the contract taken care of?"

"Yes, I got it over to legal."

"Anything I can do for you?"

"Um, yes, actually there is. Could you make reservations for me and Ms. Fulton for six at . . . the Bahamian Club. Yeah, let's do the Bahamian Club." She rubbed her temples. "Sorry. I'm so brain-dead, I can't even think."

"Sure. Anything else?"

"Yeah, could you ask them to move a little quicker between courses? I'd love to catch at least a little of Gabby's recital."

"Sure. I'd be glad to. Again, I'm so sorry about the misunderstanding today."

Riley shook her head. "No, it's okay. It was my fault. I didn't give myself enough time."

"Well, we're a team, remember, and it's my responsibility to help, not hinder."

Riley gave her a smile. "Thank you, Mia. I really need a friend out here."

Mia's smile broadened across her face. "Me too. So no worries. We'll have each other's back."

"Thank you."

"I'll make that reservation now."

"Sounds good. I'm going to make sure our other guests are doing okay and then sneak away and see Gabby before I have to meet Laine for dinner."

"Well, your other two priorities actually made it out to the pool today."

"They did?"

"Yes, together. But Winnie didn't make it to her dolphins excursion."

Riley leaned back in her chair and chuckled. "I didn't think she would. But at least they were together. That's a good thing. For both of them, I'm sure."

"Also, Tamyra was looking for you this morning."

"Really? She okay?"

"Looked slightly distraught, but I knew you were meeting Laine, and I probably didn't need to interrupt you."

"Sure. Yeah, you're right. I left to go get the contract to legal and you would have thought I had left her for half the day." She stood up from her desk. "I'll go make sure Tamyra is okay. Sounds like if Winnie had her, she was well taken care of."

"Well, try to enjoy yourself tonight," Mia offered as she walked out the door.

"I'm thinking a trip to the gynecologist for a yearly would be more pleasant," she whispered to herself, and with that she threw her head back onto the desk.

Riley knocked on Tamyra's door but there was no answer. She walked back down the hall and pushed the Down button for the elevator. As the doors opened, Tamyra stepped off. "Hey, just the woman I was looking for."

Tamyra's eyes widened. "Yeah?"

151

Riley watched the doors close behind her. "Yeah, Mia said you came by this morning and seemed kind of upset. Everything okay?"

"Yeah, yeah . . . everything's fine."

Riley studied her, noting the hesitation. "You're sure? I'm willing to help with anything."

Tamyra shook her head adamantly. "No, everything's fine. She must have misunderstood. I was just coming to see if you knew how I could reach Winnie."

"Oh, well, good. Mia said you found her and y'all spent time at the pool."

Tamyra smiled. "We did. Had a nice afternoon."

Riley patted her arm. "I'm glad. I was hoping you could enjoy it."

"We really did. Thank you for thinking of me."

"Well, enjoy your evening."

Tamyra walked past her. "Yeah, you too."

Riley watched her walk away and pushed the Down button again. Even though she knew not one word of what Tamyra had just said was true.

Tamyra turned the handle and walked into her room. She didn't know why she had lied. There was nothing about Riley that made her feel defensive. She was just as sure now as she was this morning that she could have told Riley what happened and she would have made sure she was taken care of. But something held her back. To reveal one part of her story might mean she would have to reveal everything. And she didn't want a stranger — even if she seemed like a sweet one — to know all about her. She believed the fact that Riley wasn't there this morning was just confirmation that she didn't need to tell her. She had one more week to decide if and when she would tell anyone the whole truth. But she was certain it wasn't going to be today with Riley Sinclair.

Gabby's face lit up when she spotted Riley. She and Jeremy were sitting at a round table at Carmine's. "Hey, angel girl, how's your day been?" Riley asked, scooping Gabby up in her arms.

Gabby smacked a wet kiss on the side of her face. "It's been awesome, Mommy! Me and Daddy went shopping, and I took him to see the Dig." Her voice was full of drama as she climbed back into her chair.

"You did? Well, how fun was that?" Her eyes shot to Jeremy's.

He smiled. "Very fun. I didn't know the

Atlantis had so much to offer. We had an awesome day, didn't we, Gabs?"

Gabby nodded, then took a long gulp of her drink. She flicked the straw from her mouth. "We saw sharks and jellyfish."

"Pretty amazing, isn't it?" she said.

Jeremy turned his body in his chair so he could face Riley. "They said it's the largest open-air marine habitat."

"It's supposed to give the guests an idea of what Atlantis was like."

"Works for me," Gabby said with a shrug of her shoulders.

Jeremy and Riley laughed. The waiter brought a huge bowl of spaghetti and garlic bread and set it in front of them. Then he scooped some onto each of their plates. Gabby asked for extra Parmesan cheese and he indulged her until Riley gave him a nod. "You can eat all of that and then dance?"

She nodded as noodles hung from her mouth.

"Do you have everything already in the car?" Riley asked, going light on the spaghetti, knowing Laine was liable to order a feast.

Jeremy twirled his spaghetti. "Yeah, we've got her all packed up. We have a ten o'clock flight." He took a bite.

"You didn't want to just spend the night?

I could get you a room. I have connections, you know." She smiled.

"I have a meeting tomorrow I need to be at and it's pretty early. That's why I needed to get us back."

Riley took a bite of her dinner and then turned toward Gabby. "Honey, I have some kind-of-yucky news."

Gabby's eyes widened and she put her fork down.

"I might not make it to your recital tonight." She started back in quickly. "But I'm going to try really hard and I hope that I can at least catch the last half."

Gabby twisted her lips and crinkled her nose. "Business?"

Riley let a puff of air come out of her. "Yep, business. But with Daddy being here, I felt it was okay to go ahead and take care of it."

Gabby reached over and put her hand on top of Riley's. "No problem, Mommy. I'll have lots more."

Riley felt the lump all but block her airflow. "Yes, you will. Lots more. But I still promise that I'm going to try to make this one tonight. I'm doing everything I can."

Gabby moved her hand and picked her fork back up. "At least we got to have dinner together."

Riley nodded and looked at Jeremy. They hadn't had dinner like this in a very long time. "Well, you just know, if I don't get there, that I want you to have a great time with your daddy."

Gabby smiled. "We will. It's going to be awesome! And I'll get to see Amanda."

Riley couldn't help but smile at the sincerity of Gabby's pure love for Amanda. "I know. She'll love to see you. And so will Mimi and Granddaddy. I talked to Granddaddy today and he said they can't wait!"

"They're all looking forward to seeing her," Jeremy said, then reached his hand over and placed it on top of Riley's. "She'll be fine."

Riley couldn't speak. The lump had taken over. She nodded instead. She glanced at her watch and knew she had to go. Kissing Gabby, she left without a long good-bye.

Everything about the Bahamian Club carried the ambience of an old cigar lounge or a gentlemen's club. Riley walked in grateful she had dressed for the occasion this morning because she hadn't had any time to go home and change. Laine walked in right behind her.

"Did you get some rest?" Riley asked.

"I feel fine."

Riley waited for something else. But nothing else came. Laine instead turned her head to look at the hostess. Riley took her cue. "There will be two of us. We should have a reservation under Riley Sinclair."

The hostess looked down at her large white ledger and scanned it. The red tip of her fingernail, as vivid as a taillight, traveled the reservations. "Right this way, ladies."

Riley was so grateful for Mia. She wasn't sure she could handle another scolding today.

Their shoes clicked on the shiny oak floors beneath them. The deep forest green walls and heavy wood moldings encompassed the two women with their warmth as they made their way to their table. Riley tried to let the environment soothe her nerves as well as her senses.

"Thank you," she said to the server who was standing by her pulled-out chair, her napkin in his hand.

"You're welcome, madam." He walked over to Laine's chair, which was already pulled out, then picked up her napkin and extended it to her as well. His white starched apron virtually blended into the crisp white tablecloth, making his Bahamian skin seem even darker as he stood there so dapper and refined. "Will it just be the two of you this evening, ladies?" His accent was thick and smooth.

Laine responded, her voice now warm and her countenance softened. "Yes. Just the two of us."

Riley relaxed into the leather cushion of her chair.

He extended a menu. "Here is our wine list. I'll give you a moment to decide what you would like and I'll be right back."

Laine took the list from his hands and perused it. Riley watched her eyes as they scanned up and down the list. "Ooh, they have Penfolds Grange. I'll get us a bottle of that. Those are hard to come by."

Riley knew that wine very well. It was a brainchild of Max Schubert and it was expensive. It was also wonderful. "I'm sorry, Laine. I appreciate it. But I'll just have water."

"At a restaurant like this you're just going to have water?" Her warmth was gone, her condescension back.

"Yes. Just water. But thank you. That is a very nice wine."

She set the menu down and looked at Riley. "Why don't you drink?"

Riley felt the intimidation of this woman sweep over her. She looked at Laine, unable to figure out how she possessed the ability to make her feel like a child.

"It was a simple question, Riley. Why don't you drink?"

Riley lifted her chin and met Laine's gaze head-on. "Because I choose not to. It's just a decision that I've made. But again, thank you for the offer. I'll stick with the water."

Laine never responded; she simply looked at her. Riley offered her nothing in return. She couldn't. Laine had already drained her today. If she made it to bed sane, she'd collapse in gratitude. When the waiter arrived back at the table, Laine ordered, not even asking Riley what she wanted. She ordered a bottle of wine, the seafood extravaganza appetizer (for two), the onion soup gratin, the club house salad, and the mixed grill house specialty (for two). Riley ordered herself a Caesar salad and the Bahamian conch chowder, which was one of her favorite items.

In fact this dinner was far different from last night's. Laine didn't talk to her during the rest of the meal. She simply took out her little notebook, ate a few bites of each item, studied the layout of the room, questioned the servers and wine stewards, and wrote down whatever she deemed important in that leather-bound book of secrets. Riley nibbled, glancing at her watch and grieving over each fifteen-minute increment that passed, her appetite gone. Laine had pretty much ruined her appetite. By the time Laine ordered dessert, the bottle of wine was gone, a glass of cognac had arrived, and most of her questions were slurred. By the time Laine was through, it was almost eight o'clock.

When Riley was certain she was finished, she got out of her chair to help Laine up. "I canth gif myfelf outh this thair." Her voice was loud through the restaurant.

Riley stepped back. Laine stumbled slightly from her chair and headed toward the door, her journal still sitting on top of the table. Riley grabbed the journal and followed her out the door. "Laine, let me walk you back to your room," she said, reaching for her arm.

"I donth neef yur helf!" she shouted once they reached the corridor.

Riley wasn't going to have this on her head too. "I know you don't. But it's my job to make sure you're taken care of." And she did, with Laine fussing and cussing all the way. She got her to her room and settled her on the sofa, setting the journal on the coffee table. Riley sincerely hoped she'd remember none of it in the morning, because somehow she knew Laine would make it her fault.

"What are you doing out here this late?" Christian's voice cut through the distant sound of waves crashing against the shore a couple floors below.

Riley stepped out into the main foyer of The Cove and looked at her watch. It was now almost eight thirty. Gabby's recital was over, she was certain. She had missed so much in the past two years, she hadn't wanted to miss anything else. But Laine's self-absorption had caused her to miss another piece of her little one's life.

She looked up at Christian, the sight of him taking her breath for a moment. His deeply tanned skin was breathtaking against the baby blue of the linen shirt that hung over the top of his white linen shorts. She hoped he didn't notice that she had just checked out his gorgeous legs. "I've been working."

"That writer killing you?" He laughed as he walked toward her. His eyes were all but dancing. They always looked at her that way. At least they seemed to.

"Yes, and these shoes." She walked over to one of the teak benches and tugged at the clasp on one of her shoes.

Christian sat beside her. "Here. You're too

161

tired to even take off your shoe." He bent down, lifted both of her feet up onto the bench, and unbuckled each shoe. His hands against her skin made her tremble. "Cold?"

"Um . . . yeah, chilled, I think." She was so lying. She scooped up the hem of her dress, pressing it against her legs. He set her shoes down on the floor next to them.

"I'd give you a jacket if I had one."

"It's okay." She slipped her feet down quickly and rested them on the warm wood floor. Then her hands went for the knot in her neck.

"Want to talk about it?"

Riley's head darted up quickly. "She's unbelievable! She's condescending and arrogant! She's mean and snippy! She's a beast! She caused me to miss Gabby's recital and she's my responsibility for five more days!"

Christian laughed. "Guess that would be a yes."

"I could have reached across the table tonight and slapped her. I wanted to. Honest, I did." Her words sounded more like Gabby's than her own. She leaned against the side of the bench and took a deep breath, trying to calm her own nerves. Her voice came out calmer when she spoke the next time. "She got drunk tonight. That's why I'm here. I had to all but tuck her in bed. She drinks all the time. But tonight she was just out of control."

Christian leaned against the end of the bench. "I'm sorry about that. Those can be difficult, I know. I've had a couple. But I've figured out pretty quickly that the drinking is just a by-product of something deeper going on. I usually try to get to the bottom of that. I learned half of my job is being a counselor."

Riley smiled. She pulled her feet back up on the bench and tucked her dress around her legs, then leaned back so she could face him. The candle behind him flickered light against the right side of his face. She felt her tension begin to release. "I know. I don't know what it is about her, though. She's not nice sober, either. And she's intimidating. It's like I'm this ignorant schoolgirl when she's around, even though I'm the one giving her the information. But it's like she thrives on making me feel like an idiot."

"Anyone that is around you for a moment, Riley, knows you're not an idiot."

Riley shifted against the wooden beam, and her foot slid against his knee. She pulled it back quickly, but the effect was already done. "Tell that to me when I'm with her." She wrapped her arms across her chest. "So what are you doing here so late tonight?"

"Me?" He smiled as he crossed his ankles and folded his arms across his chest. "A guest had a rough day. Just thought I should check to make sure their evening was going better than their day had gone. Not much different from you, I guess."

"Yes, it's different. I had dinner with her because I didn't have a choice." She cocked her head at him, studying him in the dim light of the evening. "You did. And you chose to take care of your client. And you're not sitting here lambasting them when they can't defend themselves. I'm horrible." She set her chin on top of her arms.

He laughed. "You're tired. We all have our days."

"But I shouldn't. Not with her . . . and not over this." The last words were spoken more to herself. Hoping he hadn't heard, she changed the subject. "So what brought you here? This man from Greece coming to Paradise Island."

No words came for a moment. He simply kept his black eyes on her. Then he finally spoke. "Healing."

Her foot slipped and brushed his leg again. She crossed them underneath her so it wouldn't happen again. "What would you need to heal from?"

"A marriage that should have worked but didn't. I've been in Miami for the last ten years. A year after I arrived, I met a woman who stole my heart. Loved her the best I knew how, but sometimes that isn't enough. After eight years of marriage, she had another plan."

The pain that still existed in his heart became evident on his face. She knew that look. "What kind of a plan?"

"The I-don't-want-to-be-married-anymore plan. The this-isn't-the-life-I-want plan. You name it, she said it."

"Any children?"

"No, she changed her mind about that after our second year of marriage. That was the first time I realized that we were in trouble."

"What did you do?"

"Kept hoping. Kept praying. Kept believing for a miracle. That I could love her enough to fill whatever this hole was inside of her. But you can't. Learned that a little too late, but you can't fill something that was made for something eternal. So eventually she packed her bags in search of something she thought was 'out there.' When all along it was 'in here,' " he said, tapping his

165

chest, the linen shirt moving beneath his touch.

"I'm sorry, Christian."

"Me too. Wasn't in the plan. Mine, anyway."

"So how's it going? The healing part."

He smiled. "Good. Got a great counselor early on and just said, whatever is in me that got me here, I want it out of me."

"Doesn't sound like there was anything in you."

"Yeah, I thought that too. Realized just thinking that was part of the problem. I thought I could be enough. Realized that I tried to play rescuer. Didn't work too well. Codependency looks a lot like incredible love. Turns out it's just an excuse for not wanting to confront things that are wrong in your home. So you just avoid them. I avoided confrontation all the way to divorce court. I'd say there was a lot in me to get out. I had completely shut down my voice. Took a while to get it back. That is just as damaging as the person who doesn't know how to silence theirs."

"So then, back to the healing part. How's it going?"

"Can't say I don't grieve at times. But I don't live broken anymore. Found my voice again. Realized I actually did enjoy life and

166

that there was a life out there to live. And right now I'm enjoying this."

His look unnerved her. Unease washed over her with the warm breeze that flowed through the foyer.

He must have noticed too because he changed the subject quickly. "So where did you take her for dinner tonight?"

"The Bahamian Club."

"Ooh, good food."

"I could hardly eat. I'm starving."

"Who's got Gabby?"

"Her dad. He came today and took her for some time together." She looked at her watch, the sorrow of what she missed washing over her again. "They're on their way to the airport by now."

He stood and reached out his hand. "Okay then, come on. Let me take you to get something to eat."

She looked at the hand that was extended to her. She wanted to go. She really did. But she couldn't. Divorced or not, he wouldn't understand her stuff. No one would. She put her hand in his and let him help her to her feet. "Thank you again. But honestly, my mind is so tired, I wouldn't be great company."

"You just were," he said, nudging her slightly. "You can just eat. I won't even

167

make you talk anymore."

She laughed. "No, really. Thank you." She leaned down and picked up her shoes, letting them dangle from her fingertips. "I'm just going to go home."

His eyes didn't hide his disappointment. "I'll ask again. I got my voice back, remember."

She chuckled. "Okay. You can ask again." As she walked away, she hated herself for being such a coward. But she still knew something he didn't. And something Laine didn't. And something she wished she weren't. But something that, no matter how much she wished it away, would always be a part of who she was.

8

Monday morning . . .
Laine rolled over and tumbled to the floor. Her eyelashes were stuck together and she struggled to open her eyes. When she cracked them apart, the side of the sofa was all she could see. She spat an expletive at it, then jerked the blanket down and wrapped it around her. Two days in a row she had awoken with her head pounding. Two days in a row she had slept on the sofa in a suite that cost an exorbitant amount per night. Two days in a row she had wanted to pull the covers over her head and hide.

She reached up, grabbed the side of the sofa, and pulled her body up. She walked into the bathroom and stared at her haggard image in the mirror. She had made a fool of herself last night in front of Riley. Perfect Riley. Miss "I don't drink. I don't cuss. I don't rat my hair. I'm Sandra Dee" Riley. There was something about that woman that she loathed. She didn't know what it was, but her niceness couldn't be as real as she tried to make it seem. Southern or not, there was no way she was that "good." She was as nauseating as that sweet tea Winnie craved. And if Laine weren't so ridiculously obsessed with not eating alone, she wouldn't have Riley around at all. She was going to have to find someone else to eat with. Someone who didn't make her crazy.

She unplugged her iPhone from the charger that sat on the bathroom counter. She checked it again. Nothing. She knew in her gut he wouldn't call. She longed in her heart that he would. But she knew she would tell him the same thing, so it was ridiculous that she was obsessing over the fact that he hadn't. But the calls had at least let her know he was there. Without the calls there was nothing. Books — sure. Money — a lot of it. Fans — everywhere. Happiness — gone. Life — meaningless. It vacated right along with Mitchell.

She popped four ibuprofen and headed out to run, hoping one day she could outrun the hatred she had for herself. Then maybe she could find something worth living for.

Winnie's gray walking pants with the pink sequined stripe up the leg and her pink shirt with complementing sequins made her as hard to miss as Dolly Parton's cleavage. Her round behind moved side to side in rhythm as she greeted the new morning with a brisk walk. She had joined a boot camp class in her neighborhood about a year ago, so her heart was in pretty good shape. Granted, she did more "camping" than "booting," but she enjoyed the music and the company. Plus, she didn't feel quite as guilty about what she ate anymore.

She looked out over the ocean, the sight breathtaking. Morning had arrived with elegance and grace, and the song of the ocean could have rivaled a Nashville picking fest. Her angst over seeing Albert yesterday was absorbed by the tranquility of this majestic site. This place was big enough that she could avoid him for the next five days. She looked at a young woman who jogged below her on the beach with headphones on, confirming this generation was incapable of appreciating the music that heaven played. She'd confiscated enough iPods in various sizes and colors to open a pawnshop.

She walked down the concrete walkway, admitting she was thoroughly enjoying herself. She hadn't realized how much her mind and body had needed a getaway. And that Tamyra. That girl had stolen her heart.

Her walls were slowly coming down, and Winnie knew she wasn't far away from getting to the heart of what that young woman was going through. She had talked her into going with her to dinner last night, and Tamyra had shared a little about her pageant experiences and her family. But Winnie knew that something was incredibly broken in the soul of that young girl. She was just trying to be patient to let her reveal it when she was ready. Taking care of the hearts of young people for years had taught her that every soul has its seasons.

The jogger who had passed her a few moments ago headed back in her direction. It was Laine Fulton. *The* Laine Fulton. Winnie still couldn't get over the fact that she had met a celebrity. As Laine was about to pass below her, their eyes connected and Winnie gave her a huge smile and wave. Laine stopped and slipped her earphones out of her ears as she walked up from the beach and onto the sidewalk that ran the perimeter of the Atlantis property.

"Good morning, Miss Winnie. How are you today?"

It was useless to hide her excitement. "I'm having the best time and just loving your book. Sugar, you are so talented. Those stories you tell . . . well, they just rip the heart right out of me. Have me crying like a two-year-old. How is your research going?"

Laine fidgeted. "Good. Yeah, good. A lot to discover around here."

"They haven't tried to get you swimming with the dolphins yet, have they? Lord, have mercy, they've booked me for that thing again. I didn't show up yesterday. I told them I'm not a fish. Never wanted to be a fish. Don't plan on acting like a fish."

Laine laughed. "I'll probably have to try it out so I can know how to describe it to my readers. I think I'm headed there tomorrow. I have a private session. You're welcome to join me if you'd like. Might not be as daunting with a partner."

Winnie spread her arms out. "Honey child, a wet suit can't handle all of this."

"Well, the invitation is open. I'll tell Riley that there's no need for her to come since you will be with me. And you can invite that other young woman who joined us too, if you'd like."

"You're very kind to include us in your experience. Thank you."

"Well, I'd better get back to this jog. Got a lot packed into the day."

Winnie looked at the path ahead of her. The side of the Beach Tower peered out from the other building in front of her.

"Ooh, yeah, I need to get back too. Don't really want to walk down there."

"Something wrong?"

"You read expressions too?"

Laine laughed. "I watch people all the time. You just look like something unsettled you."

She tossed her hand behind her. "Just have a few memories down there, that's all. And not a one of them do I feel like remembering today."

"Okay then." Laine turned to go, then stopped. "Um, Winnie, any chance you're free for dinner tonight? You're welcome to join me for that, too."

Winnie cocked her head. She knew this was far more than a friendly invitation. "You don't like eating alone, huh?"

Laine's eyes widened. "It was just an invitation. I travel alone all the time."

Winnie pressed further. "You're not enjoying Riley's company?"

"Riley is very professional."

Winnie raised an eyebrow and gave the woman a nod. "Okay then, since you're enjoying yourself so much but just want this crazy old fan to have dinner with you tonight and swim with the dolphins with you tomorrow, I will oblige. But just know, sugar, famous author or not, you're still a woman. And I'm thinking you haven't found a dining companion you are enjoying yet, so I'll be glad to be there."

Laine's demeanor shifted as she shifted her weight on her feet. "You don't have to come; I was just offering."

"Oh no, I'm coming, baby girl. I'm coming. My pleasure. I'll see you tonight."

"I'll have Riley call you with the time and place. Enjoy the rest of your walk."

Winnie watched as Laine jogged around the bend of the sidewalk. Laine Fulton was proof that neither money nor notoriety afforded companionship. But she'd be her companion, especially if she was buying everything on the menu again. Winnie studied the lean body of Laine as it disappeared up the beach. She had no idea why she attracted women with flawless bodies. Maybe to show them all what they could become. She laughed at the thought. Then she hastened her steps too, putting as much distance as possible between her and the memory of her past.

"Mr. Takashito, how is everything with your stay?"

"Oh, lovely . . . lovely, Ms. Sinclair."

Riley patted the arm of the gentleman who stood almost shoulder-to-shoulder with her. "Please let me know if we can get you anything."

"Will do."

Riley looked at her watch, grateful that there were no distractions this morning that kept her from being on time. After last night she could have killed Laine, but just talking about it with Christian had soothed some of that angst. And as she stood on her balcony earlier this morning and stared out over the vastness of the ocean, she'd had a talk with God about it too. She figured if He could create something as amazing as those waters in front of her and tell them where to stop so they wouldn't cover the earth, she could trust Him to help her endure Laine Fulton.

She'd talked with her mom too. Everyone was safe, and Gabby was going to have lunch with them that afternoon. She was sure she'd get an update before the day was over.

Mia rounded the corner, her phone up to her ear, the hem of her green and white dress moving as she walked. Her voice was rushed and tense. "I can only do so much. Honestly, Mom, could you lay off?"

She pulled the conversation to a quick close when her eyes caught Riley's. "I've got to go. I'll talk to you later." She closed the phone and the furrow of her brow loosened as a smile stretched across her flawless face. "Good morning, Riley. Hope last night was better than the first part of your day."

Riley smiled. "How about, it was just as interesting as my day."

"Alright then." Mia's energy was buoyant as they walked down the open corridor of The Cove.

"You okay?"

"Me?"

"Yeah, you. Wasn't eavesdropping, honest, just sounded like a tense conversation."

Mia swatted her hand. "Oh, it's nothing. My mother is stressed out over some things and just needed to vent. She doesn't realize how busy I am."

Riley stopped and turned to Mia. Mia almost passed her but realized Riley wasn't following her. She turned and looked at her. "Mia, if you need to tend to something with your family, I want you to know you can take the time to do that. I've had you going as frantically as I am."

"Nonsense, Riley. This is what I came here to do. To work. My mother will be fine. Mothers are always fine."

Riley laughed. "You never met mine."

Mia laughed with her. "Now back to work.

What do you need today?"

"Well, if you could check on Mr. and Mrs. Reynolds this afternoon. They had some questions about Thursday night's concert."

"Sure. I'll call them this morning."

"So what's on your agenda today? Anything you need to tell me?"

"No, just some new guests arriving later and a reception for that larger group that gets in at noon."

"Sounds good. I can't be at the reception, though, because of Laine. Can you handle that for me?"

Mia brushed away a long strand of wavy blonde hair that fell across her face as the wind swept through the hall. "Absolutely. Christian and I have already gone over everything this morning, and he is coming too. Then I think he and I are grabbing some lunch before the afternoon heats up."

Riley felt a slight pang in her chest. "Oh, well, good. It sounds like you've gotten everything taken care of."

"You just take care of Ms. Fulton, and we'll get through this week."

"I appreciate that. I'll see you later."

Riley shook away the heaviness that had taken up residence on her chest. *It doesn't matter if Christian is hanging out with Mia. It's not like I'm planning on going to dinner with him. Maybe he'll turn his attention on her, and I won't have to continue to find excuses not to have dinner with him.* She played ping-pong with her thoughts all the way over to the Water's Edge, where Laine was meeting her for breakfast.

The incredible smell of pancakes shifted her attention toward the growling in her gut. "Oh, my word, that smells good."

She took a seat by the door to wait for Laine and repeated to herself a hundred times, *It's going to be a great day.* By one hundred and one, Laine still wasn't there. She repeated it a hundred more times. Because she was certain the first hundred didn't take.

"Are you sure she's coming, ma'am?" the hostess asked Riley.

Riley looked at her watch. Laine was never this late. She had been a few minutes late that first evening, but it was already nine thirty. She had checked her phone multiple times to make sure she was at the right restaurant. At nine fifteen she had called Laine's room and there was no answer. Then she had called Laine's cell and got no answer there, either. "I'm not sure. I think I'll go see if I can find her. If she should come, let her know I went to look for her and call me."

"Sure."

Riley was way past panicked. If she had screwed up the time or the place, she was going to fire herself. But she had put it in her phone as soon as she and Laine had decided where to meet so something like this wouldn't happen. She stopped in the spa and checked the fitness center on her way back to The Cove, but Laine hadn't been either place. She called Mia twice on her way there to see if she had heard from her. That was when Mia told her that Gerard had seen Laine in her bathing suit, apparently headed out to her cabana.

"Oh. Okay. I'll go out there and see what's going on." Riley's aggravation was evident in her walk. She headed straight to Cain and over to Laine's cabana. Laine was laid out on one of the lounge chairs overlooking the ocean. Her eyes were closed when Riley arrived.

"Can I help you, Riley?"

Riley was glad Laine's eyes were closed because then she wouldn't see the flush of anger that had settled over Riley's face. "I was just checking on you. I had been waiting on you at breakfast and wanted to make sure you were okay."

Laine never opened her eyes. "I hope

you're not irritated. I changed my mind. I grabbed some breakfast and decided to come out here."

Riley swallowed and made every effort to relax her voice. "Okay, well, that's fine. This is why we got you the cabana, so that you could enjoy it. Anything else I can do for you this morning? Would you like me to schedule lunch for you somewhere?"

"Sure, plan on meeting me back at that restaurant for lunch. I'll be ready to eat around noon."

"Okay, noon it is. I will meet you there then. If you need anything else, just give me a call." She hoped the tightness in her voice wasn't betraying her.

"I won't need anything else, Riley. Just lunch." And with that she turned her black-bikini-clad body away. It was clear Riley had been dismissed.

Tamyra stared at her phone. There hadn't been another call since the one yesterday. That had allowed her nerves to settle slightly. She had talked to her mom for a little while when she had gotten up to let her know she was okay and would be home Saturday night. Her mom's relief was evident. She walked out onto the balcony and removed her bathing suit from the railing.

She let the sun wash over her and warm her skin. Her eyes closed as she lifted her head toward it.

"I know I've been really mad at You."

The warmth increased on her skin.

"But I just wanted to thank You for Winnie."

A breeze swept over her.

She opened her eyes and blinked them at the blue sky. She was certain the sun winked.

Tamyra walked across the glass bridge as the waterfalls that flanked it welcomed her to the soothing world she was about to enter. All the elements of nature that ran throughout The Cove seemed to converge at the Mandara Spa. Winnie's kids had given her a day of spa treatments, and she had asked Tamyra to join her. Tamyra enjoyed the company. And with the way Winnie talked so incessantly, it gave her brain little time to consume itself with her stuff.

The hostess greeted her and led her up a spiral staircase at the edge of the foyer. Winnie had already gotten to the "relaxation" part of the relaxation lounge when Tamyra arrived. She sat sprawled out on a large lounge chair, white terry cloth robe covering her body, bottled water in her right hand, head leaned back, eyes closed, and the gentle sounds of her snoring filtering through the otherwise-tranquil atmosphere.

"I think we found her," Tamyra said to the young woman.

"Good. They'll take you back for your massages in a few minutes. Your wraps will be after that, and then you can soak in the pool for a while, grab some lunch, and we'll finish you off with your manicure and pedicure."

"I can't think of a more perfect day."

She left Tamyra with her companion.

"Sleeping beauty," Tamyra whispered.

Winnie snorted and rolled over, the water bottle falling from her hand and rolling underneath her chair. The commotion of it all woke her from her sleep. "Oh, my. Please tell me I wasn't sawing logs."

"Not quite. More like a gentle puffing."

Winnie sat up on her chair. "I puffed?"

"Kind of puffed. Sputtered. Something like that."

"Huh? That sounds a lot more feminine than what I imagined I did."

"Well, I'm glad I could bring you some peace regarding your snoring habits," Tamyra laughed. "How long have you been here?"

"A while. I wanted to make sure I could get here without Albert seeing me."

"He seemed harmless."

Winnie squinted at her. "He's a man. Have you ever met a harmless man?"

Tamyra's skin bristled but she was rescued.

"Ladies, we have your room ready," a petite Bahamian said as she entered the lounge. "Follow me this way. You can get a robe in there if you'd like." She pointed to the women's locker room.

"Sure. I'll be right behind y'all." Tamyra slipped out of her clothes and into a robe, then moved down the hall to the door where Winnie had disappeared. Winnie was already laid out on her table, face looking down at the floor through the hole that held her head.

"We're about to be pummeled." Her words came out slightly muffled.

"I thought massages were supposed to be relaxing," Tamyra said as she laid her robe on the chair beside her table and climbed underneath the sheet.

"I asked for the Swedish massage. And from what I hear, those Swedes can kill you."

The door opened, hopefully bringing in their masseuses. "You ladies ask for Swedish massage?" Their Asian accents were evident.

"How do Asian women know how to do Swedish massages?" Winnie asked.

Tamyra laughed.

"We'll show you."

And show them they did. For sixty straight minutes they kneaded and rubbed, and at moments Tamyra was certain her masseuse had rearranged her muscle tissue. Winnie groaned on more than one occasion and not from pleasure. It was clear she was getting what she asked for. Tamyra couldn't help but grimace a time or two, but by the way the lady stayed at her shoulders, it was evident that the stress of the last two months had taken up permanent residence there.

An hour and a half later both of them were slathered head to toe with mud. Tamyra turned her head to look at Winnie. Winnie must have sensed it because she turned at the same time. Tamyra burst out laughing, the mud on her face cracking all over. "You look like a raccoon."

"I don't know why you think I look so funny. You look the exact same way."

"What would your kids say if they could see you now?"

"I can't say it." She started giggling.

That made it even funnier. "Come on, why can't you say it?"

"Because I've never said a cussword in my life. I'm Baptist, remember?" she spat out through her laughter.

Tamyra was trying to hold her face still. "You've got to tell me."

"I can't. It's horrible. Sam would die."

That cracked Tamyra up uncontrollably. Winnie couldn't contain herself either. "Sam's already dead," Tamyra announced. Laughter spewed from her gut.

Winnie let out a whoop as her hands flew up in the air, the laughter preventing her from breaking her seventy-two-year no-cussing streak. And with that, the mud that was all over each of them cracked like a seismic plate shift in the earth, making the one hundred and fifty dollars of mud they had slathered over their bodies worth every penny. Whether it had done anything for their complexions or not, it had already done wonders for their souls.

9

Monday afternoon . . .

Laine's body was sprawled across a large, sand-colored sectional. Her head was propped up by vibrant orange and yellow pillows, giving her an unobstructed view of the pool. She was tempted to sleep out here. One of twenty cabanas that ran along the perimeter of the pool, it had everything she could need. There was an entertainment center behind her with a flat-screen television fully equipped with a DVD and CD player. There was a daybed, a beautiful bathroom, a patio dining table, and a magnificent view of the Atlantic Ocean. With the teakwood louvered doors open, she could see all the way to the end of the world.

The cabana butler had already brought a tray of fruit, a sandwich, and a glass of wine and placed them on the sea grass–woven ottoman that sat in front of her. And from her throne she was able to watch the rich try to get richer, the tan try to get more tan, and the lovers try to fall more in love. Had she only had to endure the first two, she would have enjoyed herself a little more. Her iPhone sat at her side; her assistant had already called four times this morning, and she had sent her to voice mail. Laine was surprised her assistant kept trying to call her after being ignored for two straight days.

She had avoided Riley too. After last night it was easier for her to gain back her control by being the diva she could tell Riley already assumed that she was. Laine had no intention of having lunch with her and knew it when she said she would meet her. Ate a hole in her gut too. Despite what Riley thought about her. But she couldn't help it. The last thing she wanted was just the two of them at a lunch where she would be reminded of how completely inadequate she really was. She already knew that. She pulled one of the pillows from behind her head and threw it over her face. If she could smother herself without having to suffocate, she'd press it in and not let go.

Unfortunately that pillow over her face caused her to miss Riley heading her way. She heard Riley clear her throat.

"Yes," she said from behind the pillow.

"I see you've been taken care of for lunch."

Laine tried not to squirm beneath the pillow. But she knew if she kept her head under it, she'd look like a two-year-old trying to hide from her mother instead of like the prolific author that Riley was responsible for catering to. She moved the pillow back under her head as she fluffed it on the sides.

She looked straight at Riley. "I decided I wanted to eat out here. I needed the fresh air."

"Laine, please don't think because of last night you have to avoid —"

Laine cut her off. "I don't avoid anyone."

She could see Riley steel herself slightly. "Well, I do understand —"

"I don't need your understanding. I simply need your assistance in gathering the information that I came here for. That's all." The words came out icier than even Laine knew she was capable of. She saw the change in Riley immediately.

"Okay, then, how can I take care of you for dinner?" Her words now carried an edge of their own.

"I invited Miss Winnie and her friend to dinner. We'd like to go to Café Martinique tonight."

"Would you like me to make the reservation for just the three of you?"

Laine could sense this was what she really

wanted to do. "No, I want you to join us. It's your *job,* remember. *I'm* your job this week."

"Well, *all* the guests are my job, Laine. But it will be my pleasure to join you. I'll make reservations for six."

"Yes. For *six.*" She stated it because she needed it to sound like it was her idea. She was officially a two-year-old.

"I'll see you at dinner."

Laine watched as Riley made her way across the walkway and through the lounge chairs of the guests. Men's heads turned and followed her petite figure, outlined to perfection in flowing white trousers and a short-sleeved, buttoned-up black shirt with a ruffled collar. The two-inch white wedges she wore gave her legs a longer look than her height afforded her. And that black hair. The perfect curls made Laine tug at the back of her short blonde locks.

Laine pounded her hand against her head. *You're horrible,* she chided herself. *She's been nothing but nice and you've been a jerk. You are a jerk.* She mumbled the last line to herself. "She doesn't deserve that no matter what you think of her."

She reached over to the patio table and grabbed an apple. She bit into it with determination, hoping that wouldn't curse her more than she already felt, because apples sure hadn't done Eve any favors.

Riley tried to stifle her furor. "That little, pompous . . ." She had a thousand colorful adjectives she could pepper Ms. Fulton with. But none of them would be crass enough. True enough. She was just evil. Downright evil. Riley had no idea how someone could completely disregard another person the way she had. What made it so frustrating was Riley knew Laine was capable of being nice, but twice today she had intentionally stood her up. She hadn't been stood up since that Valentine's Day in high school when she had gone to school with an oversize card and a larger-than-life chocolate bunny, and her "boyfriend," Ralph, told her to take them home with her and he'd pick them up later. She ended up eating the chocolate bunny herself three months later. Riley knew in her gut that Laine's behavior was because she was embarrassed over last night. But if she had allowed Riley the opportunity to finish a sentence, she might have realized that Riley understood and was glad she could help her. At least she *had* been glad.

The sound of Riley's shoes hitting the stone floors reverberated through the tall ceilings of the corridor. As she neared the front walkway, she saw Mia and Christian headed down the hall. She thought for a moment Mia saw her, but apparently she hadn't, or she would have returned her wave. She watched as Mia ran her hand up the back of Christian's shirt and playfully ran her fingers through the thick black waves of his hair. She could hear their laughter all the way down the hall to where she was. The yuck in her gut grew to nausea. Frustration at herself churned just as aggressively. And the desire for her hand to be the one running through Christian's hair even she couldn't deny.

Tamyra leaned back and closed her eyes as her toes received their finishing touches. The French pedicure matched her fingernails. "It's been a perfect day."

"Perfect." Winnie slurped her virgin mango daiquiri. "I'm like a pig in slop."

Tamyra cocked one eye open and looked at Winnie. The nail technician was rubbing lotion into her calf, and her body moved up and down with the vibration of the massage chair beneath her. "How many of those have you had today?"

"I'm on vacation. I'm not counting. Calories don't count this week, so I'd appreciate it if you take no worries in what this here voluptuous frame consumes," she said, running her free hand across her stomach.

Tamyra closed her eyes. "I'll remember that."

"That means tonight when Laine orders one of everything off the menu, you are to pay no attention to what I consume. I won't talk about your ridiculous eating habits, and you just pretend I'm chomping on lettuce."

A chuckle slipped from Tamyra's throat. "You got it."

They lay there with the sweet aromas of the lotions and the soft ambience of the music and lighting as the techs finished up their day of beauty and left them in a state of serenity.

Tamyra opened her eyes and rose up to look at Winnie. It was just the two of them. She rubbed the soft cream leather arms of her chair and leaned back, closing her eyes again. "Winnie?"

Winnie didn't move. "Yeah, sugar."

"I bet you're really great with those kids at your school."

"I am." She sighed heavily. "I was made for the difficult cases. Just part of God's calling, I guess."

"Yeah. I guess."

Winnie was silent for a few moments, then

spoke softly. "So when did you find out you were HIV-positive, honey?"

Tamyra's body bolted upright. Every ounce of blood rushed from her face. Had she been standing, she wouldn't have been for long. Winnie knew. How? She was so private. So guarded. So careful. "How did you . . ." Her words seemed to lodge in her throat.

Winnie didn't move. "I told you, honey; I work in the inner city. I know what the face of HIV looks like at first. I know its voice. I can read its hopelessness. And you could be its poster child."

Tamyra sat there dumbstruck, staring at Winnie. Her body wanted to run. But she couldn't move. The only person who had ever said those words to her had been the doctor who told her. And Winnie just lay there, as if she had said something as casual as "What do you want for lunch? the turkey or the ham?" This woman was like no one she had ever met.

Her heartbeat slowed. The blood slowly moved back to its rightful place. Over the last two days Winnie had made Tamyra feel like she could tell her anything. She slowly lay back down, turned her body toward Winnie, and leaned on her elbow. "No one knows."

Winnie finally opened her eyes and turned her head. "They do now, baby girl." She raised her glass and took a long swig, then rolled over and mimicked Tamyra's position. "You haven't told your family?"

"No." She paused. Her eyes began to burn with tears. "I don't know how to tell them."

"Tell them like you told me."

She sniffed and swatted at her tears. "I didn't tell you."

Winnie chuckled and reached down to grab a towel from the table beside her. "No, you didn't, did you?" She handed the towel to Tamyra. "Do you want to tell me?"

The blood began to pump harder. She hesitated. Then finally spoke. "Yeah. I do."

Winnie nodded.

"I met Jason two years ago. He plays in the NFL. We met on a blind date and that was pretty much it. He swept me off my feet, and I thought my life was as wonderful as a life could be, until I won my title, anyway. As soon as they placed the crown on my head, my life changed. I had to spend a year traveling the state and I wasn't as available. That was when I noticed that he was acting distant. I questioned him about it, of course, and he answered me with an engagement ring. A four-carat, radiant-cut stone set in platinum. He said the 'distance' was all in my mind because I just wasn't around as much."

"Did you believe him?"

"At first I did, yeah. But when the new season started and he was on the road, I got a call from one of my close friends who I had gone to college with. She lives in Dallas and had seen him with a woman at a bar when his team was in town to play the Cowboys. When the team got home, I called one of his team-mates, Ben, a guy with impeccable character, and just asked him if it was true. He didn't respond at first, part of that teammate oath or something. But I begged him to be honest with me and he finally broke. He said there was rarely a city they went to where Jason didn't have someone to spend an evening with, whether she was free or purchased. He asked me not to tell Jason who it was that had told me."

Winnie shifted her weight and leaned in farther. "Are you still planning the wedding this whole time?"

"No, I stopped everything. But he had no idea because he had left it all up to me anyway, as if he were doing me a favor."

Winnie puffed.

"So as soon as I got off the phone with Ben, I immediately went to my doctor to get tested."

"Had you ever been tested before?" Winnie asked.

Tamyra's voice constricted. "I had never been intimate before. He had been my first and my only." The tears were hot down her face. She wiped at them with the back of her hand.

She watched as pity flooded Winnie's expression. Winnie's stubby, soft hand reached over and patted Tamyra's. It was the same kind of touch her mother would have given her. "Go ahead, baby."

"So I went to get tested and then waited. It was the longest week of my life. I had to avoid Jason's phone calls and was doing pretty good at it until he showed up banging on my front door. But I even skirted around all of it that night too. The next morning I got the call from my doctor that changed my life. I went in to see her and she told me I was HIV-positive. That my T cell count was 889. And my viral load was 100,000. She announced my death sentence as if she were giving me results from uneventful, routine blood work."

"Did you tell him then?"

"Yeah, I told him. I was in a blind rage. I don't even remember driving over to his place that morning. All I remember is a depth of anger that I didn't even know existed in me. I banged on the door of his loft like a crazy woman. When he came to the door, I went for his throat."

Winnie's eyes widened. "Like, fingers wrapped around his throat?"

"Oh yeah, I was screaming and yelling and crying. I told him I had given him everything and he had taken everything from me. I was honestly like a wild animal. I told him I hoped he died and that I was going to tell anyone who would listen that he had given me this. And that was the first time he ever hit me."

Winnie wanted to respond. Tamyra could tell by the way she slightly jumped from her seat and the way she chewed on the inside of her mouth. "Where did he hit you, baby girl?"

"The first time he hit me, it was in my gut. He hit me so hard it took the wind right out of me and I fell back onto the sofa just trying to get air, any air. That was when he grabbed me by my arms, squeezing them until they almost went numb, as he was talking to me in this voice . . . this voice, it was so controlled, so evil. I had never seen him this way before. He pulled me from the sofa and threw me on the floor. Then he kicked me in my side. He said if I told anyone, he'd kill me and that he had no reservations about doing it now since both of us were going to die eventually. He'd kill me and then just take his own life. He let me know that I *would* go through with the wedding and I would do everything else he told me too. The final kick left me in a ball on the floor. He walked out as if we had discussed the weather."

"Did you ever think about going to the police?"

Tamyra shifted on the lounge chair. "No, all I thought about was getting as far away from him as possible, where he'd have no idea where I was. I went straight to my apartment, listed all of my furniture on craigslist, and had a lot of things sold by that evening. I took the rest to a storage facility, dropped my car off at the airport for my sister to pick up, and called my parents to tell them I just needed some time away. I had an old college professor who I knew had a place in Puerto Vallarta, called him from a pay phone, and he said I could spend six weeks there to do whatever I needed. I tossed my phone and got one of those prepay phones, where no one could get my number, and called my mom when I got there just so she would know I was safe. And until this morning I thought I was."

Winnie sat up in her chair. "What do you

mean, until this morning?"

Tamyra sat up too, her hands starting to shake slightly. "He called me. On the phone that my mother doesn't even have the number to. He found it. And if he found that, he'll find me."

She watched that sassy little swing come into Winnie's shoulders. "So what have you decided?"

"What do you mean?"

"I mean you've run away for almost seven weeks. In those seven weeks what decisions have you made for your life?"

"I don't have a life, Winnie. I have a death sentence no matter how it comes. In all honesty, if he did kill me, it would just end the misery faster."

Winnie pursed her lips. "You'd better thank God almighty I didn't just slap you. Truth is, you need to be slapped. People are living longer with HIV now than they ever have. But you've got to have a will to live. And as far as I'm concerned, the only thing dying around here is that piggy they're going to cook for my dinner. Now, you have one of two choices: you can cower the rest of your life out in fear, or you can face Mr. Fancy Pants head-on and get your life back."

Tamyra felt herself shrinking into her shell

again. What had come alive over the last two days was about to go back into hiding. "You don't know him, Winnie."

Winnie must have seen it because she quickly leaned in closer to her and put her hands on top of Tamyra's. They were quivering. "You, Tamyra Larsen, have been called to live. You have not been called to die. And the only way you will ever live is to get out of the shadows. You did it with me, but there's a lot more to do."

Tamyra dropped her head. "I've done all I can do."

"You've done all you're *willing* to do. You haven't done all you *can* do. Now look at me."

Tamyra kept staring at the cream leather of her chair. It looked so smooth. No cracks. No age.

"Look at me," Winnie said louder.

Tamyra raised her gaze.

"Do you trust me?"

She nodded.

"Then hear me. It is time to face your fears. You can't continue to hide, baby girl. And you're not going to die. We'll do it together. Nothing until you're ready, okay? I promise. Nothing until you're ready."

"Promise?"

"Promise. So come here." Winnie held out

her arms and Tamyra slipped from her chair and crawled into them. They felt as comforting as her mother's. "You did real good, honey. You did real good." Winnie's whispers ran through Tamyra's ears.

Even though fear had swarmed through her again like a hive of angry bees, she still knew that what she had done was a huge step. That alone had lifted something. And being here in Winnie's arms had healed something. Maybe there was healing in these waters after all.

10

Monday evening . . .

Riley was having déjà vu. This marked the third time today that she had stood in the entrance of a restaurant waiting on Laine. Her bets were on being stood up again and spending the evening with Winnie and Tamyra, which would be far more enjoyable, she was certain. The peaceful music from the Steinway settled her nerves. She looked out over the breathtaking marina, the sun descending in the sky, and she couldn't help but breathe a prayer of thankfulness that she had made it through the day. Truth be told, she had gotten a lot of work done and had enjoyed her Laine-free afternoon.

"Magnifique!" Winnie announced as she entered the front of the restaurant. Her lime green denim outfit sparkled like the sun on water. Riley watched her carefully scan the restaurant.

Tamyra was right behind her, her long, lean body covered in a simple black dress. "Hello, Riley."

"Good evening, ladies. I'm glad you could join us." She looked at Winnie oddly. "Are you looking for someone, Winnie?"

Winnie turned her head back around quickly. "Me . . . um . . . no, I'm not looking for a soul. Just you. I guess you've figured out by now Laine doesn't like eating alone," she announced.

"Well, I was eating with her," Riley informed her.

"I don't think she's crazy about you, Riley, for whatever reason."

Tamyra grabbed her arm. "Winnie."

Riley stood there dumbfounded.

"It's not about you, Riley. This lady isn't happy, and she's simply trying to get through the week. Anyway, I think she just wants a warm body at the table that doesn't remind her of her 'stuff.' Apparently, you remind her of her stuff and I don't."

"Am I interrupting something, ladies?" Laine asked as she approached their circle of three.

Riley felt her head start to pound.

"Not a thing, sugar. We were just talking about what a lovely evening we're all going to have. Weren't we, ladies?"

Riley and Tamyra nodded obediently. Winnie took matters into her own hands and told the hostess they were ready to be seated. They were led to a beautiful table in the back of the room next to the glass-enclosed wine cellar that carried the most celebrated vintages French and California wineries had to offer. Winnie's rhinestone-covered outfit lit their way.

"I swear that woman must carry a BeDazzler in her pocket," Laine whispered.

Tamyra stifled her laughter.

"How is this, ladies?" the hostess asked.

Winnie gave her a pat. "It's fine, sugar. Just fine."

The women all stood at their chairs awkwardly.

"Sit, girls."

They all sat like schoolchildren under their principal's watchful eye.

Laine picked up her menu as she spoke. "Are you sure I didn't interrupt something?"

Riley picked up her menu and stuck it in front of her face. "No, we were just talking about all we've discovered today. Apparently, Miss Winnie here is a perceptive one."

"She doesn't miss a thing," Tamyra added.

Riley looked up as Tamyra raised her eyebrows at Winnie.

Laine ordered almost as extravagantly as she had their first evening together, and between Winnie and Tamyra's tales of their "day of beauty," Riley needed to contribute little. By the time Laine paid the check, Riley had watched her fill up at least five pages of notes. She was pretty certain Winnie would have her own complete story line in Laine's next book. Truth be told, if Laine wanted her book to write itself, she could have walked around and recorded Winnie for seven days.

Winnie stood to leave, and Riley and the other women followed suit.

"I'm looking forward to our dolphin experience tomorrow," Laine said.

"Oh, about that," Tamyra said, "I'm not really into swimming."

"You'll love it," Laine assured her. Her smile was gracious and her voice irritatingly tender.

Riley wanted to slap her.

The fear was evident on Tamyra's face. "I don't know."

Laine walked over and put her arm around Tamyra. "Trust me. It will be the experience of a lifetime. Now, you ladies go get some rest and I'll see you tomorrow afternoon." She hugged them both before they left.

She turned to Riley as they disappeared up the hall. "I won't need you for that tomorrow, Riley." The old Laine was back.

Riley was grateful to not have to spend the afternoon with her, but the way Laine said it made Riley's entire body bristle, though she refused to let it come through her words. "No problem. That's fine. We've got your appointment all set up. Do you need me to meet you for breakfast or schedule anything else for you?"

"I'd like you to meet me at Mosaic for breakfast at nine. And if you could bring with you all of the answers to the questions I had yesterday, then I can make some final notes and we can begin our tour of the rest of the facility after our dolphin adventure." With that, she turned to go. There was no *good night.* There was no arm around the shoulder. There was no hug. There was only the backside of one Laine Fulton, who needed a swift kick in the . . . When Riley knew Laine couldn't see her, she stuck out her tongue. She had grown so much since she'd been here.

11

Tuesday morning . . .

"Hey, Daddy."

"Hey, angel girl. You missing *your* girl?"

Riley leaned against the railing and let the breeze wash over her face. "Like crazy."

He chuckled that deep laugh she loved. "She's doing good. You know your mother; she'll have every part of that child dolled up by the time she gets back to you."

"You driving?"

"Yeah, headed down to the office."

"I knew I could catch you up this early. You're the only person I can call at the crack of dawn and find up and at 'em."

"Well, you know, the sun don't shine on the same dog's tail all the time."

She laughed. "Still afraid the sun is going to quit shining on you? You've been doing this for almost forty years."

"Never know when they're going to want some new blood."

"Strom Thurmond was still a senator when he was in his nineties. You're only sixty-seven."

"Strom Thurmond was old as dirt and the sun quit shining on him quite a few years before he realized. Can't say I want to be that old guy either."

"Well, I think you've got a lot of sunshine days."

"My girls are what bring out the sun."

Riley rubbed her toes on top of her other foot. "Thanks for taking care of my angel girl."

"You take care of *my* angel girl."

She felt the burning start in her eyes. "Love you."

"See you soon, okay?"

"What? You're going to actually take a vacation?"

"Been thinking about it. Don't under-estimate the old geezer. I still surprise your mama every now and then."

"I can't wait."

She hung up the phone and stared out into the first burst of morning. She prayed for a grace to match her day. With Laine Fulton as a part of it, she decided to pray that prayer twice.

When she walked into Gabby's room, Ted was fast asleep on his rocky throne. She placed some lettuce inside his cage. "How you doing, Teddy? Missing our girl?"

Ted was motionless, his eyes closed.

"I know. Me too." She nudged him with her finger to make sure he was at least alive. His eyes popped open. "Good boy, Teddy."

His stubby legs moved slightly on his perch.

"Your princess will be back soon, I promise. Until then you're stuck with me."

He got his footing and closed his eyes again.

She shook her head. "Oh, if only getting rid of people were that easy. I'd walk around with my eyes closed all day."

The Cove was still quiet at seven o'clock. Without Gabby at the house, Riley couldn't sleep. But at least she was completely prepared for her day. She had spent most of the night and the wee hours of the morning finishing up the answers to all of Laine's questions and officially OD'ing on Dr Pepper. Somewhere around 3 a.m., when The Cove was laying to rest its reds and magentas and awakening its yellows and oranges, she fell asleep. She wouldn't awaken until The Cove began to play its piano and strings. Those were the sounds that were wafting through the breezeways while the staff flitted about like conductors of a new day.

A warm breeze blew through her soft curls, and the skirt of her red dress fluttered around the tops of her knees. She patted the double layer of matte gold beads that hung from her neck and straightened her collar. With as little sleep as she had last night, she was simply grateful she had been able to dress herself at all.

She headed to the far end of the entrance that presented a panoramic view of the grounds of The Cove and a breathtaking view of the ocean. She wanted to see it one more time before the day officially began. She placed her hands on the railing and leaned over slightly, closed her eyes and breathed in deeply. The salt air clung to her lungs and brought to mind every cherished memory of her childhood.

"You aren't going to jump, are you?"

She opened her eyes and looked up to heaven quickly. She'd never heard an audible voice from above before. And she thought if God was omniscient and all, He'd know jumping hadn't been on her Tuesday agenda.

"Riley." Christian touched the back of her arm.

She almost jumped out of her skin. "Oh,

my stars! You scared the living daylights out of me."

He laughed. "Stars and living daylights?"

She leaned back against the railing, trying to steady herself and slow her heartbeat. "Yes, those are old sayings."

"Well, you looked mighty serious leaning over the railing like that. I didn't know what you might be planning."

"Rest assured it wasn't jumping. I'm petrified of heights."

He turned and leaned against the railing too. They both stared at the long expanse of the lobby. "What are you doing here so early?"

"Trying to get some work done before Laine Fulton determines the rest of my day."

"Still keeping pace with the writer, huh?"

She turned her head toward him. "She stood me up twice yesterday. She hugged Winnie and Tamyra. Hugged them! Oooh, she makes me crazy!" Her hands gripped tighter on the railing that she now held behind her. Her face scrunched up. "See? Just talking about her gets me all riled up."

"You Southern women. You're loud and passionate. You're a lot like the women from my family."

"I'll take that as a compliment."

He laughed. "You obviously haven't met the women from my family."

She couldn't help but laugh too.

"You watching this storm?"

"Get updates periodically. How's it looking?"

"It turned into a tropical storm yesterday afternoon, and if it stays on course, it looks like we'll be in its path. The swells have really increased and the waves are coming in quicker. So there is definitely something out there."

"When did you find out it had been upgraded?"

"This morning."

"Maybe Laine will fly out sooner."

He smiled, his dimples deep and adorable. "From the sounds of Ms. Fulton, I can imagine her sitting on the beach, sipping a martini while it roars around her."

"You've met her, then," Riley quipped.

He shook his head. "So, lunch? Dinner? Midnight picnic on the beach before we pack away the umbrellas and lounge chairs?"

"Lunch and dinner will be determined by Ms. Fulton. And midnight, I pray, will find me comatose, since I was awake last night at midnight."

"I should have called you then, huh?"

"Yes, you should have called me last night," she said, smiling. He was undeniably charming.

"I hope you have a wonderful day, and I hope Ms. Fulton realizes how lucky she is to spend her meals with you."

"Thank you. I'm really not crazy."

"I know. You just play one on TV," he said, offering her a wink as he headed through the lobby.

Riley covered the day with Mia, cleared all the messages awaiting reply from her desk, and headed to Mosaic to meet Laine for breakfast. By nine thirty she knew she had been stood up again, and something inside of Riley snapped. There was only so far she was willing to allow a customer to go. She didn't care if Laine's face was plastered across the backs of thirty million books. At this point Riley also didn't care if she lost her job. And she wasn't calling anyone to get permission. She was simply finding Laine Fulton.

Laine sat out on the balcony of Sea Glass. She had grabbed a croissant and a coffee and was enjoying the breeze coming off the ocean. She brushed crumbs from her breakfast off the mother-of-pearl and copper mosaic tabletop, then leaned her head back on the gray suede cushion, scooting her feet farther out in front of her.

"I dare you to say you forgot."

She knew immediately who it was, although the fire behind the voice was slightly contrary to the Riley she knew.

"There's no need to dare me," she said, eyes still closed. "I didn't forget; I simply changed my mind."

She heard a loud puff of air come out of Riley. "What is it, Laine? Have I offended you or something? Because I have tried to do nothing since you've been here but serve you and make sure that you had every resource at your disposal to make this a productive and pleasant trip for you. So what is it? What have I done to make you act so incredibly rude?"

Laine raised herself from her seat. She turned her head to see Riley's black curls bouncing slightly on the edges of her shoulders, her hands on the hips of her red dress, and her black eyes blazing. Her voice, however, was completely calm. "I don't owe you any explanation, to be honest with you, Riley. If I decide to change my mind, I decide to change my mind." She could tell by Riley's expression that didn't register well.

"I have other guests I'm responsible for,

215

Ms. Fulton." Now she was Ms. Fulton. "Guests who appreciate my service and attention. So, forgive me, but yes, if you're not going to show, I would appreciate a phone call. A common courtesy. I don't care where you're from; decency is decency."

Laine felt her own anger rise but maintained control. "You know what, Riley? I simply don't like you." There. She said it. And it felt as awful as it sounded. "You and your little perfect life, flitting around here as if you are doing the world a favor." She motioned with her hand. "With your senator daddy and your fancy name."

"Perfect? You think I'm perfect? You're mad at me because you think I'm perfect?" Riley's rage seemed to escalate with each rhetorical question.

"I believe that's what I said."

Riley moved in closer to Laine. She invaded her space to an uncomfortable level, but Laine refused to move. She could see the tears that now lay at the edges of Riley's eyes. Laine wouldn't let her face betray her, holding her glare steady.

"Okay, Laine, since you know me so well and are such a discerner of people, just tell me what exactly made me so perfect. Huh?" Her anger was palpable now, and her words were engorged with passion and furor.

"Was I perfect when the car I was driving ran over a little boy, Laine? Was I perfect when I snuffed out the life of a three-year-old right in front of his mother? a little boy who was doing nothing but chasing a ball out into the road? Was I perfect then, Laine?"

Laine sat there, stoic. She wouldn't even let herself blink.

"Or, no, wait; oh yes, I know." She watched as Riley slammed her hands together. "I was perfect when I became so depressed that I consumed enough alcohol to drown my self-loathing and destroy my family. Was that perfect woman the one you were talking about? Or was I perfect when my husband left and had full custody of my child because I didn't have a waking moment that was sober? Was I perfect then, Laine? Tell me, because I really want to know. Is that the perfect woman you were talking about? the one you — oh, how did you say it? — 'simply don't like'?"

Laine's jaw pulsed as she clenched her teeth.

Riley's tears were free-falling now. "Was I perfect when even my own daddy —" she all but spat the words — "knew it was best for my husband to raise my baby? Was I perfect then, Laine? Or no, maybe it was when I stole from my own parents just to have another bottle of booze, and they finally had to kick me out of their house too." Her hands shot up to the heavens. "That has to be when I was perfect!"

Riley swatted at her tears and appeared to gain control of herself. Her voice was now almost a whisper. "You have no idea, Laine. You want to talk about perfect, let's dissect your life. But don't you dare — and I mean, don't you dare — ever judge me again. And I don't care if I lose my job. Because I'd rather lose my job than be treated with the level of disrespect you have shown me over the last couple of days. But you can rest assured it stops here."

She turned and walked out through the lobby, leaving a wake that all but took Laine under.

Laine refused to move until Riley was no longer in her view. Then she bent down slowly, picked up her bag, and walked to her room. It wasn't until the door was closed neatly behind her that she collapsed onto the floor. She was now officially everything she hated. Which seemed fitting for a person who hated herself so completely. Her tears fell on the plush taupe carpet with abandon. She didn't care what stain they left because it would pale in comparison to the stain that rested on her soul. To the *A* that was sewn on her chest. To the demons that clawed at her mind. She had been mean. She had been cruel. She had been downright evil. She had hurt Riley to her core. It was evident. And she had deserved every ounce of Riley's anger.

She'd had no idea. She had no idea what Riley's past looked like. Riley saw the contempt Laine had for her. What she didn't see was the contempt Laine had for herself. Riley had never been anything but kind. Not once had she judged her. Not once had she avoided her, even when Laine treated her with complete disrespect. The crying started from her gut and the wails grew until her body shook with sobs. There were no words, just groans from someplace so deep and dark and broken that the intensity of it would have dropped her to the ground had her face not already been buried in the carpet.

Tears rushed down her face in such rapid tandem that the carpet beneath her was wet against her cheek. Her body lurched forward and back with each gushing wave that rolled through her. And with each surge of un-leashed regret, the groans crescendoed. In her entire life she knew she had never been more desperate or more completely vulnerable than she was this moment. It felt unavoidable and emptying. And somewhere in the middle of it, a whisper penetrated her cries and traveled straight to her heart.

"You're never so far that He can't find you."

They were Mitchell's last words to her the day she had moved out of the house. Those words had driven her crazy for the last year and a half. His faith had driven her crazy. Especially after Dubai. But now, right now, in a strange room on an island in the Atlantic Ocean, in the ruins of what had once resembled a life, she wished it were true. She wished so many things. The words ran through her mind again. *"You're never so far . . ."*

She felt worlds away from everything. Yet she spoke anyway. "I want to be found," she cried. "Can the lost be found?"

As soon as the words fell from her lips, a breeze blew past her. Her head rose quickly, the air against her wet face making her aware of every track a tear had left. She looked at the glass door to see if it had flown open, but it was closed. Tightly. She laid her head back down on the carpet. "Please, please find me."

The breeze blew again. This time harder, swifter. And she knew. She knew she had been found. The breath of heaven swept over her. She lay there, letting it make its way to every empty cavity of her soul. It was as if she could feel it coursing through her very veins, bringing life to places in her being that had never lived. The warmth of it was real and raw and transforming. She wept at its gentleness and prayed it wouldn't hasten its departure. It felt strange yet familiar. It felt kind yet authoritative. It felt consuming yet forgiving. And it felt as if it knew her inside out. As if it created her. As if it had been waiting for this moment, and when she had relinquished herself, it was there to finally take up residence in the soul of her. The soul it had created.

When the healing of every broken place inside of her had rested from its work, she turned over, lay on her back, and stared at the ceiling. In that moment she knew that Mitchell was right: you could never travel so far that heaven couldn't find you. And Roy had been right too: you had to admit you were diseased before you could ever be healed.

Two hours passed before she raised herself up off the floor. But when she got up, something inside Laine Fulton was no longer lost. No, something — if she was willing to be honest — had been found. She just never dreamed she'd have to come to a place called Paradise to find it. But she knew that there really was healing here, if you were truly willing to admit you were sick. She could only hope that it wouldn't stop there, because there was so much left to redeem.

Winnie sat on a thick-cushioned chaise in the lower lobby breeze-way that connected The Cove and The Reef. She leaned back into the deep cushion and pulled her tennis shoe–clad feet up on top. She took a sip of her grande mocha Frappuccino and pulled her blueberry muffin from the vellum brown bag. She had walked a couple miles and once again avoided the Beach Towers. She took a bite of her muffin and chewed as she looked out at the immaculate tropical paradise in front of her. Nature was singing to her and she loved every minute of it. At some point she might even tell her kids how absolutely wonderful this entire trip had been. Once she was home and had success-fully avoided Albert.

"Beautiful morning, isn't it, baby?" She spoke to the air.

Birds chirped as they flew from palm tree to palm tree.

"I knew you'd think so. Can't believe I let

you get me addicted to these Starbucks thingamajigs. I wouldn't look so voluptuous if you hadn't turned me on to them."

She giggled.

"I know you like me this way."

She took another sip of her coffee and dabbed at the corners of her mouth. She quieted her conversation when she heard someone round the corner.

"Winnie Harris? Is that you?"

Winnie turned her head and all but choked on her muffin.

"Oh, sorry. I didn't mean to surprise you." He reached out to pat her on the back as she leaned up and coughed.

"Albert Wilson, what on God's green earth are you doing here?"

He laughed and ran a tanned hand over his pink polo shirt. "Probably the same as you. Getting a little R & R for a few days. My kids kept telling me I needed to get away."

Winnie set her coffee and muffin on the little copper drum she had pulled up next to her to serve as a side table. She threw her feet over the side of the chaise and sat up straight. What she had been avoiding she now sat directly across from.

"Mind if I sit down?" He motioned to the other end of the chaise.

She eyed him, trying not to seem as suspicious as she felt. His stature was still tall and lean for his seventy-five years. His white hair was trim and neat and his blue eyes as piercing as Winnie's own. Maybe that's why she didn't trust him. That and the fact that he was almost as handsome as Leslie Nielsen, who had made her husband laugh so ridiculously in that *Airplane!* movie. She scooted to the edge of the chaise, tempted to grab one of the cushions and put it between them. "No. Sure. It's fine."

"You look beautiful, Winnie. Seems like the sun is agreeing with you." He tugged at the ends of his khaki shorts as he sat.

She dabbed at her cheeks. "I guess so, yes."

"So what brings you here, to this exotic piece of paradise?"

She had no idea why he used the word *exotic*. It came out downright sultry with his rich Southern drawl. "My kids bought the trip — to torture me, I'm beginning to think." She raised her right eyebrow.

He laughed. "Our kids must be very similar."

"Similar how?" she inquired. She knew he was in on the whole thing.

"Worried about us. Mine won't let me breathe anymore without knowing where I am. I was glad to get away just to get out from under their prying eyes."

"Speaking of getting away . . ." She glanced at her watch as if it were going to declare some place she had to be. She didn't have to be anywhere. "I still have a few more things to do before an appointment I have this afternoon."

He stood up as she did. The true trademark of a gentleman. "Well, it was absolutely delightful to get to see you, Winnie. Maybe we could grab dinner or something one evening."

"Yeah, yeah. . . . Well, I'll see you around." She scooped up her coffee and her leftover muffin and threw her hand up in a farewell gesture. Her short legs scurried as quickly as they could around the corner and darted up the stairs to the main level, her sequin-striped britches all but starting a fire as the sequins rubbed rapidly between her legs. She didn't stop until she reached her room, where she locked the door behind her and declared to stay until her flight on Saturday. As soon as the bolt clicked, she let out a primal scream. She would not cry. But screaming was absolutely appropriate. Because she would officially kill all of her children when she got home. Until then, she'd harass them by phone, starting with the oldest.

Tamyra wiped the perspiration from the back of her neck with the towel provided by the fitness center. She came every morning and ran for an hour, for both her body and her mind. She stepped off the treadmill and walked through the store that sold fitness gear for forgetful vacationers and out the front door of the club. The morning was already warm and yet not as humid as Savannah. The breeze coming off the water seemed to remove any stickiness from the air.

She needed to call her mom. She had stayed up most of the night debating it. Winnie was right; she did have to start confronting things. She couldn't hide forever. She couldn't allow Jason to keep her separated from her family, especially now, when she needed them most. She walked into her room and continued her internal dialogue as she showered and dressed.

Winnie thought she was going to get her to climb into a pool with dolphins today, but there was no way. She had been deathly afraid of water since a near-drowning event white-water rafting a few years back. Jason had been there that day too. Had it not been for him, she would have drowned. Ironic.

He had saved her, only to be the one who would kill her. So the last thing in the world she was doing today was getting in a tank full of water. That's why, if she was "fixed" up, Winnie just might leave her alone.

She stepped into the sitting room, picked up the phone, and dialed home.

"Hello." The voice on the other end immediately made her voice choke.

"Mom?"

"T, honey, is that you?" The relief in her mother's voice was undeniable.

She tried to control her emotions. "Yes, Mama, it's me."

"How are you doing?"

She walked over to the sofa and sat down. "Doing okay."

"You don't sound like it."

She felt the lump rush to her throat. "It's bad, Mama."

"You're alive and on the other end of this phone. The only thing that could be truly bad is if you were dead. That is what I couldn't bear."

Tears burned at her eyes. The lump had become so thick, no words could move around it.

"What is it? You can tell me anything."

She swallowed hard, the words coming out

barely louder than a whisper. "I'm going to die."

Now there was no word on the other end.

Tears began to fall down her face. "Say something, Mama."

Her mother was incapable of hiding her emotions. "What did he do to you, honey?"

"He gave me HIV."

The gasp was real and deep.

Tamyra fell against the cushion on the end of the sofa. Her tears were rushing as fast now as the heaves from her chest. "I'm so sorry, Mama! I'm so sorry!"

"Hush, Tamyra. . . . Hush. It's alright."

"But it's my fault. I made the choice to do something I never wanted to do. I made the choice to sleep with him when I had committed to save myself for marriage. I made the choice, and this is God's punishment!"

"Now you be quiet one minute and listen to me. God hasn't been standing up there figuring out how to strike you down because you made a horrible mistake. Your *choice* opened the door for HIV, not God. And don't you ever forget it."

Tamyra sniffed hard. Gasps still stuttered through her, and she felt like a baby who cried itself sick. "But He must be so mad at me."

"He may be heartbroken. Disappointed. Weeping with you. But He's not mad at you. If I, your mama, am not mad at you, then you can rest assured, He's not mad at you."

"You aren't mad at me?" She pulled the pillow up closer to her face.

"No, baby." She could hear her mother's tears now. "I'm not mad that you are HIV-positive. But I am furious that you didn't tell me this six weeks ago when you ran off to hide! Now that makes your mama very mad!"

Tamyra couldn't help but chuckle. It started as a sputter. But then it burst through her like a spigot turned on high. The laughter was contagious because in a minute her mother was doing the same thing on the other end. Tamyra finally broke it with her words. "We're crazy, Mama."

"Yeah, we are, honey. But I'm so glad you called me. So very glad."

They talked for another two hours. Tamyra told her all about Winnie, and her mama couldn't wait to meet the woman who had helped heal the heart of her girl. They wept together some more. They laughed together some more. They prayed together. And when they were done, Tamyra felt as if the door to her cage had been opened.

"You're going to have to come back home

and deal with this, honey."

"I know. I fly out on Saturday."

"And you're going to have to forgive him. You know that, don't you?"

She felt a furor strike through her blood. "I'm too angry to forgive him, Mama. I hate him. I hate everything about him." The words came out with a rage that surprised even her.

"I know, honey. I understand."

Her mama stopped there. But Tamyra knew she hadn't stopped. She had simply changed audiences. She wouldn't address it with Tamyra. She'd just address it with Jesus. She'd been bringing Tamyra before Him for a long time, and this time would be no different.

"They're worried about you at the pageant. They think you might not show. I told them you keep your word. Always have. Always will."

"I will. I'll be there."

"I know, honey. That's what I told them. So I'll see you Saturday night?"

"Saturday night." The mere thought caused a smile to come across her face.

Her mother paused for a minute. "You're not going to die, honey girl. You're going to live."

"Well, telling you is a step in that direction."

"Thanks for calling me, honey. We'll tell your father together, but I'll let him know we talked and you're going to be just fine."

"Thank you. Wish I could hug you, Mama." Tamyra leaned back into the cushion of the sofa.

"You just wrap your arms around yourself and you know that Mama has you encompassed all about. All about."

"I love you, Mama." She hung up the phone. There was much left to do. Much left to face. And Jason couldn't be avoided. Well, technically, he could be for the next four days.

Laine picked up her phone and dialed. The panicked voice of her assistant answered.

"Alison, it's Laine."

"Yes, Ms. Fulton. I've been trying and trying to reach you."

"I know. I know. Listen . . ." Her voice caught. This was harder than she thought. "I don't want you to quit."

The line went silent.

"Are you there?"

"Um, yes, ma'am. I'm here."

"I was really hard on you Saturday. We all make mistakes from time to time. So let's

231

you and I try to communicate better and we'll see how things work out. But for today, let's forget about the whole new assistant thing."

"Okay. Well, I don't know what to say, honestly. But thank you. Thank you very much."

Laine sat on the edge of the bed. "You're welcome. So how about you take the rest of the week off. If I need you, I'll call you." She was sure the girl would recheck her caller ID when she hung up.

"The week off?"

"Yeah. Take a break. I'm sure it's been a stressful couple of days."

"Thank you."

She was certain the girl was close to a nervous breakdown. "I'll see you when I get back."

The sniffles were audible. "I'll be ready to go first thing Monday morning."

Laine hung up the phone and fell back on the bed. She hoped there wasn't going to have to be a lot more of that. She'd had mammograms she had enjoyed more.

12

Tuesday afternoon . . .

Riley swiped at her tears when she heard footsteps coming toward her office. Mia's boundless energy swept into the room but stopped abruptly.

"You've been crying. What in the world did that woman say to you now? She must simply be a beast."

Riley dabbed a tissue at her eyes. No matter how hard she tried, she hadn't been able to stop the tears falling for almost two hours. It was as if the announcements of her past had loosed some great reservoir that had been building inside and now the dam had finally burst. She didn't tell her story often. She only told it when it needed to be told. And she had never told it the way she had regurgitated it all out to Laine. But something about that woman's arrogance had unglued her.

"No, she's not a beast," Riley said, blowing her nose.

Mia sat down in one of the chairs across from her desk. "You're being too kind. Anyone who has the ability to make your eyes look like that has to be a beast."

"I'm a mess, huh?"

"Frightful. If I'm being honest." Even Mia's Australian accent didn't help that statement go down any better. "Let's get out of here and get some lunch. Did you even have breakfast?"

Riley shook her head. The thought of how Laine had stood her up again made a few more tears fall. She dabbed madly. "This is crazy. I haven't cried like this in years. I don't understand why this woman has had this effect on me."

Mia stood and motioned toward the door. "Come on. I'll buy you one of those Dr Peppers you love."

Riley gave a polite smile. "I'm really not hungry, Mia."

Mia walked over to Riley and pulled her from her chair. "I know you're not hungry, but you need food and you need a friend. So come on; I can help with both."

It was true. Riley had been here for almost six months, and besides a few acquaintances at church and The Cove and Bart's proposals of marriage, she hadn't even had time to make a real friend. She had no one to hang out with, watch a chick flick with, or get to know other than Max and his wife. She yielded to Mia's tug. "You're right. I'd like that."

"Want to go to Mosaic?"

"No, I want junk food. I want a burger with blue cheese and French fries."

Mia smiled wildly. "I knew I liked you."

They took a seat at one of the bistro tables by Cain pool. Riley watched a few of the men, their walks slow and easy. She was certain that their cadence on a workday would be completely different. She settled into her chair and was grateful for the ease of life this place offered. People ate slower here, talked longer, reconnected with the people they loved, and stopped for a few days to forget about the pressures that existed back at home. It didn't matter where they were from — north, south, east, or west — one thing was common among each of them: Paradise Island slowed them down enough to experience life instead of simply watching it pass them by.

Riley ordered enough lunch for two men. She sipped her drink while her ears caught the sounds of pulsating music as it pushed the morning a little farther from her mind. "Thank you, Mia. This really is what I needed."

Mia wrapped her hands around her Diet Coke and nodded. "My pleasure. No one should cry alone."

Riley laughed. "You know, I haven't really made a good friend since I've been here."

"That's because you work all the time." She brushed her wavy blonde hair over her shoulder, a stark contrast to her black silk, button-down, short-sleeved shirt.

"I do work a lot, but I'm still new here. But none of it will matter. I'm sure I'll be fired by evening."

Mia's blue eyes widened and her eyebrows rose sharply. "What are you talking about?"

"Oh, trust me. The way I talked to Laine, I'm surprised I haven't already had a call from Max to pack my bags." She took another sip and then moved her drink as the waitress set her burger down in front of her. "Maybe if I stay away from my phone, I can keep my job a couple more days." She stared at the burger, her appetite suddenly gone.

Mia leaned over her plate of seviche and looked intently at Riley. "Do you want to tell me what happened?"

Riley leaned back in her chair. "Yeah, I do."

"Tell me, then. I want to know." Mia's

words rang as a friend's would. A real friend, who until that moment Riley didn't know she needed and at the same time didn't know how she had lived without. She spent the next hour sharing her entire history with Mia — the accident, the depression, the alcoholism, the loss of Gabby, the loss of her marriage, Max's friendship, and how he offered her this job to get her away from her past. When they had finished everything on their plates, she was pretty much finished with her life story. Mia had to set her fork down for much of Riley's story. Horror, compassion — the full range of emotions had played across Mia's face. When Riley was done, Mia reached over and laid a hand on top of hers.

"I'm so sorry, Riley. For everything. And there is no way you will lose your job over this. We'll just have to let Max know everything that happened."

"Oh, Max knows me well enough to know. It's the others who don't know me that will force his hand. And I can't have him perpetually looking out for me. The contract the other day could have been a nightmare. No, it's my fault. I have more self-control than that, and I still chose to act like a beast. Laine didn't make me do any of that. I just allowed her to get to me. At the end of the day my actions are my responsibility. If I've learned anything through this journey of mine, it's that."

"You're an amazing woman, Riley Sinclair."

She laughed. "I'm a mess."

"Thank you for sharing your story with me."

"It's your turn next. For a friendship to work, we have to know each other's stories."

"I'll look forward to that."

Riley wiped her mouth and set her napkin down beside her. "Well, since Max hasn't fired me yet, we'd better get back to work."

"May our other guests require far less maintenance."

"I'll drink to that," Riley said, and they both raised their glasses one more time.

Tamyra rushed into Riley's office, startling her. "Riley, Winnie's bolted herself in her room and won't come out."

Riley skirted around the side of her desk. "Is she feeling okay?"

Tamyra was halfway out the door. "She won't tell me anything. She asked me to leave her alone and to tell Laine that she wasn't swimming with dolphins and that she wasn't coming out of her room until she leaves on Saturday."

Riley shook her head as she followed Tamyra out the door. "That doesn't sound like her. Wonder what happ—" She stopped in her tracks as Laine opened the main door.

"Oh, Laine, glad I found you," Tamyra blurted out. "Winnie won't come out of her room. I have no idea what's going on. I came down here to get Riley to help me, but I'm not sure we'll be joining you for the dolphin experience."

Laine's expression was slightly startled. "Oh, okay. Well . . . I was just coming by to talk to Riley . . ."

Riley felt the thud in her gut. "You know, if it can wait, I think I really need to go see what's wrong with Winnie."

Laine stood there awkwardly. "Sure, yeah . . . sure. But let me come with you."

"Well, come on then, you two," Tamyra said, pushing past them and scurrying down the hall toward the elevators in The Cove's lobby.

"Gerard, come with me," Riley said as they swung through the lobby.

"Sure. Everything okay, Miss Riley?" he asked, following behind their sprinting high heels.

Riley pressed the button for the fourteenth flour and the doors closed behind them. "Not sure yet, but we'll find out."

Tamyra ran her hands through her black hair. "This is so odd. She was fine when I left her last night. She was excited about being with Laine this afternoon. So I don't know what in the world happened in less than twenty-four hours. Though there was that brief incident at the pool yesterday."

The elevator doors parted, and the four of them exited wildly and darted up the hall. "What do you mean by *incident?*" Riley asked.

"A man. Some neighbor from home or something. She freaked out about it."

They came to Winnie's door and Riley turned, the other three stopping abruptly as she did. "Now, we've got to calm down. Just let me talk and we'll be fine. Okay?"

They all nodded obediently. She tapped lightly on the door. No answer. She knocked a little harder and leaned her ear to the door. Tamyra scooted her over so she could hear too.

"Winnie, it's Riley. Tamyra was concerned about you and I came up to check on you."

They could hear movement at the door. "That's very nice of you, Riley, but tell Tamyra I'm fine. Just not feeling real well right now. I honestly only want to be alone. And I can see Tamyra's shadow right there beside you."

"She was just concerned. If you're sick, Winnie, maybe we can get something sent up to you. Or I could take you down to the clinic and have the doctor check on you."

"What I've got, a doctor can't fix." Her voice was harsh. What Riley was able to hear of it, anyway.

"Miss Winnie, please let me come in and sit with you. I won't bother you; I just want to make sure you're okay."

Riley thought for sure Winnie had her head leaned up against the door. "I'm fine." Her voice was calmer. "Honestly, girls, I don't need anything. I'm just an old woman who is used to time alone and needs some of it now."

"This is ridiculous," Laine muttered from behind Riley.

Riley turned her head quickly to Laine and raised her right eyebrow. "We don't need commentary." She turned back to the door. "Do you promise you'll let us know if we can bring you something? We want you to have whatever you need."

"I have everything I need. But thank you." Riley could have sworn her voice cracked.

Tamyra turned and paced in the hall. "She's crying. I can tell. She's in there crying and we have no idea why."

Laine turned around. "She's a woman. We

cry all the time and people have no idea why. Shoot, half the time *we* have no idea why."

Riley turned toward all of them. Gerard backed up. "Well, she wants to be alone, so let's give her some space."

"Give me that key, Gerard," Laine said, holding out her hand.

"We're not going in on her, Laine. She sounds fine, and we're not intruding into her privacy," Riley said, the authority in her voice obviously understood by both Gerard and Tamyra.

Laine didn't budge. She stood there, hand outstretched, pointed straight at Gerard. "Give me the key, Gerard."

"Don't you dare, Gerard."

Riley almost felt sorry for Gerard. He looked like a rat caught in a catfight. He turned slightly toward her, which gave Laine the access she needed to his back pocket and the key. In a second she had swiped it from his shiny white pants and stuck it in the lock of Winnie's door. No one even realized what she had done until they heard the clicking of the handle.

"We're coming in, Winnie, whether you want us to or not," Laine announced as she bounded into the suite.

Winnie was sitting on the edge of the sofa;

her head darted toward the door. "I told y'all to leave me alone!" she shouted. "I just wanted some peace."

Laine walked over to her. "You're on vacation; who needs peace on vacation? If there's something so horrible that it has you stowed away in your room, we need to know about it."

Tamyra walked over and knelt at the edge of the sofa. "Miss Winnie, please tell me what happened."

Riley gave Gerard's key back to him and motioned for him to leave the room. She knew he was grateful. Riley stepped into the sitting area, walked over to the sofa, and sat down on its arm. "Winnie, I'm sorry. Ms. Fulton took Gerard's key and busted in your door."

Winnie glared at Laine. "Well, she shouldn't have. Fancy schmancy author or not, a woman deserves her privacy."

Riley glared at Laine. "You're right; she shouldn't have. And we are all now leaving to give you some time to yourself."

She tugged Tamyra up off the floor and pulled at Laine to follow her. They were walking toward the door when Winnie finally spoke. "Albert found me this morning."

Riley and Laine exchanged glances.

"The incident," Tamyra mouthed.

They nodded and stepped back into the sitting area. Apparently Winnie wanted to talk.

"I know my kids planned all this out. They just couldn't leave well enough alone, and they went and planned Albert a trip here too. And he acted like he didn't even know I was going to be here. But he knew." Her eyes squinted, the fire behind them unavoidable. "He knew.

"I told them I'm not ready to date. I'm happy being alone and they sent me all the way out here to Paradise Island to try to hook me up. I'm going to kill them! I tell you there were days when they were little I knew I needed to beat the living daylights out of them, but you can rest assured, when I get home, they're getting the poundings of a lifetime."

"What did he say?" Tamyra asked, moving in closer.

Winnie furrowed her brow and stood. "What did he say? He said all the things a little conniver would say. Acted like he didn't have one iota of an inkling I was even here. He must think I'm dumber than all get-out."

"Than what?"

"Get-out!" she hollered at Laine. *"All get-*

244

out! My word, woman, have you never heard a Southerner talk?"

Laine crinkled her nose. Riley tried not to laugh. "Well, is he cute?" Laine blurted out, obviously trying to defuse some of Winnie's hostility.

"He's old, like me. And I know what old men want! They want women with round heels."

"They want what?" Laine asked, the puzzlement on her face incapable of being hidden.

Tamyra furrowed her brow too.

"You girls are ridiculous. They want women with round heels so they can just plop right into the bed whenever they stand up. Old men are crazy that way. You think it's young men, but I'm telling you it gets worse with age."

Laine's laughter started before Winnie had even quit talking.

Tamyra had to cover her mouth.

Riley laughed softly too. "I doubt that is what he is after, Winnie. And you're not old either. You're mature. And beautiful. And I'm not surprised if he finds you extremely attractive."

"Well, he may as well not find me anything. I don't want anything to do with him. That is why I am staying here until I leave.

He had the audacity to ask me out to dinner. Can you believe that? The man is delusional."

"He might be lonely," Tamyra said.

"Well, I'm sorry, Miss Tamyra, but I am not the woman to fill up his 'lonely' social calendar. I am a married . . ." She stopped herself.

No one spoke. Her words said it all. This wasn't about Albert. This was about Winnie. About Winnie and Sam.

"How about you go put on that bathing suit of yours," Laine said, taking Winnie by the arm and walking her toward the bathroom. "And let's go see what the dolphins are doing this afternoon. It will get your mind off of everything."

"I don't want to go," Winnie protested, her feet still moving.

"It will be good for you, Miss Winnie," Tamyra assured her.

"Yeah, and we'll even make Riley go." Laine flitted a glance back to Riley.

Riley stammered. "Um . . . well, that's really nice and all . . . but, um, I have to work."

"I am your work," Laine responded tersely, not turning back around.

Riley tried to temper her seething. Because

it was apparent Laine still hadn't called Max.

"So it's settled; go get your bathing suit on and all four of us are going to swim with some dolphins."

Winnie turned and looked at Tamyra and Riley. "Thank you, girls. . . . I don't know how I found you, but thank you." She waddled on into the bathroom.

The three of them plopped down on the foot of the bed onto the tropical coverlet.

"I don't do dolphins," Tamyra announced.

"You do now," Laine informed her as she patted her leg. "You do now."

The four of them walked silently to Dolphin Cay. Riley knew it was an incredible experience — she and Gabby had come before — but this wasn't how she wanted or needed to spend her afternoon. And Laine had said nothing. Not one thing to her. She had just been her pompous self, dictating everyone's day, and had apparently decided to blackmail Riley silently.

She went into tour-guide mode without thinking. "Dolphin Cay is one of the largest and most progressive facilities for dolphins in the world."

Winnie lifted her eyebrows.

"Yeah, the lagoon itself is designed over

fourteen acres and holds over seven million gallons of salt water."

Winnie spoke. "Good grief, that's a pile of water."

Tamyra piped in. "I heard that sixteen of the dolphins actually survived Hurricane Katrina and were brought here after that."

"Yes. We call them 'Katrina dolphins.' And now they have three calves here too. Those are Gabby's favorite." Riley missed her angel girl. Saying her name made her heart ache.

They walked into the wet-suit area, where their guide was waiting for them. Lines of lockers were placed throughout the open cabana. "Are you ladies ready?" a young girl asked, the top of her wet suit hanging at her waist, her black bikini top serving as her cover-up.

Riley noticed Tamyra's face contort.

Laine rubbed her hands together. "Okay, Miss Winifred, it's time to get you suited up."

"Let's see how you're going to get all of this in not-so-much of that," Winnie announced.

"You can pick up a wet suit here." The guide motioned to two hanging rods that were lined with wet suits of all sizes. "Grab a bottled water from the bar over there. And put your belongings in any of the lockers we have here."

Riley watched as Tamyra walked hesitantly behind them. "You okay?"

Sweat was beading on her forehead. "Yeah, yeah . . . fine, fine."

Laine looked at Tamyra. "You sure? Because for a black girl, you have just lightened three shades."

Tamyra gave a weak smile. "I'm fine. Really."

Winnie's voice boomed from the other side of the room by the wet suits. "I'm telling you, there isn't one of these things big enough to stuff all of this into."

"We'll find one that suits you perfectly," the young Bahamian guide assured.

Laine and Riley suited up while Tamyra thumbed through the wet suits like she was sorting through garbage from a Dumpster.

"Here's one just right for you," the young woman said to Tamyra as she extended a suit from her dark hand.

"Thank you." It came out more as a whisper.

"She's scared to death," Laine whispered to Riley.

"She said she was fine."

"That doesn't look like the face of fine. That looks like the face of scared sh—"

Laine stopped herself. "I'm just saying she's scared."

"This is insane." Winnie puffed as she tugged at the rubber. The suit was stuck at midthigh.

"Here, let me help you," Laine said. She came over to Winnie and tugged on the right side of her suit. She pulled up one time as hard as she could and all but tipped Winnie over on her side. That got Laine tickled. "Oh, I'm so sorry."

"What are you doing? Trying to make me a roly-poly?"

Laine motioned to the other side. "Riley, grab that side and pull."

Riley walked over to Winnie and grabbed the other side of her wet suit. "On three," Laine said. "One, two, three."

On three, both of them tugged on the sides of Winnie's wet suit so hard they picked her slap up off of the ground. She let out a squeal as she rose. But at least the rubber scooted up around her waist. "My Lord have mercy, I cannot believe my behind is squeezed in this thing." She waddled over to a mirror, her legs inches apart. "I look ridiculous."

Laine finally zipped up the front of her own suit and looked at Tamyra, who was still standing there with her suit in her hand.

"Are you sure you're okay, Tamyra?"

"She's fine." Winnie swatted the air. "She's going to enjoy every minute of this. If I'm squeezing my tub of lard into this thing, you can bet Miss Beauty Queen of the South over there is going to put her skinny butt into hers. She was the one who wanted me out of my room, so she got me out." Winnie pulled up the top of her wet suit and dug her arms inside. She pushed at each breast until it was safely stuffed inside; then she zipped up her suit. Both arms stuck out from her sides, and Riley would never tell her, but she looked a whole lot like the Michelin Man.

A college-age kid came to gather them up. "Okay, ladies, we're going to watch a short instructional video. It will give you all of our safety instructions before entering the lagoon."

"Safety instructions?" Tamyra asked.

His deep brown eyes caught the stunning beauty and it was clear that he was enamored. A brief swagger hit his step as he walked toward her. "And it tells you a little bit about our dolphins. You'll love it. I promise. I'll guide you personally."

Tamyra zipped up her suit, his personal attention offering her no apparent comfort. The video introduced them to the dolphins, told them some of the history of Dolphin Cay, and then began to go over the dolphin experience. It told them when they would use their masks and snorkels and showed a tourist kissing the dolphins. Riley watched as Tamyra fidgeted oddly in her seat, sweat now dripping down the sides of her temples.

The back door opened, filling the room with sunshine. The instructor had them all stand and divided them into groups. About the time they headed into the aisle to walk out the back door and into the lagoon, Tamyra made her break. She ran straight out the front door and back toward the lockers.

"You've got to be kidding me," Laine said, no longer trying to be Miss Personality for her other friends. Riley headed out the door after Tamyra, Laine and Winnie on her heels. "Not scared, huh?" Laine announced.

Tamyra ripped wildly at her wet suit. By the time they reached her, she had pulled it from her body. Tears fell rapidly down her cheeks. "I can't do it, ladies. I'm sorry. I just can't get in the water."

Winnie waddled over to her, her arms still extended slightly from her sides. "Baby girl, you should have told us you were this scared. I wouldn't torture you."

"It's just, years ago, I almost died white-water rafting. Ever since then I just haven't been able to get in water."

"Do you bathe?" Laine asked.

Riley tossed a furrowed brow in her direction.

"I'm sorry, really. I'm sorry," Tamyra said, her tears still falling.

"It's okay, Tamyra," Riley said, wrapping her arm around Tamyra's shivering body. "Just come out here and sit and watch us. You'll at least enjoy seeing the dolphins. I promise. We will not make you get in the water. But we want you to be with us."

Riley felt her breathing steady, the panic attack lifting. In a few minutes the four of them were headed back out to the lagoon, where their instructors and the other guests waited. They placed Tamyra safely on the sandy beach and the rest of them headed into the water.

Riley, Winnie, and Laine followed the instructors and donned their snorkeling attire. In a few minutes, manned with electronic fins, they were diving underwater right next to some of creation's most amazing creatures. Winnie giggled like a schoolgirl. Laine was enjoying herself, research or not. Riley had heard Tamyra laughing at them multiple times. And she had to admit she was going to miss this place when Laine finally did tell Max how she had spoken to her.

Back on shore the instructors gave them the how-tos of riding a bodyboard while two dolphins pushed them across the water by their feet. And when it came time to kiss the dolphins and get their pictures made, Riley watched as the cute instructor who had been smitten earlier walked over to Tamyra, who sat on the makeshift beach with her toes buried in the sand.

"They'd love to kiss you, you know." His Bahamian accent was heavy.

"No thank you," she said politely.

"I will hold your hand the whole way and you'll stay in knee-deep water. I promise, you will love it." He extended his black hand.

She tilted her head slightly. Riley could tell by her expression he almost had her. Tamyra caught Riley's eye, and Riley lifted her leg to show her how shallow the water really was. "Only right there at the edge." Tamyra pointed.

He dipped his hand again. "Only right at the edge, beautiful lady."

She gave a wide smile and reached for his hand. He helped her from the sand and she brushed at the back of her cover-up. Her pace slowed as she neared the edge of the water.

"You'll love it, sugar," Winnie said, her wet suit wet and adhering relentlessly.

Tamyra dipped her toes in the water and jerked them back out. "Oh, it's cold."

The instructor took her by the elbow and led her farther in. "You'll get used to it." He blew his whistle. "What's your name?"

"Tamyra."

"Michelle, meet Tamyra."

A gorgeous dolphin leaped from the water and extended her flipper toward Tamyra, flapping it wildly. Tamyra reached out and tapped her. Then she laughed with the excitement of a child.

He blew his whistle again and two dolphins rose in unison from the water and glided backward across it on their tails as if it were a sea of glass. The women couldn't help but be amazed. Riley watched her guests as they stared in wonder at the animals. The young man finally got Tamyra to kneel down, and Michelle came right up to her and kissed her. By the time they were through, all four had held Michelle in their arms and had their picture taken. A picture of all four of them. Together.

As they exited the locker room, hair wet,

smiles blaring, Mia rounded the corner. "Hey, I've been trying to call you."

"Sorry, I had to be here with these ladies." Riley tried not to lay the blame at Laine's feet.

"Sure, yes. Hello," Mia said, tossing up a wave.

"Mia, this is Laine Fulton, and I think you've met Winnie and Tamyra," Riley said.

"Yes, a pleasure to meet you, Ms. Fulton," she said, extending her hand to Laine and shaking it wildly. Her normal manner. "And nice to see you, ladies. Looks like you had a wonderful adventure."

Winnie rubbed the towel against her short white hair. "Besides having the circulation of most of my body cut off for almost an hour and a half, it was a delightful time."

"Well, if you'll excuse me one minute. I need to grab Riley. We've had a guest with a slight situation."

Laine looked at her watch. "How about we meet for dinner at six, ladies, at Casa D'Angelo."

Riley saw Laine looking at her as if waiting to know she would be there. She clapped her hands together. "I'll make our reservations and see you all there at six."

"How did you get roped into that?" Mia asked as the women walked away.

"Long story," Riley said, dabbing her own wet ringlets with a towel. "What's up? Max hasn't been looking for me, has he?"

"Actually he called and I told him I had just left you and you should be right around here. He said he had been trying your cell phone for an hour and hadn't been able to reach you."

"Of course he did. I should have known." Riley dug for her phone in her bag as her pace quickened toward her office. "She calls him to get me fired and then traipses me off so I won't get the call when he does call to fire me. She is such a control freak. I've never met anyone like her." She checked her phone and saw that Max had called her four times. She stopped in the middle of the walkway and leaned her head back. "I can't believe she can be so in control and I lost my control like that. It's just been so long since I've done something like that."

Mia wrapped an arm around her. "It's okay. Honestly, it's going to be okay. I'll do anything I can for you."

"Well, I need to go face the music. It is what it is at this point. I'll be there in a few minutes to pack up my stuff. I'm just going to call him out here."

Mia reached out and gave her a hug. "I'm so sorry, Riley."

"It's okay. Thank you. For today. For listening. I so appreciate it."

Mia released her. "I'll be in the office."

Riley watched her as she walked away, then pressed Max's number on her speed dial. He picked up on the second ring. "Riley, where have you been? I've been looking all over for you."

"Max, I know what this is about. And I just have to tell you how sorry I am. You have been so good to me and for me to lose control like that is just completely out of line. And I understand. I'm going to pack up my office now."

"What are you talking about?"

She paused for a moment. "I thought you were calling about . . . What were you calling about?"

"I was calling to tell you that our three sets of VIPs have turned into six, so we'll need three extra rooms and six more tickets for the concert. Also, I was thinking let's make reservations at Mosaic for lunch and Nobu for dinner. Then we'll take them to the night-club for a little while after the concert. I'll want you to be there waiting on us when we arrive. I want you to shine in all of this. Now, what in the world were you talking about a minute ago?"

She closed her eyes and bit the top of her

lip. "I was talking about something so completely not important." She laughed a ridiculous laugh. "So you don't worry your head about a thing. What time do you think they'll get in?"

"I'm meeting them at the airport at noon."

"Well, you just have a great day and we'll take care of everything. It will be perfect."

"Honestly, I'm not worried about you as much as I am this crazy weather. Looks like there's real potential for this storm to hit us. Might even end up having to fly them all back Thursday evening if it looks like this thing is definitely aiming for us. And by the looks of it, it could be ugly."

"Well, I can't change hurricanes, but I can make sure everything else comes off without a hitch."

"I want you to e-mail me all of their reservation information as soon as you get it ready. And I wanted to send it to them by the end of the day. That's why I was trying to find you. Where were you anyway without your phone?"

"Our author in residence, Ms. Fulton, wanted me to go with her to swim with the dolphins."

"My word, she wants you everywhere. Is she incapable of being alone?"

"Max, she's capable of just about any-

259

thing, so I'm not sure why she wants me with her everywhere."

"Well, thanks for taking such good care of her. She called me just this afternoon and told me what a wonderful job you were doing."

Riley felt the breath go out of her. "She . . . she did?"

"Yeah, she said you were excellent at what you did and had taken superb care of her. I can't ask for more than that, Riley. So thank you. You don't want someone writing a fiction book about your place and trashing you in it. My wife reads fiction. Half the time she thinks those people are real." He laughed.

She let out an odd, nervous laugh. "Thanks, Max. Thanks for telling me. I'll make sure you have what you need within the hour. Call me if anything changes."

"You too. Take care."

Riley stuck her phone inside her pocket and shook her head. What in the world was Laine Fulton up to now?

13

Tuesday evening . . .

The scents of Casa D'Angelo filled Riley. She loved this restaurant. Especially chef Angelo Elia's herb-crusted rack of lamb. It was one of his signature dishes and her favorite. And his tiramisu . . . Well, let's just say women didn't need men with food like his. She sat at the bar to wait for Laine.

Laine arrived promptly at six thirty. She looked beautiful in a pair of flowing black pants and a black silk sleeveless blouse. Her blonde hair was pulled back behind her ears, and a few wispy pieces hung softly around her face. Her beauty really was arresting. Riley hadn't noticed until this moment just how beautiful Laine Fulton was.

Laine walked up next to her and pulled out a stool. "Are the others here yet?"

"No, not yet."

"Good, because I wanted to give you a heads-up. I think you need to watch yourself with that Mia girl. There's something about her that I wouldn't trust." She turned her head to the bartender and ordered a club soda.

"Excuse me? I'm not sure that reading people is your primary gift." Riley couldn't hide the sarcasm.

She signed her receipt and turned back to Riley. "Touché, and honestly, I wanted to —"

"Good evening, ladies," Winnie said as she came up beside them. "I don't know if any of you checked out our pictures after our little excursion today, but if one of you so much as thinks about buying one of me in a wet suit, well, let's just say the next book being written won't be Laine Fulton's. It will be a murder mystery written by yours truly."

"Don't pay her any attention," Tamyra chided. "In fact, she even said it was slimming."

"I said it was vacuum-sealing. I said nothing about slimming."

They couldn't help but laugh as they made their way to the table. "A little piece of Tuscany in the Carribbean," Laine noted as they walked to their seat. The stucco walls and hand-painted ceiling gave all the diners a little visual Italian flavor. The intimate setting, delicious food, and expansive wine collection provided a flawless evening for anyone wanting a good meal and an inviting atmosphere.

Riley watched Laine all night. She was acting odd. Lighter, more amusing, kinder even. She was a sociopath for sure. Riley knew that was exactly how sociopaths acted before they went in for the kill. She may have fooled Max, but she hadn't fooled Riley one bit. Laine Fulton was undeniably crazy; she was certain of it. As they finished up the final bites of their tiramisu, Riley felt someone approach behind her.

"Good evening, ladies. It looks like you are getting a taste of some of that Mediterranean fare that I love so much."

Riley looked up. Christian stood over her looking like an angel with his white button-down hanging loosely over white linen slacks. With his black wavy hair, he simply took her breath away. "Oh, hey. How are you?"

"It's been a long day, but this is a wonderful way to end it. Looks like you ladies had the same great idea."

"Uh-huh." Winnie cleared her throat.

Riley stood. "Oh, yes, Christian, let me introduce you. This is Ms. Tamyra Larsen, Mrs. Winnie Harris, and Ms. Laine Fulton."

Christian went around the table and shook each woman's hand. Riley could tell by their expressions that each of them were enjoying the new landscape. As Winnie chatted him up one side and down the other, Christian smiled warmly and finally excused himself. As he did, he caught Riley's elbow, causing the soft terra-cotta leather of her jacket to rub against her skin. Its three-quarter sleeve grazed her elbow.

"I'm thinking breakfast would be good," he whispered.

She laughed. "I can't. But soon."

"I'm holding you to that," he said, then turned back to the other women. "Wonderful to meet each of you. I hope you enjoy the rest of your stay here at the beautiful Atlantis resort."

Tamyra let out a soft sigh and nodded like an obedient puppy. Laine leaned back in her chair with a weird smirk on her face. And Winnie simply got up and gave him a hug as if he were one of her sons who had finally come home.

He obviously loved every minute of it.

Riley sat down and tugged at the bottom of her navy tank, then wiped her hands down her dark denim Seven jeans.

"He is completely crazy about you," Laine blurted out.

"Smitten," Winnie added.

"Gorgeous," Tamyra interjected.

Riley cocked her head. She grabbed her water and took three large gulps before she set it down. "Well, thank you for your evaluation on Christian, but we are nothing more than good friends."

"You're crazy; he is beautiful. And he's crazy about you. And you're completely crazy about him," Laine said. "So what are you so afraid of? Have breakfast with him tomorrow."

Riley looked at Laine and raised her right eyebrow. "I assumed I would be having breakfast with you."

"I don't need you tomorrow. And I would leave me for a man who was that crazy about me."

Winnie spoke up. "You can tell he is really taken with you, Riley, and he is completely charming. Seems like a precious young man."

Tamyra came out of her trance. "That is one of the most beautiful men I have ever seen. And if I had someone look at me the way he looks at you, with such kindness and admiration, well, girl, I can tell you this: I would tell Laine Fulton over there to fetch her own breakfast."

They all laughed. Riley got up from the

table to make it clear that the conversation was over. When they walked outside, as in previous evenings, Tamyra and Winnie headed up to their rooms and Riley waited for Laine's personality shift and her demands for the day to come.

"You should really meet him for breakfast tomorrow." Her tone and her words were nothing like Riley expected. "What are you afraid of?"

Riley stood there staring at her. "Who do you think you are, really?" She crossed her hands awkwardly and finally put them on her hips. Two times in one day wasn't going to win her friends or influence people. "First, you don't even acknowledge our conversation this morning . . ."

"Well, in all honesty, this morning wasn't a conversation."

Riley looked at her incredulously. "Whatever you want to call it, you didn't acknowledge it, or the fact that I revealed to you this morning some of the most private parts of myself. Then you tell me to watch out for Mia, a really nice girl who took time today to listen to me have an emotional breakdown because of you. And since we know how good you are at reading people, I honestly wouldn't make telepathy my new occupation. And now you can't let Christian go. What is with you? Do you major in making people crazy while minoring in 'researching' novels?" She used her fingers to emphasize the word as if she were in middle school.

Laine mimicked her finger punctuation. "First of all, you look like an idiot doing that. Secondly, I was going to acknowledge it this morning in the restaurant before Winnie showed up. But she interrupted me. Thirdly —"

Riley wasn't going to let her off that easily. "How were you going to acknowledge it?"

Laine took in a deep breath and blew it out. Riley watched as her stature deflated slightly, taking with it the air of aloofness that accompanied Laine as easily as pineapple rings accompanied breakfast plates around here. "You're right, Riley. I have been unkind and . . ."

"Mean. You've been mean."

Laine raised her eyebrows and nodded. "Okay, you're right. I've been mean. And I did misread you. But only slightly. You are perfect. You might have had some issues — and I do mean serious issues — in your life, but there is something inside of you that is just so pure and kind and . . . well . . . perfect." Laine started walking through the corridor of the hotel.

Riley assumed that meant she wanted her to follow.

"You're not like me, Riley. You're still Southern and gracious. I'm cynical and . . ."

"Dreary," Riley added.

"Excuse me?" Laine stopped.

"Well, you are. The all-black thing really is overdone and it just makes you look moody and . . . well, dreary."

"Dreary? Okay, that's the first time I've heard that one." She started back up the corridor. "I wasn't always this way, Riley. In fact, if you had met me about two years ago, you wouldn't know I was the same woman."

"Do you want to tell me what happened?"

Laine breathed a deep sigh again. "Yeah, I do. I owe you that much after what I've put you through these past few days." Riley watched her hesitate before the story began to flow out of her. "It was the last night of my research trip in Dubai by myself. I have taken research trips like that for years. Gone alone, while Mitchell stayed back in L.A. to make sure the rest of my life functioned okay. He would give me a week by myself, and then he would come and join me the next week for a getaway. We would do this for all my research trips. It was kind of our reward to each other for me getting my work done."

Riley could see the complete change in Laine's demeanor when she talked about Mitchell. Her words were spoken through her smile. "He's a good man, isn't he?"

Laine turned to her, her face soft in the flickering movement of candlelight at The Cove. "He is a wonderful man. But I did a horrible thing." Pain etched its way across her face immediately.

Riley felt sympathy swell to the surface. "You don't have to tell me any more if you don't want to, Laine; it's okay."

Laine shook her head. "I want to tell you."

Riley nodded. "Okay. Go ahead."

"Well, I had finished having dinner in my room. Because I hate to eat alone in a restaurant, in case you haven't noticed." She laughed slightly.

Winnie's words rang in Riley's head, but she didn't need to justify herself anymore.

"So I went downstairs and heard music. I walked out to the back patio of the hotel. They had this terrific band; people were dancing and sitting at tables all around. I found a quiet little spot and was having a good time watching everyone, when a man, a gorgeous man, came up and asked me to dance. I love to dance. Mitchell hates to dance. And honestly, I didn't think a thing about it. Everyone was having such a great time and it all seemed so innocent. We introduced ourselves, began dancing, and for the next five hours we talked and laughed and danced. He was with a group of other men on a business trip. He told me about his family. I told him about mine and we were just enjoying ourselves. We closed the entire event down that night at about three in the morning. When they cut the lights out, we were standing there on the dance floor. That's when he leaned over and kissed me." Laine paused and rubbed her hand down the side of her face. "It was so stupid."

"But it was just a kiss, Laine."

"No, it started with a kiss and ended up in my bedroom. And it was a ridiculous one-night stand with a complete stranger."

Riley felt the thud in her gut and a deep compassion for Laine.

"I mean, I have this amazing husband who I am totally crazy about, who I had never one time thought about cheating on, and who was going to be there that afternoon. I was a wreck. A complete basket-case wreck. I threw up all day. By the time he got there, I was in bed and couldn't do anything but cry and puke. He begged me to tell him what had happened. He thought I had been raped. He honestly didn't know what to make of how I was acting. He called a private jet in and had me out of there by that evening."

"Did you tell him when you got home?"

Laine finally stopped walking and sat down on one of the benches in the lobby. "I spent a week in bed. I knew I was officially dying. I mean, honestly, I felt like my heart was breaking inside of my body."

"I completely understand," Riley said.

Laine looked up at her and Riley could tell by her expression Laine knew that she did. "One day when he was at work, I packed up all of my things, put them in the car, came back inside, and sat down on the sofa until he got home. When he walked through the door, I told him everything. I told him how sorry I was, but I knew that he could never forgive me and I wouldn't ask him to. I told him he could have the house and everything in it, that none of it mattered to me, and I walked out the door and moved into the Beverly Wilshire."

Riley sat beside her. "What did he do?"

"He begged me to come home." Laine's voice couldn't hide its emotion anymore, nor her tears. They began to fall freely, landing on her trousers. "Told me he could forgive me if I knew this would never happen again. Assured me he loved me and didn't know how this had happened. But that we could get counseling and work through everything and that he'd go with me anywhere to get whatever help I needed."

"And you said . . . ?"

"I told him not to call me anymore."

Riley stood back up. "You told him what?"

"I told him that he could never really love me again. Never really trust me again."

"You told him *what?*"

"Excuse me. I think you just asked me that."

"Laine Fulton, this has nothing to do with Mitchell. What you mean is *you* can't love you again. And *you* can't trust you again. That's what you're really saying."

Laine stood quickly and swiped at her tears. "No, that's not what I'm really saying."

Riley stood there unmoving.

Laine broke. "That's exactly what I'm really saying." The tears flowed again. "I told him when I got here never to call me again, that it was over. I'm such an idiot. I love him with all my heart. And I realized today that I hadn't forgiven myself. I hadn't let go of blaming myself and hating myself for what I did. He forgave me a long time ago. But today, with what you said to me, Riley — it just struck me in my deep place, and something Mitchell said to me a long time ago came back to me, and today, finally, I was able to let go of my own shame."

Riley walked over and put an arm around Laine. Laine let her head drop onto Riley's shoulder. "I don't have a lot of friends, Riley."

"I'm not surprised."

Laine laughed softly. "I only needed Mitchell. He was my world; that's why the affair was so devastating to me. I didn't know how I could let that happen. But today I realized it. I was so broken inside, Riley. So self-sufficient, so self-absorbed. And when you live your life that way, you open yourself up to anything. And I did. It was my own selfishness that led me into an affair. It was my own distorted sense of importance that allowed my heart to believe the lie that for one brief moment the only person in the world that mattered was me. I broke the heart of the man I love because I believed life was about me."

"You've got to call him, Laine. If you love him, you've got to call him."

"I know. I know, really. And I'm going to. I settled that in my heart this morning. I mean, something happened this morning that I don't even know what to do with. It was beautiful and powerful and different from anything that has ever happened to me. And . . ." She pulled away from Riley and looked her in the face. "I'm really sorry if I hurt you. I was mean and ugly and all those things. And I'm really sorry." She was all but blubbering again.

"I'm not really sure what to do with you in this state. You're not a pretty crier."

Laine lightly punched her and laughed through her tears. "You need to listen to me. I'm telling you, seriously, you need to watch this Mia girl. It's just something I feel in my toes. And you need to go out with this Christian guy. I mean it. Go have breakfast with him. I don't need you."

"Excuse me."

"Well, I mean, I don't like to eat alone, but I've got Winnie and Tamyra. Until I can hopefully get Mitchell here," she said with a smile.

"I'll think about it. But you don't worry about Christian or Mia. Mia has been an angel for me this week. Since you have monopolized all my time, I wouldn't have even gotten through this week without her. And I can go out with Christian anytime. Because, after all, I do work for you for this week, remember."

"Well, I'm telling you to have breakfast with him."

"And I'm telling you, you don't get to boss me around anymore."

They both stood there and stared at each other. Then the laughter broke free through the heaviness of the moment. "Thank you, Riley. I haven't told anyone that story."

"Thank you for trusting me with it. I promise it won't go anywhere."

"I know that. I do."

"I'll see you in the morning, okay?"

"Okay. See you in the morning."

Riley listened as the sound of Laine's heels faded on the stone and wood floor. She pulled out her phone and looked at the time. It was nine thirty. She dialed her girl.

Jeremy answered.

"Hey, is Gabby asleep yet?"

"No, your mother took her out this evening and just dropped her off. I think Gabby OD'd on sweet tea."

"She knows I don't let her have sugar this late."

"Hey, Mom!" Gabby's voice was vibrant and high-strung.

Riley sat down on the teak bench. "How is my angel girl?"

"I'm great, Mom! Me and Amanda went

and had shrimp and grits at Poogan's Porch, and then Mimi picked me up and we went over to see Granddaddy at the men's club, where they were smoking cigars and all those things old men like Granddaddy do, and then Mimi brought me back here to Daddy."

"You had a lot of sweet tea, huh?"

"Mimi said it was the Southern lady's drink. And you know I want to be a Southern lady, Mommy."

Riley laughed. "Yes, I'm sure you do."

"She said she was going to send me to finishing school, but I told her I didn't need finishing. That you said I was fine just the way I was."

Riley chuckled again. "And what did she say to that?"

"She said, every Southern girl has a few rough edges. I have no idea what she was talking about, so I said, 'Okay' 'cause you've always told me to be polite."

Riley laughed, but she could tell Gabby was squirming. "Well, that was a good girl. Are you enjoying your time with Daddy?"

"Yeah, we've had a great time." She paused. "But I sure wish you were here too, Mommy."

Riley felt the lump rise. "I know. Me too. But if all goes well with this storm, Daddy can bring you home Saturday and we'll have Sunday all to ourselves."

"That sounds great! But, Mommy . . ."

Riley steadied herself for more of her old-soul six-year-old.

"I've really got to go pee."

Riley laughed. "Well, go, go. I'll talk to you tomorrow."

"Love you, Mommy!" The line went dead.

Riley leaned against the small back of the teak bench and stuck her phone in her pocket. A warm breeze swept through the open spaces and fluttered over her. She pulled her arms around her chest and leaned her head back. "Thank You," she whispered to heaven. "Whatever You did to Laine or for Laine, thank You."

She was certain heaven responded. Yes, she was absolutely certain.

14

Wednesday morning . . .

"Looks like a storm is headed our way, Miss Riley," Bart said as he greeted Riley on her arrival.

"So it's certain?"

"It got upgraded to a hurricane overnight. Weatherman says if it keeps its projected path, it should be here by Saturday afternoon."

"Well, we will just get everyone here, have a great concert Thursday night, and fly them out as soon as we can." Riley patted him as she headed to her office.

Mia stood behind the counter, a Starbucks cup next to her as she rapidly thumbed through papers. She looked up, slightly startled. "Good morning, Riley."

"Good morning. What you got there?"

"Oh, well . . ." She looked down oddly at the papers in her hand. "Just confirmations for our VIPs coming in tomorrow for the concert tomorrow evening."

"Oh, good. Put them on my desk so I can go over them. That isn't something we can allow anything to go wrong with." Riley turned and started toward her office, Laine's words reverberating in her head.

"So everything went okay with your conversation with Max?" Mia asked as she followed her to the door.

Riley set her briefcase and purse down beside her desk and looked at Mia. She studied her to see if there was any reflection of Laine's concern. She saw nothing. And why would she? This woman had done her job perfectly since she had arrived. "It went well. Laine called him and sang my praises. He has no idea, so it looks like we will get to work together a little longer." A smile spread across her face as she considered the absurdity of it all.

"Well . . . that's wonderful!" Mia said, clapping her hands together animatedly. "I knew you'd be okay. You're great at this. Absolutely great."

Riley sat down in her chair, scooted up to her desk, and looked at Mia again. "Thank you. And thank you for yesterday. You know, just for listening. I needed that. A place where I could share what was going on inside of me."

"We all do, Riley. Glad I could be there."

"Oh, and our tropical storm has become a hurricane. Not sure yet whether we'll be in its path, but we'll need to make sure that we have all our procedures in order to take care of our guests."

"Oh, I know. Do you think many of them will be flying out?"

"Yes. We'll probably be bombarded today and tomorrow. But a few will wait to see what category they are qualifying it as."

"I heard this morning it could be a three or greater."

Riley shook her head. She obviously needed to watch the news more. "That big?"

"Yes, it sounds pretty daunting."

"Then, yeah, we may see some leave today, but the majority will probably head out tomorrow." This was an entirely different beast. The concierge and her office would be swamped with flight changes, questions about refunds, and panicked guests. Sadly, Charleston and its turbulent waters had prepared her for times like these.

"Well, I'll keep you updated on who is staying, and we'll make sure all goes well. Let me know if there is anything else."

"Thank you again."

Mia closed the door, and Riley leaned her head back against the leather headrest of her chair. Laine wasn't as good at reading people as she thought. Mia was a really sweet young woman, a great asset to the team, and might end up being a really good friend to Riley long after Laine was gone.

Riley walked into Mosaic. A stone and glass water wall stood behind the hostess stand like an ocean wave, lit by a blue agate pool below it. Water was everywhere at The Cove, but here it was mixed with modern touches of polished chrome, wenge wood, and limestone, and its light followed the same pattern of storytelling as the rest of The Cove.

Riley took a booth and waited. Just like she had yesterday.

"I told you not to be here," Laine spouted as she climbed into the other side of the booth and laid her Dolce & Gabbana sunglasses on the edge of the table.

"You don't like to eat alone, remember?"

Laine smiled. "No, I don't. So thanks. I haven't heard from those other two this morning and I was starving. Last night about did me in."

"Not used to crying on women's shoulders?" Riley chuckled.

"Not used to crying."

They walked over to the buffet, and each

took a plate from the silver, tiered plate holder. "Did you talk to Mitchell?"

Laine took a slice of watermelon and ignored her.

"Laine," Riley persisted.

She shook her head. "He's never home on Tuesday nights. It's his standing night out with the boys. I'm going to call him tonight. I promise. I'm going to talk to him tonight."

"You promise."

"Okay, just because I cried on your shoulder doesn't mean you can turn into my mother. Plus, I'm still the boss of you for the next three days." She waited for a crepe to be placed on her plate.

Riley put some mango on the side of her plate. "First of all, I'm too young to be your mother. Little sister, maybe."

"Little sister, my —"

Riley laughed. "Secondly, you are not, nor have you ever been, the boss of me."

Laine simply turned and gave her one of those up-and-down looks and puffs of air. Maybe the devil used to wear Prada, but he had officially switched to Dolce & Gabbana.

Their water glasses were filled and orange juice was waiting at their table when they sat down. Their plates were stacked with the best food the Bahamas had to offer. As soon as she picked up her fork, Riley's phone vibrated on her side. It was a hotel number. "Hello."

"Riley, it's Christian."

Riley felt her heart sputter slightly. "Oh, hey. Everything okay?"

"Just wanted you to know that we are definitely in the path of this storm."

"It's him, isn't it?" Laine mouthed.

Riley raised her right eyebrow as she talked. "Didn't know it was certain."

"Yeah, so corporate has scheduled a meeting early evening for us to go over procedures."

"What time?"

Before she knew it, Laine had reached out and jerked the phone from her hand. "Yes, she will have dinner with you tonight. I will not be needing her services. So I will make sure she is there. What time would you like her to be there?"

Riley grabbed for the phone.

Laine wouldn't let go. "Oh, there's a meeting tonight. Okay, well, take her out after that."

Riley reached for the phone and snatched it back. "Excuse me for that, Christian." She bugged her eyes out at Laine, who stuck a big bite of pineapple in her mouth and grinned from ear to ear.

Christian laughed. "Not a replay of the

other night?"

"No, no. So what time is the meeting?"

"It's at 5:30 in the Poseidon Room at the conference center. And then I'll take you to a great little place off the island that I know you'll love."

"Oh, Christian, I . . ."

Laine scooted to the edge of the booth as if she were coming over to snatch the phone away again.

Riley changed her tune suddenly. "I'd love to. That sounds wonderful."

"Great! I'll see you tonight. Looking forward to it."

"Me too. Yes, it will be nice." She closed her phone and put it back on her hip. "I can't believe you."

"I can't believe *you*. What in the world is wrong with you? This amazing man is apparently crazy for you and you keep brushing him off like dander on a suit coat."

"Horrible metaphor for a writer."

"Don't be snide."

Riley leaned back in the booth. "I don't know why I keep brushing him off. Honestly, I really like him. He is so ridiculously nice and charming . . ." She smiled involuntarily.

"And gorgeous."

Riley laughed. "Yes, he's gorgeous."

284

"So what is it?" Laine leaned against the leather seat and crossed her arms. "What is it really, Riley?"

Riley took in a deep breath. "I just don't think I'm ready."

"Ready, schmeady." Laine's words stopped abruptly. Riley watched as a flash of recognition of some kind swept over her face. "Oh, my word." Laine leaned into the table and placed her elbows on top of the dark wood. "Here you are preaching to me, and you are just like me. You haven't forgiven yourself either. Everything I was telling you last night, you are. Living in perpetual regret. Refusing yourself happiness. Like you don't deserve it or something. Oh, my word! You are me!" she announced with laughter as if it were the best discovery she'd made in years.

"I've completely forgiven myself."

"Hogwash." Laine slapped her hand over her mouth. "Oh, my word, now I'm Winnie." Her words were muffled through her fingers. She dropped her hand. "We've spent so much time together, we're becoming each other."

Riley shook her head. "I'll believe it when you give up your mourning."

"This isn't about my attire. This is about you. And you have not ever forgiven yourself." Laine leaned back again, her body softening. "Tell me what happened, Riley. I know Winnie's story. I'm pretty certain I know Tamyra's even though she won't give up any of it. And I know your brief outbursts. But I want to know your story. Your whole story. What happened?"

Riley felt a surge of emotion start somewhere near her gut. The fork shook in her hand. She set it down quickly on the edge of her plate. The memories were fast and fluid. Her chest began to rise and fall more rapidly. Laine reached across the table and grabbed her hands. "It's okay. I promise. I will not make you a character in my next book."

A laugh bubbled up and broke through her lips; tears followed right behind. Riley removed her hands from under Laine's and swiped at them. "You're crazy." She leaned against the smooth padded leather booth and took in a deep breath. She had recounted this story to Mia yesterday through her torrent of tears that were laced with anger at Laine. But these tears were different. Laine had pegged her and she knew it.

"It was a beautiful summer afternoon. Gabby and I were coming home from the grocery store to get dinner ready. I had just pulled into our neighborhood. The speed limit was only twenty miles an hour because of all the children. Gabby was two, and since having her, I did everything differently. Drove slower. Ate better. Far more cautious about everything in life. But I never saw him. He apparently darted out from behind the front of a car that was parked on the side of the street. He was chasing a ball. I thought I had just run over something in the road until I looked and saw the horror on his mother's face. She had watched me run over her son.

"She was screaming wildly by the time I could get out of the car. I ran over to where she was." The stinging from hot tears burned at the top of her nose. "He was still breathing in her arms, though the tire had gone right over his little body. The rest is a blur. We called 911. Neighbors came out from everywhere. The ambulance got there and rushed him to the hospital, and that was when I fell completely apart."

She dabbed at her face with her napkin.

"My neighbors got me home and Jeremy was there in just a few moments. I don't even know who called him. Then one of my neighbors took Gabby until my mother could get her. I pulled myself together enough for Jeremy and I to get to the hospital. But the baby was pronounced dead two hours later." She twirled her napkin mindlessly in her fingers. "It was all downhill from there. I couldn't get it out of my mind. The feeling of his little body underneath the car, the look on Janet's face."

"Did you and she ever talk?"

"Yes, she and her husband were precious. I couldn't get out of bed for days. Didn't go to the funeral. Couldn't take care of Gabby. About a week after the accident, both Janet and her husband, Craig, came over to see me. They told me that they forgave me. That they knew it was an accident and that I had in no way been careless. And the four of us just sat in our family room and wept. It was the most horrible — and most precious — moment of the entire journey."

"Why wasn't that enough?"

Riley looked at Laine, her head moving slowly from side to side. "I just couldn't make it quit playing in my mind. Then it became all the what-ifs. 'What if it had been Gabby?' 'What if I was that mother?' 'What if I really was speeding?' Every night it plagued me. I couldn't sleep. I had no appetite. And the only way I could shut down my mind was to drink. Crazy, because I had never been a real drinker. Would rather have calories in a glass of sweet tea than in a glass of wine."

"Were you drinking wine?"

"At first. But Jeremy put an end to that really quick. So I went to vodka. I would hide it in the house. That's when you know you're in bad shape, when you begin to hide it."

"Did he find it?"

Riley smiled softly at Laine's compassion. It was on her face. It was in her voice. "Oh yeah, he found it. One day he came home and I was so drunk. And it was just Gabby and I there. Here I was trying to drink away the torment of thinking that it could have been my baby that died, and I'm putting her in danger anyway. It was crazy. And that was his final straw. He told me I couldn't live there anymore if I was going to drink. That he would take me anywhere. Get me any help I needed."

"Did you go?"

"Yes, I went. For two weeks. And then got kicked out for getting drunk. I just couldn't stop the scene in my head. It tormented me."

Laine leaned across the table. "I'm so sorry, Riley."

"Me too. Jeremy wouldn't let me come back home, so I moved in with my parents."

"How long were you there?"

"Two months. My parents tried everything. My mother had the ladies from her church come over and do an intervention. My dad tried to talk me through it. But they kicked me out when my mom came home one day and found me stealing from her. Here my parents are, some of Charleston's premier citizens, and I, their once-respected daughter, was now crashing on friends' sofas."

"Did you ever try AA?"

"Yes. My dad took me to AA himself. Sat right there in the meetings with me for a month. But I didn't want any part of it. The lowest point came one night when I was in this run-down hotel off of King Street in Charleston, and I walked out into the street with nothing on but a T-shirt and my underwear. It's pouring down rain and I beg God for someone to hit me. Run me over. I wanted to end the pain the way it had all begun."

Laine wiped at the tears that were falling down her cheeks.

Riley laughed softly. "The manager of the hotel ran out into the street and told me I could get back inside, that there wasn't any of that happening while he was on duty."

"What got you sober?"

"Reality. One day my dad came and picked me up at the hotel. He had someone keeping tabs on me most of the time. He took me out to a restaurant to feed me and told me that Jeremy had filed for divorce. That it wasn't because he didn't love me, but he needed to protect Gabby, and that he and my mother had encouraged it."

"That must have devastated you."

"It was the best thing that happened to me, honestly. When he dropped me back off, all I wanted was a drink. I walked down the street and heard this loud music. I thought there must be a bar nearby, so I kept following the sound. But when I got closer, it was a black church with the doors swung wide open and music pouring out. I was drawn inside like a praying mantis draws its prey. I sneaked into the back row and started crying. At the end of the service everyone had left, but I couldn't move. That was when my old nanny Josalyn found me. It was her church. Of all the churches in Charleston, I had walked right into hers. She had been our nanny for years and years. She had retired just a few years earlier and had been kept up by my family about what was going on with me. I was curled up on the pew like a baby when she got to me. She said two words: 'You ready?' I knew exactly what she meant."

"What did you tell her?" Laine asked.

"I said, 'Yes. I'm ready.' She put me in her car, took me to her house, prayed over me, fed me, read the Bible to me until the wee hours of the morning, and I never had one moment of withdrawal."

Riley picked up her glass and took a drink of water. Laine didn't say a word.

"Not one night sweat. Not one seizure. And not another craving. Josalyn let me know that it was time to let it go. She reminded me of everything I knew, but somehow hearing her say it, it all made sense. She took me to church, where they danced a Holy Ghost jig all around me."

Laine wrinkled her nose. "I've heard about that stuff."

Riley laughed. "They were harmless. Happy, but harmless. Those precious ladies in white loved me back to wholeness. I spent a month with Josalyn until she finally told me it was time to go home. She walked me right up to Mama and Daddy's door. We all sat in the living room and cried together. Jeremy came over to see me and asked if he could watch me for the next couple months before he brought Gabby back around. I completely understood his hesitation. But Josalyn took him by the shoulders, said, 'My baby's gone and been set free and knows it's fine time she needs to be seein' her baby too.' He knew she would know. And the next day he brought Gabby over. That was the beginning of putting our life back together."

"And he never tried to keep her from you?"

"Not one day. He knew she needed her mother as much as her mother needed her."

"So how did you get here?"

"Max had known my family for years. He and my dad go way back. I was working as head of guest relations at the Kiawah Resort's Sanctuary Hotel, and Max called me with the offer to come here. I saw it as a real chance to start fresh, no skeletons, no whispers over dinner at 82 Queen. A real beginning. And everyone agreed. So here we are. Two years sober. And Josalyn still checks in often. She talks me off my ledge every now and then, prays over me, and sends me back out to face the devil." Riley smiled slyly.

"Please tell me I didn't almost send you back to the bottle or that you just called me the devil."

Riley bit her lip slightly. She could never tell Laine how frustrated she had really made her. "No, you almost sent me to a psychiatric ward, which is much less destructive. And there were moments where you could have been the devil himself."

"I'm so sorry, Riley. I had no idea. You'd never know you have been through all this to look at you."

"Nor would you know it to look at you."

Laine gave her a soft smile. "Can I ask you another question?"

"We both know you will regardless."

"Why didn't you ever put your home back together?"

She shook her head, put her napkin back in her lap, and picked up her fork, though her food was way past cold. "He'd been through enough. It was really for the best when he decided to marry Amanda. I had hurt him enough."

Laine shook her head vehemently. "That's a lie. It's you. It's like I said in the very beginning. You haven't forgiven yourself; that's why you never tried to work things out with Jeremy."

Riley let the words fall on her ears. They sounded all too familiar. Josalyn had said the same thing to her over and over. She studied Laine. She'd come so far in her healing, but a sense of shame remained. Could she even get past it? Laine made it sound like she could. And Laine should know.

"You've got to let it go, Riley. Once and for all. Then maybe you'll be free to love again. I know I'm hardly the person to be giving advice on this topic, but there it is."

The tears rushed out of Riley again with even greater force this time. "I think you're right. That's why I never went back." She'd never admitted the truth before, but now it seemed so obvious. "I never went back to him because I felt like he deserved so much more than me. That he didn't need to spend the rest of his life with a tainted wife on his arm."

"Oh, Riley. What messes we've both made of our love lives. But it's not too late. I'll go get Mitchell and try to undo what I've done, and you can start living again by going out with this beautiful man who is crazy about you."

Riley felt a smile creep across her face. The cold trail on her cheeks moved as she did. "I really like him."

"I can see that you do. So go."

Riley picked up her napkin and dabbed at her face again. "I should, shouldn't I?"

"You absolutely should."

"I haven't had a date in ten years! What do you wear? What do you do? How do you act?"

"I don't know. I haven't had a date in fifteen years. Just an affair. Now if you asked me who the man in my life was, I'd say it was Google. That's who I spend most of my time with."

Riley's eyes bugged. Then laughter permeated the restaurant. And the storm brewing on the horizon was completely forgotten.

15

Wednesday afternoon . . .

Tamyra had sneaked away from Winnie long enough to set her plan in motion. Winnie was basking in the glow of her third virgin watermelon daiquiri and was on such a sugar high, she was entertaining strangers. Proof that you didn't have to be drunk to loosen up. Tamyra had called Albert that morning and asked him to meet her in the lobby at one thirty for a few minutes. He had been undeniably gracious, and his Southern kindness seeped through the receiver. He was also prompt, she noticed, as he stood waiting when she rounded the corner.

Albert extended his hand. "You must be Tamyra."

Tamyra looked at the dapper older man almost at eye level. With her two-inch heels, she virtually matched his six-foot stature. He was neatly packaged — pressed khaki shorts, ironed blue Izod short-sleeved shirt, and refined leather loafers. His white hair and crystal blue eyes were as striking as Winnie's and his skin just as olive. How Winnie could have freaked out over this kind and distinguished gentleman was beyond her understanding. It had been three years and Winnie still hadn't let go. Well, she had told Winnie her story and had felt for the first time in two months like the world might not actually end. Now it was time for Winnie to live her own life.

Music and wind whipped around them. She took Albert's hand and wrapped it in both of hers. Something she had done since she was little. She always wanted people to know they mattered. Two hands said, "You really matter." She hadn't put two hands around someone else's in two months. The revelation made her smile. "Thank you so much for meeting me." She nodded toward the other end of the hall and began to lead him along the wide corridor toward the overlook of the ocean.

"Well, you said you were a friend of Winnie's. Though I had the assumption she was traveling alone."

"Oh, she is. We've only met since we've been here. But she has told me about you." Well, it wasn't a lie.

He cocked his head toward her. "She did, huh? That kind of surprises me because she acted like a scared schoolgirl the other day when she saw me."

Tamyra patted his arm. "Oh no, she was just surprised. Just caught her off guard seeing you all the way over here."

"She's a wonderful lady."

"Yes, she is. She's a treasure."

"So y'all just met?"

Tamyra laughed at the absurdity of it all. The way she felt about this woman was as if they had known one another forever. "About four days ago. Or three and a half."

His look registered no surprise. "She has a captivating way about her, doesn't she?" He couldn't hide his regard.

"*Captivating* is a perfect word. So I was thinking —" she nudged him slightly — "Winnie is still kind of shy and every-thing . . ."

"Winnie shy?"

She bit her lip, hating that she had just used that word. "Well, no, not shy. . . . I mean, she just wouldn't want to intrude on you during your stay, but I know she would love to have dinner with you."

"I've been Winnie's neighbor for years. I've never known her to care about intrud-ing."

Tamyra wasn't doing too well. "Well, you know, she is mellowing in her . . . mature age."

He smiled. The deep wrinkles in the corners of his eyes stretched out like waterways. "Good choice of words."

"So tonight, I was thinking, maybe I could make you some reservations at Seafire Steakhouse at six. Winnie loves beef, so I'm sure it would be right up her alley."

He stopped and turned toward Tamyra. "Are you sure Winnie Harris would want to have dinner with me?"

Tamyra wished she had been an actress instead of a beauty pageant winner. "I'm certain. She hasn't really said it just like that, but I can tell."

"So basically you're saying you're setting this whole thing up and she has no idea."

She was so busted. She bit the inside of her lip. She was going to need reconstructive surgery before this conversation was over. "Yes, but . . ."

He shook his head slowly. "You're a sweet girl with good intentions, I'm sure. But I can't be a part of that. But you are very kind to offer. Now, it's been nice to meet you, Miss Tamyra." He gave her a genuine smile and turned to go.

Before she knew what she was doing, she

grabbed him by the arm. His skin was warm beneath her fingers. "I know. I know it's probably not the best idea. But she needs this. She doesn't realize all that she needs. Trust me. Most of us broken people don't know until we get it. And she needs to laugh, Mr. Wilson. She needs to have a good conversation with a gentleman. It will be healing for her. Look at it this way: you will be doing her a favor whether she asked for it or not."

He raised his gray eyebrows at her. "You're incorrigible."

"I'm hoping that means yes."

"If she runs out of the restaurant, I will blame you."

"I'll blame me too. But I know, if I can just get her there, she will enjoy herself."

"Six o'clock, you said?"

"Six o'clock."

"Seafire Steakhouse?"

"Buy her half a cow and she'll be your friend forever."

They both laughed. "You should go into the matchmaking business, Miss Tamyra."

She laughed out loud. Yes, the woman who picked out men who abused her and left her with terminal illnesses. Oh yeah, match-making was definitely her calling.

■ ■ ■ ■

A stack of papers was waiting on Riley's desk. All of the new reservations had been taken care of for Max's special guests. An additional table would be set up for the concert and all would be well in the world of VIPs. She pulled out the final e-mail printout and realized quickly it was a personal message to Mia. She didn't intend to read it, but the abruptness of the first line jumped out at her.

You know what is expected of you. We didn't let you travel halfway across the world to be someone's assistant.

She scanned it briefly and caught the signature. It was from Mia's mother. Riley heard Mia's voice coming from the foyer. She quickly stuck the e-mail back on the bottom of the pile, picked up the stack, and headed to the door. She walked into the lobby, where Mia was talking with a guest.

"Excuse me, ma'am," Riley said to the lady standing in front of the frosted glass counter, then turned to Mia. "It all looks good. I think there was something personal in there for you, but I just left it at the bottom. Didn't want to be nosy. Have a great night."

"Thank you," Mia said.

Riley walked into the lobby. Mia's mother must be a tyrant. She should be happy with what her daughter had accomplished. They'd had fifty applicants for this job. Mia had outshone them all. If she could see her in her position, she'd know that Mia did her job well. Very well. If Riley ever talked to the woman, she'd tell her just that.

16

Wednesday evening . . .

Riley's closet looked like the aftermath of a hurricane. The real one headed their way couldn't do as much damage as what surrounded her. Clothes lay in crumpled piles at her feet, shoe boxes were scattered about, and she sat in the middle of it all.

"I haven't had a date in ten years," she said to the shoe she held in her hand. "I don't know how to act, let alone how to dress. This is crazy." She picked up a green shirt from the pile, held it in front of her, and then tossed it to the side.

She felt a lump form in her throat. Laine was right. She had never thought she was worth loving. Not after all she had done. All she had screwed up. Even though Josalyn had told her for years that "If Jesus could love you, no one else has any excuse worth giving not to."

She didn't necessarily agree with that and

hadn't believed it. She still didn't believe it. Not really. If Christian — or any man for that matter — truly knew her, he couldn't love her.

She picked herself up off the floor and tugged at a pair of jeans. At least she had part of her outfit picked out. By the time she left the house, she had picked out a shirt too, which, from where she had begun, was no small feat. The polished cotton, puffed sleeve, wraparound blouse complemented the white stitching in her jeans. A blue stone cross hung from her neck, and her black hair hung in abandoned curls. With the tightness in her chest, it was a good thing something was abandoned tonight, or Riley would make for a very dull girl.

Mitchell's voice mail greeted Laine — again. The second time today. She was afraid he was avoiding her. Unlike him, she knew. He didn't avoid anything. But after their conversation on Saturday, she couldn't blame him. He had no idea why she was calling and probably was tired of hearing anything she had to say. But he had said, "The next call will have to be made by you."

She hung up again without leaving a message. She just couldn't. These things could not be told in a recorded voice mail. If she couldn't tell him face-to-face, she at least needed to connect with him in person on the phone. Maybe she should just wait until she got home to tell him. She shook her head at the thought. If the man who had called her Saturday still had an ounce of love for her, she knew he'd want to know this now. Plus, she had never been good at waiting. That's why when she did things, they were usually swift and extreme. She had never been good at doing things in halves. She was a whole kind of girl. She slipped the phone into her purse and headed out the door to meet Tamyra and Winnie for dinner. She thought briefly about Riley and her date. She looked at her watch. He would have picked her up by now. It had been a long day for Riley. Shoot, it had been a long week for Riley and it was only Wednesday. She had tortured the poor soul the entire first part of it.

Laine slipped out the door, glanced to the ceiling. "Give her a good one, please. She really deserves it."

Tamyra fidgeted in the foyer of the suites. "You okay, ma'am?" Gerard asked.

"Yeah, yeah. Fine, fine."

He nodded, though she could tell he wasn't convinced.

She stuck her fake nail in her mouth and chewed, making a mental note that when she gave her crown away, everything fake about her was coming off. She dropped her hands when Laine rounded the corner.

"Hi," Laine said.

"Hey, have you heard from Riley?"

Laine smirked.

"She's going on a date?"

"Gave her no choice."

Tamyra smiled. "You're evil."

"I'm persistent."

Tamyra nudged her. "I'm evil too," she said, throwing her hands up to her mouth and giggling.

Laine's brow furrowed. "Oh, my word, what have you done?"

"I have a dinner companion for Winnie waiting at the restaurant, and it's not me and it's not you." She pointed at them both as she spoke.

"She will kill you."

"She'll be in public. She's a principal. She won't make a scene."

"She's Winnie. She always makes a scene."

Tamyra cleared her throat when she caught sight of Winnie rounding the corner from the elevators. Her outfit illuminated the hallway.

"Well, hello to my lovely dinner dates this

evening. I hear steak is on the menu to-night." Winnie laughed as they headed out into the night air to walk over to the Royal Towers.

"You're on the menu," Laine whispered.

Tamyra nudged her.

Laine got in her ear. "Did you ask Albert if he likes Porter Wagoner?"

Tamyra's eyes bulged out at her.

"Well, I know you Southerners and the Grand Ole Opry. You might have wanted to make sure he was into all of that."

"Where's Riley?" Winnie asked.

"She's got a date," Tamyra blurted out spastically. She had to get control of her nerves.

"Good for her. I'm glad she decided to do that. She needs to get out like that. She's young and beautiful. And . . . well, that's just wonderful."

"I think dating is good for people who aren't married," Laine chided.

Winnie turned toward her. "Not everyone has the need to date, Laine."

Tamyra caught her message loud and clear, and beads of sweat formed at the top of her lip. She exhaled deeply when they walked through the doors of the steak house. Deep wood paneling and beams cre-ated an immediate coziness in the atmosphere. Her eyes darted around the room until they caught sight of Albert's white head of hair. Laine gave her name to the hostess, and the three of them followed her across the gold, cream, and gray modern-designed carpet, straight toward his table. A gasp came from Winnie, but Tamyra placed a hand in the small of her back and all but pushed her toward him.

She leaned over and whispered in her ear. "He's here to have dinner with you and you don't need to cause a scene."

Winnie turned around quickly, a fire of Southern wrath blazing in her eyes. Tamyra flinched slightly but knew she couldn't show any sign of weakness with this little fireball. She grabbed her by the shoulders and hoisted her back around. Laine just kept walking past the table to one on the other side of the room. Winnie went to follow her, but Tamyra grabbed her arm and pulled her to a halt right in front of the deep wood table with its crisp white plates and debonair guest.

Albert stood beside the table. "Wonderful to see you, Winnie. You look beautiful."

Winnie tugged at the waist of her purple jacket, her hands clasping the rhinestone trim. If it wouldn't have given away her plan, Tamyra might have encouraged Winnie to go with a little less vibrant color and a little less flash. But she knew Winnie liked her jewel tones, and besides, Winnie without rhinestones was like the Ryman without Little Jimmy Dickens. Winnie's hand reached up and patted the purple and royal blue scarf that was tied around her neck. "Good evening."

"I know you didn't know about this dinner. So I completely understand if you're not comfortable," he said, his hand resting on the back of a wood and leather chair. Tamyra watched as his hand nervously patted the gold leather.

"That's very kind of you. And actually —"

Tamyra interrupted, placing her hands on Winnie's shoulders. "Actually, she is tired of our company and needs someone educated and entertaining to give her some decent conversation. We can be simple and boring and very one-dimensional. None of which Miss Winnie is."

His face resonated his agreement. The flush on his cheeks rose with his smile. "That she is not."

Winnie brushed Tamyra's hands off her shoulders. "Well, thanks to both of you for knowing so much about me, but I —"

Tamyra leaned over in her ear. "Be nice. You're a Southern lady, remember. It's just dinner."

She heard Winnie sigh. "Albert, I would be delighted to have dinner with you. Tamyra is right; I'm tired of *simple* and *boring* people." She looked over her shoulder and crinkled her nose like a schoolgirl at Tamyra.

Tamyra patted her back and smiled a huge and satisfied smile. "Enjoy your evening." She gave no time for retractions. She was at her table in less than four long strides.

"You're worse than me. At least Riley knew what she was doing," Laine said with a laugh as Tamyra jerked her napkin from the table and patted it multiple times in her lap, her back toward Winnie.

"What is he doing?"

"Pulling out her chair."

"Is she sitting?"

Laine leaned onto the table. "Do you want to change seats?"

"Just answer the question," Tamyra snapped.

"Ooh, beauty pageant girl isn't all bea-u-ti-ful," Laine quipped.

"Sorry, I've just never done anything like this before." She picked up her water and didn't quit drinking until the ice jingled at the bottom of the cup.

"It's two people on a date, Tamyra. It's

happened before."

She swiped at her mouth with the back of her hand.

"You're falling apart. Think I could get you to eat meat tonight?"

Her quirky grin made Tamyra laugh. She could only hope she'd still be laughing when Winnie got through with her.

Winnie felt the tightness in her chest slowly make its way around to her back. She was certain her bra strap would pop when the tension finally released. If Tamyra hadn't only recently decided she was going to actually live, Winnie might well have killed her. She took the crisp white napkin from the table and laid it across her pants. The white all but bounced off the purple denim. She lifted her hands and ran them along the straight edges of the stark white plate in front of her and finally willed herself to lift her eyes to Albert.

"You really don't have to stay, Winnie. I completely understand. Tamyra was pretty persistent and I don't want you to be uncomfortable in any way."

She could see the sincerity in his clear blue eyes. She almost felt sorry for him. "No, no." She flapped her hand at him. "It's fine. Really. We've got to eat, don't we?" she said with a nervous chuckle.

His smile expanded across his face, accentuating the deep wrinkles around the corners of his eyes. Despite a few on his forehead, he still held a strong sense of his youth. "Well, good, then. Let's order big ol' steaks, because I'm starving."

The vise around her released a portion of its pressure, and she raised her menu. "That would be great."

By the time the waiter brought their drinks and took their order, they had settled into a conversation about children, the neighborhood, and the pesky yapping poodle who lived two doors down that Winnie had threatened to neuter on multiple occasions. "I told him all his manly wiles would be gone if he didn't put a lid on it." She chuckled.

She watched as Albert cut into his steak, laughed at her jokes, and made conversation easy. "I'm glad you took this vacation, Winnie. I know it's been a rough season for you."

"I'm sure it's been a rough season for you, too. Death is a painful process. Especially when you loved someone so long like we did."

"Yeah, doesn't go away, that's for sure."

"No, I think about Sam every day."

"Yeah, can't say there's a day that goes by that Judith doesn't enter my thoughts. But that is the beauty of love, isn't it? And the depth of the pain is a reflection of the depth of the love, I suppose."

She set her fork down and smiled. "That's a good way of putting it." It was so nice to be with someone who understood. She could tell he did. He had loved Judith so deeply. She could see that. And that was the beauty of that kind of love. You could just hold on to it. You didn't have to let go.

Albert cut into another piece of his steak. "I know Sam would be really proud of you. For moving on with your life and living again."

Her smile dropped and her voice thinned. "What do you mean 'moving on with my life'?"

His head snapped up. "I just meant —"

"I don't know what you think. But I have no intentions of *moving on* —" she added a slight snap of the head as she emphasized her words — "with my life with you, if that is what you were insinuating."

"I wasn't insinuating anything, Winnie. I was . . ."

She picked up her napkin and wiped her mouth, then slapped the napkin beside her plate and scooted her chair back with one

314

quick motion. "Tamyra, my side. You and Tamyra were in cahoots with this entire dinner. It was probably as much your idea as it was hers to take advantage of a grieving widow." She stood up abruptly, her words breaking through the soft Muzak and offering entertainment of another sort to those in the room. "You will not take advantage of this grieving widow. And you should be ashamed of yourself. Your wife would roll over in her grave thinking you were taking vacations just to hit on women like me."

She snatched her purse from the edge of the chair. It caught hold of the side and wouldn't release with her tug. She jerked back slightly and tugged it again. This time the chair flew over on its back and her purse fell right underneath the weight of it. This wasn't quite the exit she wanted. Albert was up and out of his seat, trying desperately to help her. She pushed away his hands and snatched the edge of the chair, finally unhooking the strap of her purse. As she rose, her eyes caught Tamyra's, which were as wide as a hoot owl's, from her table across the room. Winnie furrowed her brow at her, gathered her Southern dignity, and stood. Her scarf had slid around to the back of her neck, all but choking her. She jerked it around quickly and headed for the door.

By the time she made it into the hallway, she was running with more gusto than her thighs and calves had seen or felt in the last twenty years. They'd all be hating each other by morning. Just like she hated this entire trip.

"Hungry?" Christian asked as they walked out of the meeting room in the Atlantis Conference Center, a one-billion-dollar expansion that had added two hundred thousand square feet of meeting space for everything from trade shows to board meetings.

"Haven't met a French fry that wasn't my friend," Riley said as she walked through the large main hall.

He laughed. "My kind of girl."

"Hey, you two, where you headed?" Mia asked as she came up beside them.

Riley breathed in hard. She was not ready to say she was about to go on a date.

Christian saved her. "Just going to grab a quick bite."

"Oh, I'm starved," she said, throwing her head back in her animated way. "Mind if I join you?"

Riley saw a possible moment of salvation. "That would be —"

Christian jumped in. "You know, I've been

316

trying to steal this woman away for dinner for almost a week now. So if you don't mind, maybe we can all hang out another night."

Riley glanced at Mia. Her eyes flickered momentarily. Riley was sure it wasn't anger. Momentary surprise, she assured herself. But just as quickly as the look came, it was gone. Mia patted Christian's arm and nodded at Riley. "You take care of this special lady; she's had a difficult couple of days. She deserves a night out on the town."

Riley smiled. "Thank you."

"Yeah, thanks, Mia. That's exactly what I'm going to give her."

Riley couldn't help it. "Everything good for tomorrow night? All the rooms ready to go?"

"Absolutely. I took care of everything. They will be treated like royalty."

"Let's meet in the morning at eight and go over everything just to make sure we're on the same page and to make sure all the guests that are heading out are taken care of."

Mia placed a hand on her hip and smiled coyly. "You don't trust me, Riley."

Riley smiled. "I absolutely trust you. Just can't risk anything for my own sake."

Mia swatted her hand. "I'll see you at

eight. Now, no more thinking about work. Christian, make her not talk about work. It's all she does."

Christian grabbed Riley by the arm and pulled her toward the exit. "Rest assured, we will not talk about work."

Riley's stomach fluttered at his touch. And in that moment she was very grateful that Mia was not joining them for dinner.

"Get up!" Tamyra yelled, yanking Laine from her chair.

Laine's knife and fork, which had just cut into a perfect piece of medium-rare filet mignon, were still sticking in the meat when she flew out of her chair. "My dinner!" she said as she reached for her purse before Tamyra caused her to lose that too.

"You eat enough! We've got to get Winnie."

Laine was almost out the door in less than four strides. How women like Tamyra ran in stilettos was still beyond her. Poor Albert followed right behind, and by the time they all made it to the hallway, Winnie was nowhere in sight.

Tamyra stopped by the door for a brief second. "Let's head to her room." Before Laine could speak, Tamyra was a blur.

Laine turned to Albert. "Don't worry about Winnie. We'll take it from here. She's an ornery old cuss. Sorry if it messed up your dinner. Better go. Those long legs are no match for mine."

"I'm sorry. I tried to be so careful."

The worry in his eyes touched Laine. She patted his arm. "It's okay. She's just having trouble letting go. It's not you."

He patted her hand. "Go. Go. I'm fine."

She let his approval release her to hightail it down the hall. Fortunately she was wearing wedges, so she made up a little ground. Her wide-leg black pants kept whipping each other at the hem as she ran. When she came to the foyer of The Cove suites, Gerard was standing there as if he had been waiting on her. He simply pointed to the elevator.

She raised her hand. "Thanks."

He called out as she rounded the corner to the elevators. "Should I be expecting Miss Riley, too?"

"No, she's got a hot date!" She knew Riley would kill her for that. "I'm the last of the posse." The door opened and Laine pushed the number for Winnie's floor. When she exited the elevator, she could hear Tamyra banging and screaming from down the hall. She ran to her and grabbed Tamyra's hands away from the door.

"Leave me alone!" she heard Winnie yell.

"We're going to, Winnie," Laine said.

Tamyra slapped at her. "No, we're not, Winnie! We're coming in there just like we did earlier."

"You are not! I'll block the door with the sofa!"

Laine wrapped her arms around Tamyra's waist and pulled. "My word, woman, you're big," she said as she dropped her in the hall away from the door. She stared up at Tamyra and pointed her finger. "You're going to listen to me even if you have to look down at me. We're leaving her alone."

"But we can't —"

"I said, we're leaving her alone. She has to come to terms with this herself. This is a place she has to deal with. You can't do it for her. Just like she couldn't do it for you. You had to break down and get honest with her over the fact that you're dying."

She saw Tamyra's eyes bug out. "She told . . ."

"She didn't tell me a thing. Your actions told me everything I needed to know. I study people for a living, Tamyra. You were an easy one. Now, we are leaving her alone." Laine leaned against the door and spoke to the woman behind it. "We're leaving, Winnie. You just take your time. We won't bother you anymore. Just know if you need us, we're here."

There was no sound from the other side.

Laine grabbed ahold of Tamyra's arms and pulled her down the hall. "Come on. Let's go." She pulled her across the carpet and down to the elevators.

"It's all my fault."

"Yes, it is all your fault. You set the woman up. On a date she didn't want to go on in the first place."

Tamyra removed her wrist from Laine's grasp. "Don't hold back, Laine. Tell me what you really think."

"I will. But you know what? It was good for her. Maybe this is what she needed to finally let Sam go."

"So you don't think I've destroyed her?"

Laine pushed the Down button for the elevator and laughed. "No, Winnie's a big girl. No pun intended. She will be fine. But Albert, on the other hand . . ."

Tamyra walked into the elevator and slapped her hand over her mouth. "Oh, my word. What I did to him was horrible."

"Yes, now that was horrible."

Tamyra rolled her eyes at her.

"You need to go apologize to him."

The elevator doors opened and they walked back out into the foyer. Gerard was still standing there. "All is well, Gerard. All is well," Laine informed him.

"So Miss Riley really had a date, huh?" Gerard asked, following her to the doorway.

Laine turned and gave him a big smile. "Yes, with that Christian Manos guy."

His black eyes widened and his white teeth overtook most of his face. She was shameless.

Riley licked barbecue sauce from her fingers.

"Southern girls like ribs, huh?" Christian laughed.

She could feel her face flush. Bertha's Go-Go Ribs was a local hangout on the island. And had the best ribs in town. "I'm sorry; I hope I'm not embarrassing you." She picked up her napkin and wiped her hands.

"You're not embarrassing me. I did a little research and found out what Southern girls like. Guess I got it right."

Charm seeped from him. Right along with sincerity. An odd pairing. "Fry it or barbecue it and we eat it."

"Tell me about growing up in the South, Riley."

He picked up another rib and took a bite. But his eyes came straight back to her. They had been on her all night. And she had determined about thirty minutes ago that if there were going to be eyes on her, she'd couldn't think of any she would rather have than these. She shook her head. "It is a world all its own. In the South all girls 'come out.' " They both laughed at that. "That's too long a story for this pile of ribs. Fathers are icons. Mothers are . . . How shall we say it? *Involved.*"

He laughed. "Involved? That is new to me. Do you go home often?"

"Haven't been back since I left. But that's because I needed to settle in here. I think my parents are coming to visit soon, and I've got some old demons back there I'm not ready to confront." She gave a cautious laugh.

"Old demons?"

"Another long story."

He raised his napkin and wiped his mouth. "One I hope you'll tell me someday."

Riley leaned back in the booth. Music from the jukebox played hits of the eighties. "Why have you been so persistent?"

He took a drink and leaned back. "Persistent? What do you mean?"

"About having dinner with me."

She caught his coy grin. "I see something in you, Riley. Something I don't see in many women."

"What? I don't swoon over you?" His expression registered his uneasiness. Her words had been careless. She leaned forward quickly. "Sorry, Christian. I didn't mean to insinuate that you are a womanizer. It's just evident by the way women look at you that most find you extremely attractive."

"Attraction is easy to come by, Riley. Depth, not so much."

She laughed. "Okay, so now *really* why me?"

"I've watched you. Even when you didn't know I was watching. The way you care for your guests. The way you care for Gabby. You have a way about you. A sensitivity that only comes from knowing pain. At least that's what I've discovered. Most people are so self-absorbed because they've never really known what hurting was like. But once you know what it's like to hurt, you're different. Your compassion is richer. Your eyes are more aware. I see that in you. And one day I hope you'll share some of that with me."

She shook her head. "I doubt you could handle my story."

He leaned in. "One day I hope you'll trust me enough to try me."

She didn't say anything. She couldn't. The leaping in her heart had her too concerned that if she said anything in that moment, she would officially spill her entire life and not come up for air until every last detail had been unearthed from even the deepest graves.

He pulled twenty-five dollars from his wallet and set it on the table, then grabbed her hand, rescuing her from herself. "Come on. I want to take you somewhere else."

She slipped out of her side of the booth. "Where?"

"It's a surprise. Your first step in learning to trust me."

Little did he know that his last statement had already cracked open that door. This would be her second step.

The room was closing in around Winnie. She jerked open the sliding-glass door to the patio and stepped into a rush of warm, salty air. Her fingers fumbled frantically with the scarf around her neck as if it were a noose only moments from ridding her of all known life. When she was finally free, she flung it to her feet, where the wind whipped it and flew it like a kite over the manicured lawns of the resort. "I don't care!" Winnie wailed. "The saleslady talked me into you anyway!" But her heart knew she wasn't talking to the scarf.

She dropped her head down on the railing. Her bangle bracelets clanged against the railing as her arms dropped too. There was nothing rhythmic about her tears or her rage. They were fierce, violent, surging.

"I don't want to move on, Sam! I don't! I don't! I'm fine with the way it is. I have you all to myself every night." Her tears dropped in scattered puddles on the concrete beneath her feet. "We talk. You listen to my day." She snorted hard, trying to stop the faucet of her nose. She had kept this pain at bay for three years, knowing that if she ever allowed it to break free, it would consume her. It had. It was. And she had nothing in her to stop it this time.

"I don't want to move on!" Her voice was desperate, pleading.

And then words were whispered to the very center of her soul. *It's time.*

She jerked her head up. "Who's there?" Her head darted from side to side as she looked at both sides of her balcony to see if someone else was out. There was no one. At least no one she could see in the darkness. She shot her gaze downward. But no one was below her. She turned her head upward in the most contorted way, but there was no one there, either.

"Don't toy with me! I'm not in the mood!" Her blue eyes blazed out at the darkness.

She was sure that a passing ship would mistake them for the lighthouse that stood at the end of the harbor.

It's time, Winnie. It's time.

"No! No! You can't! You can't leave me!" She felt a tearing in her heart. A knife went in and sliced her in two, and she crumpled. Her jacket caught the side of a chair as she fell and pulled it up around the back of her neck. She fought with her right sleeve until she finally set herself free, and there she hung, one arm stuffed inside the sleeve of her bedazzled denim jacket and the other sleeve wrapped in a knotted mess around the chair. Pretty much the way her insides felt. "You already left me once! I won't make it if you leave me again!" Her body heaved as the pain of her grief coursed through her.

It's the only way you will make it.

Her hands tried to grip the concrete beneath her. Gravel slid underneath her fingernails. "But I need you! I need you so bad!"

You need to start living. And you can't live holding on to Sam.

The word *Sam* startled her. "Why are you talking about yourself in the third person?" she sputtered through her tears.

A flutter went through her heart. And in

that moment she knew it wasn't Sam talking to her.

Sam's voice had always been in her head. There was only one voice that swept through her heart.

The wailing ceased, but the tears were relentless. She looked up into the moonlit sky as if she were going to peer into heaven itself. But she didn't have to. Heaven was whispering in her heart. Tugging her. Wooing her. She had found Jesus on a wooden bench at vacation Bible school when she was six years old. Anytime He talked to her, it was always in her heart. But she had stopped listening after Sam's death. Now she knew why. She was mad at Him.

"It's not fair, you know."

Yes, I do know.

"I miss him."

And I miss you.

She shifted on the concrete, the solidness of it doing nothing for her old bones. "He's all I've been thinking about."

The whisper in her heart came again. *For a long time.*

She sniffled again and wiped her runny nose with her sleeve. No one ever had to know. "You've missed me?"

Like crazy.

"I haven't known what to do without him.

I've been so mad at You."

I know. And I've tried to get your attention. I've wanted to hold you, comfort you, show you some new things.

She blinked hard; tears gathered on her eyelids in bulging droplets. The moon swelled in her sight, its beauty almost new. As if she hadn't seen it in a while, either.

"But I've been too angry, huh? Caught up in all these old things, the past."

Buried.

"A part of me died with Sam."

I know it did. That is what happens when you've become one. Your pain shows the depth at which you've loved. But you didn't die, Winnie. You're here. And I want you to live.

The ache started again in her chest. "I've lived with the kids at school."

Yes, you have. You have loved them beautifully. And I'm so glad. But I have more for you.

"I don't want another man! I just want Sam!"

She felt the flutter again, stronger. As if He were laughing. Not mockingly. Knowingly.

I'm not sending you down the aisle. I'm asking you to open your heart. I'll give you what you need, but I can't do that if the opening to your heart is so tight you need a tub of lard to grease anything through it.

She chuckled. "I knew You were Southern. . . ."

I'm shamelessly in love with you, Winnie. And I want you to come into this season with Me. I want to show you things. New things. Things that you can only find when you're single.

"What if Sam thinks I've forgotten him?"

I'll assure him you'll never forget him.

"Promise?"

I Am the Promise, Winnie.

Winnie let her head drop. Tears flooded through her and over her and fell around her until she was certain there would be no tears for the next decade. And when she was spent both in body and soul, she walked back inside and closed the door. Roy was right. You had to face your fears before you could truly heal. She had stared hers down tonight.

When her head finally came to rest on the pillow, she began her evening conversation. But this time she wasn't talking to Sam. This time she was talking to the Ultimate Companion. When she fell asleep in the wee hours of the morning, she was positive she had effectively worn God out too. She was almost certain the moon flickered.

■ ■ ■ ■

As soon as Christian opened the door to his Jeep, Riley could hear the music. The little white church stood with its doors flung open wide, windows propped up with sticks of wood, and light streaming out from every open cavity into the darkness of the evening. He didn't have to tell her where they were. She just didn't know why they were there.

He grabbed her hand and pulled her toward the front door. "You'll love it, I promise."

They walked into a tiny foyer no bigger than a closet. Two wrinkled ushers — eyes closed, heads rocking back and forth to the rhythm of the old Negro spiritual coming from inside — greeted them from folding chairs flanking each side of the door. Well, kind of.

Christian smiled and patted one on the shoulder. "Wake up, Tiny, or you're going to miss the robbers when they bust in the door."

Tiny's eyes popped open, revealing coal black. A grin spread across his face, his wrinkles running like speed racers, as his eyes registered Christian. His remaining teeth were seen through his openmouthed smile. He chuckled, closed his eyes, and went right back to swaying.

Christian led Riley to the back row. About the time her legs hit the edge of the pew, the final chords of the song ended. Her heart sank slightly. She loved music — especially this kind of music because it reminded her of Josalyn. It took her back to a place she loved and to the woman who had helped heal her soul. An elderly pastor climbed the two steps covered in worn red carpet. She was certain its muted shade was a reflection of the knees it had held and the tears it had received.

He asked the congregation to sit. She and Christian followed. "You okay?" he whispered.

She couldn't think of any place she'd rather be. "I love it."

He wiped his brow in mock relief.

The pastor gave a fiery message, seemingly more fit for a Sunday morning than a Wednesday evening, but it was received with just as much enthusiasm as if he were speaking to a stadium of twenty thousand. He mopped sweat from his brow, and after forty-five minutes of organ-accompanied preaching, he collapsed in an exhausted heap in the front row. The organ music didn't stop, though. And when it hit a familiar chord, as if directed but completely uninstructed, every member of the congregation rose to their feet and began the first stanza of "Amazing Grace."

The words and melody soared through the breeze of a perfect Bahamian evening and didn't stop their journey until they settled right across Riley's soul. She had heard this song a thousand times. She knew every word by heart. But until now she had never heard those first four lines the way she heard them in this moment. " 'Amazing grace! how sweet the sound that saved a wretch like me! I once was lost but now am found, was blind but now I see.' "

And that was what seemed to happen. As those words washed over her, so did Laine's words from that afternoon. *"You have not ever forgiven yourself."*

She knew that she hadn't. And now she could see — really see — that it had been unforgiveness that had caused her to lose her husband. The man she had loved since she knew how to love. It was that same unforgiveness that could possibly cause her to miss this wonderful man next to her. And something in that moment let her know she didn't want to live under her own load of shame anymore. That everyone at their core was wretched. Sure, society had its own measuring scales, but in the light of this kind of grace, all were wretched beyond deserving. But now she realized that's why it's called grace. Because you can't earn it. You can't ever be good enough for it. And in that moment, everything the past four years had blinded her from she could clearly see.

Her body felt glued to the pew. Christian had stood earlier, but she couldn't move. Nor was there a power great enough to stop the overwhelming emotion that rose like a welling tide to the surface. She leaned her head against the back of the wooden pew in front of her and didn't try to stop the heaving sobs. Four years of shame wasn't washed away with a tiny stream; it was accompanied by a torrent. And though it felt as if it would consume her, and though there was a desire for dignity, she refused to dam it up. Not in this moment. Because when you've been blind for four years and you finally see . . . well, you don't care who's watching. She had thought she no longer hid, but she still hid from so much. But not now. All things had come out of hiding.

And as they came out of hiding, it was as if pieces of her soul opened up. As if the thick anchor of shame that had wound itself around her soul, taken up residence inside the core of her, was pulled away; the weight she had carried was removed. She hadn't even realized a heaviness had been buried in her chest for the last four years until it was gone. She felt lighter. More free. Alive. If she hadn't been holding on to the pew in front of her, she might have lifted off.

She thought she had been living since she had put the pieces of her life back together, but she knew that what was happening here, on this tiny pew, surrounded by the beautiful water of the Atlantic Ocean, was life changing. She had been anchored to shore for way too long. And this final release was about to let her heart see what the open waters actually offered.

She felt a soft hand slowly rub her back. She couldn't imagine what Christian must be thinking, but there was no stopping this. Though there was no sound, she was sure the shaking of her shoulders could have caused an earthquake. When the rush of all the emotion finally subsided so she could catch her breath, she swiped and dabbed at her face in a desperate and vain attempt to not look like Norma Desmond in *Sunset Blvd.* A black hand came from underneath her and held out two neatly folded tissues. She reached for them with gratitude and blew hard.

She raised her head to find three black faces hovering over her. Their smiles were as rich and warm as the healing balm that still flowed through her.

"You look beautiful," the thin-faced one said, her smile wide as her gold looped earrings swung.

Riley felt the hand slip from her back and knew now it must have been hers. The rounder one with short hair and bright red lips spoke next. "Felt the Spirit, sugar? You know, He always shows up here. And He was flowing all over you."

"Mmmm. Love that Holy Spirit," the one on the other side with a flowered head scarf and pink lips responded, rolling her head as she closed her eyes.

Riley smiled at her new group of friends. Laine would be jealous. She chuckled to herself. "I hope I didn't make a fool out of myself." She dabbed at her nose again and looked around casually but couldn't find Christian.

"Christian's here. He's outside with the men. And if you're going to make a fool of yourself, honey, this is the place to do it. Jesus loves fools."

"Mmmm . . . Loves them fools," Flower Scarf said, eyes still closed, head still bobbing.

Riley placed her hands on top of the ones that rested on the pew in front of her. "Thank you. Thank you for praying with me."

"We love that, sugar," Red Lips replied. "You come join us anytime, you hear?"

Riley stood and dabbed her face again. "I will. I promise." And she meant it. She so meant it.

The ladies walked her out under the night sky. She was grateful it was dark; that way Christian couldn't see the flush in her cheeks. They felt like they were on fire. The elderly gentlemen scattered from the side of the car where they had been talking. One tipped his hat at Riley as Christian opened the door. The ladies patted her and kissed Christian before they finally pulled out of the parking lot.

She sat quiet for the first mile. What should you say after something like that? *Is this where you take all of your dates? Sorry I was a blubbering idiot back there.*

He rescued her. Again. "You are a wonderful woman, Riley Sinclair. I'm not sure what you've gone through all your life, but it has made you into a terrific woman." He reached over, placed his hand gently on top of hers, and squeezed it softly, then moved his hand back to the steering wheel.

His touch sent another fire roaring through her. His words had done more than that. "Even after I cried like a baby in there?"

"It takes a strong woman to let go of her emotions like that."

She laughed. "Is that what you'd call it?"

He laughed too. "Not your typical first date, huh?"

She turned to look at him, his face lit by the passing streetlamps. "No, but thank you. I just can't thank you enough. Honestly, I haven't cried like that in a very long time, but that song . . ." She turned her gaze back to the front windshield. "I've heard that song more times than you can shake a stick at, but tonight I really heard it. And something just went through me and I don't know —" She stopped herself. "It just touched me in a really deep place. So thank you."

" 'Shake a stick at'?"

A chuckle came out softly.

"Your sayings. It's like learning a whole new language."

She leaned her head against the headrest. She felt spent. "We're odd little creatures that way." Those were her last words. She had no idea when she fell asleep.

Christian nudged her gently. "We're home, Riley."

She jerked awake. He was crouching beside the open car door.

"I did not fall asleep."

He nodded. "You so fell asleep."

"I'm the perfect date, aren't I? I eat like a man. Cry like a baby. And fall asleep like a child."

"Do you cuss like a sailor too?" He laughed. "That saying I know."

She laughed. "I have my days."

He took her hand, helped her from the car, and walked with her toward her house. "Thank you for finally agreeing to have dinner with me."

"I'm sorry for taking so long. I really had a lovely time." She fumbled through her purse for her keys and finally felt them beneath her fingers. She turned at the doorway. This was the awkward moment she did not want. Once again, Christian took all awkwardness away.

He leaned over and kissed her softly on the cheek. "I hope that means you'll go again."

"I'd love to. Thank you."

"Good night, Riley."

"Good night." She opened the door and walked inside her cozy and inviting home.

When she laid her head on her pillow, she realized the tightness she had carried in her chest for the last four years was gone. She had thought she was free before. She'd had no idea.

Tamyra's pillow was soaked. She had cried from the moment Laine had pushed her inside her room and demanded she leave Winnie alone. She had been stupid. Presumptuous and stupid. Winnie wasn't ready. She was finally away, having a great vacation, and Tamyra had completely screwed it up for her. Not to mention what she had done to poor Albert. Set him up wonderfully to be dumped at dinner.

It made all her self-doubt return. She had created this mess for both Albert and Winnie. Maybe she had created her mess with Jason too. Maybe she deserved the hits. Maybe she deserved AIDS. She had spent years being foolish and stupid, and her insensitivity tonight just proved that she moved too quickly. Made decisions too hastily.

Jason had told her that so often. In fact he had called her stupid more times than she could count. Maybe he was right. Stupidity deserved punishment. And if she were being honest, she'd rather have the pain of Jason's fists right now in this moment than the pain of her own shame at hurting her precious new friend. The one woman who had opened her up and helped her begin to heal.

"I need a drink," Laine said as she slipped onto the sofa. She knew it was right in that refrigerator. She looked up at the ceiling. "These women are crazy. They would drive a sober man to become an alcoholic. I'm telling You, I've had characters in books less crazy."

She hadn't realized until that moment how strong the urge to drink had become. She glanced at the clock on the DVD player and decided to sidetrack herself by trying Mitchell again. He didn't answer. She factored in the time difference and determined it was about 5 p.m. in California. He was always home by five o'clock. Maybe he was sending her straight to voice mail because he simply didn't want to talk to her.

She was past desperate now. She had been patient to an extreme that had shocked even her. She clicked the text icon on her phone. *Call me,* she typed. Then added, *Please.*

17

Thursday morning . . .

Laine's iPhone sat by her head, staring at her with mock indignation. She must have fallen asleep with it there. She pushed a button and the screen burst to life. No missed calls. No missed texts. That said pretty much everything. Apparently her push on Saturday had been the final one. Right before she let the words come out of her mouth, she knew she could be sealing her fate. Yet her shame — no, her downright arrogance — had let them fly anyway. Jesus might have raised Lazarus, but she was pretty certain there would be no grave-clothes flying today.

She sat up in bed. After her breakthrough the other day, she had finally bid adieu to the sofa. She pushed a button beside the bed, and the wall of draperies began to slowly open, letting in the morning. The sun had yet to make its official break, though her heart might. She grabbed a pillow beside her and pulled it tight against her chest, wrapping her arms around it in a symbolic act of need. She loved Mitchell more than she knew she was capable of loving anyone. And she had hurt Mitchell more than she knew she was capable of hurting anyone.

But in the midst of this horrific reality, she couldn't deny a strange peace. A strange sense that everything was going to be okay. She let her cheek fall against the soft, expensive pillow-case. She knew now that Mitchell would never hold her again. But she had a sense she was being held even now. She lifted her hand and rubbed her eyes. They burned from too little sleep. She climbed out of bed, slipped on some workout clothes, and headed out to begin her day. It was sad to think that the remainder of her days would be spent without Mitchell by her side, but it was the only option she had.

Winnie woke up and rolled over in her bed to take in the sun rising above the ocean. The view was breathtaking, except for the large mass of ominous-looking clouds that seemed to be approaching. She had a feeling that at this rate the sun would be gone before long. Her sleep had been peaceful. Even though she knew her eyes were as swollen as Laine's ego.

One more thing. The soft whisper fluttered through her soul.

She clutched the pillow next to her. "No, no more. I'm taking the day off."

Get up. One more thing.

She knew what it was. She didn't even have to ask. And she didn't want to do it. Not one part of her wanted to do it.

Trust Me. I have something to show you.

She pushed herself off the bed and slipped into a lime green jogging suit with rhinestone-accented sleeves. In ten minutes she was standing at the edge of the beach entrance to the Beach Towers, the wind brushing past her and the sound of crashing waves providing background music. The very towers she had successfully avoided for almost a week were about to come into view. She would have been perfectly content to avoid them for the last two days of her visit too.

Trust Me.

She could hear a jogger behind her but didn't turn around. Instead, she walked slowly around the corner. But what she saw was not what she had expected. The once-pristine pool with rocky caves, billowing boulders, prestigious waterfalls, and an inviting lazy river was now all dried up. The only things left were water stains and cracked concrete. The once-towering white gazebo stood with far less pride, its white weathered and its wood rotting. The restaurant looking out over the pool, which fifteen years ago had afforded her and Sam some of the best food they had ever eaten, was boarded up. Boarded up. Every window was boarded up.

Old memories closed, heaven whispered. *Time to make some new ones.*

The magnitude of the moment brought old Winnie to her knees much the way last night's encounter had done, though this time was different. This moment was a gift. She had a vision in her mind, a memory she didn't want to let go of. And it would always be there. But it was time to cease the perpetual revisiting and reenter the land of the living. She would never have had this closure if she had stayed away. Seeing the state of this place, here, now, had released the final piece of her heart to live. To heal.

Laine had come up quietly on Winnie. She watched her walk slowly over to the old, boarded-up hotel. She felt like she was intruding in some way and had turned to go when Winnie fell to her knees in a heap of tears. Laine knew there was no way she could leave her there by herself. Not like that.

She walked over, knelt beside her, and wrapped her arms around her as best she could. She might have fed her a little too much this week. "It's okay, Winnie. It's okay."

"I know," she whispered. "I know."

Laine had not let a woman cry in her arms in a whole lot of years. Shoot, she had done things this week she wasn't sure she had ever done. She laid her head on Winnie's back and patted her hands softly. "I'm sorry you lost him, Winnie. I'm really sorry."

"But I got to love him. That was worth the losing," Winnie said. "I've got to start living now, honey. No more living in the past. I've got to let Sam go and start living my life."

Laine raised her eyebrows but didn't lift her head. She had been right. Winnie had needed last night to herself. "I'm proud of you."

Winnie chuckled. "If someone sees us, I don't even want to know what they are going to think."

Laine laughed too. She was from Los Angeles. She knew exactly what they would think. "Well, you're a little old for me."

Winnie elbowed her. "I'm not too old to beat your tail, which is what you need."

Laine stood and helped Winnie to her feet. "You'd better go see Tamyra. She was pretty traumatized by what happened last night."

"Bless her heart. I'll go see her." She looped her arm through Laine's and pulled her sleeve up to wipe her face.

"Why do you all say that?" Laine asked as they walked.

"Say what?"

" 'Bless her heart.' I heard that means, 'Ain't she stupid.' If that is what it means, I don't want you ever blessing my heart."

Winnie laughed. Laine could tell it came from her toes. And Winnie didn't stop. And Laine didn't want her to.

Riley stared at the sky before she walked back into her office. The day was beautiful, making it hard to believe that a hurricane could be blowing through here by Saturday. The wind was so calm. She had noticed this morning that the waves had grown a little higher, but other than that it seemed like another picture-perfect day in paradise. There had been a mass exodus of guests last night, and today would prove just as crazy. On top of that, Max's VIPs were heading in, along with Harry Connick Jr., but all were flying out tonight as well since the latest indicator was that the storm was picking up speed. Good, in that it wouldn't be over the island very long; bad, in that it might not impress vacationing VIPs. Each one Riley's responsibility. She had hit the ground running at 5 a.m. Had checked and rechecked rooms, concert tickets, table arrangements, and it didn't look like she had missed a thing. By eight o'clock she had already consumed a blueberry bagel with cream cheese and three Dr Peppers. She had so much sugar running through her veins, she would probably register positive on a drug test.

As soon as her butt hit the chair, Mia tapped on her door. "Did you have a good evening?"

Riley could not control the smile that took over her face. She had thought about the experience at church until she finally drifted off to sleep. When she woke up, she was thinking about it all over again. "It was wonderful. Magical, almost."

"My, my . . . Christian must be quite the ladies' man."

Riley felt her face flush. "I wasn't talking about —"

"You'll have to tell me details at lunch.

I've got to take care of some guests who are heading out early. And some more guests who want to snag their concert tickets. But I want to hear all about it. Not one juicy detail do I want you to leave out." With that, she was gone.

Christian was wonderful, but the evening had been about so much more than Christian. Riley shrugged it off and knew she'd have the opportunity to tell Mia later. Her cell phone buzzed. She retrieved it from her hip.

"Hey, Max."

"Hey, Riley. Everything good?"

"It's all ready to go. I've checked and rechecked and checked again. We've got every detail prepared for them. The gift baskets are absolutely extraordinary. Mr. Connick arrives at ten this morning and we're expecting your guests at one.

"Yes, I'm meeting them at the private airstrip at twelve. We will be back here by twelve thirty; then I'll take them to Mosaic for lunch at one."

"I have dinner arrangements at six thirty at Nobu. The show starts at eight. It should be a great evening."

"Well, it sounds like you've taken care of everything. Their flight leaves at midnight, so we'll show them a fabulous day and then they will get home in time to be safe from the storm."

Riley scribbled on the pad in front of her. "Anything else you can think of?"

"No, sounds great."

"Okay, then I'll see you at one."

Riley hung up the phone and lifted her head to see Christian's face at her door. "Busy day?" he asked.

"Crazy day."

"We're pretty quiet next door. Most of our nesters have flown the coop. Don't want to risk a hurricane. So if you need any extra help, I've got some extra hands."

"Thank you." She stood from her desk. "I'll let you know if I do. Right now I think we're good, though. Just waiting on Mr. Connick to arrive. That sounds weird, doesn't it?" She half laughed.

"You'd rather call him Harry?" His brown eyes scanned hers.

She shook her head. "No, that sounds weirder." She walked around to the front of her desk. "I'm going to go check his room one more time. Want to walk with me?"

"Oh, my, now you're inviting me somewhere."

She walked past him and raised an eyebrow. They walked from her office into the lobby of the office suites. Mia was standing in the doorway. Her expression registered oddly with Riley. "Anything wrong?" she asked.

Mia's smile took over. "No, no . . . everything is perfect. Just a few frazzled guests. Trying to calm their fears and assure them the hurricane isn't hitting today."

"Well, let me know if you need me. I'm going to go check Mr. Connick's room real quick, then talk with Gretchen at the theater. I think she's getting him after lunch. Did you make his lunch arrangements?"

"He requested a private lunch in his suite with his family."

Riley and Christian walked to the door. "Did you get his children passes for Aquaventure?"

"Yes, they should be in his room, and he has already given me his lunch order and we will have that delivered promptly at noon."

"Thanks, Mia," Riley offered with appreciation.

Christian nodded. "Good to see you, Mia."

"You too."

Riley and Christian talked about their previous evening as they made their way up to the suite. The conversation was natural, easy. When they knew everything was ready for the Connicks, they parted ways with the knowledge they would see each other at the concert. Riley watched him as he headed back to The Reef. He was truly a charming man. She bit her lip and wrinkled her nose, an involuntary act of contemplation. And she had been contemplating all morning, between her tasks, how much she enjoyed his company.

Mia was standing in the doorway and appeared to be watching him too. But then an elderly couple approached the office door and Mia waved them toward her. Riley hated that Laine had made her suspicious. Mia had been nothing but an angel, a friend, and a tremendous help during this crazy week. She smiled at her as she headed to her office to await the arrival of her first guest.

Tamyra pulled the handle of the slot machine mindlessly. In the span of an hour she had lost five hundred dollars. A smarter gambler would have changed machines. But she wasn't smart at anything. She deserved the loss. And with each coin that was sucked into the bottomless abyss, her thoughts of worthlessness were affirmed.

She swatted at her cheeks. Tears had been falling since last night. And the casino noise hadn't distracted them. Of course there weren't many people at ten o'clock in the morning to pay much attention to a woman crying on a barstool in front of a slot machine. An elderly woman had looked at her oddly as she had passed through on her way to breakfast. Breakfast. Tamyra felt her stomach growl. She had hardly put a fork in her food last night when Winnie had split, and she hadn't eaten anything since. But years of beauty pageants had taught her how to deprive herself despite even the sharpest hunger pains, so she didn't offer it much condolence either.

"There you are." Winnie's voice penetrated the few clanging bells already ringing in the casino. "I've been looking all over for you this morning. And — Lord have mercy," she said, grabbing the cup that held a couple fleeting coins. "How many were in here?"

Tamyra pulled the handle again. "Lots."

Winnie waved her hand in front of Tamyra's face. "You have officially OD'd on a slot machine. I knew those things weren't good for you, and you are proof. Now get your hind end out of this chair and get to the gettin'." She pulled at Tamyra's sleeve until she had her out of the chair.

Tamyra looked at her little friend. "I'm so

sorry, Winnie." Tears fell freely again. "I should have never done what I did last night."

Winnie swatted at her and pulled her down the hall. "No, you shouldn't have. But it's okay. It was good for me on so many levels, but obviously bad for you on . . ." She paused and studied Tamyra again. She was still in her same clothes from last night. ". . . on sooo many levels. Have you been in here all night?"

Tamyra rubbed her swollen eyes. "No, I tried to sleep but I couldn't. I finally came down here this morning and just thought I'd do something mindless."

"Well, you've let this get way out of hand."

"But I do that a lot. Get in the way. Insert myself. Voice my opinion. That is probably why Jason hit me."

Winnie released her arm quickly and was in her face — well, close to her chest — before she could even take a step back. "If I ever hear you say something like that again, I'll whup you myself. That is the most ridiculous, inane thing I have ever heard. No woman ever deserves to be hit. Do you hear me?" Her hands were wrapped around Tamyra's arms now. "Do you hear me?"

"Yes, yes. I hear you."

"You are a beautiful, talented, engaging,

and passionate woman. A man should never stifle that. He should only enhance it. If a man shows up trying to shut you down, it's because he isn't secure himself. A secure man wants a real woman. That kind of woman makes him alive. Brings out the best in him. A man that is threatened by a strong woman is no man at all. And don't you ever forget that."

Tamyra wrapped Winnie in her arms, all but lifting her off the ground. "Thank you. I was so afraid you would never speak to me again."

"I can't breathe," Winnie muttered.

Tamyra released her and couldn't hide her laughter.

Once Winnie caught her breath, she shook a finger at her. "You are afraid of too much."

Tamyra caught something frightening in Winnie's eyes. "What?"

"Go get your bathing suit on."

"Winnie, you know I don't —"

"I said, go get your bathing suit on. You tortured me last night. Granted, it was probably for the best, but this will be for the best too. Now, go. Don't stop. Don't talk. Don't say a word. Go get your bathing suit on and go get it on now. Meet me at the elevators in thirty minutes. I'll have Riley and Laine, and you, my dear, are about to get over some fears."

Spidery veins of fear began at the base of her neck, until she felt as if they would poke her eyeballs out of her head. "I can't. . . ."

Winnie spread her feet apart and put her pudgy hands on her cushy hips. "You will, and you will now. I won't debate. Now go."

If it hadn't been for Winnie all but dragging her to her room, she would have never been able to do it. But for such a petite sister, Winnie could wield one big stick.

18

Thursday morning . . .

The doors to the elevators opened and Riley stepped off. Mr. Connick and his entourage were safely in their rooms and everything had run smoothly. An on-time arrival, a smooth delivery, and room service was scheduled to arrive promptly at noon. It was only ten thirty, so the other VIPs from Miami wouldn't be arriving for another two hours. Riley all but ran smack-dab into Laine as she rounded the corner dressed in a blue and white Ralph Lauren knit bathing suit. The halter top tied around her neck, and her white terry cloth pants had a matching polo player in blue on the edge of her waist.

"Well, finally. Go get your bathing suit on. You're needed at Aquaventure."

Riley kept walking, and Laine joined in step. "Laine, this is the busiest day of the week. I just checked Harry Connick Jr. into his room, I have twenty VIPs arriving here in two hours, and I have to make sure everything runs perfectly for them. I do not have time to go to Aquaventure."

"Are you still my host?"

Riley turned and gave her a quick glare. "Do not even try that today."

"I will tell. I will call Max right now and tell him you are not doing your job."

She watched as Laine reached for her phone. "You wouldn't dare."

"I got you a date with Christian last night; don't tell me what I would and wouldn't do. You are needed at Aquaventure for an intervention."

"You are needed in a program for 'pains in the butts.' "

"I'll take that as a yes."

"One hour, Laine. One hour is all I have. If anything goes wrong, I really will lose my job. Honestly."

Laine wrapped an arm around her as they both continued to walk. "Sweet little Southern belle. I promise you, if you lose your job, I'll give you a new one. You can be my assistant." She smirked.

Riley pointed a finger at her. "One hour."

Laine stopped in the middle of the corridor and raised her hands in mock surrender. "I still want to hear how that date went." A smile broke out across her lips.

"And for the record, you're not wearing black." Riley turned before Laine could say a word, but she knew she was scanning her attire rapidly at this point, and it allowed her a small taste of satisfaction.

Mia was standing over the fax machine reading a piece of paper when Riley walked into the lobby. "I'll be back in one hour, Mia. Please make sure everything goes smoothly. No one should be here before I get back."

"You're leaving for an hour?"

"It's Laine. She's demanding that I go with her somewhere."

"You couldn't tell her what a busy day this was?"

Riley walked into her office and rummaged through her bottom desk drawer. "I did. I told her everything I could possibly tell her. I will be one hour. I promise. Just one hour," she called. Her hands caught her black bathing suit and she stuck it in her bag. She walked back to the door.

Mia looked hesitant. But no more hesitant than Riley felt inside. "Can I reach you by phone?"

"No, not for the next hour. I promise. One hour and I'll be back."

■ ■ ■ ■

Riley found the ladies waiting for her at the entrance to Aquaventure. For an African American, Tamyra was as white as Riley had ever seen her. "What are y'all doing to her? She's going to have a heart attack."

Tamyra shook her head wildly.

Winnie took over, her voice as bold as the red bathing suit she had on. "This is for her own good. It's time for this woman to get past her fears." Winnie bent down, getting nose to nose with Tamyra, who had a death grip on the edges of a lounge chair. "All of them."

Winnie tugged at her.

She didn't budge.

"Come on, Tamyra," Laine coaxed. "This is for your own good. It's your last hurdle to overcome."

Tamyra still wasn't budging.

All sympathy left Riley in that moment. She walked over to Tamyra, grabbed both of her hands, pried them from their death grip, and in three quick steps had her in the wave pool. She snatched a two-person inner tube, then used all of the power in her thighs, along with the buoyancy of the water, to hoist Tamyra onto one side of the tube. She shoved another two-person tube to Laine and Winnie and said, "Get on!" By this point everyone was obeying.

"Gracious. Someone must not have put sugar in her tea today," Laine said.

Riley's head snapped to Laine, and she raised a finger. "Not a word from you. Do you hear me? Not one word." She pulled the inner tube toward the conveyer belt that would send them to one of the towers, down a course of waterslides, and into the wave pool that coursed through the entire property of the hotel. It was a favorite of most guests, but she could tell by the look on Tamyra's face she could have left and never missed it. She grabbed hold of Tamyra's legs, which dangled from the inner tube. "I will be with you the whole way. You're going to be fine. Just breathe."

Then she hopped onto her side of the tube, convinced that she hadn't convinced Tamyra at all. So she didn't plan on telling her that she was surrounded by twenty million gallons of water or that this was a pretty long ride.

The technology was rivaled by very few: inner tubes laced their way up conveyer belts, through meandering funnels of water, up water escalators, and were pushed through canals by water surges. The scenery was breathtaking, and the color in Tamyra's face and knuckles had even begun to come back. Right until another conveyer belt came into view that looked as if it ended at the throne of God Himself. That was when the slow, guttural moans began.

Riley turned to Winnie. "If she jumps off, you're going after her."

Winnie crinkled her nose. "It's okay, Tamyra. Just imagine you're in your bathtub."

That was about the time that something unleashed, and a prison door broke open inside Tamyra. The tiara came off, and with it self-control. "This is not my bathtub! This is death! You are sending me to my death!" Her voice was shrieking and her terror was unmistakable. "I know I'm dying already, but my word, woman, I wasn't planning on doing it today!"

Riley reached over and tried to grip her hand. Tamyra jerked it away but then seemed to realize that also removed it from the handle she had been grasping for dear life. She flung it back onto the handle and gave Riley a dirty look. Riley withdrew her hand and looked back at Laine and Winnie. "You two are unbelievable."

Laine tilted her head in that cocky way she had. "Well, *you're* here, aren't you?"

If Riley were in the habit of flipping people off, this would have been the prime opportunity. Tamyra's groaning started as they came to the top of the final conveyer belt that would deposit them at the waterslides. "Honestly, Tamyra, it will be over in a minute. And you don't ever have to get back in water again." Riley hoped the words would soothe her.

But Tamyra was no longer responding. She had gone to the place of fear where breathing was altered and eyes were glazed. A young lifeguard pushed them to the top of a chute that would propel them down a waterslide. Riley had wisely placed them in the lane that took them to the most elementary slide, but she knew that it would still be far more than Tamyra had ever wanted to experience.

Without time to say a word, they shot through the darkness of a tunnel, their inner tube bouncing and colliding with the walls, the water surge beneath them carrying them through the blackness until it pushed them into the open slide. Riley looked back and saw that Tamyra's eyes and fists were clenched so tight, she wasn't sure what it would take to eventually pry them open. The tube continued to bounce and careen down the slide with rapid speed, and

Riley felt the adrenaline of the thrill rush through her. Gabby loved this ride. She would fly through here with the shrill squeals of a six-year-old and beg for more when they finally came to the bottom.

As the tube made its final plunge from the slide into the wave pool, Riley reached over to touch Tamyra's hand. "It's over, Tamyra. Now it's just the wave pool."

About that time she heard Winnie and Laine scream as they were spit out a few yards behind. She turned and couldn't help but smile at the rapture on the faces of those two mongrels. She looked back to see Tamyra opening her eyes.

"It's over?" Her voice was barely audible.

"Yeah, it's over."

"I did it?"

Riley patted her. "Yeah, honey, you did it."

"I did it? I really did it." The excitement grew with each personal revelation.

Winnie called out. "Way to go, Tamyra baby! I knew you could do it!"

Tamyra was slightly laughing now. She turned toward Winnie. "I did it, Winnie. I did it!"

Riley watched as Tamyra's eyes grew huge. Riley looked back and saw a large wave headed straight for them. She had forgotten about that. The ride was far from over. Now came the wave pool.

"What's that?" Tamyra's voice squeaked.

"Um, you might just want to hold on."

That was when the wave came up underneath them and projected them heavenward and then placed them back down with a massive, but somewhat-gentle, surge. It brought Laine and Winnie alongside them.

Tamyra's eyes were huge. "Whew!"

Laine and Winnie were cackling like hens.

Riley couldn't help but laugh too.

About that time Tamyra's eyes grew wide again. No one had to look this time. The next wave overtook them and lifted them again with reckless abandon. That was when Tamyra screamed and then slowly raised her hands in the air as if she were riding a roller coaster. Riley studied the delight that appeared on Tamyra's face. Another wave lifted them. Tamyra screamed as her hands shot straight up to the heavens.

With each wave that roared beneath them, Tamyra seemed to let go of another piece of the tormenting fear that had held her. With each powerful wave, another bar on Tamyra's prison door was broken. Until finally, a primal scream burst forth from her lips, and tears began to rush from her eyes. And with every surge of water beneath them, a fresh surge came from inside of Tamyra. All Riley, Winnie, and Laine could do was watch her. Not one of them spoke. There was something holy and cleansing and profound about this moment, and to speak would lessen it, cheapen it. And they knew it. So they simply rode each wave with her — those that were physical, those that were emotional, and those that were spiritual. And Tamyra's hands never came down from their outstretched place until their inner tubes made it back to where they started.

Riley slipped from the tube and passed it to Winnie and Laine. "Take her again if she wants to go. I'll see y'all at dinner. I made reservations for six thirty at Nobu. The show starts at eight."

Laine reached out and grabbed Riley before she could exit the water. She mouthed a silent thank-you. Riley left them in the waters of Tamyra's baptism.

Tamyra wasn't sure when it happened. Maybe it was when the fear became so suffocating that it was breathe or die. Maybe it was when the wave lifted her up and raised her body and it felt as if heaven lifted her up and raised her soul. But somewhere in the middle of a wave pool at a resort in the

Atlantic Ocean, this simple Southern girl believed. She believed that healing, real healing, was possible. Whether she died tomorrow from AIDS or was healed miraculously, the greater healing had occurred. Her soul would never be the same. Old Roy had been right after all. And now she believed it.

Riley didn't have time to dry her curls. But she had a good hour for them to dry on their own before she met Max and his guests for lunch. She flung her wet bathing suit into her bag, exited the locker room, and made her way to her office. Mia met her as she walked through the door. "I'm glad you're back. You're not going to believe —"

But the voice behind her cut Mia's sentence short. "Riley, there you are."

Riley turned quickly, stunned to see Max staring at her. "Max, hey." She walked to him and gave him a hug.

He returned it warmly. "Mia said you had been sidetracked with Laine, but she has handled everything beautifully for us. I'm just sorry you couldn't be here at our arrival. I wanted your face to be the first face they saw. But we have pushed up lunch, and I want you to join us. Meet us at Mosaic in fifteen minutes."

Riley tried to refrain from revealing her complete shock and rising horror. "Sure, yes. I'll see you there in fifteen minutes. And I'm sorry too that I wasn't here."

He looked over her shoulder. "Well, you've got a great team. Mia here made sure everything came off without a hitch."

Riley turned. Mia's face was beaming. She turned back to Max, grateful for Mia's diligence. "I'm sure she did. She has been an amazing asset to this team."

"See you in fifteen."

"Sure, yes. Fifteen."

Max headed to the door and then turned back. "You look wonderful, Riley, honestly, but your hair?"

She had forgotten her hair was still soaking wet. "Long story."

He smiled, shook his head, and then the door swung silently closed behind him.

Riley turned back to Mia. "What happened? When did their plans change?"

"A fax came through right after you left. I tried calling you, but you said you couldn't be contacted, and you didn't answer."

Riley fumbled frantically through her bag and pulled her phone from it. Sure enough, there was one missed call from the office. She leaned against the counter, the emotions feeling as if they might overwhelm her. "So everything was perfect?"

"Yes. It went off without a hitch? I think that is what Max said." She laughed. "You Americans and your sayings. Anyway, I just told them that you had a Laine emergency only you could handle, but that we had everything all ready for them. Christian came over and our teams escorted each VIP personally, and not a glitch was found." Mia walked over and placed her hand on Riley's shoulder. "No worries, Riley. I've got your back."

Riley hugged her. "Thank you. I honestly can't thank you enough. I don't know what would have happened if you hadn't been here." She released Mia.

"Well, we don't have to worry about that. I was. And it was all perfect. I've rescheduled the luncheon, so you go dazzle them and all will be fine."

Riley ran her hands through her hair. She rushed into her office and jerked open the top drawer, her hand scouring for a hair band. Mia held one out to her from the other side of the desk. Riley looked up and let out a large sigh, the tightness in her neck released. "That's what I was looking for. Thank you."

Mia gave her a few minutes so she could

freshen her makeup and pull her hair back, and in ten minutes she was ready to go. She walked out to the front of the offices. "So you've got everything here."

Mia nodded from behind the desk. "Yes, finalizing things for tonight. Got a large group of guests out this morning. So we're all good."

"And Christian helped?" Riley tried to hide her smile.

"He was glad to."

She nodded. "Okay, then. Thank you again." She ran her hands across her navy cotton twill dress and stuck her master key and lip gloss in one pocket and her phone in the other. She breathed in deeply and thanked God as she exhaled that Mia and Christian had just saved her behind. Again.

Lunch with the VIPs couldn't have gone better. In spite of being kidnapped by Laine earlier, Riley knew every detail of the visit so far had been rendered exquisitely. She could still wring the woman's neck. But she was too grateful to be angry. Her phone vibrated in her pocket. It was a hotel number. "Hello? Riley Sinclair."

"Hello, Riley."

She smiled; her shoulders relaxed. "Hey, Christian. I hear I owe you an immense thank-you for what you did for me this morning."

He chuckled. "It was my pleasure. I told you I would help. Just thought you'd be there too."

"It's a long story. I seem to have a lot of those."

"The demanding Laine Fulton."

"Yes, she is my perpetual long story. But thank you. Thank you so much."

"No more thank-yous. It was no problem. Honestly. So did you make it to the lunch?"

"Yes, we just finished. It was as smooth as could be. All of the guests are ready to go crash on lounge chairs on the beach and stare at the ocean in this gorgeous weather, where they will sleep until it's time to eat again." She paused, hesitant to make the move she was about to make. But she pushed through anyway. "Would you like to join a group of ladies tonight for dinner and then go to the concert with us?"

"I would love that. Okay if I bring along at least one other male with me to even out the testosterone slightly?"

"That's right; you've met my ladies." She laughed.

"I have." She could practically hear him smile.

"Please. Bring anyone you like."

"One of the guys here was going to go with me."

"Sure. All the ladies are single. Bring him along."

"But you aren't looking, are you? I mean, not right now."

The phone felt warm against her face. Or it had just gotten hotter outside. "You know, I actually met this really charming man last night."

"Oh, you did?"

"Yes, I made an idiot out of myself while I was with him, but he didn't seem to notice."

"I hear he likes idiots."

"Well, that's a good thing. . . ."

"Dinner is at . . . ?"

"Six thirty. Nobu."

"I will see you there."

Riley smiled as she hung up the phone. A rather eventful day had just gone to another level of eventfulness.

Laine raised her head up off the lounge chair in her cabana. The ocean was no longer playing a lullaby. Instead it had changed to a more forceful concerto. Wind whipped around them, causing the curtains of the cabana to flap against the wood plank walls. Winnie and Tamyra were facedown in their lounge chairs next to her with no idea they were in the world and no idea that the sun had been completely overtaken by an overcast heaven. Laine only knew they were alive because of the atrocious sounds coming from Winnie that competed with both the wind and the waves.

There were times she wished she had met Sam. He must have been one great man to put up with the "interesting" character traits of this woman. She chuckled softly and laid her head back down. Aquaventure had wiped these three out. None of them had any idea just how much of an adventure it was going to be. Nor did they want to leave early. But the hurricane had changed all of their plans. And it seemed to be coming in even quicker than they had thought. They would each be heading out in the morning. So tonight Harry would have to sing their swan song too.

19

Thursday evening . . .

Nobu sat at the edge of the casino in the Royal Towers, right beneath the nightclub. It was Japanese cuisine at its finest. Riley had arrived thirty minutes early to make sure the tables and menu were set for the VIP guests. She knew Max would arrive early too. He was always early. She smiled to herself, thinking she should have taken that into consideration this morning. She still had no idea how he had corralled twelve people an hour early.

The chef was preparing his omakase for them. It was a multicourse dinner of his choicest cuisine. A guest could never go wrong with it. And she knew Max and his guests would love it. At twenty after, Max walked through the doors. She handed him a watermelon martini. He loved them.

"You know me too well," he said, taking the glass from her hand and leaning in to give her a kiss on the cheek.

"Sorry again about today."

"No apologies. I know with the hurricane coming in fast things are crazy around here. The good news —" he took a sip of his drink — "you have an incredible team who executed everything to perfection."

"Well, tonight should be no different." She raised her water to him. "Thank you for this opportunity, Max. I am enjoying my job immensely."

He let the edge of his glass clink against hers. "Gabby seems to be doing great too."

"She's adjusting very well. The school has been very good for her."

"I love seeing her."

"I know. I sent her home with Jeremy this week. After Hugo, I don't want anyone to have to go through one. I can't believe any of the guests are staying."

"People take their vacations seriously. But this thing has picked up speed. The wind is really whipping out there now. People who are leaving really do need to get out of here tonight. You should tell your other guests that. They've increased flights and will be running them through the night, until they can no longer fly."

"They should leave tonight?"

"Yes, the storm is coming more quickly

than they originally thought. So we need to be diligent about getting the rest of the guests notified. Reception was leaving messages for all of the remaining guests. But the ones who were staying for this concert might not realize that if they don't get out tonight, they will probably be riding this one out. The surge is already getting much higher."

Riley spotted Laine walking through the door and their discussion of the storm stopped. She glanced at her watch. Laine was a few minutes early. My, how things had changed. "Come here. I want you to meet someone." She took Max's arm and they walked toward Laine, who looked stunning in a black sheath dress with a complementing V-neck and a pair of yellow slingbacks. Riley was certain they were Jimmy Choos and she was shocked they weren't black.

"Laine, I would like you to meet my boss and friend, Max Magiano. Max, this is our author in residence, Laine Fulton," she said with a smile.

Laine gave her a smile in return and took Max's extended hand. "It's a pleasure to meet you, Max."

"And it's a pleasure to have you at our hotel. I hope you have enjoyed your stay."

"It's been perfect. The property is extraordinary. The food exquisite. And the customer service —" she stopped and glanced at Riley — "matchless."

Max patted Riley softly on the back. "This is a special lady."

"She has been a wonderful hostess, I assure you."

"Well, I'm glad you have had everything you need. Please accept my apology for not saying hello before now. Between some upcoming contracts, this event tonight, and this storm, I have been too busy." Riley watched as Max caught sight of his guests beginning to come through the doors of the restaurant. "We'd love for you to join us for dinner tonight if you'd like, Ms. Fulton."

"Please, call me Laine. And I think I will stay with Riley and our other friends this evening since we're all headed out tomorrow. But thank you for the invitation."

"Riley, take good care of them. Get them whatever they want, on me."

Riley smiled and patted Max. "Thank you. We'll see you at the concert. Your tables are all ready for you in the front, and don't hesitate to let me know if you need anything."

"Thank you. Well, if you'll excuse me, ladies."

Laine nodded as Max headed toward the door.

"Thank you," Riley said, pointing Laine toward their table.

"For what?" She put her hand mockingly to her chest. "Were you afraid I was going to say something to embarrass you?"

Riley raised an eyebrow. "You? No. I figured you'd just snatch me away again and make me miss something else important."

Laine's eyes widened. "What happened? Something else?"

"The VIPs all showed up an hour early today."

She could see it was registering. "And I had you at Aquaventure."

Riley nodded. She let her marinate in it for a moment.

"I'm so sorry. Was he mad?" Her anxiousness was evident.

Riley laughed, not wanting Laine to drown in the torture. "No. Thankfully I had everything ready, and Mia executed everything just like I would have."

Laine nodded slowly. "Of course she did."

"Stop it, Laine. You're being nice tonight," she said, sitting at the table. "And I'm ordering dinner tonight. Not you."

"My, my, you've gotten bossy."

"Just trust me."

Laine looked down at the table. "Why are there all these plates?"

"We have extra guests."

"So you took care of the roster, too?"

"Yes, this is my evening. You had your morning. The evening is mine."

Laine crinkled her nose.

"Sit. You don't always have to be in control, Laine. It's an illusion anyway. There is no such thing. Now sit." She smiled.

Laine obeyed. Twice in one day she had sat when told. Maybe miracles did still happen.

"And where's your notebook?"

Laine raised her head in mock indignation.

Riley smiled. It was no longer about work for Laine. My, how far they had come.

Christian walked through the door with a young man who matched his six-foot frame. When they reached Laine and Riley, he introduced his friend. Lance Tyson had been working at The Reef for the last two months. He was still getting used to the job and to the area. He had moved here from Boston and his heritage came out with every syllable. He couldn't have been more than twenty-five, and his biceps bulged slightly beneath the pressed sheen of his white cotton button-down.

Christian slipped into the seat beside Riley. His chocolate brown shirt only made the deep brown of his eyes more immersing. "You look beautiful," he whispered.

Riley fingered her curls. She ran her hands nervously down the front of her khaki and white linen sheath dress. "Thank you."

They were interrupted by the arrival of Winnie and Tamyra; Mia followed only a few moments later. When all the seats were taken and all the introductions made, the feast began to arrive. They would start with sushi.

Tamyra passed a plate in front of Winnie. "Taste it."

Winnie eyed the raw tuna. "I do not eat food that has yet to be killed. I was raised on a farm, Tamyra. We wrung the chicken's neck before we ate it."

Tamyra didn't move the plate. "I got in water today, Winnie. Eat the tuna." Then offered her a cheesy smile.

Winnie pursed her lips and twisted them to one side. Tamyra took her own fork and placed a piece on Winnie's plate, then politely passed the dish. The entire table tried to pretend they weren't waiting to watch Winnie eat the tuna. But they were. Finally Laine broke the silence.

"For pete's sake, Winnie, eat the blasted

tuna. You've done things you never thought you'd do this week. No need to stop now."

Winnie cocked her head at Laine, stabbed the tuna with her fork, and popped it in her mouth, chewing intentionally, all while staring Laine straight in the eye. Laine offered a satisfied smirk.

"I can see you ladies have had an interesting week." Christian laughed.

Laine shook her head. "Christian, *interesting* doesn't even begin to define the week we've had."

All four paused for a moment. Then laughter erupted around the table. As the food came like a revolving door across their table, their conversation transpired virtually the same way. Tamyra and Lance were engaged in conversation, Laine prodded Christian mercilessly, Winnie braved the conch seviche, and they all devoured Chilean sea bass, black cod with miso, and shrimp and lobster with spicy lemon sauce. Riley couldn't have asked for a better evening.

"So, Mia . . . ," Laine began. Riley involuntarily began to hold her breath. "Riley tells me you saved the day today."

Mia laughed casually. "I wouldn't say that. I'd say we have a great team." Riley didn't miss the glance she threw across the table toward Christian. Obviously Laine didn't either.

"That's what Riley keeps telling me. In fact, after her date with Christian last night, she was telling me just how grateful she was that she worked with such talented people."

Riley kicked her under the table. Hard. Laine never flinched. Obviously she had been kicked under the table before. Riley had told Laine nothing. She had barely had time to breathe in the last twenty-four hours, never mind tell Laine about her date with Christian. "Don't underestimate yourself, Mia," Riley said, hoping to put a stop to wherever Laine was headed.

"Yes, you should —" Laine hesitated when Riley cut her off with a raised eyebrow, then continued. "Yes, you should be proud of the job you did today. It sounds like it saved Riley's a—, uh, job."

Christian interjected. "Riley had everything handled and ready to go. All we did was get them there a little early. She had worked ridiculously hard to make sure every detail was taken care of and nothing was missed. That made us more like concierges than anything."

Riley turned to look at this man who seemed too good to be true. He was incredibly gorgeous, way too generous, and inexplicably kind. And right now he was looking right at her. "Well, again —" she turned back to Mia — "I couldn't have done it without both of you."

Winnie entered the conversation. "Okay, I'm glad everything went okay with y'all today, but I just need to know, do we have to walk through the casino to get to the concert? Because I had to do that this morning to save Tamyra from herself and you know, I'm Baptist —"

Riley, Tamyra, and Laine cut her off immediately. "And Baptists don't gamble."

Their unison response tickled the snot out of all of them. Even Winnie had to laugh.

They walked from the restaurant and into the casino. Winnie eyed the blackjack tables and craps tables as if the devil himself were going to jump off of them.

"We're giving money away tonight like candy," one of the dealers said as Winnie stopped to stare. She scooted to the center of the aisle as if he were going to grab her and tie her to a chair, forcing her to roll a die.

Riley walked in the front with Christian. "Thanks for joining us."

"I see you and Laine have broken through your communication barrier."

Riley rubbed slightly at her head. A gnawing pressure had been building throughout dinner. "*That* sounded like we had broken through something? I think we're just broken. That woman is crazy. She'd drive a sober person to . . ." She stopped herself. She hadn't made a remark like that in a long time. "Well, she'd drive a sane man crazy, let's just say." She rubbed her head again.

"You have a headache?" Christian reached over and cupped the back of her neck with his hand. Every part of her body tingled at his touch. He rubbed gently. She wanted to lean in like a dog would when you scratch behind his ears, but she didn't think that would be too attractive in the middle of the casino.

"Just a nagger. It started coming on before dinner. Probably was hungry. I'm not sure that I've eaten much all day. I hardly touched lunch. So maybe once the food all settles, it will ease off."

His fingers began to press at the base of her neck like a trained masseur. "I'll go get you something."

She reached for his hand. "No, honestly, I think I'm all right. It will ease off. I'll just go into the concert and see how I feel. If it doesn't subside, I'll get something after it's over."

They came to the door of the concert hall.

She stepped back to make sure everyone was there. Each one passed by her to enter the theater. Each one but Winnie. When Tamyra got to the door, she stopped her. "Where's Winnie?"

Tamyra turned. Laine looked too. "I don't know. She was right here with us."

"Oh, great, you've lost a Baptist in the casino," Riley said as she walked past them and headed back toward the casino.

Laine followed at her heels. "Don't tell Winnie, but I'm certain I spotted a couple other Baptists in there and they were enjoying themselves."

Riley just shook her head and kept walking. About twenty feet into the casino, she spotted Winnie's bejeweled denim ensemble and her pink cowboy hat. She was as hard to miss as a charismatic at Catholic Mass. She was standing at a craps table, hands on the side, head tilted down, and eyes transfixed. Riley scooted up beside her, followed by Tamyra on her other side and Laine breathing down her neck. "God sees you everywhere you go, Winnie."

Winnie swatted at Laine behind her. "I'm just watching."

"Interesting, huh?" Tamyra asked.

"Incredibly confusing. He told me the rules, but I don't have one idea what in tarnation that man said."

Laine stepped back. "She did not just say *tarnation*. Please tell me you Southern people don't still say *tarnation*. Do you still preach hell and damnation?"

Winnie turned and looked at Laine. "Do not cuss. It's bad enough we're standing in the middle of a casino and y'all are watching a game called 'craps,' " she said, her hands flying out at them. "We sure don't need you aiding and abetting by cussing." She pushed past her and headed toward the theater.

Tamyra laughed. "You'll learn, Laine. You'll learn."

"Good luck with that," Riley quipped.

Laine mimicked them all from behind, but Riley knew exactly what she was doing. She had learned Laine well.

About halfway through Harry Connick Jr.'s second set, Riley thought her head would split open. The tables for the VIPs and her guests sat in front of the stage. She rubbed her temples fiercely, unable to remember the last time her head had hurt this way. Mia slipped a hand around from behind her and handed her a bottled water, the lid already off. It wasn't Goody's headache powder, but hopefully just the distraction of something to drink could get her mind off of the pain shooting through her head. Fortunately she was listening to Harry Connick Jr. and not Aerosmith.

Laine leaned over. "You okay?"

"Just have this killer headache I can't get rid of. But I'll be fine. I'll grab something when we leave."

Riley took a long drink and rubbed the back of her head. When she lifted it, she caught Winnie's smile. It shone as bright as the rhinestones on her outfit did when they caught the lights from the stage. She looked at Tamyra. The young woman who didn't even want to look you in the eye five days ago now didn't take her eyes off of the stage. Their deep blackness was lit with a brightness of one who was living. She turned toward Laine. She hadn't mentioned if she had talked to Mitchell, but then again, Riley hadn't stopped long enough to ask. But whether she had or not, the woman sitting next to her was not the beast who had arrived less than a week ago.

She smiled to herself and took another long drink from the bottle. Her friendship with these women made no sense. They had all wanted to kill each other at some point. Wanted to hug each other at times. Laughed during all the moments they weren't crying or yelling. And somewhere in the middle of all of it, her heart had connected to these women with an intensity few of her friendships had ever produced. She had known she would enjoy her job, but she had never known she could enjoy it this much.

One of those "divine setups," as Josalyn would say. Yes, she had been set up perfectly. She glanced at Christian. He caught her eye and winked at her. The kindness from that man overwhelmed her. She couldn't perceive anything in him to contradict this deep, genuine kindness. He had admitted his faults in his marriage, was candid about his imperfections, and she was sure they were there. But there was also this sweetness that couldn't be masked. Riley glanced over her shoulder; Mia gave her a quick wave and one of her bouncing smiles. This girl had saved her behind all week. She would be a friend long after the others were gone, and this was just another reason to be grateful for where life had her now. For more than a moment Riley had forgotten the pounding in her head. Maybe she was just thirsty.

The concert ended with two encores and three hundred satisfied guests. Max sidled up next to her. "They want to go to the nightclub for a little while before they head out."

"Yeah?"

He touched her arm softly. "I'd like you to join us, just because it would be good for business, but if it would be too difficult, I don't want you to put yourself —"

She patted his hand, stopping him in mid-sentence. "It's okay. I can handle a night-club. I still like to dance," she said, giving him a reassuring wink.

Obviously his guests wanted more fun before they flew back to Miami. And it wasn't the alcohol that would bother her. It would be the music that could possibly ramp up the pounding in her temples. Riley turned back to her ladies. "Would any of you like to go to the nightclub for a few minutes of dancing?"

Riley glanced at Winnie, whose hand had quickly flown to her chest. Tamyra pulled her hand away and looked at Max. "We'd love to. Winnie loves to dance."

Winnie's eyes darted to her.

Max clasped his hands together, still at Riley's side. "Great. We'll see you on the dance floor."

"Tamyra Larsen, I do not dance."

Tamyra wasn't going to be deterred. "Have you ever tried it? And if you say, 'I'm

389

Baptist,' I promise you I will scream. Have you ever once danced?"

Winnie tugged at the edges of her pink denim jacket. "Once. I danced. Well, okay, five times. Sam always wanted to take dance lessons, and so he finally talked me into five lessons at the Arthur Murray Dance Studio."

"And you never danced again?" Tamyra pressed.

She dropped her head slightly. "No. We never danced again."

Laine interrupted. "The question is, did you like it?"

Winnie gave her that Winnie eye and paused for a moment; then her nose turned up along with the edges of her smile. "I really did. I loved every minute of it."

Tamyra's face showed an almost pity for her new friend. "Then why didn't you ever go back?"

"Sam got sick. We couldn't."

Tamyra wrapped her in her arms. "I'm so sorry, Winnie. I'm so sorry." She let her go and stepped back.

Riley reached out a hand. "Tonight you will dance, Winnie."

"Yes, Riley knows all about dancing," Laine spouted. "She went to one of those Holy Roller churches when she lived in

Charleston. She knows all about dancing. And no telling what else, from what I hear about them."

"Keep it up, Laine, and I'll make you go with me," Riley quipped from over her shoulder.

As they left their table, Riley spotted Albert about the same time he spotted Winnie. She looked behind her and saw that Winnie had seen him too. "Why don't you ask him to join us?"

Winnie turned sharply to Riley. "Join us?"

"I bet he'd enjoy it."

"You owe him far more than dancing after what you did to him last night," Laine said.

Tamyra elbowed her.

"I don't mean that. I just mean she owes him . . . coffee . . . shuffleboard . . . whatever people her age do."

Winnie stepped away from all of them and made her way to Albert. None of them heard what she said to him, but as they walked out the door, Albert was walking with Winnie. Apparently he was joining them for some dancing.

Riley took a few steps and felt a strange heaviness wash over her. She grabbed a chair and looked around. Thankfully, no one saw her. This must be a migraine or something, though the throbbing had eased off a bit. She caught Christian's eye. He walked toward her. "Max has asked us to come up to the nightclub for a minute," she told him. "It's not my first choice for how to spend an evening, but I think Winnie needs to dance, and he would like me to be able to say hello to his guests. I might even see if I can get them to play something more up Winnie's alley."

Christian laughed. "Blaming it on Winnie, huh?"

She smiled. "Yeah, that would sound much better than me being too old for nightclub music. But we won't be there long."

"I'd love to join you."

She knew he meant it.

The music was felt from the stairwell as if it pulsated the very ground. Winnie turned when she got to the door. Tamyra pointed her back around.

"I really don't think this is for me," Winnie protested.

Riley wasn't sure it was for her either. Not the music, but her body. She had to pull against the railing to even get herself up the stairs, as if her body was washed-out. She tried to act normal as she and Christian walked through the doors of the nightclub.

Strobe lights moved to the beat of the music.

"This isn't Arthur Murray," Laine said in Riley's ear.

"No, it sure isn't."

"You sure you need to come in here? I'm sure Max would understand if you didn't think you should."

"He asked me already. I'll be fine. Thanks, though."

Mia was already inside talking to Max and the other guests who surrounded his tables. Drinks were flowing all around, and Riley felt as if she were drowning. Her head was fuzzy and heavy, and the whole scene brought back a lot of memories. She hadn't been to a nightclub in a long time, where drinks flowed freely, bodies collided, and where, when the lights finally came up at the end of the night and people got a look at what they were dancing with, most ran for cover.

She touched Christian's arm. "I'll be right back. I just need to go to the ladies' room for a minute."

"Sure, I'll be right here."

She walked into the ladies' room and leaned against the sink; turning on the faucet, she dropped her hands beneath its rapid flow. The coolness of it jolted her slightly. She pulled her hands from the water and patted them softly against her face. She blinked her eyes rapidly, trying to get the blood flowing through the fog.

Mia came through the door and saw Riley standing there, hands pressed against her face. "Riley, are you okay? You don't look that good."

Riley shook her head and reached for a paper towel. "Just feel kind of strange. That headache got me, I guess," she said as she wiped her hands.

"Here, I've got this extra-strength headache reliever." She turned the pill in her fingers. "At least I think that's what it is. Let's go out and get you something to drink and you can take it."

"You know, my head really isn't hurting that badly anymore. I think I might just need caffeine or something. It's been a long day. Maybe when I finally sat down, I realized how tired I was."

"Well, come on, let's go get you a Coke."

They sidled up next to the bar, and Riley looked at the amber-colored liquids that lined the wall. She stared at them, remembering.

Mia nudged her, a martini already in front of her. "Riley, he's asking you what you want to drink."

Riley hadn't even heard the bartender

speak to her. "Oh, sorry. Could I have a Dr Pepper please? Just need some caffeine."

"Dr Pepper it is."

"You sure you don't want this?" Mia asked, pushing a nondescript white pill in front of her.

Riley's head throbbed slightly behind her eyes. "Yeah, sure. I still have a little nagger." When the bartender set the drink down in front of her, she took the pain reliever capsule and chugged her drink, hoping it would give her the boost of energy she needed.

"Thank you. You've been there every time I've needed you this week."

Mia patted her on the back. "It's been a pleasure, Riley. Really, I'm sorry Laine has stressed you out so much this week. That woman is a handful."

Riley rubbed her head again and laughed softly. "She's really a great woman. You just have to get her to let her guard down. I've become quite fond of her and you, too. You haven't really told me any of your story, Mia. How did you get here?"

Mia shifted on her stool. Her smile tensed. "My mother . . . well, she felt like I should get out and explore the world. She has really high ambitions for me, you know."

"Sounds like most mothers."

Mia's laugh sounded forced. "Yeah, sure. Most moms are that way. But I was working in the hospitality industry in Sydney and heard about this opening and thought it might be nice to get away from home for a while. Just couldn't get away from . . ."

Either her words trailed off or Riley just couldn't focus. She blinked her eyes hard.

"How are you able to come in here tonight with the bar and everything?"

Riley blinked hard again. Her body was beginning to feel even more out of control. She shook her head. "Man, I just feel weird. You sure that was a headache pill?"

"Yeah, it has to be. That's all I carry in my purse."

Riley blinked again and looked at Mia. Her vision doubled. She heard her laugh coming as if from across the club. "I feel like I'm drunk and I haven't had a thing. That will teach me to get more sleep and to not let myself get so stressed out." She took another drink of her soda and that was when she heard the music change.

The DJ's voice broke through the intense chatter of the club. "And a special request goes out for some of the ladies in the house. We bring you an old classic, not our typical music flavor, but it is from the icon himself, Frank Sinatra." The first melodic line of "All the Way" began to take over the nightclub. A brief cheer went up. Obviously she wasn't the only one who enjoyed a change of pace every now and then.

She looked up and Christian was beside her, hand extended. "Would you dance with me?"

She looked at Mia. Her face registered something. Something she hadn't seen on her before. Mia was jealous and in that moment she knew it. But it was just a moment. Mia turned quickly to Riley, flashed her engaging smile, and said, "Go. Go dance."

She turned back to Christian. She spoke, but it felt as if her words were slower. Slurred, even. "I'd love to."

As they made their way to the dance floor, Riley stumbled slightly.

"You okay?" Christian asked.

"Yeah. Fine." Even as she spoke, it felt as if she were exiting her body. She could see Winnie and Albert already on the dance floor; Tamyra was dancing with Christian's friend Lance. Max and his wife were on the other side of them, and a few more of the guests and their spouses had taken to the dance floor as well. But Riley knew something was terribly wrong. With all of her might she wanted to pull Christian toward her and tell him something was seriously wrong, that she needed to get home. As they got to the dance floor and he took her in his arms, her body disconnected from her mind. Her hands began to slide their way up his neck and around his back. Every part of her being desired him.

She wanted to push away from him and run, but she didn't. She couldn't. Her mind was crazed, but her body was alive. She began to move seductively.

Christian took her arms from around his neck and let out an uncomfortable laugh. "Riley, what's up with you?"

She pushed her body toward him again, her words now slurred as her hands moved up and down his back. "I just want to be close to you. I just want to dance with you. Can't I dance with you?" Even as the words came out of her, she felt no ability to stop them.

He pulled her hands from his back. "Riley, come on. This isn't like you. What are you doing?"

She felt a heat rise up inside of her, and this one wasn't from passion. Her words came out loud. She could tell. Though they didn't feel like hers. It was as if her mind and her body had been taken over and everything was happening outside of her control.

"What's wrong with you?" She could tell by his expression he wasn't sure what to do with her.

Laine was across the room when she saw Riley head out to the dance floor. She had watched her conversation with Mia at the bar and didn't know how she had even been able to come in here. She knew Riley thought she had beaten this thing. But the woman she was watching on the dance floor wasn't Riley. That woman was a drunk. She knew she should have pulled her away from the bar. And now Riley was about to make a fool of herself in front of everyone if Laine didn't stop her and stop her quick.

She sidled up beside her and slipped an arm around her. "You know, Christian, my friend here has had a really long day. I think I just need to get her home and let her get some sleep."

Riley jerked free from Laine's hold. "I'm not going anywhere with you!" Her words were biting from her drawn lips. She turned back to Christian and wrapped her arms around him again, pressing her head against his chest. "I want to stay here with Christian." She sounded like a child. A drunk child.

Laine grabbed her with a little more force.

"I said, we're going, Riley."

Tamyra came up beside her. "You need some help?"

"Riley, are you drunk?" Christian asked.

Laine felt as if she herself had been slapped. If Riley had been coherent enough to know what was going on at this moment, Laine knew she would be sick. "Christian, she's just had a long day. I promise, she is just exhausted."

Max finally noticed the commotion and came over. Exactly what Laine had been trying to avoid. "Riley, is something wrong?"

Riley jerked free from Laine again. "Yes!" The word came out as if it had three syllables. "This woman has driven me crazy all week!" She swung her arm wildly at Laine. "She's mean and angry and sad." Riley all but spat her last words.

Laine tried to refrain from her desire to slap Riley. Slapping a drunk wouldn't help them. Though she'd feel a lot better.

Max interrupted her. "Riley, have you been drinking?"

She let out an arrogant puff. "I don't drink." Her slurred words in no way confirmed her declaration.

Max shook his head. Laine could see the disappointment on his face. "I shouldn't have let you come in here. This is my fault."

His last words were more of a whisper. "I'm sorry, Ms. Fulton."

Riley's head jerked toward Max. Laine hadn't seen that much fire in her eyes since she had let her have it the other day. But that time Riley had seemed hurt. Tonight she was like a wild animal. "Don't apologize to her!"

Laine watched Max's face shift to stern and fatherly. "Riley, your behavior is unacceptable. Laine Fulton is our guest and you will give her your respect."

Riley let out a drunken puff. "She doesn't deserve anyone's respect. She's an adulterer, you know. Yeah, that's right. She couldn't keep her marriage together because she is an adulterer." Laine felt a slap in her gut and hoped Riley's words were slurred enough that the others couldn't quite make out what she was saying.

"That's right! Slept with a stranger. A stranger!" Riley stumbled slightly as the last words came out.

Laine was grateful that Frank's song was over and the club was now pumped with the sounds of rap.

Winnie had walked over as Riley finished her last announcement and steadied Riley back on her feet. "What in the world? Riley, what is wrong with you?"

Riley jerked free from Winnie and stumbled again yet continued her maligning of Laine. "Yeah, that's why she's so angry and demanding. Always telling me where I should be and when I should be there."

Max stepped up and took her by the arm. Laine saw the hurt on his face. But he was resolved. "Riley, you will have your office packed up by morning and I will expect you on the first flight out after the storm blows over. I'm very disappointed in you." He spoke his next statement under his breath, but Laine was close enough to hear him. "I'm sorry. I should never have let you come in here." He dropped her arm.

Laine took Riley by the arm one more time, and this time Tamyra and Winnie helped her. "We'll get her back to her condo."

"I can have Mia take her back," Max said, motioning for Mia to come over.

Laine eyed the woman. "No," she stated clearly. "*We* will get her back."

"Yes, we want to handle this," Tamyra said to Max.

"I'm going to beat your tail, young lady," Winnie added.

Max nodded at them and left the dance floor. Christian's face came into Laine's view. "I'm really sorry, Christian. This isn't like her."

"I wouldn't have thought so. But apparently it is." The hurt on his face was unmistakable.

Riley jerked beneath her hold, but Laine squeezed harder. She could tell Tamyra had a strong hold on the other side.

"I've got the rear," Winnie announced. And together they escorted Riley off the dance floor. Bodies closed the gaping hole where they'd been as if nothing had even taken place.

Laine looked back as the bouncer opened the door for them to exit. Mia was standing by Christian. She raised her cup in a mimicking motion of one who had hit the bottle a little too hard. Laine watched her a moment longer, then turned to take this pitiful creature squirming beneath her grasp back home.

Riley squawked her protests as they carried her down the stairs. When they got to the bottom, Winnie came around to the front of Riley and swatted her thigh. "You hush up."

Riley stopped squirming and leaned back, her eyes blinking hard at Winnie.

"I don't know what in the world has gotten into you, or what you've gotten into, but we are not going to carry you through this hotel. You are going to get yourself together and walk through here without looking like a drunk. Now straighten up," Winnie demanded.

They watched as Riley tried to stand up straight. Tamyra let go of her side and Riley tottered.

"Stand up straight now." Winnie was adamant on how this was all going to take place.

Riley tried to steady herself again. Laine felt like she could let go.

"Now, we will be right here with you, but you are going to get to your room like a lady, not a tramp."

"She's the tramp." Riley pointed at Laine and all but fell over.

"I'm going to slap her," Laine announced.

Winnie stepped into Riley's space. "Don't you say another word. Don't speak. Don't mumble. Don't hum. We want nothing. You've done enough damage tonight and you will do no more."

Laine and Tamyra eyed each other.

Winnie stepped aside and motioned in front of her. "Now, go."

Riley took a faltering first step and Laine reached out and steadied her. She jerked her arm from Laine's grasp, caught her footing, and stood up straight. And they walked through the casino.

"You're good at this, Winnie," Tamyra said.

"This is what I do."

"Deal with drunk women?" Laine quipped.

"Deal with desperate people," Winnie reminded. "This is nothing but a desperate means of avoiding the real issue."

She had Tamyra's curiosity. "What is the real issue?"

"Fear. It's always fear."

Laine and Tamyra walked beside Riley all the way to her condo, ready to steady her at any moment. When they got there, they led her into her bedroom and lowered her onto the bed. She fell over immediately. "She never should have gone in there tonight," Laine said.

"It's just a nightclub."

"She's an alcoholic, Tamyra," Winnie said.

Laine jerked her head toward Winnie. "How did you know that? Did she tell you?"

"Didn't have to. I know what one looks like."

"Just like you knew what I looked like." Tamyra was getting it.

"This is what I do," Winnie said.

"Well, do you put pajamas on grown women?" Laine asked. "Because I don't."

Winnie laughed, then knelt and pulled off

Riley's shoes. She sent Laine in search of pajamas and Tamyra in search of a cold rag. When they came back, she put Riley's pj's on her and tucked her beneath the covers. Riley opened her eyes for a brief moment.

"I loveth you. I loveth you all," she announced.

"Get some sleep, Riley," Winnie said as she scooted the other two out of the room.

Laine fell onto the sofa. "I can't believe this. She just lost her job tonight."

"If you both knew that was her issue, why did you let her go in there tonight?" Tamyra asked.

"I asked her if she needed to, and she said she'd be okay. She just kept complaining about that dumb headache."

"When did she get so much to drink?" Tamyra interjected again. "We weren't even there that long."

Winnie walked over to the couch and sat down. "You don't have to be at a nightclub to get a drink, Tamyra."

Laine took off her heels and rubbed the bottom of her feet. "Yeah, she could have gotten one early and we just didn't see her or something."

Tamyra sat in the chair beside the sofa. "Well, you should have been paying attention is all I'm saying."

The three women sat there, heads leaned back, feet propped up on Riley's sea-grass ottoman. "I ran right out on Albert again. Two for two. Boy, that's a track record for a woman who hasn't had a date in fifty years."

Tamyra laughed. "This one wasn't my fault."

Laine crossed her feet at the ankles. "Mine, either. I'm just a pitiful adulterer, but I had nothing to do with you running out on Albert again."

Winnie reached her hand over and patted Laine's leg. "You're a good woman, Laine Fulton. A good woman."

Laine changed the subject. "Did you see Christian's face? He was heartbroken."

"I did see Christian's face," Winnie replied. "My question is, did you see Mia's face?"

Laine sat up quickly. "You saw that too?"

"She's up to no good."

Tamyra sat up. "How do you two see all this? Please tell me. I don't see anything and you two don't miss anything."

"It's because we're Baptist," they said in unison. Their raucous laughter didn't stir Riley from her drug-induced sleep.

Laine walked along the concrete walkway that skirted a sandy beach and wove around the properties of the Atlantis. The wind had really picked up and whipped the edge of her dress around her legs; the ocean seemed to have gone to a steady roar in the background, though she couldn't see it. She had left Tamyra sound asleep in the chair and Winnie killing it on the sofa. But she couldn't sleep. The Mia thing was killing her. Laine had pushed Riley in extreme measures this week, but she also knew something had happened on that date with Christian. Granted she had known Riley less than a week, but long enough to know she was irritatingly honest. Laine knew she herself was irritatingly honest as well, but they were very different in their delivery. And the self-control that Riley had shown simply in dealing with Laine made her all but certain she wouldn't have gotten wasted like that tonight. Not with everything that was at stake for Max and his guests. None of it made sense.

The only thing she knew was that Mia irritated her. There was this feeling that had nagged her from the moment she met her, and Mia's immediate gravitation toward Christian confirmed it. Laine hadn't been a sleuth before, but she'd written about one. So she had plans to see what she could find out.

"Where are you going without me?" Winnie's voice startled her.

Laine turned. The crashing waves warred behind them in the cloud-covered night. "It's just bugging me. This whole thing tonight."

"It's in your craw, huh?"

Laine shook her head. "In my what?"

"Up your butt. In your craw."

This woman and her words. "Sure, yeah. All of that crazy stuff. So the only way I'm going to get it out of my . . . craw . . . is to go see what I can find out."

Winnie put her pudgy hands on the edges of her white studded belt, the belt buckle visible even in the shadows of nighttime; then she grabbed the edges of her jacket and pulled it around her. Her white hair whipped in front of her face. She pushed back at it forcefully. "What are you going to do? Break into their offices or something?"

"I have no idea what I'm going to do. But I've got to do something." Laine turned back and started walking toward The Cove. Winnie's tiny heels followed at a steady click until they caught up to her. "I didn't wake you up when I left, did I?"

Winnie handed Laine her phone. "No. Your phone did."

Laine took it. "Who would be calling me

at this time of night?" She looked down. *Missed call. Mitchell Fulton.* Laine felt a rush of heat flood through her. "It's my husband, Winnie. . . ." Her voice softened. "I mean, my ex-husband."

Winnie tilted her head.

Laine bit her lip hard.

"Go call him, sweetie. I'll go back to Riley's and get out of this wind. You go call your . . . You go call Mitchell, and when you get back, we'll straighten out Riley's life."

"We were supposed to leave tomorrow."

Winnie shook her head. "We're not leaving until we get that baby girl in there out of this mess she's in. And I'm not getting her out by myself."

Laine gave her a smile and nodded. "No, I won't leave until we get this figured out. She's done too much for me to leave her." She felt her pulse quicken. "Okay. I'm going to call him back real quick and then I'll come get you."

"Go on," Winnie said, giving her a flutter of her hand.

Laine looked at Winnie, her face serious, her words as sincere as any she had spoken in a long time. "Winnie, would you pray?"

Winnie gave her a smile and a wink. "I'll be praying until you get back. Just don't take too long now. 'Cause even the disciples couldn't pray for an hour."

Laine laughed nervously. "Okay. I'll be there in a minute."

Winnie left her alone. The sounds of the roaring ocean and the wind were no contest for the pounding of her heart inside her ears. He had left no voice mail message. She pressed his name and his number lit up on the display screen of her phone. His picture took over every remaining piece of black space behind it.

"Hello?" Mitchell's voice sounded tired.

Laine walked farther away from the ocean. "Hi, Mitchell. It's me."

She could hear him stir. "Hi." She could picture him sitting up and turning on the light. For some reason he couldn't talk on the phone in the dark. "I've been out of town and I just got all of your messages. Sorry that I'm just getting back to you."

She found a small bench by the koi pond in front of Riley's condo. She sat down, crossing her legs underneath her and wishing she had brought a jacket. "No, it's okay. I just thought maybe you didn't want to talk to me. You know, after our last conversation."

He stirred again. "No, baby. No. I would talk to you anytime. Anywhere. I am so sorry. But after our conversation I just had to get away from everything. And I did. I drove up the coast. Left my phone, laptop, and told the office I'd be back at the end of the week, that there would be no reason to try to contact me because I wasn't even going to check in. Then I got home and saw that I had missed you so many times, so I called you right away."

Her heart rate began to slow. Burning tears filled her eyes, and the lump in her throat made her wonder if speaking would even be possible. "I'm so sorry." Her words came out soft and choppy.

"Baby . . . it's okay."

Her tears were falling now and she didn't try to hide it in her voice. "No, it's not. I hurt you so much. I was so stupid."

"Laine, you don't have —"

She stopped him. "Yes, yes, I do. And I need you to let me. I need you to let me say everything I need to say. I was so stupid and foolish. It was like when I was in Dubai and I met him, I let down my guard. One guard, then another guard. First it was a look. Then a conversation. Then a dance. And with each thing I did, I knew. I knew I shouldn't be doing it. But with each step I took closer to the fire, my resistance weakened. And by the time I had any sense about me, it was too late. And I'm so sorry." Her tears had become heaves now.

Mitchell was quiet, respecting her yet again.

"And I wouldn't blame you if you never wanted to see me again. Or talk to me again. Or love me again. I wouldn't blame you for any of that. And no matter what, I'll be okay now. I know that. Something has happened to me this week, Mitchell. Something I can't explain. It's like I can see things clearly. I can feel my heart coming alive again. But I want it to be alive with you. I want to share this journey with you. You have done nothing but love me. You've loved me so well."

"And I still love you." His words came like an agent of healing as salt water pours over a wound. They stung as the declaration of what she had violated, but they soothed as a declaration of what could be restored.

"You do?"

"I love you with all my heart, Lainey. I've never stopped loving you."

"But can you forgive me?"

"I forgave you immediately. I was angry. Could have wrung your neck. But I forgave you. I knew you had to forgive yourself. And I knew that was the real barrier, not you loving me."

"But with everything I said the other day,

how can you love me now?"

"Because everything you said the other day was just another way of protecting yourself. Of staying in your shame. And I don't want you to stay there, baby. I want you out of your shame."

She sniffed. "I feel like I am. Honestly, the other night I came back to my room and I had been a real a—, um, butt, and a woman here had said some really hurtful and incredibly truthful things about me, and for the first time since all of this happened, I was able to see myself, really see myself. And all of that stuff that you've told me about healing and forgiveness, it just all seemed real in that moment. And it was almost like heaven itself reached down and took an eraser and erased all of the shame from my soul."

"I love you so much. I'm so sorry you've hurt, baby."

She looked up and laughed through her tears. This man amazed her. This man whom she had all but destroyed, completely disregarded, was sorry she had hurt. "Forgive me for hurting you."

"You are completely forgiven. Now get home so I can marry you all over again and we can start this life we were supposed to be living."

She sniffed hard and wiped at her face with the back of her hand. She would have given anything for a Kleenex, not even caring that her hair had blown completely free of its ponytail holder. "I can't come home yet."

"You do know there's a hurricane headed right at you. They're saying it's a Category 3. That's bad, Laine. You need to get home. Where are you right now? It's so loud."

"I'm outside."

"Is that wind?"

"Yeah, it's gotten pretty bad today. I don't think they expected it to pick up this quickly."

"Like I said, get out of there now."

"I will. I promise. But I can't yet. And by the time I can, I doubt there will be any more flights even heading out. I have a friend I have to help before I can leave, babe. It's a really long story, but honestly, I've given her an incredibly hard time and I owe her this."

"You have a friend? I don't think I've ever heard you call anyone a friend. Is this really the woman I love?"

She laughed a half snort, half cry.

"Yep, it's her," he said. "Well, I'm coming to get you, then. You're not going to endure a hurricane without me."

415

"No, baby. You can't come here. It's too dangerous. I promise, I'll be home by Sunday. It's supposed to start heading in by tomorrow evening, and then, Lord willing, I can get out of here by late Sunday. If the airports are moving people in and out and the damage isn't too bad."

"Well, you hunker down and don't be foolish. And when you get home —" he paused — "I'm going to marry you."

She held on to that phone as if it were a lifeline. "Promise?"

"I promise. I'm so proud of you."

"I'm so grateful for you. I love you, Mitchell Fulton."

"You've always loved me," he declared.

And she knew it was true. Another reminder of how completely he knew her.

Laine poked her head back inside Riley's condo. Winnie was stretched out on the sofa, back to inhaling most of the Bahamian air. Apparently she couldn't tarry one hour either. It was then that Laine realized how tired she really was. The gamut of emotions she had just run through had drained her completely. She walked into the other bedroom and stretched out across the hot pink comforter, and in a matter of minutes she was sound asleep.

20

Friday morning . . .

Laine could smell coffee and bacon. She opened her eyes and had no idea where she was. Her eyes focused on a glass container, where a small turtle slowly made his way over a rock. She watched him for a moment. The intent movement with such little progress made her feel sorry for the little guy. She looked down at the pink comforter beneath her and remembered. An overwhelming pity for Riley rose inside of her. The woman had aired her dirty laundry across a dance floor for anyone and everyone to hear, and yet she still felt sorry for what had happened last night.

She lifted herself from the bed, her black dress creased like an accordion now, and walked into Riley's living room. Tamyra pulled orange juice out of the refrigerator while Winnie stood over the stove, flipping bacon. "Tamyra, if you eat one piece of that,

I swear I'm going to my balcony and jumping."

Tamyra opened the carton and poured juice into one of four glasses that sat on the counter. "Don't worry. Your life is safe today."

Laine pulled out a barstool and sat. Tamyra handed her the glass she had just poured, and Laine took a drink. "Is Sleeping Beauty still sleeping?"

"Haven't heard a peep," Winnie said as she laid a plate covered with bacon in front of Laine. She studied the grease-stained paper towel and wondered how that could be good for her.

"Why do I love that stuff?"

"Because it is so good," Winnie offered.

The wind whistled through the invisible cracks of the sliding-glass door. Laine turned and looked out. Rain was blowing past the window in sheets.

Laine scooted her stool back. "Gracious, it's getting fierce out there. Guess we missed our ticket out of here."

"You think?" Tamyra retorted.

"Yes, smarty-pants. I think. Now, while this hurricane is blowing paradise away, I'm going to check on Miss 'Tell All My Business' in there and make sure she's breathing."

"Breakfast will be ready in just a few minutes," Winnie said. "Just pull her out of there and bring her on in here."

Riley could hear sounds coming from what seemed like a world away. A fog sat over her head and felt so heavy she didn't even know if she could open her eyes. She rolled away from the windows and the sound of the wind that seemed to blow against them and felt the weight in her head blow to the left side of her brain. She reached her hands up in agony. There hadn't been a morning in over two years that she had woken up feeling this way.

"Get up and face the world." The voice boomed from behind her and felt like a pounding bass drum against her skull.

She stirred to try to get away from the pain.

The bed dipped beneath the weight of her guest. A hand rested on her shoulder and turned her over. "Get up, Riley. We've got a lot to talk about."

Riley knew it was Laine. She tried hard to open her eyes. "What happened last night?"

"Well, from the looks of things, I'd say you got sloshed. Wasted. Trashed. Would you like me to go on?"

Her words tried to register with Riley's

brain. She forced her eyes open and tried to lift her body up. "There's no way."

"How else would you explain how you feel?"

She finally raised her body up and leaned against the padded headboard. She blinked hard to get her eyes to focus on Laine. "I don't know. I don't even remember last night."

"Lucky you. I'm not surprised. And honestly, it's for the best, and I'm hoping to forget most of it myself. Now come on and get up and let us get some food in you."

Riley realized then how hungry she actually was. "That would be good. I'm starving."

"You're hungry?"

"Yes, I'm famished." Riley scooted to the side of the bed and pushed her body out. "I don't remember throwing up, either. And I used to throw up a lot when I got drunk." Riley stood, and immediately her head began to swim. Everything she felt was reminiscent of a thousand hangovers. But she usually remembered drinking — at least once she was able to open her eyes. And she had no recollection of last night at all. She rubbed at the sides of her head. "My head feels like a freight train has just crashed through it. But if I had been drinking, I would remember," she said, walking into the kitchen. She stopped when she saw Tamyra and Winnie there.

"What's going on? Why are all of you here?"

Winnie turned the water off at the sink. "You mean, you don't remember a thing about last night?"

Riley looked at them, dumbfounded. "I don't remember a thing. And trust me, I've been drunk many times." She lowered herself into a chair at the breakfast table. "And I may not remember everything about an evening, but I do remember some things. Usually the worst things . . ." Her voice trailed off.

Tamyra came over and set a glass of juice in front of her. "So you don't remember telling the entire disco that Laine was an adulterer?"

Riley's expression immediately registered horror.

Winnie set scrambled eggs on the table and pulled out a chair. She motioned for Laine to sit too. "And you don't remember gyrating on that dance floor around Christian like a pole dancer, except he was your pole?"

Riley's hands went to her mouth. Tears

immediately flooded to the surface. "Oh no."

Laine came over and sat beside her, reaching for her hand. "It's okay. Listen. It's okay."

Riley dropped her hand and shook her head rapidly. "I said that about you?"

Laine shook her head again. "It's okay, Riley."

"No! No! It's not okay. I'm so sorry!"

Winnie put her napkin on her plate. "I don't think it's Laine you should be worrying about."

Tamyra patted her hand. "No, I think it's Christian."

Riley's eyes widened further. "What did I do to Christian?" Her voice was weak and trembling.

Laine scrunched her nose. "It's not important."

"You acted like a hoochie mama," Winnie said as she spooned two helpings of eggs onto Riley's plate.

Laine tossed her a glare. Riley saw it but still couldn't believe what she was hearing. "Tell me it isn't true," she said, her face turning to Laine, her heart pleading.

Laine let out a sigh and her shoulders lowered but she gave Riley a compassionate look she knew she didn't deserve if everything they were saying was true. "It was bad, Riley. It was really bad. You got drunk. You got out on the dance floor and acted in a way that I know you never would have otherwise. Then you got belligerent, said some rather nasty things, and Max heard you and came over and told you to pack up your office and leave."

Tears were falling freely down Riley's face now.

"And you can't remember a thing?" Tamyra asked.

She shook her head slowly, the cries audible now.

"Did you have drinks with Mia at the bar?"

Riley's scattered thoughts tried to grasp for a memory. Any piece of last night that she could grab hold of. But all she remembered was the concert and the piercing headache. "I don't remember drinking anything but a bottle of water that Mia gave me. I just had that brutal headache. And I don't even remember anything at the nightclub."

Laine pressed further. "You were at the bar with Mia. You were drinking something, I know that for sure. And then by the time Christian got you to the dance floor, you were out of control."

Riley wiped at her tears. She couldn't believe all she was hearing. She had felt so good. So alive. It was as if for the first time in the last six years she was free from all her demons. Healed. And ready to see what was on the horizon for her and Christian. She had been so excited about her job too. And now it was all gone. She couldn't believe it. She couldn't believe any of it. And on top of all that, she had disgraced Laine. She reached her hand out to Laine quickly. "I'm so sorry. I can't believe I said that about you. Please, please forgive me. I am so sorry."

Laine shook her head. "Riley, honestly, it's okay. I know you weren't yourself."

"I would have never said those things, Laine. Even when I used to get drunk, I was never belligerent. So I don't know what would have made me do that last night. Or act that way. Usually I just shut down and became a recluse. I've never done anything like what you've described last night."

"Well, let's just eat breakfast and we'll figure this out one thing at a time, okay?"

They all jumped when the umbrella on the back patio came crashing against the glass-paned door. "We'd better get what isn't nailed down out there put up," Winnie said as she took a bite of bacon.

Riley jumped up. "My guests. Oh, my word, I've got to go make sure my guests are okay. And you! Y'all have to get out of here before this gets any worse! You are all supposed to leave today."

Tamyra grabbed her arm. "Riley, we're not leaving. All the flights out of here are done. Plus, we're not leaving you. And you can't help your guests. You can only go clean out your desk."

Riley's arm dropped at the recognition of how her life had completely changed in the course of one evening. "This can't be happening," she said as she collapsed back into her chair.

Winnie put a homemade biscuit on her plate. "Try to eat, baby girl. Try to eat."

But Riley couldn't eat. All she could do was bury her head in her hands and weep.

Riley pressed her umbrella out toward the blowing rain. It was doing little to cover her body, but at least the rain wasn't beating her in the face. And maybe if she couldn't see people, they couldn't see her. She wanted to hide like a child. But she wasn't a child. She was a grown woman who had made her own bed and would face the consequences of her actions. And this time it would be different than it was four years ago. When she made it beneath the covering, she lowered her umbrella and shook her entire body. Water flickered from her raincoat and umbrella like sparks from a sparkler. She raised her head and Bart was right there with his award-winning smile. That one look assured her that at least everyone didn't know about last night. The staff moved quickly around her, locking up everything that usually stood out front to welcome visitors to this small piece of paradise.

"This week, Miss Riley?"

"Definitely this week," she said and smiled as best she could. She rushed to the glass doors of the office and struggled to open them against the wind that blew at her back. Mia stood behind the counter when she came in. Her eyes widened when she saw Riley. She laid her papers down and came around the counter, her face full of sympathy. "I'm so sorry, Riley. What a tragedy all of this is."

Riley leaned in and gave Mia a hug. Mia returned it. "It's horrible. And whatever I said or did last night, please know I am so sorry. I have no idea what happened, but with my track record I must have been incredibly intoxicated not to remember anything."

"You don't remember anything?"

Riley shook her head. "No, it's just crazy. And I have been inebriated to extremes before and remembered at least snippets. But I don't remember anything. After the concert everything else is just gone."

"So you don't remember being at the bar drinking and me trying to get you to stop?"

Riley felt the burning sensation of embarrassment sweep through her. She reached her hand up and rubbed her head, then shook it slowly. "No, I had no idea."

Mia shook her head; her hand patted Riley's arm. "I tried so hard to get you away from the bar after what you had told me. I knew it wasn't a good idea. And I had given you a pill for your head and it probably wasn't a good combination."

Riley looked up. "I can hardly take an ibuprofen. So if you gave me something for my headache, that and the alcohol probably explains why I can't remember anything."

Mia's face registered her apology before she even spoke. "Oh, Riley, I would have never given you that pill if I thought you were going to drink."

"I don't even know why I would want a drink. I haven't wanted one for two years."

"You just said it had been so stressful. And that Laine had ruined the morning and then with the guests arriving early and maybe with the pressure of Christian . . ."

"Christian? Did you talk to him?"

She cocked her head again. Pity registered. "Yeah, he was pretty upset about it all. I walked back here to the office with him so he could at least have someone to talk to. He had so enjoyed your time together. He just never dreamed . . ."

Riley walked to the door of her office. "I never would have dreamed either. But it's done." Her resolve was settled. "Now I get to clean out my office."

Mia walked to her office door and leaned against it as Riley walked around her desk and opened the top drawer.

"I guess they'll put you in here," Riley said, not looking up.

"Well, Max has asked me to step in until they decide what they want to do. I think my being here yesterday morning just kind of . . ."

Riley looked up. ". . . let him know you were more than capable. And you are. You'll do a wonderful job, Mia. A wonderful job." She gave her a sincere smile and began to pull personal items from her desk.

Mia fidgeted at the door. "Do you need some boxes?"

"Yes, that would be great."

"I'll go get you a few and be right back."

Mia left Riley alone. Riley looked down at the picture of her and Gabby that sat in a seashell frame on the edge of her desk. She picked it up and held her angel girl in her hands. She was so grateful she hadn't been here. The mere thought of her being there with Riley in that state made tears rush to the surface again. Her little girl had been through so much. And if she couldn't even remember what had happened, what would she have done if Gabby had been there? She could have put her little girl's life at risk, and there was nothing that would be more horrific than something happening to her and it being Riley's fault. She couldn't even trust herself. How in God's name could she let her daughter be with a woman who could lose such control that she didn't even remember the night or remember drinking? The thought petrified her.

She set the frame down and noticed a manila folder on top of her desk. She opened it and recognized immediately the termination letter in front of her. A card was inside and she opened it.

I want to see you sometime today. We need to talk about what has transpired here. Sign this today and have it faxed to me. I should be back in the office by mid-afternoon. I'm extremely disappointed, Riley. But please know I love you. Max.

"Ms. Sinclair, a couple is wanting to see you." Clint, a beautiful Bahamian man, and the one in charge of all hurricane preparations, stood in Riley's doorway. "They decided to ride out the hurricane, and now that the weather is getting rough, they're getting scared. But the airport is shut down for good. So they want to see you."

Riley walked into the lobby. Mia was nowhere to be found. And Riley still had a responsibility to make sure all the guests were safe. She looked down at the termination letter that requested she leave immediately. And she would. Immediately after she took care of her guests. "Where are they?"

"They're in room 626."

She walked to the doorway and he stepped back. "Walk with me and let's go over all the preparations." As soon as the doors opened, the reality of what awaited outside swept over her like a tsunami. She pressed her petite frame against the driving wind and walked out into The Cove. Everything in the expansive open breezeways had either been removed or bolted down. Benches and cushions had been stored. Candles and sconces had been put away and all that remained were the gorgeous floors, the bronzed artwork, the magnificent ocean, and prayer. "Everything shut down at Cain?"

"Yes, ma'am. The outdoor casino is closed up, the chairs are all put away, and the bungalows are locked up tight."

Wind whipped through the open corridors and rain was able to reach them like a mist, yet they both knew it was only a taste of what was to come. "The other pools too?"

"Yes, ma'am, all pools are taken care of."

"Has someone checked all the roofs?"

"Yes, maintenance did that the first of the week."

"All the signage has been secured? garbage cans?"

"Yes, ma'am. All taken care of."

"And all the remaining guests have directions to The Cove meeting rooms and the time they need to be there?"

"Yes, everyone has been given their instructions multiple times."

The wind whipped at the skirt of her dress and she pressed it down with her hands, grateful she had pulled her hair back. "When did this storm pick up this much speed?"

"It just got over the open water, Ms. Sinclair, and seems like it took off. Took off straight for us."

"Well, we've got our work cut out for us, then, don't we. Because quite a few of our guests were still planning on leaving today. Food is on hand?"

"Yes, we have food ready." They walked into the foyer of The Cove. Gerard was standing at the concierge desk.

"I'm going to close these doors here in the next hour or so," he reported to Riley as she passed through. "Then as soon as we get all of the guests to the ballroom, I'll pull the shutters and bolt it."

"Thank you, Gerard. And you too, Clint. You both have done great jobs. It's been a pleasure working with you."

Gerard laughed. "You sound like you're going somewhere, Miss Riley."

She wasn't going to address it. "Right now, we've got a hurricane to get through."

Laine, Winnie, and Tamyra had sneaked out right after Riley. They had work to do. By the time they made it to Starbucks to concoct their plan, they were windblown, wet, and frazzled.

"How are we going to prove this woman

has done something to Riley?" Tamyra asked.

"Girl, you have been in the world of the pretty for too long," Winnie said, her white hair pressed against her face. "Deceitfulness reveals itself."

"And it's usually stupid, too," Laine said, pulling a black ponytail holder out of her soaked purse and tugging at her wet hair until she looked sleek.

"Obviously y'all have never met some of the women I've competed with."

Winnie and Laine looked at each other. "Touché," Laine responded.

"So we're just going to go into the office and look through Mia's stuff and find everything we need and save the day like in some pathetic novel," Tamyra scoffed.

Winnie chuckled, and the Styrofoam cup she held in her hands shook with her. "I think she just dissed you."

"I don't know if I'm more horrified over the fact that she called novels pathetic or that you just said *dissed.*"

Tamyra wrapped her hands around the arms of her white pin-striped suit jacket. "This is crazy. All of it. We're about to go through a hurricane. We're still in our clothes from last night. We're about to break and enter."

"I have no intentions of breaking any-thing," Winnie interjected. "I have an ap-preciation for nice things."

Laine laughed.

"You two laugh. But I'm not going to jail."

Laine pushed lightly on her arm. "My word, woman, you're wound tight. I thought you got set free over there on that water ride."

"Well, I can't do anything without brush-ing my teeth," Tamyra said. "Are y'all not at least going to your rooms to freshen up?"

Winnie and Laine scanned each other again. They both shrugged their shoulders. "Have you seen yourselves?" Tamyra ques-tioned.

Winnie answered. "We're about to go through a hurricane, Tamyra. I don't think the fact that our breath stinks or that we've been in the same outfits for almost a day is going to be of any real significance."

"And with the hurricanes we've been through this week, I'd say the welfare of my teeth isn't high on my list of to-dos either. Plus, I just fixed my hair," Laine retorted.

"Well, all I can say is, if you two question Mia looking and smelling the way you do, she'll give you whatever information you need with no problem." Tamyra immediately noticed the glint in Laine's eyes. "I'm not getting in trouble, Laine Fulton."

"No, but if you're going to your room, that will be the ideal cover. When you get there, call Mia and act like you've had an emergency. That will give me and Winnie plenty of time to get in there, see what we can find out, and then get out without having to confront her."

"And what, pray tell, am I going to have an emergency about?"

"A broken nail?" Laine huffed. "I don't know! What do beauty queens have emergencies over? Be demanding. Be obnoxious. Tell her your peanuts are out and no one refilled them. Dump your Coca-Colas down the drain and tell her you can't go two hours without one. Be creative. Surely world peace is not the only thing you can talk about."

"I can talk about pitiful romance novels," Tamyra quipped.

"Children. Enough," Winnie intervened. "Tamyra, you go to your room. Call Mia in about ten minutes and tell her that you are freaking out about the storm. You wish you had gone home. But now you can't get out. But make sure she is the one you get. And tell her you want her specifically. Not to send anyone else up."

"Then stall," Laine said.

"I'll give you ladies thirty minutes. And if

you can't get it done in thirty minutes, you need to make sure you don't quit your day jobs."

"She's sassy for a swizzle stick," Laine said.

"We have our assignments." Winnie was well into the act.

Tamyra shook her head. "Go live out your fantasies, ladies."

Winnie giggled as she pulled Laine down the breezeway, the wind all but picking up her pudgy frame. If it hadn't been for all the rhinestones, she would have surely flown away.

Tamyra slid her key into the door and the light turned green. She heard the bolt dislodge and turned the handle, entering the tranquility of her room. The real hurricane headed for them was nothing compared to the storm that had blown through last night. She mumbled beneath her breath at the two women who were forcing her to lie. She hated lying. That was part of the reason she had run away. But avoidance felt as much like lying to her as telling a bald-faced one. And just when she had decided she wasn't going to avoid the truth anymore, they were making her lie all over again.

She set her key down on the small console

table against the front entrance wall and walked into her room, dimly lit by the cloud-covered view. She noticed that the beds had yet to be made. Probably with the storm, the staff was exceptionally taxed. Her eyes scanned the sitting area. Her blood all but stopped flowing when she saw a figure sitting on the sofa. Everything that accompanied terror swept through her body: her pulse quickened, sweat broke out on her forehead, and her feet wouldn't move. He spoke first.

"You're a hard one to find, Tamyra." Jason stood. His six-foot-five, three-hundred-pound frame all but shut out what light was coming from the sliding-glass doors.

She tried to get out a sound, but her voice was gone. Fear had stripped it bare. She reached over and grabbed ahold of the table.

He took a step forward. "I thought you'd rush over here to see me."

Her mind tried desperately to calculate how quickly she could turn around and get out of the door and into the hall screaming before he reached her.

He stepped closer. She knew it was now or never. She turned as quickly as she could, grasped for the door handle. It slipped from the sweat that already encased her palms. She reached for it again in a frantic attempt and pulled down hard; the click of it unlocking reverberated as loud in her ears as shots from a twenty-one-gun salute. She pulled it open, sensing a moment of freedom as the air from the hallway rushed in, but before she could get her head out and make her feet follow, Jason was on her and had the door slammed shut. She panted as both of his hands flew above her head and held the door in place. Her head fell against the wood of the door. Tears wanted to follow the fear, but she wouldn't give him the satisfaction.

His hands reached for her arms and jerked her around. Before she could stabilize herself on her feet, the back of his hand connected with the side of her head and sent her spinning into the table by the door. It thudded loud against the wall as her head connected with the corner and gashed a two-inch slit right through her forehead above her left eye. Blood gushed quickly down her face as she grabbed for the corner of the table and tried to pull herself up.

He didn't wait. He jerked her up and pulled her toward him. The rapid movement and loss of blood left her certain she was about to pass out. She wished she had. "So you thought I wouldn't find you?"

"I prayed you wouldn't find me," she whispered.

He pushed her into the bedroom and threw her across the bed. She pushed herself back frantically and grabbed at a pillow, pulling it in front of her. She moved quickly to the side of the bed, put her feet firmly on the floor, and stood up quickly.

"Well, looks like your God is laughing at you, wouldn't you say?"

She felt an intense anger rise up from somewhere inside her soul. An anger she had never known. It was extremely passionate. Righteous, even. The boldness of it made her find her voice even though her body was trembling. She wiped at her chin, where the blood had fallen. Her words came out solid and steady. "You lie to me. You give me a disease that leads to death. And then you come in here thinking you can beat me?" She stepped toward him.

He stepped around the side of the bed. "No, Tamyra, I came in here to kill you."

The second blow sent her reeling. Her body tumbled across the bed and landed on the other side. Another gash opened up below her left eye. But the pain shooting through her body had her gasping for air. She tried to open her eyes but couldn't even will them open. He came around the other side of the bed and jerked her to her feet once again.

He threw her back on the bed. She screamed out in pain. The full weight of his body straddled her. The vileness of his words spewed across her while the pummeling blows he pounded her with broke most of the bones in her face. She was sure she could hear them as they cracked. She prayed she would die. And when his large hands came around the base of her slender throat and sucked all the air from her lungs, she was certain she would. When she blacked out, she hoped for death. "God, help me" leaked from her lips. It was the last thing she remembered.

Winnie sat on a bench in the reception lobby, a magazine stuck in front of her face.

"Winnie, Mia has had dinner with you. Trust me, she's going to recognize you. There is no need to hide. That's why we have to wait until she's gone."

Winnie talked from behind her *Southern Living.* "But I've always wanted to be a private investigator. Didn't you write about a private investigator once?"

"A long time ago, and she didn't hide behind magazines. And it sure wouldn't have been *Southern Living.* Where did you get that anyway?"

"From my room. I brought it with me. And thank you for giving me five minutes to change. Wet denim can chafe your thighs."

"Yeah, I was tired of that black dress. I just didn't want to give Tamyra the satisfaction of knowing I needed to change."

Winnie dipped her head down and stared at Laine from behind dark sunglasses.

"Seriously, we haven't seen the sun for two days; do you not think those are a little dramatic? Plus, my characters would never hide behind such a ridiculous getup."

"Oh, that's right. Your last character hid behind her sexual prowess."

"Are you calling her a slut?"

"No, I would call her a hussy, tramp, floozy, but you're the author."

"And you're the devoted reader, Miss Baptist." Laine fidgeted on the bench. "What in the world is taking her so long? This is ridiculous. She had one little task. Make a phone call. Tell a lie. And get on with it. You'd think we asked her to feign death."

"She doesn't like lying. You ought to have seen her trying to get me to dinner with Albert. Plus, she's pretty pitiful at it. Why did we pick her for that part anyway?"

"Because she's a beauty queen. They all lie about something. So have you talked to him today?"

She raised the magazine back up. "No, I haven't talked to him since last night. Doubt he'll ever want to talk to me again. I've left him standing there completely alone twice in one week. Would you want to talk to me again?"

"I'm sure he figured out it wasn't about you last night."

"Yes, I think Riley's inability to keep her hands to herself and the announcement of you being an adulterer let him know I was pretty mild in comparison."

Before Laine could react, they watched as Mia took off past their window and down the hall toward the suites. "Gracious, she must have come up with a doozy," Winnie said.

"Who cares what she told her. We don't have much time." Laine got up and snatched Winnie off the bench. Winnie dropped her magazine and followed Laine. They entered the glass doors of the offices and looked around. All the offices were empty.

Winnie walked around the counter, then looked at Laine. "What are we looking for anyway?"

"I don't know. I just write about detectives. Look for anything that looks suspicious — faxes, e-mails, anything. And take those fool glasses off," Laine said, walking around the counter too.

Winnie took the glasses off and pulled a large stack of manila folders from beneath the counter, each immaculately labeled. "She has excellent penmanship."

Laine sighed heavily. "Winnie, seriously."

"Well, she does. It's hard to find that nowadays."

Laine muttered, "So is good help."

"I heard that."

"I'm glad."

Winnie picked up a folder labeled *E-mails* and began to rummage through them. Nothing looked worth anything. She picked up the folder of faxes and found one from Thursday morning at nine, stating that Max's guests would arrive earlier than expected. "What time did Riley join us yesterday to take Tamyra down the rapids?"

Laine shook her head. "I think it was around eleven, wasn't it? Isn't that when we went down to the pool?"

"Yes, I think so."

"Mia told her the fax had come through right after she left."

Winnie pursed her lips, shook her head, and dangled a piece of paper in front of her.

"Well, she lied. It came in at 9 a.m."

Laine looked up from the papers she was rummaging through. She snatched it from Winnie's hand. "So she would have known before Riley even left that they were coming. She deliberately didn't tell her so she could look like the woman who saved the day."

"That's what I'm thinking."

She was enjoying this whole sleuthing bit. Until she saw Laine's eyes change as she pushed her slightly out of her way. "Is that her purse?"

Winnie turned; a black Chanel bag sat in an open drawer.

Laine snatched it out and set it on the floor, knelt down and dumped its contents out, splattering them across the carpet in front of her.

"Oh, my side, you are not going through that woman's purse."

"You want me to just sit there and look at it? I told you she was a conniver."

Winnie and Laine noticed the bottle of pills about the same time. Laine picked them up and turned them over. Winnie knelt behind her and squinted to read the label. She leaned back.

Laine stood and held the bottle in her hand. "Oh, this stuff can be brutal."

"What is it?" Winnie asked.

"It's an antianxiety drug. Sometimes used in fighting depression. I researched it heavily for a book two years ago."

Winnie remembered. "Yeah, the one about the flight attendant having an affair with the pilot and they were on a flight when the plane almost crashed, which gave her terrible anxiety for flying, so the doctor prescribed her this antianxiety medication until she could get over her fear."

Laine shook her head. "I need to take you on the road."

Winnie smacked her on the arm. "You need to quit writing about people committing adultery. I just realized that's a running theme."

"Can we have our morality discussion later? I did so much research on this drug. Sometimes it can make a person seem inebriated. And they can lose all inhibition if too much is taken. This could have been the 'headache reliever' she slipped Riley."

"Are you serious?"

"I could have been a pharmaceutical rep for this drug after all the research I did for it. I wanted people to know I knew what I was talking about." She shook the bottle in front of Winnie's face. "This is all I need."

"What are you going to do?"

Laine walked around the counter and over to the cream leather sofa against the far wall. "I'm going to sit here and wait for Mia to come back. And then the three of us are going to have a little talk."

Winnie clapped her hands. "Like a shake-down."

Laine rolled her eyes. "Oh, you've got to be kidding me."

Riley walked down the stairs to make sure the pool nestled between The Cove and The Reef was secure. She came down the long corridor that connected the two buildings and turned to survey the grounds. Her thoughts were on her guests and how grateful she was that most had taken the advice of FEMA and the local rescue officials and left the island two days ago. She wished Laine and Winnie and Tamyra had gotten out. And if they hadn't been so focused on her, maybe they would have.

"I see you're alive." Christian's voice stopped her thoughts.

She didn't want to turn and face him. She wanted to hide in a hole and pretend he wasn't there. But he was. And he deserved an apology. She turned. His face was kind but his eyes were sad. She dug her hands deep into the pockets of her khaki cotton twill dress and walked toward him. "Yes, I'm alive."

He didn't say anything. He didn't rescue her this time.

"From what I hear, I owe you a tremendous apology."

"That sounds like you don't remember." His words held no accusation.

She shook her head. "No, for the life of me, I don't remember anything. But please, please accept my deepest apologies for anything that happened last night. I am so very, very sorry. I thought . . ." She stopped herself. He didn't know her story, and after what she had done last night, it was no time to start defending herself. She was a drunk, plain and simple. A drunk who inevitably couldn't be trusted.

"You thought what?"

She could see in his eyes a sincere hope. *Be honest. Completely honest.* "I just thought that it was all very sad. And I'm very sorry."

"I accept your apology, Riley. I just don't want you going backward. I mean, that's what the other night at the church was all about, wasn't it? Moving forward?"

His words struck deep. How did he know so much when she had shared so little? "You're right. It was." She wanted to say more, but she didn't. "I really need to go, though. I've got to pack up my office and make sure everything else is secure and ready. Sounds like the winds are going to be pretty heavy by early evening and downright evil tonight." She stopped and looked at him. Really looked at him. His face held no guile. No indictment. Just questions. Questions she could never answer. "It was really good getting to know you, Christian. You are a truly wonderful man. And if I was a better woman, I would hold on to you and not let you go." She heard the crack in her own voice, gave him a soft smile, and walked past him.

He reached out and took her arm, pulling her toward him. The tears she had been holding back with all her might rushed to the surface and fell rapidly down her face. "You are an amazing woman, Riley Sinclair. Despite your past. Despite what happened last night. There was something in all of that that was crazy and so different from our night before. But when I looked at you last night, it wasn't you. It was something, but it wasn't Riley. I don't know your story. I can tell there's been a lot of pain, but I know this, the Riley that I saw last night wasn't you. It wasn't this Riley. Trust me, I'm not a man looking to rescue a woman with issues. But I am a man looking at an incredible woman who gives herself way too little credit for the woman that she is."

She shook her head. "You see what you want to see, Christian."

"And you see what you were."

She slid her arm from his grasp and turned away. She didn't stop until she got to the top of the stairs. That was when she leaned against the wall, and the choking sobs came once again.

Riley dashed through the open doors of The Cove Suites. She pounded on the Up button of the elevator as if that would hasten its arrival. Mia's panic-stricken voice on the phone had driven Riley back to reality. She kept running the room number through her mind . . . 575 . . . 575 — that one was so familiar. When the elevator doors opened, she propelled her body through them and poked the fifth-floor button with a jolt. When her finger jabbed the round button, she realized whose room it was. It was Tamyra's.

The door was held open by a frantic house-keeper. "What's going on?" Riley asked, her own panic rising as she rushed into the room.

The housekeeper was on her heels. "I

came in to clean her room, Ms. Sinclair, and he was on top of her. I screamed and it startled him. He jumped up, pushed me out of his way, and ran out the door."

Riley stopped at the foot of the bed. "Oh, God." The words slipped from her throat at the sight of the body before her. Mia was pounding frantically on the phone. "Oh, God, please help us."

Riley climbed gently onto the bed. Tamyra was not moving. Her face was hardly recognizable. Blood was caked everywhere and had created a puddle around her head. "Get me a warm wash-cloth now." Riley tried to hide the panic in her intense whisper.

Riley took Tamyra's dainty wrist in her hand and felt for a pulse. "God, please. Please let there be a pulse." Nothing. She moved her fingers again, her body pleading. "Oh, please, God, please." The faintest thump came beneath her fingers. She exhaled the breath she hadn't even known she held.

"Yes, we need an ambulance at the Atlantis resort now! Room 575," Mia said, her voice high-pitched with fear.

The young housekeeper's hand trembled as it extended a warm, wet washcloth to Riley. She took it and began to wipe as gently as she could across Tamyra's forehead.

"Hey, Tamyra, honey. It's Riley. We've got an ambulance on the way. They're coming for you, okay? Now you just hold on and we're going to take really good care of you. You're safe now. You're completely safe."

Riley raised her head to Mia. Mia stood there, her face contorted with fear, the receiver still in her hand. "Mia." She didn't respond. She just stared through Riley. "Mia, come on now. I need you to focus. Get back on the phone. Call security. Have them contact the police immediately. This guy can't get off the island without us finding him. Now come on."

Mia turned toward the receiver and began dialing the number for security.

Riley continued to wipe as gently as she could. Tamyra's face was already swollen to the point that Riley didn't know how she could even breathe. Tamyra gurgled. "It's okay, honey. I'm right here. Riley is right here. I've got you taken care of and the ambulance should be here any minute." Her words came out as soothing as any mother's would be to her own child. "Mia, go on down to the lobby and wait for the ambulance so you can bring them right up."

Mia stood there. Unmoving.

"Mia, go on now. I need you to make this as smooth as possible. Tamyra doesn't need any delays."

Mia put the phone back on the receiver and headed out the door, doing just as Riley told her.

Tamyra moaned.

Riley kept wiping and kept praying. The only two things she was capable of doing.

Laine saw Mia as she rounded the corner. "Okay, Winnie, we're on." Laine leaned back on the sofa, waiting for Mia to walk through the door. Both she and Winnie watched as Mia ran right past the office and stood at the main entrance.

"Looks like we're on hold."

Laine stood. "Oh no she doesn't. She's not going to avoid this any longer," she said as she burst out the door.

She heard Winnie's fresh and dry denim pants swish together as she followed her. She was certain if her rhinestones rubbed together too hard, they'd have a fire on top of the hurricane.

"Mia!" Laine called out, her voice sounding almost hollow against the wind.

Mia turned. "Hey, oh, my goodness. You've got to get up to your friend Tamyra's room right now!"

Winnie covered up a snicker. But she quickly tried to regain her composure.

Laine shook her head. "Well, she can wait a minute. Right now we need to talk."

The sound of sirens began to filter through the wind and rain. Mia's voice was loud and strained. "I can't. I'm waiting on the ambulance."

"Who's the ambulance for?" Laine felt as if she were yelling.

"It's for your friend Tamyra!" Mia was getting irritable. "I told you. You need to get up there now!"

Laine looked at Winnie. "Looks like our friend went a little over the top."

"I'd say. Sounds more like a lie I would tell."

Laine turned back to Mia. "Listen, I'm sure Tamyra will be fine. There is really no need for an ambulance. Honestly. You know beauty queens. They can be a little overemotional."

Mia turned, her look one of horror. "I'm sorry. But if someone's face has been pummeled until they are unrecognizable, I'd say they need an ambulance."

Laine's expression changed, and she stepped forward. "What are you talking about?"

"Your friend. A man attacked her in her room. He has nearly killed her. So I'd say our conversation can take place another time. Right now, I need to get the paramedics to her room."

The screaming siren blared now as an ambulance pulled up in front of them. Laine and Winnie stood there stunned, watching as the passenger door flew open and a young paramedic exited.

"Oh, Lord, have mercy!" Winnie said.

"Come on, Winnie! Come on!" Laine didn't wait for Winnie to follow. She took off down the hall.

"Oh, Jesus, help her! Help her, Jesus!" Winnie knelt by the bed. Her hands lay gently on Tamyra's shoulder.

"They'll be right here, Tamyra. You just hold on, okay?" Laine said, trying to keep from throwing up. She hadn't seen a face so injured in her life. She fought back the thought that she had sent Tamyra up here. If she had just let her stay with them, if she had thought of something else, then maybe Tamyra wouldn't have come up here.

As if she could read her expression, Winnie called out to her. "He would have been here no matter when she came to her room, Laine. Jason's been looking for her. This is not your fault."

Riley still wiped her face gently.

The paramedics came through the door,

and the women all stepped back. The paramedics worked swiftly but gently with Tamyra's pummeled body. She moaned a couple times, but Laine knew she was barely conscious. The women followed the stretcher downstairs and through the open corridors.

"You ride with her, Winnie. We'll meet you at the hospital," Riley said, patting Winnie on her shoulder as they followed the stretcher.

Wet streaks lined Winnie's cheeks. "Okay. We need to call her mother. And the police. Tell the police to look for her ex-boyfriend — Jason something."

"I will. I'll take care of that. But her mother can't get here until this storm has passed, and that won't be until sometime tomorrow evening. I don't even know when they'll start letting flights take off again."

The paramedics lifted the stretcher into the back of the ambulance, trying to keep Tamyra covered from the pulsating rain. Winnie climbed in with one of them. The other closed the doors tightly and disappeared around to the front of the vehicle. Riley and Laine stood underneath the building's entrance, shock sweeping through them with each gust of wind that blew. The ambulance's sirens came back to life as it sped from the resort.

"I can't believe this," Riley said, finally able to let her guard down. Her body began to tremble.

"What happened?" Laine asked.

"Apparently she came back to her room and a man was waiting on her when she got there. Thank God the housekeeper hadn't cleaned her room yet. Because when she opened the door, he was on top of Tamyra, choking her. Honestly, Laine, if she hadn't come in . . ." Riley's voice broke.

Laine felt a surge of horror rush through her. Tears came hard against the brim of her eyelids. "But she did. She did come in."

"It's a miracle, Laine. Honestly, it's a miracle. Of all the rooms she could have cleaned, she went to that one."

Laine reached out and took Riley's arm. "Listen, go on to the hospital. Go sit with them and I'll be there in a little while."

"You sure? You don't want to come?"

"No, I've got something to take care of here, and then I'll be right there."

Riley nodded. Laine was grateful she didn't press. "If you're sure. I just need to go hear what the doctor says once he looks at her. Then I'll come back here and make sure all of the guests are okay."

"I thought you were fired." Laine regretted saying it as soon as it came out, but she needed to get Riley out of here for a minute.

"I haven't signed my termination letter yet."

Laine breathed a sigh of relief.

"So legally I'd say I'm still responsible for my guests."

Laine smiled. "You'd be responsible for them even if you had signed it. That's just who you are."

"I'll call you if I hear something before you get there."

"Sounds good. Now go." She swatted at her. She watched as Riley made it to her car, the wind sweeping wildly at her petite frame and the rain beating against her. Laine would be grateful when Riley finally could feel the wind at her back and not beating her in the face. Speaking of beatings . . .

Laine turned back and caught sight of Mia's blonde hair in the office. She took a deep breath and headed straight for the glass door.

21

Friday afternoon . . .

"Someone has been in my purse," Mia said as Laine walked through the door. Mia's head disappeared behind the counter.

Laine walked to the other side of the counter and leaned against it. A fury rose inside of her. Everything in her wanted to make Mia responsible for what had just happened to Tamyra. If they hadn't had to protect Riley, they would have all been home by now. But something inside her wouldn't let her blame even Mia.

"Look at this. Everything in my purse has been dumped out on the floor!" Laine watched as Mia frantically ran her hands through the exposed contents of her handbag. "They were obviously looking for something. Maybe it was the same guy who did that to Tamyra."

"Did they steal your wallet?"

Mia picked up her wallet, unable to hide

her irritation. "No! My wallet is right here."

"Something else missing?" Laine coaxed.

Mia grabbed her handbag and crammed her hand inside; she fumbled wildly through the empty purse. "No, no. I'm sure it's all here. If they didn't take my wallet, I can't imagine what else they would have wanted." She tossed the purse down and leaned over to peer beneath the counter.

"Wouldn't be looking for these, would you?"

The look on Mia's face when she raised her eyes and saw the bottle of antianxiety medication dangling from Laine's fingers gave her a small sense of satisfaction amid all this mess. Laine only wished the girls could see it with her.

"Where did you . . . ?" Mia stood quickly.

"Out of your purse."

Mia made a desperate attempt to grab it from Laine's hand.

Laine pulled the bottle out of her reach. "I don't think you will be getting these back anytime soon. In fact, I think you need to grab a seat right there on that sofa and tell me everything you've done. To be honest, that is about the only thing that will keep you out of prison at this point."

The fear that flew across Mia's face made that statement so worthwhile, whether there was any validity to it or not. "I want to know everything. How many of these did you give to Riley?"

"You're crazy!" she barked. "Just because you write fiction novels doesn't mean you can walk in here creating it."

Laine stepped back and decided she'd sit on the sofa if Mia didn't want to. "Drugging someone's drink is a crime, Mia. Pure and simple. Ever seen what happens to pretty girls in prison?" She was being ruthless but she didn't care. Tamyra was in a hospital room with a face that resembled a prizefighter's, and she doubted Tamyra had had the privilege of landing a single blow. "They eat women like you alive in prison. Trust me, I've written all about it." She smirked.

She could hear the trembling in Mia's voice. "I don't want to go to prison."

"You should have thought about that before you drugged someone."

"I wouldn't call two pills drugging someone." She laughed nervously.

"You gave her two?"

Mia came around the counter. The arrogance in her shoulders slowly seeped away. "Please promise that if I tell you, Riley won't press charges."

"Of course not. Riley won't press charges."

She knew she couldn't be sure. But she was pretty confident Riley Sinclair wouldn't press charges against anyone. "But you'll write it all down, and you'll call Max while I'm standing here. Now sit," Laine said as she stood, walked over to the counter, and got a pen and paper. "I want you to write everything that you've done to Riley from the moment you arrived. I know more than you can imagine. So leave one thing out and any promise I've made to you will be as void as what rests between your ears."

Mia sat, took the pen, and began writing. Laine sat down in the leather chair beside the sofa, placed her hands atop its chrome arms, and let the coolness of the metal alert her to how real this day actually was. If she had written this as a story, she wouldn't have even thought of this ending.

Laine stood there as Mia told Max everything. Even as she recounted it all, Laine couldn't believe how quickly Mia had begun her sabotage against Riley. She had known in her gut that this girl was up to no good. But Riley was so trusting. And Mia had maliciously used that trust against her.

Mia handed the phone to Laine. "He wants to talk to you."

Laine took the receiver. "Hello."

"Thank you, Ms. Fulton. I'm sure this isn't how you planned to spend your research trip."

"Well, no, not exactly. But I'd say it's been a very informative week, to be honest with you."

"I'm sending security over to make sure Mia gets her stuff and gets out immediately, and they will call the Bahamian police. I'll call Mr. Manos and ask him to take care of both The Reef and The Cove until Riley can get back. And I'll call Riley and apologize to her and see if I can get her to take her job back."

"From the way she was handling the guests this morning, I'd say her heart has never left this job. And I don't think you have her termination letter yet, do you?"

He laughed. "No, I didn't figure she'd be in a hurry."

"I'm headed to the hospital now. But could you give me a little time with her first before you call? She needs to hear what's gone on from someone in person. She's beaten herself up mercilessly, and I just don't want her to have to hear this over the phone. I'm thinking she's going to hear it straight from the horse's mouth," Laine said, her glare not leaving Mia's face.

Mia dropped her eyes at Laine's stare.

"Well, thank you. I'll call Riley this evening. I heard what happened to Ms. Larsen as well, and I called the hospital and asked them to keep me informed. We will be hoping for a miracle. And I have also talked to the chief of police. They've received a picture of the suspect, so thanks to this storm — can't believe I'm saying that — he won't be able to leave the island without being seen."

"Tamyra will be grateful. Thanks for everything, Max."

"Sounds like the thank-you goes to you, Laine. And after what Riley said last night, I'm kind of surprised you would have been willing to help her."

Laine laughed slightly. "Riley is an odd little creature who gets under your skin. You just can't seem to shake her."

Max laughed. "She's been under my skin for years. She's been like a daughter to me. My heart was broken last night. I knew she had come so far. And I couldn't believe what had happened. I felt like it was my fault, but I still couldn't let it go without repercussions."

"Well, now we know that she has come far. Very far."

"She deserves a huge apology from me. I shouldn't have assumed the worst."

"Don't beat yourself up, Max. We all had those initial assumptions. Thankfully, we were incredibly wrong."

Two security personnel entered through the glass doors. "Security is here, so I'd better let you go."

"Thank you again, Laine."

Laine hung up the phone and watched as the guards hovered over Mia like vultures while she emptied out her desk. "A police escort is waiting outside, ma'am," one of them said to Laine.

"You said no police!" Mia quaked.

"I said no charges. I didn't say no police. And honestly, Riley will decide what charges will be pressed against you. So that is why we're going to the hospital and you get to tell her everything that you've done," Laine said as she walked in front of Mia to the door.

Christian opened the door as Laine reached for it. His eyes grew wide when he saw the security guards behind her escorting Mia with her brown box of belongings. "What's going on, Laine? Max didn't give me a lot to go on."

Laine touched his arm. "Let's just say last night wasn't all it seemed, Christian. We'll explain later, but right now Mia and I have an appointment at the hospital."

"She set Riley up, didn't she?"

"Almost perfectly," Laine responded.

Mia walked out the door and passed Christian without so much as looking at him. He grabbed her arm as she stepped in front of him. "Did you erase that message from Riley, Mia? The day we were at the meeting? I left my cell phone on the table when I went to the restroom. Riley said she called. Did you see it and erase it?"

She looked at him with no expression. "Yes," she said flatly. Then she jerked her arm free and walked beside the security guards to the waiting patrol car.

Laine got in first and let out a heavy sigh. She found herself praying for Tamyra. She hadn't "found herself praying" in a very long time.

Riley and Winnie paced the waiting room. The doctors had taken Tamyra into surgery immediately. The damage to her airway was extensive and they had no time to waste. Riley turned when she saw Laine come through the door.

"How is she?" Laine asked.

Winnie wrung her hands. "We don't know. No one has been out since they took her to surgery."

"They took her straight to the OR," Riley

confirmed.

Laine shook her head. "It's horrible, isn't it?"

Riley nodded. "Yeah, it's pretty bad."

"Well, I know this isn't the time or place, but could you two come outside for just a minute?"

Riley watched as Winnie looked at Laine and Laine gave her a nod.

"How about you take Riley and I'll wait here to make sure we don't miss an update from the doctor. I promised her mother I would call her as soon as I heard something."

Laine gave her a soft smile. "That sounds good." She nudged Riley toward the door.

"What is it?" Riley asked as she followed Laine to the exit.

"Something that will set you free."

The glass doors opened automatically and she saw a patrol car to one side of the covered entrance. Mia stood beside it. "Laine, tell me you didn't demand a police escort."

Laine shook her head. "No, Mia demanded the police escort. Didn't you?" Her words were tossed to Mia and not to Riley.

"Mia, who's taking care of the guests?"

Laine interjected. "Max has asked Christian to handle it until you get back."

Riley couldn't hide her confused expression. She let out a half laugh. "Until I get back? What's going on here? Honestly, someone needs to tell me now."

"Tell her. Now," Laine said.

Mia looked at Riley, her eyes flat and cold. "I drugged you, Riley. I gave you two anti-anxiety pills. One in your water. The other you took yourself at the bar."

Riley's head was spinning. What was Mia saying? She rubbed her head, then looked back up. "You did what?"

"I drugged you. You weren't drunk, Riley. I gave you something that made you seem inebriated. You weren't drunk last night."

Riley felt the words slam into her chest. She tried to suck in the air that had just been sucked out of her. "You mean . . . you . . . you took advantage of what I told you and used it against me?"

"She wanted your job, Riley," Laine said. Then, to Mia, "Now tell her what else you did."

Mia lifted her chin in an arrogant manner. She cut her eyes at Laine and back at Riley. "I knew Max and his guests were going to show up early. But I didn't tell you." She stopped there.

Laine wasn't about to let her get off that easy. "And you . . ."

"And I sent the contracts to Max when I knew they were supposed to go to legal."

"And?"

Mia's jaw pulsed. "And the message you left for Christian, I erased."

"Any more of your conscience you need to clear?" Laine quipped.

"Only the part that holds memories of you."

"Touché."

Riley tried to digest everything she had just been told. But she couldn't believe someone could be so malicious. "You wanted my job?"

"Yes, Riley. I wanted your job." She tossed her head.

"Why didn't you just work your way into it?"

"Riley, you're so naive. You had just gotten there. I didn't want to wait until you decided to retire."

"Your mother."

Mia's eyes glared.

"This is about your mother. She pushed this, didn't she?"

Mia would offer her nothing.

"I trusted you with everything, Mia. My job. My story."

"You trust too easily," Laine said quickly, as if she couldn't keep it in.

Riley looked at her. "How did you find this out?"

Laine turned away from Mia. "I didn't trust her. Not from the first moment I saw her. And it didn't add up last night. Then I saw her with Christian. I knew there were all kinds of motives going on with this one. So Winnie and I set up a decoy." She hung her head and bit her lip. "Tamyra was going to her room to fake needing Mia. But when she got there, that man was waiting on her."

Riley let out a gasp.

"Winnie and I had no idea. So while Mia was gone to check on Tamyra, we went through her things. All of them. That was when we found a fax and the pills. We just put two and two together and I made her confess."

Riley shook her head, blinking hard. "I can't believe this. You made her confess?"

"I told her inmates would like her."

Riley shook her head again. "You did all of this . . . after what I said about you last night?"

"Riley, stop it. *You* didn't say it. You didn't slip off the wagon. You're still the incredible woman you were when you woke up yesterday morning. All of this was a horrible, despicable scheme of this woman," Laine said, tossing her head at Mia. "Now, would you like to press charges?"

Riley's head shifted back. "What? Press charges?"

Laine sighed. "Yes, this woman could get jail time for putting something in your drink."

Riley hadn't even thought about Mia's actions being a crime. She looked at Mia. Her face registered no remorse. Jail would probably do her good. But it wouldn't come at Riley's hands. An officer stood silently at the front of the car. "No. No, there will be no charges."

"Are you sure?" Laine asked.

Riley knew Laine knew she was sure. But she also wasn't surprised she asked again. "I'm sure. Mia apparently already lives in prison. She'll have to decide when she's ready to set herself free."

Riley looked at the police officer. "Officer." He walked over to her. "You can let this woman go. I won't be pressing charges."

Mia's face was expressionless.

"Are you sure, ma'am?"

"Absolutely." Riley turned her back on Mia and walked through the automatic glass doors. Laine came up beside her. "Thank you," Riley whispered. "Thank you so much."

■ ■ ■ ■

The doctor came into the waiting room
when Riley and Laine got back inside. The
three women huddled together as he began
to speak. "We've done our initial evaluation
and her nose is broken badly, there are quite
a few broken bones in her face, a couple
cracked ribs, and she will have some major
bruising, but there is no head trauma, no
swelling on her brain of any kind. Honestly,
with the way her face looks, I thought . . ."
He paused; then his training seemed to kick
back in. "Well, it is far better than we ever
expected."

Laine heard Winnie exhale. "Thank you,
Jesus," she said.

"How much longer will she be in surgery?" Riley asked.

"Another hour maybe for her nose; then a
plastic surgeon is coming in and he will
probably be with her a couple more hours.
We will come and let you know when she is
in recovery."

"Thank you so much, Doctor," Laine said.

He nodded and turned.

The three collapsed in side-by-side chairs.
"That is great news," Riley said. "When I
saw her face, I didn't know how in the world

she would live through that."

"It's a miracle," Winnie said. "An absolute miracle."

Laine nodded. Her phone rang inside the purse at her feet. She pulled it out and her eyes lit up. "It's Mitchell."

"What?" Riley couldn't hide her surprise.

"I know; I haven't gotten to tell you in all of the commotion. But I can't tell you now. You tell her, Winnie," she said as she accepted Mitchell's call and walked out of the waiting room.

"Hey."

"Hey, Lainey. Listen, if you're not coming home, I'm coming there. I don't want you going through that storm without me. It's too dangerous. So I'm flying my plane out and will be there as soon as I can."

"No!" she protested loudly. "It's too dangerous for you to come! We're in the middle of this thing, babe. The wind is blowing like crazy. Rain is coming down in sheets. You haven't been flying that long, and even experienced pilots aren't flying in this. Just stay put and I'll be home as soon as it's over. It's just too dangerous."

"I know. That's why you shouldn't be there."

She shook her head. "I had to be. Honestly, if I hadn't stayed, I don't know what would have happened." She filled him in on last night and Riley and what had happened to Tamyra. His final words before hanging up were "I'm coming. I'll be there tonight, and I love you more than you will ever know."

He was going to see her no matter what. She hung up the phone and prayed. Laine was praying.

Riley had left the hospital once Laine came back to sit with Winnie. Max had called her on the way back to the hotel, apologized, and assured her he'd get her some new help as soon as the storm passed. "Let me know if you need anything over there. I'll be at the Towers," he said.

She ran through the parking lot and underneath the shelter, her umbrella no longer any protection from the driving rain. She had lived through hurricanes before and respected them for the force that they were. It was time to start moving guests into the ballroom. There were only a couple dozen remaining, but she needed to make sure the workers stayed safe too. Her job was to protect them all. She grabbed the glass door to the offices and pulled with her full strength, her small arms no match for the wind and the leaded glass. She saw a strong tanned hand grab ahold of the door and push it open.

"Get in here. It's horrible out there."

The door closed, sending a burst of air through and pushing her right into Christian's chest. She looked up, ringlets hanging in her face, blown free from her ponytail holder. He didn't move. She didn't either. He raised his hand and brushed the hair away from her face. She felt every part of her being come alive. He let his hand slide to the back of her neck, and as he leaned his head down, he raised hers to his own. His mouth covered hers and she let it. Everything inside of her screamed to life. Her body relaxed beneath his touch, and he wrapped his other hand around her waist, pulling her even closer. She wrapped her hands around him and let every ounce of his presence engulf her. When he finally lifted his head from hers, he saw the tears that brimmed at the corners of her eyes.

"So I can make you cry too?" he chided.

She laughed and pushed at his chest playfully. But he wouldn't let her go. "You knew, didn't you?" she whispered, settling her palms against the linen of his white shirt.

"I knew that wasn't you last night. And something about Mia just didn't compute. I was, in fact, headed here to confront her when Max called me to come over. It was then I put it all together."

"I saw it in your face this morning. I saw that you didn't believe the worst about me."

"I knew what happened to you the other night at the church was real. It was like nothing I had ever seen. And I knew from the moment I met you that you were a woman who was strong and not the woman that I saw last night."

She dropped her head and let her forehead rest against his chest. His hands slid up her back and she could feel his lips kiss the top of her head.

"We've got to make sure these people are safe," he whispered.

She nodded. "I know."

"Let's round them up and get them to the ballroom, and we'll spend the night together," he said. She didn't miss his innuendo.

She laughed. "Yes, it looks like we will. Boy, I'm an easy date. One date and you get me for the night."

"I think I might want Riley Sinclair for longer than any night."

She tilted her head up, and his black eyes bored into her own. She'd take care of her guests in a minute. Right now she was go-

ing to kiss this man in front of her one more
time.

22

Friday evening . . .

Winnie pulled her luggage down the hall. The hospital had sent her and Laine back to the hotel. Tamyra was in ICU, so they could only visit a few minutes every other hour. The staff told them they would be safer riding out the hurricane at the Atlantis than at the hospital. Riley had sent all the guests to get their luggage and come down to the meeting rooms at The Cove. Winnie's Mesa Red Vera Bradley luggage looked like a cowboy's bandanna. That's why she had bought it in the first place. It matched the red bandanna she wore around her neck to complement her studded denim skirt and white T-shirt emblazoned with a red-sequined heart that took over most of her bosom. She had risked a shower and changed her clothes even if it meant being reprimanded by Riley.

The elevator deposited her at the entrance

to the ballroom. Gerard was waiting for her in the hall. He nodded toward the doorway. "He will walk you the rest of the way, Miss Winnie."

Winnie looked across the hall and saw the man. It was Albert. She couldn't believe it. "What in the world are you doing here? You should be home. You should have gotten out of here when you could," she scolded like a mother talking to a four-year-old.

"I called home and my children said yours were beside themselves when they found out you weren't taking that flight home. So I told them I would stay here with you. Now we need to get a move on," he said with a firmness in his voice that bade her to comply.

"Well, you should have gone home. I am more than capable of taking care of myself," she huffed slightly.

"You know what, Winnie Harris? You need a man who will straighten you out. You're set in your ways, and it's time you open up and let someone inside." His hand held her by the arm.

Her rigidness softened beneath his grasp. She looked at him with slight dismay.

"Yeah, that's right. You tell kids what to do all the time, but I'm not a kid. I'm a grown man. And I think you're an incredibly beautiful woman, albeit a pain in the butt. But I've handled worse than you. And we're going to the ballroom and I'm going to make sure you get home safe. And, well, dang it, I'm going to —" And with that, Albert's lips came down on Winnie's and sucked every last word from her. Her heart beat beneath the sequined one like a schoolkid's at recess. He lifted his mouth from hers.

"Now do you understand me?" he asked.

She just stood there. Head tilted back. Eyes still closed. Mouth partially open. And all she could do was nod. She heard him chuckle.

"I should have done that a long time ago, huh?"

She nodded again.

He laughed harder. He pulled her arm softly and took her large bag from her. She opened her eyes and released it to him. And for the entire walk to the conference room, she didn't say a word. Winnie Harris had been rendered speechless.

Laine paced the length of the ballroom.

"He'll call," Riley assured her.

"I told him not to come. I told him it was a hurricane, for pete's sake. No one should fly in a hurricane. He's a pilot. He knows better."

"He's flying himself?"

"Yeah, he got his license a few years back. He loves it. But this is stupid. And he doesn't have experience for this kind of weather." Laine looked at Riley. She knew her eyes had to be pleading, because her heart sure was. "He will show up, won't he?"

Riley patted her. Laine could read the concern on her face. Professional pilots didn't even have the experience for this kind of weather. It was foolish.

"Yes, he will show up. Now come on; get something to eat. Neither you nor Winnie have eaten since this morning." Riley nodded to the table where Winnie sat with Albert.

They could all hear the storm outside. In the last three hours since they had all the guests accounted for, the winds outside had grown fiercer. The last report had coconuts flying from the trees like missiles and the ocean a mass of white spray. The lights in the ballroom flickered. "Have you seen how she's been looking at him?" Laine asked as they walked to their table.

"Yes, I'm not sure what's happened, but I think ol' Albert has broken Miss Winnie-belle."

"Miss Winnie what?"

Riley laughed. "Southerners add *belle* to anything and everything."

"You are weird people."

Riley nudged her. "Well, you only wear black. Let's not talk about weird."

Laine raised her finger. "Ah . . . last night I did not have on all black."

"Unfortunately, I can't remember last night."

Laine shook her head. "Of course you can't. The one night I actually wear something that isn't black or some shade thereof and you can't remember." She sat at the table, and before she could speak again, the lights went out. The eerie blackness in front of them made the sounds outside seem even louder. If Laine were to describe it, she'd say the noise reminded her of a wolf howling for its prey. The noises of the darkness were soon drowned out by the guests' dialogue, which had escalated in pitch and anxiety. It descended rapidly, though, when the generators kicked on and floodlights illuminated what had only moments earlier been encased in black. Apparently hurricanes had a predisposition for black too.

Riley watched as Christian passed out bottled water. The staff was minimal and so were the guests. He caught her watching him and smiled. She smiled in return and surveyed the rest of the room. Cots were lined up on one side of the room and some guests had already settled in to try to sleep. Tables were lined up on the other side, where some guests planned to eat their way through the storm or entertain themselves until it was over. Some played cards. Others carried on conversations. All attempted to forget what was going on beyond the windowless walls around them. The fact that the ballroom was belowground made all that was going on outside easier to ignore. But some of it still couldn't be avoided. The main thing they had to be concerned about down here was flooding. And Gerard and his team were making sure that there was no sign of that. So for now everyone was okay. And that was Riley's main concern.

Christian walked over to where she stood. "You should sit down and get something to eat."

She hadn't thought about food for hours. She had for others, but not for herself. Hard to believe it had been only a day. She felt as if she had lived a thousand lives in the past twenty-four hours. Her stomach growled. "Not a bad idea."

He walked with her to a long table. The

buffet dinner that had been provided earlier had been put away. Coolers full of boxed meals now lined the table. She opened the lid of one and picked up a white box labeled *Turkey.* "Turkey it will be." Christian handed her a bottle of water, and they sat down.

She unhooked the top of the white box that was fastened like a carton of Chinese food. "Ever been through a hurricane?"

"Can't say we get many of those in Greece."

She pulled out a turkey and Swiss sub sandwich, some baked potato chips, and a brownie, then leaned back in her chair. She immediately realized how exhausted she was. He reached his hand across the table and touched her face. "You're exhausted, Riley."

She rubbed her eyes. "Yeah, I am."

"You eat; then you can grab some sleep and I'll keep watch over everything."

She sat back up and unwrapped her sandwich. "I'm fine. Honestly, I'll be fine." She took a bite.

"You'll eat, and then you'll sleep. Honestly, woman, you're hardheaded."

She laughed. "Okay, I'll sleep." Her smile dropped. She knew it was time. He deserved to hear the truth. She put her sandwich down. "I want to tell you something first."

"You can tell me anything."

"I want to tell you my story."

He smiled softly at her. And that same smile stayed on his face as she relayed every detail of her painful past. She could see at times her own sorrow reflected on his face. But that smile — that genuine, comforting smile — never left it. When she finished, he stood up and walked over to her. He bent down, lifted her chin with his fingers, then kissed her softly, gently.

He leaned back. "Thank you, Riley. Now you will never have to tell me again."

She couldn't hide her emotion. "It's a horrible story, Christian."

His hand never left her chin. "It is horrible, Riley. And sad. And I'm sorry it is yours. But it's only part of your story. Don't ever let yourself think it is the sum of your story. There is much left for you to write. And the Riley that is living now is beautiful."

She smiled at him. "Thank you."

"Thank you for sharing it."

She finished her sandwich while he talked and told her more about his life and his family. They laughed together while Hurricane Kate acted far more unladylike outside than its Southern name would suggest. Before Riley laid her head down, she looked up and checked on her friends. They were both asleep. She was surprised Laine had finally laid her head down. Her panic over Mitchell had her fit to be tied. But it had been a long day and night for her, too. Albert slept in a cot next to Winnie's, and she hoped that Winnie's unladylike noises wouldn't frighten him away. Riley closed her eyes and said a prayer for Mitchell. Then she thanked God for Christian . . . and that she wasn't more than he could handle. And she also thanked God that her story wasn't over.

23

Saturday morning . . .

Riley's cell phone vibrated her to life. When her eyes darted open, she saw Christian sitting in a chair by her side, wide-awake, sipping a cup of coffee. He apparently had never gone to sleep and must have worked all night. She was surprised her phone could receive calls now. She was even more surprised that anyone had slept through the storm. But most were still sleeping. She picked her phone up. It was Max. She sat up, shook off her sleepiness, and answered the phone.

"Looks like we've got service," she said.

Max's voice came through. "The hurricane doesn't seem to be as bad as they expected. Given its speed, it had to go through here pretty quickly. But it's still churning out there. We're probably in for another couple hours of strong winds and then a day of heavy gusts. Everyone all right over there?"

"Yeah. Everyone's okay here."

His voice wasn't right. And she knew it. "What's wrong, Max?"

"Riley, I've got some terrible news. Are you with all the guests?"

Riley looked around at the guests. A few were up; some grabbed coffee and breakfast, while others sat and talked quietly. "Yeah, I'm in the ballroom. Please tell me Gabby's okay." The panic rose in her throat and her pulse quickened.

His voice returned reassuringly. "Oh yes, Riley. I'm so sorry. Your family is fine. This isn't about your family. Can you go out in the hall?"

She pushed herself off the cot. "Sure. Yeah, I'll go out in the hall."

Christian obviously noted the panic in her voice. He got out of his seat quickly. "You okay?" he whispered.

"Yeah," she mouthed. "Something's happened."

"Tamyra?" he questioned.

She shrugged her shoulders and shook her head, then walked from the ballroom. "Is it Tamyra? Did she take a turn for the worse in the middle of the night?"

"I haven't heard anything about her. I assume that whatever word you got last night is the same. It's Mitchell Fulton, Riley."

Riley felt the knot in her gut grow. "Oh no, Max. What? Please tell me he's okay. Please."

"His plane went down last night. He didn't have a chance."

She had to sit down. She walked down the hall and sat on a bench, bent over, and put her head in her hands.

"Are you there, Riley?"

"Yeah, yeah, I'm here. I can't believe this, Max. He was coming to be with Laine. She begged him not to come. She begged him."

"I'm so sorry. But his office called. They didn't want her hearing this over the phone or on the news."

Riley looked around; the hall was completely barren. "We don't even have television in here; the power still isn't working. And I can't believe you were able to get through to me, in all honesty."

"Well, I know she's very fond of you, Riley. I felt like she needed to hear this from someone in person. They felt that way too; that's why they called me."

She shook her head again. Tears fell down her face freely now. Laine had finally gotten free from her shame. Finally she loved him the way he deserved, the way she deserved. And now this. "I can't believe this."

"I know; it's horrible. And I know with everything that has happened there this week, this might feel like too much, but you —"

"No, you're right." Riley swiped the tears from her eyes. "She needs to hear it from me. She stayed because of me. Oh, Max —" she broke completely — "she stayed because of me."

"Hey, hey . . . it's okay, Riley. It's okay. Listen, if you don't think you can do it, I will come over there and tell her."

She sniffed and tried to regain her composure. "No . . . no. I can do it. It's just crazy. It's all just crazy." She shook her head and wiped her tears away again. She looked up and saw Christian making his way down the hall toward her. She stood. "No, I can do this. I need to do this."

"Call me later and let me know how everything is over there. I know you and Christian have done a great job."

She looked at Christian and gave him a broken smile. "It's been wonderful to have him here to work with. I'll call you later." She ended the call.

"Is Tamyra okay?" he asked when he reached her. "Are you okay?"

"It's Mitchell. Laine's husband." Her voice broke as she spoke. "He was flying here to be with her. He didn't want her to be alone in the storm. His plane went down, Christian." Her tears fell freely again. "He didn't survive."

"Oh, Riley." He reached out and pulled her toward him. Her head rested at the top of his chest, nestled beneath his chin. "I can't believe this. This is horrible."

"I've got to go tell her." She pushed away from him and raised her face to look into his. "Can you take care of the other guests? She'll need me. I'll have to figure out how to get her out of here and home."

"Sure. You don't worry about anything here, okay?"

"Thank you."

Riley walked toward the ballroom door. Her legs felt like they had just finished a full marathon. Christian placed his hand in the small of her back as he opened the door for her. Laine sat up and stared at her when she paused in the doorway, unable to even step inside.

Laine knew in her gut when she had gone to sleep that something wasn't right. She didn't know how she had even fallen asleep at all. Now, as she sat looking at Riley's face, she knew for sure. Mitchell was dead. She could feel it. She could feel the disconnect from him in some way. The divorce hadn't made her feel this way. She had still felt connected to him in her very soul. But she felt this loss in a way she couldn't describe. She stood and walked toward Riley, who was still standing in the doorway. The tears in Riley's eyes glistened brighter the closer she got.

When she reached Riley, she collapsed into her arms. She felt the door brush past her as it secluded them in the hall, away from the others' eyes. Wracking sobs coursed through her body. Riley held her with a death grip and never said a word. She just held on to her until Laine's legs gave way and they both slipped to their knees onto the carpet. As much as her heart was breaking, as much as questions blasted through her head in a desperate attempt for some kind of answers, some kind of logic to this ridiculous nightmare, there was something inside of her that was incredibly stable and unwavering. She finally let all the energy drain from her body as it became limp in Riley's embrace.

Her body was drenched in sweat, and her face was covered with the brine of her tears. She wiped her face with the edge of her sweatshirt sleeve. Finally able to lift herself, she sat back and exhaled heavily. She was certain Riley's face mirrored her own. "Can you tell me what happened?" Her words came out broken, soft, and unaccusing.

"I don't know a great deal. Just that the plane went down and that Mitchell is gone, Laine. He . . . he didn't survive."

"Do you know where it went down?"

"That's all I know."

Winnie came bursting through the door. Her stockinged feet pounded heavily on the floor with each deliberate step. "Laine, baby. I'm so sorry." Winnie fell at her side and wrapped Laine in her arms.

Laine laid her head on Winnie's full chest like a baby would to its mother.

"I'm so sorry, Laine," Riley said. "I'm so sorry. You stayed because of me and I'm so sorry."

Laine leaned up. "Stop it. I don't want to hear another word. That man loved me. That man died loving me." Her words slowed. "And I would have never known he still loved me if you hadn't helped me deal with my own shame. You may be why I stayed. But his love for me is why he was coming here at all. And no one can ever take that away from me. You hear me? Not ever." Laine was amazed at the strength of her own voice. This peace resonated in her soul, somewhere deep and real. She knew that the things that had happened in her life this week had changed her to the core. And this woman sitting across from her was the main catalyst for all of it.

"Life is a painful journey," Winnie said as she reached out and pulled Riley toward her too. "But good journeys have good companions. And we are each other's companions for this journey. However long it lasts. There are no promises for tomorrow. Just today. And today we have each other." Winnie raised Riley's face. "Today we have each other."

Both women fell into Winnie's arms. And holding them there against her sequined bosom, Winnie hummed softly and rocked them gently in her arms. What had been tested in the hurricane of Laine's life had now been proven by the hurricane that still taunted outside. Laine felt Winnie's lips come down on the top of her head and kiss it, then go back to their humming. Laine reached over and took Riley's hand. And there, on Paradise Island, in the middle of the worst of life's hurricanes, she held on to the two women who had survived their own.

24

Sunday morning . . .

The beach was strewn with muck that had only two days ago lain at the bottom of the ocean. Hurricane Kate had stirred up all kinds of destruction, even though, from a property standpoint, it had been minimal to the island and gracious to the resort. Riley picked up a broken seashell and let the sharp, jagged edges prick her fingers as she rolled it over.

There had been so much brokenness here this week, so many sharp and jagged edges, that she had hardly even taken in this majestic sight that now stood as still as glass. Funny how life could pummel you with unexpected ferocity one moment and then swaddle you in childlike innocence the next.

She looked at the grounds behind her and saw limbs that lay strewn about the resort. Some things just couldn't be protected from storms. Some things simply needed to be broken off. She had learned that in her own life. And she had also learned that once old things were broken off, amazingly beautiful things could grow in their place.

She knew the ladies who had impacted her life this week felt as scattered and broken as the debris that surrounded her. But she also knew that they would begin the cleanup of their lives just as she and the staff would begin the cleanup of all of this tomorrow. And while hurricanes might be no respecter of persons, she had become a huge respecter of hurricanes and how much they could change someone.

Riley turned off the light in her office. The winds had been strong enough through Saturday that it still felt too dangerous to release everyone back to their rooms. The staff had spent the day rescheduling flights for all the guests, and the airport was said to be resuming commercial flights by nine o'clock this morning. She walked out into the lobby of the offices and saw Christian standing at the door.

"You headed to the hospital?" he asked.

"Yeah," she said, walking through the door he held open. "We're going to see Tamyra. The doctor said she's been asking for us.

Poor thing had to weather that storm all alone."

"A long weekend for her, I bet."

She nodded. "Then I'm taking Winnie and Laine to the private airport. Laine's publishing house is sending a plane for her around eight. Winnie's flying back with her. She doesn't want her to be alone." She stopped in the middle of the walkway. A gust threw her ponytail around her shoulder. She looked at Christian and ran her hand through his disheveled thick, wavy black hair. She let her thumb fall to his face, where it traveled softly across the dark circle beneath one eye. "When have you slept?"

He smiled and took her hand. "How bad is it if I say I can't remember?"

"Bad."

"I'm going to head home and get some rest now. A new crew has come in and they can handle everything from here." He pulled her hand toward his mouth and kissed it gently. Then moved it away and wrapped it behind her back, pulling her toward him. "You know I'm crazy about you, don't you?"

She felt the heat of his closeness rise inside of her. Whenever she was near him, everything inside of her felt alive. Even as tired as she was, he awakened each of her senses in ways that she had been convinced were entombed the past few years. "I think I might know that," she said, smiling.

He leaned down, kissed her softly, and then propped his head against hers. "I'll call you later."

"Thank you for everything. For your understanding, for your help, for being here. You just made every part so much easier. Thank you."

"Thank you for finally letting me."

She laughed. "You're very persistent."

He leaned back. "And you're very stubborn."

She stood on her tiptoes and kissed him again. "Yes, I am," she said with a wink and walked out the door.

"I'll see you when you get home," Albert said, reaching down and taking Winnie's hand.

Winnie felt the hairs on her legs grow an inch. She knew she should have taken the time to shave last night. "I'll look forward to that."

"You called the kids? told them what you were doing?" he asked as they walked toward the main entrance to The Cove.

"Yes, I told them I would be there as long as Laine wants me there. Trust me, when she's ready for me to leave, she'll have no problem telling me." She laughed softly. Then the ache of Laine's loss coursed through her again. "It breaks my heart, Albert."

"I know it does, Winnie. We both know what she's going through. That's why you'll be so good for her."

Winnie shook her head. "I'm not sure about that. She had a strength last night I didn't have."

"Well, there will be days she won't be so strong."

She looked at him and saw it. For the first time, she saw the pain of his own loss in his eyes. She had been so selfish. Only thinking about Sam and what she had let go of. As if she were doing Albert some big favor, when he had gone through the same tragedy she had. She stopped in the middle of the breeze-way. "Albert, look at me."

Albert stopped pulling their bags and set them upright. Then turned to look at her. His white hair made the blue of his eyes sparkle. "What?"

She reached for his hand. "I'm so sorry. I haven't even thought about your loss through all of this."

He smiled. "Winnie, I'm fine. I grieved well. I grieved hard. I plowed through it with everything inside of me. When the grief was so great I couldn't stand, I just collapsed. When the loneliness would overtake me, I would cry. When I needed to be with friends, I'd call one up. When I needed to be alone, I didn't apologize for it."

Winnie smiled.

"I'm okay. I still miss her. I miss everything about her. But we were still two normal married people, Winnie. So I haven't idolized her death either. I've just accepted it. And now I'm ready to move on to the next phase of my life. I know she would want me to. And I'd like to move on with you."

Winnie couldn't help herself. She grabbed the edges of his shirt, pulled him toward her, and planted a wet one right on his lips. When she finally let him go, she looked at him slightly horrified. "I'm not a hussy, Albert. I'm Baptist," she said, wiping at the edges of her pink lipstick and then wiping it from his face.

He laughed and shook his head, then finally pulled her hand away. He reached into his back pocket, pulled out a handkerchief, and wiped his mouth. "You are one of a kind, Winnie. You are one of a kind. Now let's get you to your car."

■ ■ ■ ■

Laine stood on the balcony and leaned against the railing. The rain had finally stopped. She closed her eyes as warm, bursting breezes washed across her face, remnants of the thief that had come in the night, still toying with her. She had found herself awash in tears every time she thought about the reality that was now hers. Mitchell was gone. She would never see his face again. Never kiss him again. Never have him hold her again. Yet every time those thoughts came to her, it was as if some hand of grace pushed through them and let her hear those final words he had shared with her over the phone. That's when some strange peace would fill her.

This week had been none of what she had anticipated. Her life would be different in so many ways because of what had transpired over the last seven days. And it was all so bittersweet. She may be a writer, but there was no way she could even begin to write the story of all that was going on inside of her. She could only hope that one day she'd find the ability to treasure all of it. She walked back into the room and closed the sliding-glass door. Gerard had already come and gotten her bags.

She ran her hands across the sofa that had served as her bed for the majority of the week. Then she reached into the refrigerator, pulled out a bottle of water, and walked toward the door. She looked down at the carpet where she had finally come to terms with herself, with her life, with her shame. And she whispered a prayer of gratitude. Then she walked out the door to the car that waited below.

They entered Tamyra's room quietly. Her eyes were closed and her face still incredibly swollen. Winnie walked around to one side of her bed, and Laine and Riley came up on the other side. "You awake, baby girl?" Winnie whispered.

Riley watched as Tamyra opened her eyes slowly. She was certain she saw a faint smile. "How are you feeling?" she asked.

"Like I've been beaten."

Her words broke the tension and they all laughed.

Tamyra started to laugh, then reached quickly for her ribs.

"Okay, no more laughing," Winnie scolded.

"How do I look?" Tamyra asked.

"You *are* through with beauty pageants,

aren't you?" Laine asked.

Riley shook her head, grateful to hear that Laine was still alive in there inside her pain. "You look bruised and swollen. You went through a horrible ordeal. But the police called right before I left to tell me they found Jason. He was trying to get a flight out today. The storm kept him trapped here."

She saw relief on Tamyra's face. She would probably rest better tonight than she had in months.

Winnie reached for her hand. "Me and Laine are about to fly out, baby girl. But your mom is coming in on a flight this evening. So she will be here with you the rest of the time, okay?"

Riley watched as tears surged to the corners of Tamyra's eyes. She reached up and, as a mother would, wiped them away. "It's okay, Tamyra. I'll stay with you until your mother gets here. I won't leave you."

Tamyra's eyes turned to Riley. "Thank you," she whispered.

Winnie bent down and kissed the top of Tamyra's head. "I'll see you very soon, sweetheart."

Riley stepped back so Laine could say good-bye. "You will be fine, Tamyra," she assured her. "And you will always be beautiful. Because beauty comes from the deepest place in you." Then Laine bent down and kissed her too. As Laine turned to walk away, Tamyra grabbed her hand.

"Thank you, Laine."

Laine patted her hand and Tamyra let go.

Riley turned to her. "Let me walk them out and I'll be right back."

Tamyra nodded and waved with the tips of her fingers as they exited her room.

Outside the hospital, they stood beside an open car door. "You call me as soon as you know the arrangements," Riley said, then reached out and pulled Laine into her arms. Laine's hand patted her back softly as she laid her head on her shoulder.

"Pray for me," Laine whispered.

"I haven't stopped," Riley said.

Laine straightened and climbed into the back of the car.

Winnie walked over and hugged Riley. "You take care of her, Winnie."

"As if she were my own."

Riley watched as the car pulled away. These three women had etched a place into her very fiber. They had come in like hurricanes and were leaving like familiar breezes. She wiped the tears that had fallen down her face with ease. Then turned and walked into the hospital to take care of

Tamyra.

When Laine and Winnie reached the tar-
mac and the private plane, Roy Rogers
stood at the bottom of the jet's stairs.

"It's that man."

Winnie nodded. "Roy Rogers. You know
him too?"

"Yeah, when I got here that first day, he
said something about the waters here being
full of healing."

Winnie smiled. "He said the same thing
to me."

Roy nodded as they approached. "I can
see you are leaving different from the way
you arrived, ladies."

Winnie stopped at the edge of the stairs
and punched him playfully in the arm.
"How can you tell?"

"You're glowing," he said.

"She glows perpetually," Laine quipped.

Roy's black eyes took her in completely.
"And you. The tough one. You've let go of
something, I believe."

The tears burned as they rushed to the
brim of her eyes. "Let go of my disease, Roy.
And found a great deal in return. Healed,
Roy. Healed."

She saw the emotion on his face. And he
nodded at them, waiting until they had

504

ascended the stairs and let the flight attendant bring them in and close the door. When Laine looked out the window to catch one last glimpse of Roy, he was gone. Roy Rogers was nowhere to be seen. She didn't know whether to be freaked out or not. Maybe with the stress of everything, her eyes were just playing tricks on her. But she did know she wasn't leaving paradise the way she had come. No, these waters had been just like Roy had said. They had been healing.

Tamyra's mother had gotten in about nine o'clock that evening. Riley had dozed on and off, fed Tamyra, talked to her when she had felt like talking, and had been told by the doctors that she would be able to go home in a couple of days. They just wanted to make sure the swelling came down in her nose so she could breathe okay. Riley felt as if her very bones ached as she pulled into the parking lot at her condo and turned off the car. She opened the car door.

"Mommy!" She heard the little voice ring from across the parking lot.

She looked up and saw Gabby run toward her. She dropped her purse and ran toward her little girl, letting her fall into her arms. She peppered her with kisses. "I've missed you so much. How is my angel girl?"

Jeremy walked out of the shadows of the darkness into the streetlight's glow. "We took the first flight out we could get. We went by the office first to surprise you and the staff said you were at the hospital. Is everything okay?" His voice was filled with concern.

She shook her head and released Gabby from her arms, then stood. "Yeah, yeah . . . everything's fine."

"Well, we decided we'd come here and wait for you instead."

Gabby tugged at her sleeve. "But first we went to Pizza Hut and had pizza and then we went to get a slush. I've got so much to tell you, Mommy! So much that we've done and all that Granddaddy did, and I just can't wait to tell you everything, Mommy!"

All the weariness left Riley. "Let me grab my purse and you can talk until you can't talk anymore." She turned to Jeremy. "I'll get you a room for the night at The Cove. We have plenty available. I'll call, and they'll have it ready by the time you get there."

"That would be great, thanks. I couldn't get a flight out of here tonight if I tried."

"Sure. You head on over there and they'll get you everything you need. Ask for Chandra; she's on duty tonight."

"I will. Thank you." He leaned over and gave her a kiss on the cheek.

"Thank you so much for taking care of her." She looked down at Gabby's beaming face.

He patted her arm. "It sounds like it's been a tough week."

"Very. But beautiful," she confirmed.

"I love you, Daddy," Gabby said.

Her daddy took her up in his arms and kissed her. "I'll see you soon, Gabby-girl."

"Very soon?"

"Very soon."

He put Gabby down and she grabbed Riley's hand. The warmth of that tiny hand in hers refreshed her entire insides. "Let's go talk," Riley said. "Let's go talk all night. I want to hear everything."

"How's Ted?"

Riley suddenly realized poor Ted hadn't been fed or checked on in two days. "Fine . . . yeah . . . I'm sure Ted is fine."

Gabby looked at her and gave her that gap-toothed smile. And with that one look, paradise was now perfect.

EPILOGUE

One year later . . .

Riley walked up to the low-country house; its charm fit like a picture in the historical district of Savannah. It felt so much like home. Balloons flew outside, and so many television cameras and trucks lined Abercorn Street that she had been forced to park two blocks over. She walked through the red-painted wood door into a bustle of activity. People scurried like ants on an invaded anthill. A young woman in front of her was busy writing notes on a notepad. She looked up as Riley walked by.

"Hello, I'm Savannah Phillips with the *Savannah Chronicle*." The attractive young woman extended her slender hand.

Riley tried to suppress her smile.

The girl shook her head and gave an amused smile. "It's okay. I get it all the time. You can say it."

Riley covered her mouth and shook her

508

head. "I won't."

"You'll be one of the first. Are you a friend of Tamyra's?"

"Yes, I am. We met about a year ago."

Savannah's all-American features registered a knowing look. "You were there during the attack?"

Riley wasn't sure how much to reveal to someone from the paper. Obviously the young woman was astute at reading people.

Savannah put her pad down. "It's off the record. I've already written that story. Tamyra and I have known each other for quite a while. My mother's into pageants, which is a whole other story, one someone should write a book about one day, to be honest with you. But Tamyra and I have crossed paths quite a few times. She's a remarkable young woman."

"Yes, she is. And yes, I was there. It was a horrible scene."

"She said she made some wonderful friendships on that trip."

"That's good to hear."

Savannah stepped aside. "Well, I won't keep you. Nice to meet you, um . . ."

Riley had forgotten her manners. She extended her hand. "Oh, sorry. Riley. Riley Manos."

"Enjoy yourself, Riley."

"Nice to meet you, Savannah."

The young woman left her. Riley saw the back of Tamyra's head and walked into the quaint anteroom where she was. Tamyra stepped to the side before Riley reached her and gave her an unobstructed view of Laine and Winnie.

Riley let out a squeal, ran over, and embraced her friends. They all did a happy dance in each other's arms, knowing it was completely childish and immature and yet not caring who in the world looked on.

Tamyra squeezed Riley's shoulder. "You look beautiful."

Winnie gave Riley a wink. "All new brides glow that way."

"You'd think we hadn't seen each other in a year," Laine spouted. "And we just saw each other four weeks ago."

Tamyra laughed. "I know, but it's never enough."

"At least you waited a decent amount of time before you went off and got hitched," Laine said, turning her attention to Winnie. "Hussy over here couldn't wait six months."

Winnie poked her. "When you're my age, Laine, you don't waste time. Plus, with the help of Viagra, we've got to take advantage of all of Albert's good years."

Their laughter erupted.

Riley turned to Tamyra. "We're so proud of you. You know that, don't you?"

Tamyra smiled and nodded. Riley saw a complete range of emotions brimming on the surface of Tamyra's face. Her shoulders were slender and smooth as they stuck out beneath her yellow linen, sleeveless dress. And her face held little reminder of what had brought them here. She reached her hand out and took Riley's. "Can I give you a tour?"

"I'd love it."

Riley looked at Winnie and Laine. Winnie shooed her with her hand. "We just saw everything. You go."

Tamyra took Riley through every room of the domestic violence center she had started. Each was immaculately designed, impeccably furnished, and filled with Tamyra's warmth. "After the trial was over and I knew Jason was finally locked away . . ."

"He got twenty years, didn't he?"

"Yes, they tried him on attempted murder," she said, her heels clicking softly on the wooden floors as they walked.

"I'm so sorry, Tamyra."

They stopped in the doorway of a children's playroom. The primary colors were bold behind Tamyra's silhouette.

"Don't be. That trip changed me in so many ways. And that experience was so profound. Here I was thinking HIV was going to kill me, and then I realized my life could be snatched away at any moment. That I had to choose to live. And so after Jason was put away, I came home and immediately began raising the funds for this place. With the medication they have now, I could live for years with HIV. But I know, at the end of the day, I won't leave this earth a day before I'm supposed to, regardless of how I die. So I decided to live. And I thought while I was doing it, it might be nice to help others do it too."

Riley enveloped Tamyra in her arms. "You are an amazing young woman, Tamyra Larsen. And I am so extremely proud of you." She finally released her. "Now let's go celebrate a ribbon cutting."

"Let's."

"Tamyra! Yoo-hoo, Tamyra, honey!" A voice came up from behind them. A woman pulled Tamyra to her and shook her as she spoke. "Oh, baby doll, I am so proud of you. Who would ever think that one of my girls would create something as wonderful as this."

Tamyra all but gasped for air upon her release. "Riley, I'd like you to meet Mrs.

Victoria Phillips. She is the head of the chamber of commerce and —"

"— and former Miss Georgia United States of America." Victoria stuck her hand out in front of Riley, the ruffles from the edge of her cream suit jacket fluttering in front of her.

Riley leaned back slightly from the rapid approach. "Nice to meet you, Mrs. Phillips."

"Oh, wonderful to meet you, darling. I just love this young woman here. And I'm so proud of her. Do you know that we —"

Tamyra stopped her. "Miss Victoria, they're about to do the ribbon cutting. We probably need to head out to the front."

"Of course, honey. Yes, let's get out there and cut that ribbon and get this house open and anorexics some food!" Her voice reverberated through the house.

"Um, this is for domestic violence."

She shook her blonde hair, almost as white as her cream suit. "Oh, right . . . right. Domestic violence. Yes, let's get those women some defense training." She looped her arm through Tamyra's and they walked toward the front of the house. "You know I had a defense training class one time and . . ."

Riley sneaked away as soon as the coast was clear.

Riley, Winnie, and Laine stood out on the lawn surrounded by cameras from all over. The Jason Weathers trial had made headline news across the nation. Tamyra had become a household name, and now she was taking full advantage of it to change the lives of women just like her.

Riley leaned over and wrapped an arm around Laine. "How's your heart?"

"Still broken."

"But I can tell you're healing."

"I am. Beautifully."

Winnie put an arm around Riley.

"You're glowing, Winnie."

"I'm in love with a wonderful man."

"Me too." Riley winked at her.

"Your wedding was beautiful," Laine said.

Riley had to agree. "It was, wasn't it?"

"Christian wrote me a note."

Riley turned back to Laine. "He did? What did he say?"

She chuckled softly. "He thanked me for driving you so crazy that week because it drove you to him."

Riley laughed. "He did not."

Laine shook her head. "No, he told me that he knew now how much Mitchell had loved me. And he was so sorry for what I had gone through. But he believed one day I'd find someone to love me that way again."

"Now that sounds like Christian," Winnie said.

"Did you write him back?" Riley asked.

"Yes, and I told him I had already found Someone who loved me that way. I found Him before Mitchell and I ever reconciled."

Riley pulled Winnie and Laine closer to her. The three stood there, arms wrapped around each other, and watched as *the* Victoria Phillips declared it Tamyra Larsen Day and presented her with a key to the city.

"Is that the mayor?" Winnie asked.

Riley shook her head. "No, Tamyra said she was the head of the chamber of commerce."

"I thought mayors gave out keys to the city," Laine said.

"I'd say this city probably doesn't need a mayor as long as she's around."

Tamyra cut the pink ribbon. Applause erupted, balloons lifted, and a whole new season began.

"Can we just slip in here for one second?" Riley asked.

Christian held Gabby's hand as Riley pointed at the bookstore. They both looked at Riley with that you-want-to-go-in-a-bookstore? look.

"Laine said it was coming out this week."

"How about Gabby and I go grab something from the café while you see if you can find her book."

"That sounds like a plan," Gabby announced.

"Sounds good to me," Riley said, giving Christian a wink. He patted her softly on the butt as he and Gabby made a beeline for the café.

Riley walked through the front of the store and down a row of wooden bookcases of new releases. She stopped in front of the second shelf, and a smile spread across her face. Her right eyebrow rose as a soft chuckle floated from her gut. She picked up the book. The four pairs of feet and a storm-strewn beach displayed on the cover, along with the title *It Happened in Paradise,* made Laine's comment make perfect sense.

"I changed all the names to protect the innocent."

Laine Fulton had never been innocent. But they had all been changed.

A NOTE FROM THE AUTHOR

The idea for this book came when a friend offered me a getaway weekend to the Atlantis resort at Paradise Island. Sitting one night at a table with three single women, I knew I was living what could be an incredible story. While I was there, I was walking through my own personal hurricane. I remember sitting on a beautiful cushioned chaise longue, staring at the ocean, wondering how people survive brutal storms. Forgetting that I was, in fact, surviving my own. It is that story of survival that I have written.

Hurricanes are different from tornadoes. There is an element of preparedness you can have for them, yet you can never be truly prepared for the force of impact. What you can prepare for is the ability to have a steadiness of soul when they hit.

This journey, traveled over the course of a week through the lives of four single women, is sometimes funny, sometimes raw, and always real. These women face real-life struggles. Real-life heart aches that many of us face every day. And yet this is more than a story of survival; it is about learning to live. My hope is that as you close the pages, you will be more aware of what real living is all about, more aware that inside your soul is the ability to survive even the toughest storms, and that paradise can always be found — even in the middle of a hurricane — if you are willing to look.

ACKNOWLEDGMENTS

I've always said nothing in life is truly ever accomplished by one person. At the end of the day all our efforts are collaborative. Which, I think, makes life a beautiful mosaic. In the course of this book there were quite a few people who helped make it what you hold in your hands today, and if you'll permit me, I'd like to take a few moments to thank them.

My agent, Greg Daniel, you came at just the right time with a belief in my stories. Thank you for walking this road with me.

To my Tyndale team: My publisher, Karen Watson, you just make me smile. I love to hear your voice on the other end of the phone, and I'm grateful for this new journey together. To Stephanie, Babette, the creative and sales teams at Tyndale, thank you for believing in *Hurricanes in Paradise* and for helping me share a little bit of my story with others. To my editor, Kathy Olson, you tweaked me, challenged me, and encouraged me. And then you just made my story better. Thank you for your time and your talent.

To my family, who consistently believes in me completely separate from what I do, and who have walked with me through some pretty brutal hurricanes. We survived. And are stronger for them.

To my new family, one thing I know is that hurricanes come, but I am certain that we will weather them well, and I am so grateful to be able to weather them with you.

To you, the reader, I never take for granted the gift you are giving me when you pick up one of my books. I pray I will be a good steward of both your time and your money. And I hope that after reading this book, you will see life a little differently, understand yourself a little better, and know how much you are completely valued and loved in a way you never have before.

And to my heavenly Father, my, what hurricanes You have brought me through. There were days I felt bruised and bloody, and You wrapped me in Your arms. There were days I was just plain scared to death, and You filled me with a supernatural peace. And there were days when I was standing in the eye of the storm, with chaos all around, and knew I was in the hollow of Your hand. Thank You for being a constant in this ever-changing flow. And for being Paradise to me in the middle of my hurricanes.

DISCUSSION QUESTIONS

1. At the beginning of the story, Laine and Riley each misjudge the other. How much credence should we give our first impressions of people? How can we wisely and charitably relate to people who initially rub us the wrong way? How should we respond if our first impressions are proven false? when they are proven true?

2. Laine is a demanding guest at times, forcing Riley to cancel some personal calendar events. How does she treat Laine with compassion and humility? What causes Riley to snap at Laine? How should we deal with difficult people?

3. Riley chooses to work in the hospitality field and takes responsibility for her guests' needs, no matter how small or nitpicky. There are times we "may be entertaining angels," so what are some practical

ways we can show hospitality to those around us?

4. Winnie seems especially attuned to the problems of others but is seemingly unaware of the "hurricane" she's experiencing in her own life. Why do you think that is?

5. Though relationship problems aren't often as extreme as Tamyra's, each of us has encountered people who, given the opportunity, might manipulate, use, or abuse us. How can we recognize unhealthy relationships? What are appropriate measures when we find ourselves in these situations?

6. Tamyra was afraid that God was upset because of her poor choices. Have you ever felt you've done something to anger God? What was the healing process like for you? If you still feel that this comes between you, what steps can you take to reconcile with Him?

7. Both Riley and Laine have difficulty forgiving themselves for significant events they were responsible for. Why is it so hard sometimes to forgive ourselves? Psalm

103:8–12 has some beautiful thoughts on forgiveness.

8. Throughout the course of the story, Winnie learns that the pain she experienced in losing Sam showed the depth to which she loved. Have you ever lost something dear to you? How did you respond in that circumstance?

9. Riley trusts Mia with her life story, only to have this information used against her. Do you agree with Riley's decision not to press charges? How do we forgive people who have deliberately harmed us?

10. Laine and Tamyra reach a point of peace about the circumstances in their lives, but both women see additional trials. Some people think if there is a God, then no one should experience any pain. So why does God allow bad things to happen in our lives, even when we're seeking Him? How should we respond when those times come?

11. Have you ever been in a desperate situation where you felt completely at the end of your rope? If you feel you ought to, share this situation with people whose

counsel you trust. What has this situation taught you about yourself? about God? about other people in your life?

12. Each of us has different places we turn to during the "hurricanes" of life. When you face difficult times in your life, where do you turn? Is that the healthiest place for your heart or should you turn somewhere else?

ABOUT THE AUTHOR

Denise Hildreth has spent the last six years writing fiction that has been hailed as both "smart and witty." Her ability to express the heart of the Southern voice has led to her being featured twice in *Southern Living* and receiving the accolades of readers and reviewers alike, but it is the simple joy of writing stories that keeps them coming. Her previous books include the Savannah series, *Flies on the Butter,* and *The Will of Wisteria.*

Denise makes her home in Franklin, Tennessee. And on her days off, she will settle for a long walk or a good book and a Coca-Cola.

Visit Denise's Web site at www.denisehil dreth.com.